THE WORLD
ACCORDING
TO BERTIE

**Center Point
Large Print**

**This Large Print Book carries the
Seal of Approval of N.A.V.H.**

THE WORLD ACCORDING TO BERTIE

ALEXANDER McCALL SMITH

CENTER POINT PUBLISHING
THORNDIKE, MAINE

This Center Point Large Print edition
is published in the year 2009 by arrangement with
Anchor Books, a division of Random House, Inc.
Originally published in Great Britain by Polygon, an
imprint of Birlinn, Ltd., Edinburgh, in 2007.

Cover illustration © by Iain McIntosh.

This book is excerpted from a series that originally
appeared in *The Scotsman* newspaper.

The text of this Large Print edition is unabridged.
In other aspects, this book may vary
from the original edition.
Printed in the United States of America.
Set in 16-point Times New Roman type.

ISBN: 978-1-60285-373-7

Library of Congress Cataloging-in-Publication Data

McCall Smith, Alexander, 1948-
  The world according to Bertie: the new 44 Scotland Street novel / Alexander McCall
Smith. -- Center Point large print ed.
    p. cm.
  ISBN 978-1-60285-373-7 (library binding : alk. paper)
  1. Apartment houses--Fiction.
   2. Edinburgh (Scotland)--Social life and customs--Fiction. 3. Large type books.
   I. Title.
  PR6063.C326W67 2009
   823'.914--dc22
  2008039741

This book is for
Derek and Dilly Emslie

1/09

WELCOME TO THE 44 SCOTLAND STREET

Meet some of its most colorful occupants, as only Alexander McCall Smith could have imagined them

BERTIE POLLOCK: A six-year-old prodigy who speaks fluent Italian and plays the saxophone like a professional but dreams of living a normal boy's life of fishing and rugby and not yoga and pink dungarees.

IRENE POLLOCK: Bertie's fantasically pretentious and wildly ambitious mother, who has grand plans for him and her newest son, Ulysses.

PAT: A twenty-something art student who takes a job as a receptionist at the Something Special Gallery in order to make ends meet. The ineffectual Matthew is her boss. She admires Bruce and befriends Domenica.

MATTHEW: The befuddled manager of the Something Special Gallery, who after an infusion of funds—to the tune of £4,000,000—from his wealthy father, is still struggling to grow accustomed to his newfound wealth. But first he must become accustomed to his changing relationship with his employee, Pat.

BRUCE: In between glances in the mirror, Bruce—the narcissistic, rugby-loving, philandering, yet infuriatingly handsome, hunk of 44 Scotland Street—floats from job to job. Surveyor, wine merchant, what's next?

DOMENICA: An artsy and wise widow who keeps a sharp eye on all 44 Scotland Street activities; that is, of course, when she is not researching contemporary pirate households in the Malacca Straits.

BIG LOU BROWN: The proprietor of The Morning After, the local coffee bar. An eternal source of caffeine and good advice for her friends, she too has love and heartbreak on her mind.

ANGUS LORDIE: Poet and painter, Angus Lordie is a man of refined tastes.

CYRIL: Angus Lordie's dog has golden teeth and an insatiable wanderlust. He has been dognapped and arrested for being a serial biter, but always manages to get in the last bark.

DR FAIRBAIRN: Bertie's psychotherapist, who may have more to gain from helping Bertie than first meets the eye. Bertie has noticed that his new younger brother, Ulysses, bears a striking resemblance to Dr Fairbairn.

ULYSSES POLLOCK: Bertie's younger brother and future co-conspirator. Bertie feels sorry for Ulysses because he knows what Irene is capable of. "Just you wait," Bertie says to Ulysses, "just you wait until she starts on you. Mozart. Yoga. Melanie Klein . . ."

Preface

The 44 Scotland Street books, of which *The World According to Bertie* is the fourth, started as a single serial novel in *The Scotsman* newspaper. When I began to write this story, I had no idea that the story would continue for as long as it has; nor had I any idea that Bertie, that engaging boy of six, burdened, as he is with his extremely demanding mother, would become so important a character. I certainly did not imagine that he would acquire so many supporters—or sympathisers, perhaps.

Bertie's problem is his mother, one of those ambitious parents who sees her son as a project rather than a little boy. Such mothers are legion, and many sons spend the rest of their lives trying to cut invisible but powerful apron strings. Bertie wants only to be a typical boy; he wants to have fun, to play with other boys, to do all the things that Irene's programme for him prevents him from doing. Instead he is forced to learn Italian, play the saxophone, and attend yoga classes for children.

Bertie seems to strike a chord with many readers. Recently I was in New York and attended a lunch where the first thing I was asked was how Bertie was doing. This happens to me throughout the world: people are more anxious about Bertie than they are about any of my other fictional characters.

They want him to find freedom. They want him to escape.

This book continues the story of Bertie—who has, quite astonishingly, remained six for the past four volumes, even while other characters have aged and progressed. But it does not deal only with Bertie—I have carried on my conversation with Big Lou, Domenica, Angus Lordie, and all the others who have walked into Scotland Street and found their place in the saga. All of these people are, in their own way, looking for some sort of resolution in their lives, some happiness, which is what, I suppose, all of us are doing. Some of them find it in this volume—or appear to find it—others will have to wait. The whole point of a serial novel is that the future is open. If freedom eludes Bertie in this book, and if Big Lou does not just yet find romantic fulfilment, then all is not lost—there is always another chapter.

Alexander McCall Smith

THE WORLD
ACCORDING
TO BERTIE

1. In Hanover Street. Watch Out, Pat, Bruce Is Back . . . Or Is He?

Pat saw Bruce at ten o'clock on a Saturday morning, or at least that is when she thought she saw him. An element of doubt there certainly was. This centred not on the time of the sighting, but on the identity of the person sighted; for this was one of those occasions when one wonders whether the eye, or even the memory, has played a trick. And such tricks can be extraordinary, as when one is convinced that one has seen the late General de Gaulle coming out of a cinema, or when, against all reasonable probability, one thinks one has spotted Luciano Pavarotti on a train between Glasgow and Paisley; risible events, of course, but ones which underline the proposition that one's eyes are not always to be believed.

She saw Bruce while she was travelling on a bus from one side of Edinburgh—the South Side, where she now lived—to the New Town, on the north side of the city, where she worked three days a week in the gallery owned by her boyfriend, Matthew. The bus had descended with lumbering stateliness down the Mound, past the National Gallery of Scotland, and had turned into Hanover Street, narrowly missing an insouciant pedestrian at the corner. Pat had seen the near-miss—it was by the merest whisker, she thought—and had winced, but it was just at that moment, as the bus laboured up Hanover Street towards the statue of George IV, that she saw a young man walking in the opposite direction, a tall figure with Bruce's characteristic *en brosse* hairstyle and wearing precisely the sort of clothes that Bruce liked to wear on a Saturday: a rugby jersey celebrating Scotland's increasingly ancient Triple Crown victory and a pair of stone-coloured trousers.

Her eye being caught by the rugby jersey and the stone-coloured trousers, she turned her head sharply. Bruce! But now she could see only the back of his head, and after a moment she could not see even that; Bruce, or his double, had merged into a knot of people standing on the corner of Princes Street and Pat lost sight of him. She looked ahead. The bus would stop in a few yards; she could disembark and make her way down to Princes Street to see if it really was him. But then she reminded herself that if she did that she would arrive late at the gallery, and Matthew needed her to be there on time; he had stressed that. He had an appointment, he said, with a client who was proposing to place several important Colourist pictures on the market. She did not want to hold him up, and quite apart from that there was the question of whether she would want to see Bruce, even if it proved to be him. She thought on balance that she did not.

Bruce had been her flatmate when she had first

moved into 44 Scotland Street. At first, she had been rather in awe of him—after all, he was so confident in his manner, so self-assured—and she at the time had been so much more diffident. Then things had changed. Bruce was undoubtedly good-looking—a fact of which he was fully aware and of which he was very willing to take advantage; he knew very well that women found him attractive, and he assumed that Pat would prove no exception. Unfortunately, it transpired that he was right, and Pat found herself drawn to Bruce in a way which she did not altogether like. All this could have become very messy, but at the last moment, before her longing had been translated into anything beyond mere looking, she had come to her senses and decided that Bruce was an impossible narcissist. She fought to free herself of his spell, and she did. And then, having lost his job at the firm of surveyors (after being seen enjoying an intimate lunch in the Café St Honoré with the wife of the firm's senior partner), Bruce decided that Edinburgh was too small for him and had moved to London. People who do that often then discover that London is too big for them, much to the amusement of those who stayed behind in Edinburgh in the belief that it was just the right size. This sometimes leads to the comment that the only sensible reason for leaving Scotland for London was to take up the job of prime minister, a remark that might have been made by Samuel Johnson, had he not been so prejudiced on this particular matter and thought quite the opposite.

Pat had been relieved that Bruce had gone to London, and it had not occurred to her that he might return. It did not matter much to her, of course, as she moved in different circles from those frequented by Bruce, and she would not have to mix with him even if he did return. But at the same time she felt slightly unsettled by the possible sighting, especially as the experience made her feel an indefinable excitement, an increase in heart rate, that was not altogether welcome. Was it just the feeling one gets on meeting with an old lover, years afterwards? Try as one might to treat such occasions as ordinary events, there is a thrill which marks them out from the quotidian. And that is what Pat felt now.

She completed the rest of the bus journey down to Dundas Street in a thoughtful state. She imagined what she might say if she were to meet him and what he in turn might say to her. Would he have been improved by living in London, or would he have become even worse? It was difficult to tell. There must be those for whom living in London is an enriching experience, and there must be those who are quite unchanged by it. Pat had a feeling that Bruce would not have learned anything, as he had never shown any signs of learning anything when he was in Edinburgh. He would just be Bruce.

She got off her bus a few steps from Matthew's gallery. Through the window, she saw Matthew at his desk, immersed in paperwork. She looked at him fondly from a distance: dear Matthew, she thought; dear Matthew, in your distressed-oatmeal sweater, so ordinary, so safe; fond thoughts, certainly, but unaccompanied by any quickening of the pulse.

2. A Conversation with Matthew: Matthew Is Troubled by His Trousers

Matthew glanced at his wristwatch. Pat was a few minutes late, but only a few minutes; not enough for him to express irritation. Besides, he himself was rarely on time, and he knew that he could hardly complain about the punctuality of others.

"I have to go," he said, scooping up some papers from his desk. "Somebody wants my advice."

"Yes," said Pat. "You told me." It had been surprising to her that anybody should seek Matthew's advice on the Scottish Colourists, or on any painters for that matter, as it seemed only a very short time ago that she had found it necessary to impart to Matthew some of her own very recently acquired knowledge of basic art history. Only a year ago, there had been a rather embarrassing moment when a customer had mentioned Hornel, to be greeted by a blank look from Matthew. Yet in spite of the fact that he was hazy on the details,

Matthew had a good aesthetic sense, and this, Pat thought, would get him quite far in the auction rooms. A good painting was a good painting, even if one did not know the hand that had painted it, and Matthew had considerable ability in distinguishing the good from the mediocre, and even the frankly bad. It was a pity though, she thought, that this ability did not run to clothes; the distressed-oatmeal sweater which he was wearing was not actually in bad taste, but was certainly a bad choice if one wanted, as Matthew did, to cut a dash. And as for his trousers, which were in that increasingly popular shade, crushed strawberry, Pat found herself compelled to avert her eyes. Now, if Matthew would only wear stone-coloured chinos, as Bruce did, then . . .

"Chinos," she said suddenly.

Matthew looked up, clearly puzzled. "Chinos?"

"Yes," said Pat. "Those trousers they call chinos. They're made of some sort of thick, twill material. You know the sort?"

Matthew thought for a moment. He glanced down at his crushed-strawberry corduroy trousers; he knew his trousers were controversial—he had always had controversial trousers, but he rather liked this pair and he had seen a lot of people recently wearing trousers like them in Dundas Street. Should he have been wearing chinos? Was this Pat's way of telling him that she would prefer it if he had different trousers?

"I know what chinos are," he said. "I saw a pair of chinos in a shop once. They were . . ." He trailed off. He had rather liked the chinos, he remembered, but he was not sure whether he should say so to Pat: there might be something deeply unfashionable about chinos which he did not yet know.

"Why are they called chinos?" Pat asked.

Matthew shrugged. "I have no idea," he said. "I just haven't really thought about it . . . until now." He paused. "But why were you thinking of chinos?"

Pat hesitated. "I just saw a pair," she said. "And . . . and of course Bruce used to wear them. Remember?"

Matthew had not liked Bruce, although he had tolerated his company on occasion in the Cumberland Bar. Matthew was a modest person, and Bruce's constant bragging had annoyed him. But he had also felt jealous of the way in which Bruce could capture Pat's attention, even if it had become clear that she had eventually seen through him.

"Yes. He did wear them, didn't he? Along with that stupid rugby jersey. He was such a . . ." He did not complete the sentence. There was really no word which was capable of capturing just the right mixture of egoism, hair gel, and preening self-satisfaction that made up Bruce's personality.

Pat moved away from Matthew's desk and gazed

out of the window. "I think that I just saw Bruce," she said. "I think he might be back."

Matthew rose from his desk and joined her at the window. "Now?" he said. "Out there?"

Pat shook her head. "No," she said. "Farther up. I was on the bus and I saw him—I'm pretty sure I did."

Matthew sniffed. "What was he doing?"

"Walking," said Pat. "Wearing chinos and a rugby jersey. Just walking."

"Well, I don't care," said Matthew. "He can come back if he likes. Makes no difference to me. He's such a . . ." Again Matthew failed to find a word. He looked at Pat. There was something odd about her manner; it was as if she was thinking about something, and this raised a sudden presentiment in Matthew. What if Pat were to fall for Bruce again? Such things happened; people encountered one another after a long absence and fell right back in love. It was precisely the sort of thing that novelists liked to write about; there was something heroic, something of the epic, in doing a thing like that. And if she fell back in love with Bruce, then she would fall out of love with me, thought Matthew, if she ever loved me, that is.

He stuffed his papers into his briefcase and moved across to Pat's side. She half-turned her cheek to him, and he planted a kiss on it, leaving a small speck of spittle, which Pat wiped off. "I'm sorry," he muttered.

"It's nothing," said Pat, adding, "Just spit."

Matthew looked at her. He felt flushed, awkward. "I'll be back later," he said. "But if you need to go, then just shut up the shop. We probably won't be very busy."

Pat nodded.

Matthew tried to smile. "And then maybe . . . maybe we can go and see a film tonight. There's something at the cameo, something Czech, I think. Something about a woman who . . ."

"Do you mind if we don't?" said Pat. "I've got an essay to write and if I don't do it soon, then Dr Fantouse will go on and on at me, and . . ."

"Of course," said Matthew. "Dr Fantouse. All right. I'll see you on . . ."

"Wednesday."

"Yes. All right." Matthew walked towards the door. Nobody writes essays on Saturday night—he was convinced of that, and this meant that she was planning to do something else; she would go to the Cumberland Bar in the hope of meeting Bruce—that was it.

Leaving the gallery, Matthew began to walk up Dundas Street. Glancing to his side, he looked through the gallery window. Pat was still standing there, and he gave her a little wave with his left hand, but she did not respond. She didn't see me, he thought. She's preoccupied.

23

3. Famous Sons and Gothic Seasoning

Matthew was wrong about Pat. He had imagined that her claim to be writing an essay that Saturday night was probably false and that in reality she would be doing something quite different—something in which she did not want him to be involved. But although it is true that students very rarely do any work on Saturday evenings—except *in extremis*—in this case, Pat was telling the truth, as she always did. There really was an essay to be completed and it really did have to be handed in to Dr Fantouse the following Monday. And this indeed was the reason why she declined Matthew's invitation to the Czech film at the Cameo cinema.

Pat closed the gallery shortly after three that afternoon. Matthew had not returned and business was slack—nonexistent, in fact, with not a single person coming in to look at the paintings. This is what, in the retail trade, is called light footfall, there being no commercial term—other than death—to describe the situation where absolutely nobody came in and nothing was sold. So Pat, having locked the cash-box in the safe and set the alarm, left the gallery and waited on the other side of the road for the 23 bus that would take her back to within a short walk of the parental home—once more her home too—in the Grange, that well-set suburb on the south side of the Meadows.

Pat's parents lived in Dick Place, a street which had prompted even the sombre prose of the great architectural historian John Gifford and his collaborators into striking adjectival saliences. Dick Place, they write in their guide to the buildings of Edinburgh, is a street of "polite villas"—a description which may fairly be applied to vast swathes of Edinburgh suburbia. But then they warn us of "Gothic seasoning," mild in some cases and wild in others, and go on to observe how, in the case of one singled-out house, "tottering crowstepped porches and skeleton chimneys contrast with massive bald outshoots." But Dick Place is not distinguished only by architectural exuberance; like so many streets in Edinburgh, it has its famous sons. At its junction with Findhorn Place is the house in which the inventor of the digestive biscuit once lived; not the only house in Edinburgh to be associated with baking distinction—in West Castle Road, in neighbouring Merchiston, there once lived the father of the modern Jaffa Cake, a confection which owes its name to the viscous orange jelly lurking under the upper coating of chocolate. No plaque reminds the passer-by of these glories, although there should be one; for those who invent biscuits bring great pleasure to many.

Pat's father, a psychiatrist, found the location very convenient. In the mornings, he could walk from his front door to the front gate of the Royal Edinburgh Hospital within fifteen minutes, and if he was consulting privately in Moray Place he could walk there in twenty-five minutes. The walk to Moray Place was something of a *paysage moralisé*—easier on the way down than on the way back, when the cares of patients would have been deposited on his shoulders, making Frederick Street and the Mound seem so much steeper and Queen Street so much longer. But apart from this undoubted convenience, what suited him about Dick Place was the leafy quiet of the garden that surrounded the house on all four sides. If they were to pass any comment on Dr Macgregor's garden, John Gifford and his friends might be sniffy about the small stone conservatory and potting shed, with its fluted and rusticated mullions; they might even describe the whole thing as "an oddity," but for Dr Macgregor it was his sanctuary, the place where he might in perfect and undisturbed peace sit and read the *Journal of the Royal College of Psychiatry* or the *Journal of Neurology, Neurosurgery, and Psychiatry*.

When Pat came home that Saturday, Dr Macgregor was ensconced in the conservatory, a small pile of such journals beside him. He became aware of his daughter's presence as she opened the French windows across the lawn, but he was so thoroughly immersed in his reading that he looked up only when Pat pushed open the conservatory door and stood before him.

"That must be interesting," she said.

He smiled, taking off his glasses and placing them down on the table beside him. "Very," he said. "Some of these articles are intriguing, to say the least. Do you know what Ganser's Syndrome is? That's what I was reading about."

Pat shook her head. "No idea," she said.

Dr Macgregor gestured to the journal lying open on his lap. "I was just reading this case report about it. A classic case of Ganser's walked through the author's door. He was asked what the capital of France was and he replied Marseilles. And how many legs does a centipede have? Ninety-nine. When did the Second World War begin? Nineteen thirty-eight. And so on. Do you see the pattern?"

"Just marginally out on everything?"

"Yes. People who have Ganser's talk just round the edge. Dr Ganser identified it and he called that aspect of it the *Vorbeireden*. They may not know that they're doing it, but their answers to your questions will always be just a little bit off-beam."

Pat looked at her father in astonishment. "How odd! Why?"

Dr Macgregor spread his hands in a gesture of acceptance. "It's probably a response to intolerable stress. Reality is so awful that they veer off in this peculiar direction; they enter a state of dissociation. This poor man in the report had lost his job, lost his wife, lost everything, in fact, and was being pursued by the police for something or other. You can imagine that one might start to dissociate in

27

such circumstances." He paused. "Anyway, you're home."

He smiled at Pat and was about to ask her what sort of morning she had had, but then Pat said: "Remember Bruce? I saw him this morning. Or at least I thought I saw him."

"You thought you saw him?"

"It may not have been him. Maybe I just thought that it was him. Maybe it was somebody who was just dressed like Bruce."

"How interesting," said Dr Macgregor. He looked thoughtful. "Fregoli's Syndrome." He added quickly, "I'm not being serious, of course."

But Pat was interested. "Who was Fregoli?"

"An Italian clown," said Dr Macgregor. "An Italian clown who never had the condition bearing his name."

4. Some Words of Warning from Pat's Father

"Yes," said Dr Macgregor. "Fregoli came from Naples, or somewhere in those parts. He found himself in the forces of an Italian general sent to Abyssinia back in the late nineteenth century. The Italians, as you know, bullied Abyssinia . . ." He trailed off. "You did know that, didn't you?" Pat shook her head. Her father knew so much, it seemed to her, and she knew so little. The Italians bullied Abyssinia, did they? But where exactly was Abyssinia?

Dr Macgregor looked away, tactfully, as any sensitive person must do when he realises that the person to whom he is speaking has no idea where Abyssinia is. "Ethiopia," he said quietly. "Haile Selassie?" He looked up, in hope; but Pat shook her head again, in answer to this second query. Then she said: "But I do know where Ethiopia is."

That, at least, is something, he thought. And he realised, of course, that it was not her fault. His daughter belonged to a generation that had been taught no geography, and very little history. And no Latin. Nor had they been made to learn poetry by heart, with the result that nobody now could recite any poems by Burns, or Wordsworth, or Longfellow. Everything had been taken away by people who knew very little themselves, but did not know it.

"Ethiopia used to be called Abyssinia," he said. "And the Italians had skirmishes with it from Somaliland. In due course, Mussolini used this as the *casus belli* for later bullying, and he invaded them. The world stood by. The Ethiopians went to the League of Nations and begged for help. Begged. But they were little men with beards, and it took some time before anyone would listen. Little dark men with beards."

They were both silent for a moment. Pat thought: he makes it all sound so personal. He thought: we have all been such bullies; all of us. The Italians. The British. The Americans. Bullies.

Pat looked at her father. "Mussolini was the one they hung upside down, wasn't he?"

He sighed. "They did."

"Maybe he deserved it."

"No. Nobody deserves it. Nobody deserves even to be hung the right way up. Whatever somebody does, however bad he is, you must always forgive him. Right at the end, you must forgive him."

For a moment, they were silent. He felt like saying to her that there were people, right at that moment, somewhere, even in advanced countries, who were awaiting capital punishment; people whose days and hours were ticking away under such sentences; such was the hardness of the human heart, or of some human hearts. But he did not say it; instead, he looked up at her and smiled.

"Yes," he said. "Our friend Fregoli impressed this Italian general—and can't you just imagine the splendid uniform that general would have had? Such stylish people. He impressed him so much with his quick-change act that he was taken off military duties and became a performer. He would appear on stage wearing one thing, nip off, and then appear within seconds wearing a completely different outfit. People loved it."

"And why . . ." Pat began to ask.

"The human mind," said Dr Macgregor, "is capable of infinite deception—both of others and of itself. If you began to think that somebody in your life was really another person in disguise, then you would have, I'm afraid, Fregoli's Syndrome. You might begin to think that I was not really myself, but was a very accomplished actor."

"How strange."

"Yes, how strange," said Dr Macgregor. "But it gets even stranger. There's another condition, one called Capgras Syndrome, where you believe that people you know have been replaced by imposters. The whole thing is a carefully orchestrated act put on by a team of imposters. That may be your best friend talking to you, but you're not fooled! You know that it's really an actor pretending to be your best friend."

Pat laughed. "But it was Bruce," she said. "Or at least I thought it was."

"Then I'm sure it was," said Dr Macgregor. "You're a very reliable witness of things. You always have been."

But now it was Pat's turn to doubt. "Isn't it true, though, that the mind can fill in the details if it sees just one thing that it recognises? One of our lecturers said something about that. He was talking about how we look at paintings."

"It's certainly true," said Dr Macgregor. "We want to reorganise the world, and that makes our brains jump the gun—sometimes. You look at a newspaper headline, take in one word, and before you know it your brain says: yes, that's what it says. But it may not."

Pat looked thoughtful. What had she seen? A

31

rugby shirt. And a pair of trousers. Perhaps her mind had filled in the rest, filled in the hair with the gel, filled in the look of Bruce.

Dr Macgregor decided to get up from his chair. He stood, and then walked over to the window and looked out over the garden. The lawn was dry.

"Don't get mixed up with that young man again," he said quietly.

Pat looked up sharply. "I wasn't planning to," she protested. "I really disliked him."

Dr Macgregor nodded. "Maybe you did. But that type of person can be very destructive. They know how powerful their charm is. And they use it." He paused. "I don't want you to be hurt. You know that, don't you? That's all that a father wants for his daughter. Or most of them. Fathers don't want their daughters to get hurt. And yet they know that there are plenty of men only too ready to treat them badly. They know that."

Pat thought that her father was being melodramatic. Bruce was no danger to her. He may have been in the past, but not now. She was like somebody who had been given an inoculation against an illness. She was immune to Bruce and his charms.

And yet she had felt unsettled when she saw him; it had been exciting. Would one feel that excitement if one was immune to somebody? She thought not.

Her father was looking at her now. "Are you going to seek him out?" he asked.

Pat looked down at the ground. It was so easy to fob other people off with a denial, with a half-truth, but she could not do this to her father, not to this gentle psychiatrist who had seen her through all the little doubts and battles of childhood and adolescence. She could not hide the truth from him.

"I think I'd like to see him," she said.

5. An Unexpected Conflict and News of Cyril

Domenica Macdonald, freelance anthropologist, native of Scotland Street, friend of Angus Lordie and Antonia Collie, owner of a custard-coloured Mercedes-Benz, citizen of Edinburgh; all of these were facets of the identity of the woman now striding up Scotland Street, a battered canvas shopping bag hanging loosely from her left arm. But there was more: in addition to all of that, Domenica was now the author of a learned paper that had recently been accepted for publication in the prestigious journal *Mankind Quarterly*. This paper, "Past Definite; Future Uncertain: Time and Social Dynamics of a Mangrove Community in Southern Malaysia," was the fruit of her recent field trip to the Malacca Straits. There, she had joined what she imagined was a community of contemporary pirates, with a view to conducting anthropological research into their domestic economy. The pirates, it was later revealed, were not real pirates after all—or not pirates in the sense in which the term is understood by the International Maritime Safety authorities in Kuala Lumpur. Although they disappeared each morning in high-powered boats, Domenica had discovered that their destination was not the high seas at all, but a town down the coast, where they worked in a pirate CD factory, infringing the intellectual property rights of various crooners and inexplicably popular rock bands. That had been a setback for Domenica, but it had not prevented her from completing a useful piece of research on the way in which the community's sense of time affected social relationships.

The paper had been well-received. One of the referees for the journal had written: "The author demonstrates convincingly that a sense of being on the wrong side of history changes everything. The social devices by which people protect themselves from confronting the truth that there is a terminus to their existence as a community are laid bare by the author. A triumph." And now here it was, that triumph, in off-print form, with an attractive cover of chalk blue, the physical result of all that heat and discomfort.

When the box containing the sixty off-prints had been delivered by the postman, Domenica had immediately left the house and walked round to Angus Lordie's flat in Drummond Place, clutching one of the copies.

"My paper," she said, as Angus invited her in.

34

"You will see that I have inscribed it to you. Look. There."

Angus opened the cover and saw, on the inside, the sentence which Domenica had inscribed in black ink. *To Angus Lordie,* the inscription read, *who stayed behind. From your friend, Domenica Macdonald.* He reread the sentence and then looked up. "Why have you written who stayed behind?" he asked. His tone was peevish.

Domenica shrugged. "Well, you did, didn't you? I went to the Malacca Straits, and you stayed behind in Edinburgh. I'm simply stating what happened."

Angus frowned. "But anybody reading this would think that I was some . . . some sort of coward. It's almost as if you're giving me a white feather."

Domenica drew in her breath. She had not intended that, and it was quite ridiculous of Angus to suggest it. "I meant no such thing," she said. "There are absolutely no aspersions being cast on . . ."

"Yes, there are," said Angus petulantly. "And you never asked me whether I'd like to go. Saying that somebody stayed behind suggests that they were at least given the chance to go along. But I wasn't. You never gave me the chance to go."

"Well, really!" said Domenica. "You made it very clear that you didn't like the idea of my going to the Malacca Straits in the first place. You said that in the little speech you gave at my dinner party before I left. You did. I heard you, Angus. Remember I was there!"

"It would be a very strange dinner party where the hostess was not there," said Angus quickly. "If one wrote a note to such a hostess one would have to say: 'To one who stayed away.' Yes! That's what one would have to write."

Domenica bit her lip. She knew that Angus had his moody moments, but this was quite ridiculous. She was now sorry that she had come to see him at all, and was certainly regretting having brought him the off-print. "You're behaving in a very childish way, Angus," she said. "In fact, I've got a good mind to take my paper away from you. There are plenty of people who would appreciate it, you know."

"I doubt that very much," said Angus. "I can't see why anybody would want to read it. I certainly won't."

Domenica bristled with anger. "In that case," she said. "I'm taking it back. The gift is cancelled."

She reached across to snatch the off-print from Angus. She felt the cover in her fingers and she tugged; but he resisted, and with a ripping sound "Past Definite; Future Uncertain" was torn into two roughly equal parts. Domenica let go of her part, and it fluttered slowly to the ground.

"Oh," said Angus, looking down. "I'm very sorry. I know you started it by writing that cruel thing about me, but I didn't mean to do that. I'm so sorry . . ."

What upset him was the destruction of another artist's work. An anthropologist was not really an artist, but this was creative work—even if a rather dull sort of creative work—and he had destroyed it. Angus felt very guilty. "I'm so sorry," he said again. "I would never have torn up your work intentionally. You do know that, don't you? It's just that I feel very out of sorts today." He hesitated, as if wondering whether to entrust Domenica with a confidence. Had he forgiven her? Yes, he thought, I have. He lowered his voice. "Something really awful has happened. It's made me very tetchy."

Domenica's expression of irritation was replaced with one of concern. "Awful? One of your paintings . . ."

Angus shook his head. "No, it's nothing to do with my work. It's Cyril."

Domenica looked past Angus into the flat. There had been no sign of the dog, who usually greeted any visitor with a courteous wagging of the tail and a pressing of the nose against whatever hand was extended to him. This had not happened. "He's ill?" she asked. As she spoke, she realised it could be worse: Cyril could be dead. Dogs were run over in cities. There were other dangers too.

"No," said Angus. "Not ill. He's been removed."

Domenica looked puzzled.

"Accused of biting," said Angus morosely. "Removed by the police."

Domenica gasped. "But whom did he bite?"

"He bit nobody," said Angus firmly. "Cyril is innocent. Completely innocent."

6. Angus Tells the Story of Cyril's Misfortune

"I think you should invite me in," said Domenica, from the hallway of Angus Lordie's flat. "Let me make us a pot of coffee. Then you can tell me about it."

Angus Lordie's earlier—and most uncharacteristic—churlishness evaporated. "Of course," he said. "How rude of me. It's just that . . . well, it's just that this business over Cyril has left me feeling so raw."

Domenica understood. She had not had a dog since childhood, but she remembered the sense of utter desolation she had experienced after the loss of the scruffy Cairn terrier, which her mother had taken in from a cousin. The terrier had disappeared down a rabbit hole in the Pentlands when they had been taking it for a walk, and had never reappeared. A farmer had helped with the search and had dug away the top part of the burrow, but all that this had revealed was a complex set of tunnels leading in every direction. They had called and called, but to no avail, and as dusk descended they had gone home, feeling every bit as bad as mountaineers leaving behind an injured fellow climber. They had returned the next day, but there had been no sign of the terrier, and it was presumed lost. The dog had not been replaced.

"I know how you must feel," said Domenica, as she went into Angus Lordie's kitchen. "I lost a dog as a child. I felt bereft, quite bereft."

Angus stared at her. "Cyril is still with us," he said.

"Of course," said Domenica quickly. "And I'm sure that it will all work out perfectly well in the end."

Angus sighed. "I wish I thought the same," he said. "The problem is that once a dog is deemed to be dangerous, then they have the power to order . . ." He did not complete his sentence, but left it hanging there. He had been told by the police that there was a possibility that Cyril would be destroyed if it were established that he was responsible for the rash of bitings that had been reported in the area.

"But it won't come to that," said Domenica briskly. "They need evidence before they can order a dog to be put down. They can't do that unless they're certain that Cyril is dangerous. He's your property, for heaven's sake! They can't destroy your property on the basis of rumour, or wild allegations." She paused, ladling spoons of coffee into the cafetière. "You'd better start at the beginning, Angus. How did this all start?"

Angus sat down at the scrubbed pine table which dominated his kitchen. "Maybe you hadn't heard about it," he said, "but there have been a number of incidents in this part of town over the last few weeks. A child was bitten by a dog on the way to school about ten days ago—nothing serious, just a nip, but enough to break the skin. The child gave a rather vague account of what happened, apparently. You know how children are—they don't make very good witnesses. But he did say that the dog came bounding out of a lower basement in Dundonald Street, gave him a nip on the ankles, and then ran off into the Drummond Square Gardens."

Domenica switched on the kettle. She glanced at the kitchen surfaces around her and sniffed. Angus Lordie's kitchen was cleaner than many bachelor kitchens, but only just. It could do with a good scrub, she thought, but this was not the time.

"And then?" she said.

"Then," Angus went on, "then there was another incident. A few days later, a man reported that he had been getting out of his car in Northumberland Street and he was given quite a nip on his ankle by a dog that then ran away in the direction of Nelson Street. The dog ripped the leg of his suit, apparently, and he reported the matter to the police so that he could claim insurance."

"The culture of complaint," muttered Domenica.

"I beg your pardon?"

She turned to Angus. "I said: the culture of complaint. We live in a culture of complaint because everyone is always looking for things to complain about. It's all tied in with the desire to blame others for misfortunes and to get some form of compensation into the bargain. I speak as an anthropologist, of course—just an observation."

"But I would have thought that it's entirely reasonable to complain about being bitten," said Angus. "As long as you complained about the right dog."

"Oh, it's reasonable enough," said Domenica. "It's just that these things have to be kept in proportion. One can complain about things without looking for compensation. That's the difference. In what we fondly call the old days, if one was nipped by a dog then one accepted that this was the sort of thing that happened from time to time. You might try to give the dog a walloping, to even things up a bit, and you might expect the owner to be contrite and apologise, but you didn't necessarily think of getting any money out of it."

Angus thought about this, but only for a very short time. He was not interested in Domenica's observations on social trends, and he felt irritated that she should move so quickly from the point of the discussion. "That may be so," he said. "All of that may be so, but the point is that Cyril is not that dog. Cyril would never do anything like that."

Domenica was silent. This was simply not true. Cyril had bitten Bertie's mother in broad daylight in Dundas Street not all that long ago. Domenica had heard about the incident, and although she was pleased that on that occasion Cyril had been so discerning in his choice of victim, he could hardly claim to have an unblemished record. It was, she thought, entirely possible that Cyril was not innocent, but she did not think it politic to raise that possibility now.

"But how did they identify Cyril?" she asked.

"They had an identity parade," said Angus. "They lined up a group of dogs in Gayfield Square police station and they asked the Northumberland Street man to identify the dog which had bitten him. He picked out Cyril."

Domenica listened in astonishment. "But that's absurd," she exclaimed. "Were the dogs in the line-up all the same breed? Because if they weren't, it would be quite ridiculous."

For a few moments, Angus was silent. Then he said, "I never thought of that."

7. Irene's Doubts Over Bertie's Friendships

While Domenica listened to Angus recount the traumatic experiences endured by his dog, Cyril, Bertie Pollock stared out of his bedroom window. Bertie's view was of Scotland Street itself, sloping sharply to the old marshalling yards down below, now a playground, which Bertie had been forbidden by his mother to enter.

"It's not so much the devices themselves," Irene had said to her husband, Stuart. "It's not the so-called swings, it's the attitudes to which Bertie will be exposed down there."

Stuart looked at her blankly. He had no idea why she should call the swings "so-called"; surely swings were either swings or they were not. There was nothing complicated about swings, as far as he could make out; they went backwards and forwards—that was all they did. And what attitudes would Bertie be exposed to in the playground?

Irene saw Stuart's look of puzzlement and sighed. "It's the roughness, Stuart," she said. "Surely you've seen it yourself. All that aggressive play that goes on. And there's another thing: have you noticed the rigid segregation which the children down there impose on themselves? Have you noticed how the boys play with the boys and the girls play with the girls? Have you seen it?"

Stuart thought for a moment. Now that Irene mentioned it, it certainly seemed to be true. There were always little knots of boys and girls all playing within the group; one did not see boys and girls playing together. Irene was right. But, he thought, surely this was natural.

"When I was a boy," he began, "we used to have a gang. It was boys only. But the girls had their own gang. I think everybody was happy enough with the arrangement. My gang was called . . ."

Irene silenced him with her stare. "I think the less

43

said about your boyhood, Stuart, the better. Things have moved on, you know."

"But have boys moved on?" It was a bold question, and Stuart's voice faltered as he asked it.

"Yes," said Irene firmly. "Boys have moved on. The problem is that certain men have failed to move on." She fixed him with a piercing stare as she made this remark, and Stuart shifted uncomfortably in his seat.

"I don't think we should argue," he said. "You know that I'm fundamentally in sympathy with the idea of bringing up boys to be more sensitive."

"I'm glad to hear it," said Irene.

"But there's no reason why Bertie shouldn't play with other boys from time to time," Stuart said. "And I don't mean that he should play in an exclusive sense. I think that boys can be encouraged to play inclusively, but with other boys, if you see what I . . ." He trailed off. Irene was staring at him again.

Irene was thinking of Bertie's friends. She had met several of the boys in his class, and she had to confess that she was not impressed. Tofu, for instance, was a thoroughly unpleasant little boy, as far as she could make out. There had been that unfortunate incident when Bertie had exchanged his dungarees for Tofu's jeans, which was bad enough, but when one added to it the fact that this transaction had taken place at a bowling alley in Fountainbridge—of all places—Tofu's influence hardly appeared benign.

Then there was Hiawatha whom Irene had come across at several school functions. There was something off about that boy, Irene thought. She had asked Bertie about it, and he had replied that Hiawatha was known for never changing his socks and that this explained the smell.

"We get used to it, Mummy," he said. "Sometimes Miss Harmony opens the window, which helps. But we don't really mind too much."

And there were other boys in the class who seemed equally questionable as suitable companions for Bertie. Merlin was decidedly unusual, even by the standards of Stockbridge, where he lived. Irene had met his mother at a parents' evening and had found it very difficult to sustain a conversation with somebody who insisted on bringing the discussion back at every opportunity to crystals and their curative properties. If Bertie were to spend too much time with Merlin, then there would be a danger that he would start thinking in an irrational way, and that would be disastrous. No, Merlin was to be discouraged.

That left that very unpleasant boy whom she had seen hanging about the school gates waiting for his father to collect him. What was his name? Larch. That was it. Irene had heard from Bertie that Larch liked arm wrestling and that nobody dared win because he was known to hit anybody who beat him at anything.

"I'm surprised that Miss Harmony lets him

behave like that," said Irene. "It's a very well-run school, and I know they don't tolerate that sort of behaviour."

"I don't think that Miss Harmony knows," said Bertie. "You see, Mummy, there are two different worlds. There's the grown-up world, and then there's the world down below, where boys and girls live. I don't think grown-ups really know what's happening down in our world."

"Nonsense, Bertie," said Irene. "We know perfectly well what's going on. And I'm sure that Miss Harmony knows exactly what Larch gets up to."

Bertie said nothing, but he was sure that Irene had no idea of anything that happened at school. And he was equally sure that Miss Harmony knew nothing of Larch's violent tendencies and all his lies too. That was the trouble with Miss Harmony, and with most grown-ups, Bertie thought. Grown-ups simply did not understand how children lied. Bertie did not lie—he told the truth—but all the others lied. Tofu lied all the time, about just about everything. Merlin made up stories about some of the things he had at home—a crystal that was capable of killing cats if you pointed it at their eyes; that was one of the lies he had told Bertie. Then, when it came to Hiawatha, he was probably lying too, if only they could make out what he was saying. There were just so many lies.

"I think you should spend more time with Olive,"

said Irene. "She's a very nice girl, and I know that you like her."

Bertie shook his head. "I don't like Olive, Mummy. I hate her."

"Now, Bertie!" scolded Irene. "That's simply not true."

Bertie sighed. When he told the truth, as he had just done, he was accused of lying. But if he lied, and said that he liked Olive, his mother would nod her approval. The world, he thought, was a very confusing place.

8. A Whole New Vista of Dread for Bertie

Bertie mused on this as he looked out over Scotland Street. Life was very dull, he thought, but would undoubtedly improve when he turned eighteen and could leave home to go and live somewhere far away and exotic—Glasgow, perhaps; his friend Lard O'Connor had more or less promised him a job over there, and it would be fun to live in Glasgow and go with Lard to the Burrell Collection and places like that. But that was daydreaming, and Bertie knew that he had another twelve years of his mother before he could get away. Twelve years! Twelve achingly slow years—a whole lifetime, it seemed to Bertie.

Yes, life was difficult, and it was becoming all the more difficult now that Irene had had her new baby. Bertie had suggested that they could perhaps have it adopted, but this suggestion had not been taken seriously.

"But, Bertie, what a funny thing to say!" Irene had said, looking anxiously about the maternity ward in which Bertie, visiting his mother, had made the suggestion.

"But they need babies for adoption, Mummy," Bertie had said. "I was reading about it in the newspaper. They said that there weren't enough babies to go round. I thought that maybe we could share our baby with somebody else. You always said it was good to share."

Irene smiled weakly. "And of course it is. But there are some things you don't share, Bertie, and a baby is one of them."

It was not that Bertie disliked Ulysses, as his mother had insisted on naming his new baby brother. When Irene had first announced her pregnancy to Bertie, he had been pleased at the thought of having a brother or sister. This was not because he wanted the company, but mainly because he thought that the presence of a baby would distract his mother's attention. Bertie did not dislike his mother; he merely wished that she would leave him alone and not make him do all the things that he was forced to do. If she was busy looking after a baby, then perhaps she would not have the time to take him to psychotherapy, or to yoga. Perhaps the baby would need psychotherapy and could go to Dr Fairbairn instead of Bertie. It was an entertaining thought; Bertie imagined the baby lying in his pram while Dr Fairbairn leaned over him and asked him questions. It would not matter at all if the baby could say nothing in reply; Bertie doubted very much if Dr Fairbairn paid any attention to anything said to him by anybody. Yoga would be more difficult, at least until the baby was a few months old. There were some very young children at Bertie's yoga class in Stockbridge—one of them just one year old. Perhaps they could try putting the baby into yoga positions by propping it up with cushions; he could suggest this to his mother and see what she thought.

Bertie's hopes, though, that he would be left more to his own devices were soon to be dashed on the immovable, rock-like determination of Irene to ensure that her two sons—Bertie and baby Ulysses—should undergo a process of what she called "mutuality bonding." This programme had two objectives. One was that the arrival of the baby should be part of Bertie's education in understanding the whole process of child-nurture, something which girls and women understood but which, in Irene's view, often escaped boys and men. The other objective was that the relationship which grew up between the two boys would be one in which there was a full measure of reciprocity. Bertie would come to know the baby's needs, just as the baby, in the fullness of time, would come to know Bertie's needs.

The first of these objectives—that Bertie should be brought up to understand what it was to look after a baby—meant that right from the beginning he would have to shoulder many of the tasks which went with having a baby. Bertie would be fully instructed in the whole business of feeding the baby, and had already been shown how to operate a breast pump so that he could help his mother to express milk for the baby should breast feeding become uncomfortable, which Irene thought likely.

"The trouble is this, *carissimo*," said Irene. "When you were a little baby yourself—and remember, that's just six short years ago—yes, six!—you tended to be a little—how shall we put it?—guzzly, and you bit Mummy a little hard, making Mummy feel a bit tender. You don't remember that, do you?"

Bertie looked away in horror; the sheer embarrassment of the situation was more than he could bear.

"Well, you did," went on Irene. "So now Mummy has bought this special pump, and you can help to put it on Mummy and get the milk out for baby when he comes along. That will be such fun. It will be just like milking a cow."

Bertie looked at his mother in horror. "Do I have to, Mummy?"

"Now then, Bertie," said Irene. "It's all part of looking after your new little brother. You don't want to let him down, do you?"

"I'll play with him," promised Bertie. "I really will. I'll show him my construction set. I'll play the saxophone for him and let him touch the keys. I can do all of that, Mummy."

Irene smiled. "All in good time, Bertie. Tiny babies can't do that sort of thing to begin with. Most of the things you'll be doing will be very ordinary baby things, such as changing him."

Bertie was very quiet. He looked at his mother, and then looked away. "Changing him?" he said in a very small voice.

"Yes," said Irene. "Babies need a lot of changing. They can't ask to go to the bathroom!"

Bertie cringed. He hated it when his mother talked about such things, and now a whole new vista of dread opened up before him. The thought was just too terrible.

"Will I have to, Mummy . . . ?" He left the sentence unfinished; this was even worse, he thought, than the breast pump.

"Of course you will, Bertie," said Irene. "These things are very natural! When you were a baby, Bertie, I remember . . ."

But Bertie was not there to listen. He had run out of the kitchen and into his room; his room, which had been painted pink by his mother, then white by his father, and then pink again by his mother.

9. So Who Exactly Are Big Lou's Big Friends?

Big Lou always opened her coffee bar at nine o'clock in the morning. There was no real reason for her to do this, as it was only very rarely that a customer wandered in before ten, or sometimes even later. But for Big Lou, the habit of starting early, ingrained in her from her childhood in Arbroath, resisted any change. It seemed to her the height of slothfulness to start the morning at ten o'clock—a good five hours after most cows had been milked—and it was decadence itself to start at eleven, the hour when Matthew occasionally opened the gallery.

"Half the day's gone by the time you unlock your door," she had reproached Matthew. "Eleven o'clock! What if the whole country started at eleven o'clock? What then? Would folk lie in their beds until ten? Would they?"

"No," said Matthew. "Most people will start much earlier than that. Nine o'clock seems reasonable to me."

Big Lou snorted in disbelief. "It would be an awfie odd day that we saw you about the place at nine," she said.

Matthew smiled tolerantly. "Reasonable for other people," he said. "What's the point of opening a gallery at nine when it's well-known that nobody buys pictures before noon, or at least before eleven? I'd just sit there doing nothing if I opened up at nine."

Big Lou rolled her eyes. "That's what you do anyway, isn't it?" she said. "And I doubt that you spend more than a few hours a day at your desk, what with your coffee drinking and those lunches you have. Two hours a day, something like that?"

Matthew shrugged. "Well, Lou, it wouldn't do you much good if I stopped drinking your coffee. You should be encouraging me, not making me feel guilty."

Big Lou said nothing. She liked Matthew, and he liked her, and these exchanges were good-natured, even if Big Lou meant every word of her criticism. But now it was time for her to prepare Matthew's coffee, and besides, there was an important piece of information for her to impart to Matthew.

While she clamped the grounds container in place, Big Lou asked Matthew over her shoulder whether he had heard of Cyril's misfortune. Matthew had not, and while the espresso machine steamed and hissed, Big Lou related the melancholy story of Cyril's detention by the Lothian and Borders Police.

"Angus will be very upset," Matthew ventured.

"Aye," Lou said. "Cyril is his only real friend."

Matthew thought this a bit extreme. "Oh, he's got other friends, I think. Domenica, for example."

"She tolerates him," said Big Lou. "But only just.

Have you heard the way she talks about him when he's not there?"

"There are people down at the Cumberland Bar," said Matthew. "He's got friends there."

"Not much use having friends in a bar," said Big Lou enigmatically. "Anyway, Cyril meant a lot to Angus. And now I expect they'll put him down. That's the way it is for dogs. Step out of line, and that's it. We had a dog in Arbroath that worried sheep and a farmer shot it. No questions. That's how it is for dogs."

Matthew half-listened to this dire prediction. He was thinking of friendship: even if Angus had few friends—which he did not think was true—then how many close friends was it possible to have? Big Lou herself was hardly one to imply friendlessness on the part of Angus; Matthew had not heard her mention any friends, and he had always suspected that her life outside the coffee bar was a solitary one, immured, as she was, in her flat with all those books.

"What about you, Lou?" he asked. "You say that Angus doesn't have many friends, but how many do you have? I'm not trying to be rude, asking this question—I was just wondering."

Big Lou reached for the polishing cloth. There was never any dirt on the bar, but that did not prevent her polishing it assiduously, staring into the reflective surface in the hope of finding a speck of something that she could rub away at.

"Friends?" she said. "Friends? I've got plenty, thank you very much, Matthew. Plenty of friends."

Matthew, leaning against the bar, took a sip of coffee. "Here in Edinburgh?" he asked. "Or up in Arbroath?"

Big Lou polished energetically, moving her cloth in large circles that threatened to collide with Matthew's elbow. "Both places," she said. "Arbroath and Edinburgh. And some in Glasgow and Dundee. Everywhere, in fact."

"Who are your Edinburgh friends, Lou?" pressed Matthew. "Not counting us, of course."

Big Lou glanced at him. "You're very inquisitive today," she said. "But since you ask, there's Mags and Neil and Humphrey and Jill Holmes and . . . well, quite a few others. I've got my friends, you know. Probably more than you have, Matthew, come to think of it."

Matthew smiled. "Maybe, Lou. Maybe." He paused. "But, I hope you don't mind my asking, Lou: who are these people? We never see them in here, do we? Who are they? Mags, for instance, who's she?"

Big Lou finished her polishing with a final flourish and tucked her cloth away beneath the bar. "Mags," she said, "since you ask, is a very good friend of mine. I met her on the corner of Eyre Crescent, on the way down to Canonmills. She was standing there when I walked past."

Matthew stared at Big Lou. "You met her on the

street? She was just standing there? And you went up to her and said . . . ?"

"It wasn't like that," said Big Lou. "Mags was working in the street when I went past. I stopped to have a word with her."

Matthew rubbed his hands together. "This gets better and better, Lou," he said. "Working in the street, Lou? What exactly was she doing in the street?"

"Working in the street," said Big Lou in a matter-of-fact tone. "You see, Mags drives one of these small steamrollers that road crews use. She was sitting on her steamroller with a cigarette in her mouth and she bent down and asked me if I had a light. I didn't, but I said something about her steamroller and we started to chat."

"Just like that?" said Matthew. "You started to chat? Two complete strangers?"

"Not complete," said Big Lou. "Mags, you see, came from Arbroath. Unlike you, Matthew, she came from somewhere."

Matthew looked crestfallen. She was right, though, he thought. My trouble is that I come from nowhere. Money, education—these give you freedom, but they can take you away from your roots, your place.

10. *Matthew Is a Sexist (but a Polite One)*

But Matthew wanted to know more about this Mags, the Madonna of the Steamroller, as he had now decided to call her. "Something interests me, Lou," he began. "What sort of woman thinks of getting a job on a road crew? How did Mags end up doing that?"

Big Lou turned from her task—emptying the grounds container—and fixed Matthew with a stare. He looked back at her, unrepentant.

"Well?" said Matthew. "It's a fair enough question to ask, isn't it? One doesn't see all that many women working on the roads."

"I thought that women could do anything these days," said Big Lou coldly. "Or have I got it wrong? Can men still tell us what we can and cannot do?"

Matthew made a placatory gesture. "Don't get me wrong, Lou," he said hurriedly. "I'm not suggesting that . . ."

"Well, what are you suggesting then?"

"All I was saying, Lou," said Matthew, "was that there are some jobs in which it's still usual—that's all, just usual—to see men rather than women."

Big Lou continued to stare at him. "Such as?"

Matthew had to think quickly. He was about to mention airline pilots, but then he remembered that on the last two flights that he had taken, a female voice had issued from the cockpit to welcome passengers. And nobody, it seemed, had been in the slightest bit surprised, except, perhaps, Matthew himself. But then the woman beside him, possibly noticing his reaction, had leaned over and whispered to him: "How reassuring to have a woman at the controls, isn't it? You do know, don't you, that women pilots are much, much safer than men? Men take risks—it's in the nature. Women are much more cautious."

Matthew had nodded. "Of course," he said. "Of course."

So now he was having difficulty in thinking of examples. Firefighters? But then he remembered having seen a fire engine race past him the other day in Moray Place, and when he had looked at the crew he had seen not the usual male mesomorphs but a woman, clad in black firefighting gear, combing her hair.

"I saw a woman fire . . . fireperson, the other day, Lou," he said brightly, hoping to distract Big Lou from the subject.

"Plenty of them," said Lou. "But I'm waiting for you to come up with some for-instances. What jobs do women not do these days?"

"It was in Moray Place," went on Matthew.

"Good class of fire over there," said Lou. "None of your chip-pan fires in Moray Place. Flambé out of control maybe."

"She was combing her hair," said Matthew. And

then, out of wickedness, he added, "and putting on lipstick. On the way to the fire. Putting on lipstick."

Big Lou frowned. For a few moments she said nothing, then: "Well, it was Moray Place, wasn't it? A girl has to look her best . . ." She paused. "Not that I believe you, Matthew, anyway. She might have been combing her hair—you don't want your hair to get in the way when you're working, do you? But she would not have been putting on lipstick."

Mathew was silent.

"Well, Matthew? I'm waiting."

"Oh, I don't know, Lou," said Matthew at last. "Maybe I'm just old-fashioned."

"Maybe you need to think before you speak," muttered Big Lou. She looked at him reproachfully. They liked each other, and she did not wish to make him uncomfortable. So she moved back to Mags. "You asked me why Mags does what she does. The answer, I think, is that she suffers from claustrophobia. She told me about it. If she's inside, she feels that she wants to get outside. So she needed work that took her outside all the time."

"And her steamroller would be open," mused Matthew. "No windows. No door."

"Exactly," said Big Lou. "That's Mags—an open-air girl."

"It's a perfectly good job," said Matthew. He paused. "But the men who work on the roads can be a little bit . . . how does one put it? A little bit . . ."

59

"Coarse?" asked Big Lou. "Is that what you were trying to say?"

Matthew nodded.

"Then you should say it," said Big Lou. "Nae use beating aboot the bush. Say what you think. But always think first. Aye, they're coarse all right. They're always whistling at women and making crude remarks. That's what Mags says."

"Very crude," said Matthew. One did not find that sort of behaviour in art galleries, he reflected. Imagine if one did! A woman might go into a gallery and the art dealer would wolf-whistle. No, it would not happen.

"What are you smiling at?" asked Big Lou.

"Oh, nothing much," said Matthew airily. "Just thinking about how different sorts of people go for different sorts of jobs."

Big Lou shrugged. "No surprise there. Anyway, Mags worked on the crew for eight years and everyone treated her like one of the boys. They just accepted her and took no special notice of her. Then, one day, she ran her steamroller over a piece of jewellery that somebody had dropped in the street. One of the men found it flattened and held it up for everybody to laugh at. But Mags cried instead. She thought that it might have been of great sentimental value to somebody, and there it was completely destroyed. She cried."

"I can understand that," said Matthew.

"Well, that made all the difference for Neil," said

Big Lou. "He operated a pneumatic drill and had been like the rest of them and had treated Mags as one of the boys. Now he started to look at her. A day or two later, he asked her out. That's how they came to be together. They're very happy, Mags says."

Matthew said nothing. He lifted his coffee to his lips and looked down into the detritus of the cup, the scraps of milk-foam. In the interstices of the big things of this world, he thought, were the hidden, small things, the small moments of happiness and fulfilment. People fell in love in all sorts of places; anywhere would do—amidst the noise and fumes of the daily world, in grim factories, in the most unpromising of offices, even, it would seem, amongst the din and dirt of roadworks. It could happen to anybody, at any time; even to me, he reflected, who am not really loved by Pat, not really. And who does not love her back, not really.

11. Bruce Goes Off Flat-Hunting in the New Town

Bruce had cut out the advertisement from the newspaper and tucked it in the pocket of his jeans. He was house-hunting, and the earlier part of the morning had been frustrating. He had looked at two flats, both of which had been unsatisfactory. The first, in Union Street, had been promising from the outside but had revealed its unsuitability the moment he had stepped inside the front door and had seen the extent of the subsidence. This was the problem with that part of town, where movement in the ground had resulted in uneven floors and bulging walls. The buildings were safe enough—this movement was historical—but the impression created from heavy settlement could make one nauseous, as if one were at sea.

"This place is subsiding," Bruce had said to the employee of the lawyers who was showing the flat.

She looked at him coolly. "There's a great deal of interest in this flat," she said evenly. "It won't be on the market long."

They moved farther into the hall. The flat had been vacated by its owners and the floor was bare: wide, yellow-stained pine boards, shipped from Canada all those years ago.

Bruce smiled at her. "That so?" he said. "Well, I can tell you that there's subsidence. Nobody will find it easy to get a mortgage on this place. Bad news."

The young woman fiddled with the top of her folder. "That may be your view," she said primly. "Others," and it was clear that she numbered herself amongst such others, "others obviously think differently."

Bruce gestured for her to follow him into the kitchen. She did so hesitantly and saw him extract a golf ball from his pocket. "Know what this is?" he asked.

"Of course I do. A golf ball."

"Right," said Bruce. "Clever girl. Now watch."

He bent down and placed the golf ball on the kitchen floor, giving it a slight nudge as he did so. Then he stood up and smirked.

The golf ball rolled away from Bruce, gathering momentum as it did so. By the time it hit the wall at the other end of the kitchen, it was travelling quite fast.

"See?" said Bruce. "That ball agrees with me. The floor slopes."

The young woman bit her lip. "These buildings are very old," she said. "The whole town is very old."

Bruce nodded. "That's right," he said. "That's why one has to be so careful."

"I take it that you don't want to see the rest of the flat?"

Bruce caught his reflection in the kitchen window and turned his head slightly. "No," he said. "I don't. Thanks anyway for showing me the place. I hope you sell it."

They went downstairs in silence.

"Coffee?" said Bruce at the bottom of the stairs.

The young woman looked at him. She was, he thought, on the verge of tears. "No," she said. "No, thank you."

Bruce shrugged. "Oh well," he said. "Another flat to look at. Sorry about that place."

She had hesitated, he thought. She had hesitated

when he had asked her to accompany him for a cup of coffee, which meant that she had been tempted. Of course she was tempted—they all were; they simply could not help themselves.

The next flat was in Abercromby Place, a basement flat that described itself as lower-ground-floor. Bruce smiled to himself as he walked along Forth Street. He remembered writing the particulars of flats when he had worked as a surveyor in Edinburgh; he had referred to lower-ground-floor flats before, and had once even described a sub-basement as a pre-lower-ground flat, well-protected from excessive sun exposure. The lighting in that flat, which had to be kept on all day if the occupants were to see anything at all, had been described as imaginative and helpful. And the atmosphere of damp he had described as cool.

The Abercromby Place flat did not take long.

"You're not seeing it at its best," said the owner. "It's not a very bright day today."

Bruce raised an eyebrow. "Oh? I thought the sun was shining when I came in."

The owner looked down at the floor. "All the wiring has been renewed," he said. "And everything in the kitchen's new, or next to new."

"Hard to see that," said Bruce.

"Well, I assure you it is."

Bruce pointed to a door leading into gloom. "Is that a dark room?" he asked. "Do you do photography?"

"It's the dining room."

The owner now became silent, and he remained silent as Bruce made a cursory inspection of the remaining rooms. Then they moved back to the entrance hall and Bruce thanked him for showing him round.

"You didn't like it," said the owner miserably. "You didn't, did you?"

Bruce reached out and patted him on the arm. "You'll find somebody," he said. "Just lower your price far enough and you'll get a buyer. I'm a surveyor. I shifted dumps like this. It's just a question of getting a buyer who's desperate enough."

"That's very reassuring," said the owner.

Outside in the street, in the light, Bruce took out the scrap of paper on which he had noted the address of the third flat he was to look at. This was in Howe Street, a street which went sharply down the hill from the end of Frederick Street and then curved round into Circus Place. It was one of Bruce's favourite streets in the Georgian New Town, and he had a good feeling about the flat that he was about to see.

It was not only a question of the address, but the name of the owner. It was a woman called Julia Donald, and if Bruce was not mistaken that was the name of somebody he had known when he had first come to Edinburgh. She had, he thought, been rather keen on him, but he had had his hands full at the time with . . . it was difficult to remember who exactly it was, but it was some other girl; there had been so many.

Bruce hummed a tune as he walked towards Howe Street. It was grand to be back in Edinburgh, grand to be back on the scene, utterly in control, the world at his feet. And what feet! he thought. Just look at them!

12. An Old Flame Flickers: as Well It May

"Brucie! So it was you!" exclaimed Julia Donald. "My God, what a surprise! I thought, you know, when the lawyers phoned and said that a Mr Bruce Anderson would be coming to look the place over, I thought: Can it be the one and only? And here you are!"

"And I thought just the same," said Bruce. "I thought, there's only one Julia D. in Howe Street that I want to see again, and here you are, it's you!"

He leaned forward and planted a kiss on her cheek. "Long time no kiss," he said. "And here's another one."

"Brucie! You haven't changed!"

"Why should I? No point changing when you've got things just right, is there?" He paused. "But you've changed, Julia."

A shadow passed over her face. "Oh? Have I?"

Bruce smiled. "You've become more beautiful. More ravishing."

"Brucie!"

"No, I mean it. I really do. Look at you!"

Julia led him into the living room. "I go to the gym, every day. Every single day."

"And it shows."

"Thank you. What about you? Do you still play rugby?"

Bruce did not. "Now and then. Not much really. Too busy."

Julia nodded. "I know what it's like. I almost got a job the other day, but I found I couldn't. I was just far too busy."

He looked about the living room. A large sofa, piled with cushions, dominated one wall. Opposite it was an ornate, gold-framed mirror above a large marble chimney piece. Bruce noticed, too, the expensive glass table piled with fashion magazines.

"You're quite a reader," he said, gesturing to the copies of *Vogue* and *Harper's*.

Julia seemed pleased with the compliment. "I like to keep my mind active. I've always liked to read."

Bruce, who had seated himself on the sofa, reached forward and flicked through one of the magazines. "No!" he said. "Would you believe it? I knew these people in London. That girl there, in the black dress, I met her at a party in Chelsea. And that's her brother there. The tall one. Terribly dim, but a good chap once he's had a drink or two."

Julia joined him on the sofa. "I can't wait to get to London," she said. "That's why I'm selling this place. One of Daddy's friends has arranged for me to work with a woman who cooks directors' lunches in the city. You know, they make lunches for the boardroom. And they cater for dinner parties. Party planners, sort of."

Bruce turned a page of the magazine. There was an advertisement for perfume, with a flap down the side of the page. He ripped open the flap and sniffed at the page. "Great," he said. "That's the stuff. It really is. Sexy, or what?"

Julia took the magazine from him and sniffed. "Mmm. Spicy. It reminds me of Mauritius."

"Yes," said Bruce. "Mauritius."

He laid the magazine back on the pile and turned to Julia. "So. London."

"Yes," she said. "London."

"When?" asked Bruce.

"Oh, I don't know. After I sell this place. Or before. I don't know."

Bruce looked thoughtful. "Great place, London," he said. "But I'm pretty glad to be back in Edinburgh, you know. It's great here too. And not so crowded."

"No," said Julia. "I've enjoyed myself here."

"The important thing," said Bruce, "is not to burn your boats. Never make a decision in a rush."

He rose to his feet, rubbing his hands together. "You going to show me around?"

Julia laughed. "Of course. I forgot. Where shall we start?"

"The kitchen," said Bruce. "You've got a kitchen?"

Julia reached out and punched him playfully on the arm. "Cheeky! It's a great kitchen, actually. All the stuff. Marble tops. Built-in wine racks. Everything."

They moved through to the kitchen. Bruce ran his fingers over the marble surfaces. "Smooth," he said. He looked at Julia. "Are you hungry? Seeing the kitchen makes me realise that I haven't had lunch. You had lunch?"

Julia had not, and Bruce offered to cook it for her, in her kitchen. "You've got pasta?" he asked. "And some butter? Parmesan, yes? Well, we're in business."

"This is fun," said Julia.

Bruce winked at her. "Better than selling a flat?"

Julia giggled. "Much better."

Bruce found a bottle of white wine in the fridge and opened it. He poured Julia a glass and they toasted one another as Bruce cut a piece of cheese off the block of Parmesan.

"I went to the place where they make this stuff," he said, breaking off a fragment of the cheese and passing it to Julia. "Reggio Emilia. Near Parma. That's where they make it. I knew an Italian girl. They lived in Bologna, but her father had some sort of farm there. Big place, with white oxen. And this great villa."

Had Bruce been paying attention to Julia's

expression, he would have noticed the trace of a frown. But she recovered quickly. "An Italian girl-friend? Very exotic."

Bruce looked at her from the corner of his eye. He appeared to be concentrating on slipping the pasta into the water, but he was watching her.

"No more Italian girlfriends for me," he said. "I've had enough of all that. It's settle-down time now. Comes to us all."

He watched her response. She had picked up her glass and was gazing at the rim. But he could tell.

"You? Settle down?" She forced a smile, but there was a real point to her question.

"I'm serious," he said. "I want a bit of quiet. I want a bit of domesticity. You know . . . going out for dinner, coming back and putting one's feet up on the sofa with a . . . with a friend. Lazy week-ends." He paused. "Long lie-ins on a Sunday. Then brunch somewhere. Some jazz. The Sunday papers."

Julia had closed her eyes, just momentarily, but she had closed them. It's working, thought Bruce: she's imagining what it would be like. And there's no reason for me to feel bad, because it really would be like that. That's exactly what we could do in this place. It's ideal. And the other great attraction of it all was that the need to find a job would be less urgent. Julia, as everybody in Edinburgh knew, was not impecunious. An indulgent father, the owner of three large hotels and a slice of a peninsula in Argyll, made sure that his daughter wanted for nothing. It was surprising, thought Bruce, that she had not been snapped up by some fortune hunter. If she went to London, there would be a real danger of that happening. And that was why he was doing her a good turn. That's what it was: an act of pure selflessness—considerate and sympathetic, pure altruism.

13. Matthew Gets Ideas from a Blank Canvas

After he had finished his cup of coffee at Big Lou's, Matthew made his way back across Dundas Street to the gallery. It was always a bit of a wrench leaving Big Lou: he felt she was the most relaxing, easy company, rather like a mother, he thought—if one had the right sort of mother. Or an aunt perhaps, the sort of person with whom one could just pass time without the need to say anything. Not that Matthew had ever had an aunt like that, although he did have vague childhood memories of an aunt of his father's who lived with them for a time and who worked all day, and every day, at tapestry. Matthew's father had told him an amusing story about this aunt's older brother, a man who suffered from a mild mental handicap and who had been taken in by Matthew's grandfather. Uncle Jimmy had been a kind man, Matthew's father said, and although there was little other contribution he could make to the household, he had been adept at fixing clocks.

"During the war, Jimmy had been largely uninterested in what was going on," Matthew's father had said. "But he was in great demand as a fixer of clocks, and his war service consisted of repairing the clocks of naval vessels that came into the Clyde. They brought the clocks round to the house because he couldn't really be left wandering around the ships unattended.

"After the war, he was disappointed that his supply of ships' clocks dropped off. He liked the shape of these clocks, and it was not much fun going back to the fixing of mantelpiece clocks for the neighbours. Eventually he asked why there were so few ships coming in and was told that the war had finished three years ago."

"Oh," said Uncle Jimmy. "Who won, then?"

Matthew's father had for some reason found this story vastly amusing, but Matthew thought: poor Uncle Jimmy, and remembered those Japanese soldiers who had come out of the jungle twenty, thirty years after the end of the war. Presumably they knew who won, or did they?

He unlocked the door of the gallery, removing the notice which said *Back in half an hour*. Surveying his desk, from which he had earlier cleared the day's mail, he realised that there was not much to do that morning. In fact, once he thought about it, there was nothing at all. He was up to date with his correspondence, such as it was; he had paged through all the catalogues for the forthcoming auctions and knew exactly which pictures he would bid for. There were no invoices to send out, no bills to be paid. There was simply nothing to do.

For a few moments, he thought of what lay ahead of him. Would he be doing this for the rest of his life—sitting here, waiting for something to happen? And if that was all there was to it, then what exactly was the point? The artists whose work he sold were at least making things, leaving something behind them, a corpus of work. He, by contrast, would make nothing, leave nothing behind.

But was that not the fate of so many of us? Most people who made their way to work each day, who sat in offices or factories, doing something which probably did not vary a lot—pushing pieces of paper about or moving things from one place to another—these people might equally well look at their lives and ask what the point was.

Or should one really not ask that question, simply because the question in itself was a pointless one? Perhaps there was no real point to our existence—or none that we could discern—and that meant that the real question that had to be asked was this: How can I make my life bearable? We are here whether we like it or not, and by and large we seem to have a need to continue. In that case, the real question to be addressed is: How are we going to make the experience of being here as fulfilling, as good as possible? That is what Matthew thought.

He was dwelling on this when he saw Angus Lordie walk past, carrying a parcel. On impulse, Matthew waved and gestured to him to come in.

"I was on my way to Big Lou's," Angus said. "And you?"

"Going nowhere," said Matthew. "Sitting. Thinking."

"About?"

Matthew waved a hand in the air. "About this and that. The big questions." He paused. "Any news of Cyril?"

Angus shook his head. "In the pound," he said. "It makes my blood boil just to think of it. Cyril will be sitting there wondering what on earth he did to deserve this. Have people no mercy?"

"They used to try animals for crimes," said Matthew thoughtfully. "Back in medieval times. I read something about it once. They had trials for pigs and goats and the like. And then they punished them. Burned them alive."

Angus said nothing, but Matthew realised that he had touched a raw nerve and changed the subject. He gestured to the parcel that Angus was carrying.

"That's a painting?"

"It will be," said Angus. "At the moment it's just a primed canvas. There's a man down in Canonmills who does this for me. I can't be bothered to make stretchers and all the rest."

"Well, don't leave it lying about," said Matthew. "It might be picked up and entered for the Turner Prize. You know the sort of rubbish they like. Piles of bricks and unmade beds and all the rest."

"But they wouldn't even consider this," said Angus. "Although it's only a primed canvas, it comes too close to painting for them."

Matthew smiled. An idea was coming to him.

"Antonin Artaud," he muttered. He looked up at Angus. "You know something, Angus. I would like to try to sell something of yours. I really would."

"You know that I don't sell through dealers," said Angus. "Even a semi-decent one like you. Why should I? No thank you, Mr Forty Per Cent."

"Fifty," corrected Matthew. "No, I'm not asking for any of your figurative studies. Or even those iffy nudes of yours. I'm thinking of something that wouldn't involve you in much effort, but which would be lucrative. And could make you famous."

"You're assuming that I want to be famous," said Angus. "But actually I can't think of anything worse. People taking an interest in your private life. People looking at you. What's the attraction in that?"

"It's attractive to those who want to be loved," said Matthew. "Which is a universal desire, is it not?"

"Well, I have no need to be loved," snorted Angus. "I just want my dog back."

It was as if Matthew had not heard. "Antonin Artaud," he said.

"Who?" asked Angus.

14. Artaud's Way Proves to Be an Inspiration

This was something that Matthew knew about. "Antonin Artaud," he pronounced, "was a French dramaturge."

Angus Lordie wrinkled his nose. "You mean dramatist?"

Matthew hesitated. He had only recently learned the word *dramaturge* and had been looking for opportunities to use it. He had eventually summoned up the courage to try it on Big Lou, but her espresso machine had hissed at a crucial moment and she had not heard him. And here was Angus making it difficult for him by questioning it. Matthew thought that a dramaturge did something in addition to writing plays, but now he was uncertain exactly what that was. Was a dramaturge a producer as well, or a director, or one of those people who helped other people develop their scripts? Or all of these things at one and the same time?

"Perhaps," said Matthew. "Anyway . . ."

"I don't call myself an arturge," Angus interrupted. "I am an artist. So why call a dramatist a dramaturge?"

Matthew said nothing.

"Simple words are usually better," Angus continued. "I, for one, like to say *now* rather than *at this time,* which is what one hears on aeroplanes.

They say: 'At this time we are commencing our landing.' What a pompous waste of breath. Why not say: 'We are now starting to land'?"

Matthew nodded, joined in the condemnation of aero-speak. At least this took the heat off his use of dramaturge.

"And here's another thing," said Angus Lordie. "Have you noticed how when so many people speak these days they run all their words together—they don't enunciate properly? Have you noticed that? Try to understand what is said over the public address system at Stansted Airport and see how far you get. Just try."

"Estuary English," said Matthew.

"Ghastly English," said Angus. He mused for a moment, and then: "But who is this Artaud?"

"A dram . . ." Matthew stopped himself, just in time. "A dramatist. He was very popular in the thirties and forties. Anyway, he painted monochrome canvases and gave them remarkable titles. It was a witty comment on artistic fashion."

This interested Angus. "Such as?"

Matthew smiled. "He came up with a totally white painting—just white—and he called it *Anaemic Virgins on Their Way to Their First Communion in a Snowstorm.*"

Angus burst out laughing. There were white canvases in the public collections in Scotland. A suitable title, he thought.

"And then," Matthew went on, "he painted a

completely red canvas which he called *Apoplectic Cardinals Picking Tomatoes by the Red Sea.*"

Angus clapped his hands together. "Wonderful!" he said. "Now let me think. What would we call a canvas that was simply blue?"

Matthew thought for a moment. "*Depression at Sea*?"

"Not bad," said Angus. "A bit short, perhaps? What about *A Depressed Conservative at a Risqué Film Convention*?"

"Except that people don't use the term 'blue film' anymore."

"But we do talk about turning the air blue," said Angus. "One turns the air blue with bad language. So how about *A Sailor at Sea, Swearing*?"

"Maybe," said Matthew. "And green? A completely green canvas?"

It did not take Angus long. "*An Envious Conservationist Sitting on the Grass*," he said. And then he added: "*Reading* Our Man in Havana."

Matthew looked blank for a moment, but then he laughed. "Very clever," he said. He was about to add something, but then he remembered how the conversation had started. "That canvas of yours," he said. "I could sell it for you. Just sign it, and I'll sell it."

Angus looked puzzled. "But I haven't begun . . ." he said.

"It's plain white," said Matthew. "Just sign it. I'll put a title on it, and we could see if I could sell it.

We could follow our late friend, Monsieur Artaud."

Angus was scornful. "A waste of a perfectly good primed canvas," he said. "We don't have a sufficient body of pretentious people . . ."

Matthew interrupted him. "But we do!" he said forcefully. "Edinburgh is full of pretentious people. There are bags and bags of them. They walk down Dundas Street. All the time."

At this, they both looked out onto Dundas Street. There were few people about, but just at that moment they saw a man whom they both recognised. Matthew and Angus exchanged glances, and smiled.

"Perhaps," said Angus.

"Exactly," said Matthew, producing a small tube of black acrylic paint from a drawer. "Now, where do you want to sign it?"

Once Angus had inscribed his signature, Matthew raised the issue of the painting's title. He held the white canvas up and invited Angus to suggest something.

"It looks very restful," Angus mused. "Something like *Resolution* might be a good title for it. Or perhaps *The Colour of Silence*?"

"Is silence white?" asked Matthew. "What about *White Noise*?"

Angus thought that was a possibility, but was just not quite right. Then it occurred to him. "*Piece Be With You*," he said.

"Perfect," said Matthew.

Angus nodded in acknowledgement of the compliment. "The subliminal message of such a title is this," he said. "Buy this piece. That's what it says. This piece wants to be with you." He paused. "Of course, we could increase its appeal simply by putting an NFS tag on it—not for sale. That message would fight subconsciously with the encouraging message of the title. And the result would be a very quick sale."

Matthew reached for one of the sheets of heavy white paper on which he typed labels for his paintings. Inserting this into his manual typewriter, he began to tap on the keys. "Angus Lordie, RSA," he said and typed. "Born . . ." He looked at Angus expectantly.

"Oh, nineteen something-or-other," said Angus airily. "Put: Born, Twentieth Century. That will be sufficient. Or, perhaps, *floruit* MCMLXXX. I was in particularly good form round about then." For a few moments he looked wistful; MCMLXXX had been such a good year.

Matthew typed as instructed. "And the price?" he asked.

Angus thought for a moment. It did not really matter, he thought, what he asked for the painting, as he did not think it would sell. But it occurred to him that if he was going to expose artistic pretentiousness—and artistic gullibility—he might as well do it convincingly. "Twenty-eight thousand pounds," he suggested.

Matthew laughed. "Fifty per cent of which will come to me," he said.

"In that case," said Angus, "make it thirty-two thousand."

The price agreed, Matthew stood up and prepared to hang the plain white canvas in a prominent place on the wall facing his desk. Then, after sticking the label and details below it, he stood back and admired the effect.

"I'm tempted to keep it," he said. "It's so resolved!"

"One of my finest works," said Angus. "Without a shadow of doubt. One of the best. Flawless."

15. A Small Sherry and a Hint of Synaesthesia

Since her return from the Malacca Straits, Domenica Macdonald had not seen a great deal of her friend Antonia Collie to whom she had lent her flat in Scotland Street during her absence. It had been a satisfactory arrangement from both points of view: Domenica had had somebody to water her plants and forward her mail, while Antonia had been afforded a base from which to pursue her researches into the lives of the early Scottish saints. These saints, both elusive and somewhat shadowy, were the characters in the novel on which she was working, and even if they had failed to leave many material traces of their presence, there were manuscripts and books in the National Library of

Scotland which spoke of their trajectory through those dark years.

Domenica's return came too early for Antonia. She had become accustomed to her life in Scotland Street and to the comfortable routine she had established there. She had no desire to return to Fife, to the parental house in St Andrews, where she had set up home after the collapse of her marriage to a philandering farmer husband; not that he had been a philanderer on any great scale—unfaithfulness with one other woman was hardly philandering, even if that woman was exactly the sort an echt philanderer would choose.

If she could not return to Fife, then Antonia would have to find somewhere else to live in Edinburgh. She would not have far to go—three yards, in fact—as the flat opposite Domenica's, and on the same landing, came up for rent at exactly the right time. It was the flat previously occupied by Pat, and the one which had been sold by Bruce when he left for London. Its coming on to the market at just the right time amounted to particularly good fortune, Antonia thought, and indeed there was to be more.

Within six weeks of her signing the lease, the owner asked Antonia if she was interested in buying it. Of course she was able to reply that the difficulty with this was that the flat already had a sitting tenant—herself—and this would require a reduction in the price. The owner had been annoyed by this claim, which seemed flawed in some indefinable way, but, wanting to make a quick sale, had agreed to take £10,000 off the price. Antonia agreed, and the flat became hers. Domenica, though, was hesitant. She was half-hearted in the welcome of her old friend: such friends are all very well—in their place—which is not necessarily on one's doorstep.

In the early stages of their being neighbours, Domenica had decided that she would not encourage Antonia too much. There had been an invitation to a welcoming drink, but this drink had consisted of a carefully measured glass in which the sherry had occupied only two-thirds of the glass, which was a small glass at that. Anything more than this, she decided, might have sent the wrong signal. Antonia had noticed. She had looked at the sherry glass and held it up to the light briefly, as if searching for the liquid, and then had glanced at Domenica to see if the gesture had registered. It had, and both decided that they understood one another perfectly.

"I know that you were about to offer me another sherry," Antonia said about fifteen minutes later. "But I really mustn't stay. I have so much to do, you know. The days seem to fly past now, and I find that I have to struggle to fit everything in."

Domenica felt slightly embarrassed. After all, Antonia had shown no signs of living in her pocket, and perhaps it was rather unfriendly to make one's concerns quite so obvious at this stage.

"You don't have to dash," she said. "I could rustle something up for dinner . . ."

"Very kind," said Antonia. "But I've made my own arrangements. You must come and have a meal with me some time soon. Next month perhaps."

There was an awkward silence. Next week would have been courteous; next month made her meaning crystal clear. And perhaps had added the belt to the braces.

"That would be very nice," said Domenica. "No doubt we shall see one another before then. On the stairs maybe."

"Yes," said Antonia. "On the stairs."

Over the next few days, they did not see one another at all. It had been an awkward way of establishing the rules of good neighbourliness, but it had worked, and after a while Antonia found herself able to knock on Domenica's door and invite her in for coffee. The invitation had been accepted—after only a moment's reflection on what the diary for that day might contain. That content was nonexistent, of course, but one should only accept an invitation immediately if one is happy for the person issuing the invitation to conclude that one had nothing better, or indeed nothing at all, to do. And Domenica certainly did not want Antonia to reach that conclusion. She was sensitive to the fact that Antonia was writing a book, and therefore had a major project, while she did not.

There was a very significant division, Domenica believed, between those who were writing a book at any time, and those who were not; a division just as significant as that between those actors who were currently on the stage and those, the majority, who were resting. For this reason, there were many people who claimed to be writing a book, even if this was not really the case. Indeed, somewhere at the back of her mind she remembered reading of a literary prize for such unwritten books, and of how the merits of those works on the shortlist for this prize were hotly debated by those who claimed to know what these unwritten books were all about.

"What are you going to do with this flat?" asked Domenica as she watched Antonia pour boiling water into the cafetière. It was the wrong question to ask somebody who had just moved into a new flat, but Domenica realised that only after she had asked it. It implied that the new place needed alteration, which, of course, may not have been the view of the new owner.

But Antonia was not offended. "A great deal," she said, stirring the coffee grounds into the water. She sniffed at the aroma. "What a lovely smell. Coffee. Certain new clothes. Lavender tucked under the pillowcase. All those smells."

Domenica nodded. "Do you see smells as colours?" she asked. "Or sounds as colours?"

"Synaesthesia," said Antonia. "My father's one, actually. A synaesthetic."

16. Domenica Is Left to Puzzle a Petty Theft

Antonia poured coffee into a blue-and-white Spode cup and passed it to Domenica. Her guest thanked her and carefully put it down on the kitchen table. The cup seemed familiar—in fact, she remembered that she had one exactly like it in her own flat, one which unfortunately had acquired a chip to the rim, more or less above the handle, just as this cup . . . She stopped herself. The cup which Antonia had handed her had a chip to the rim at exactly the same place.

She reached out and lifted the cup to her lips, taking the opportunity to examine the rim more closely as she did so. Yes, there it was, right above the handle, a small chip in the glazing, penetrating as far as the first layer of china, not enough to retire a well-loved cup, but clearly noticeable. She cradled the cup in her hands, feeling the warmth of the liquid within. Antonia had stolen her china! And if this cup had been removed, then what else had she pilfered during her occupancy of Domenica's flat?

She looked up at Antonia. It took a particularly blatant attitude, surely, to serve the dispossessed coffee in their own china. That was either the carelessness of the casual thief, or shamelessness of a high order. It was more likely, she decided, that Antonia had simply forgotten that she had stolen the cup, and had therefore inadvertently used it for

Domenica's coffee. Presumably there were many thieves who did just that; who were so used to ill-gotten goods that they became blasé about them. And even worse criminals—murderers indeed—had been known to talk about their crimes in a casual way, as if nobody would sit up and take notice and report them. In a shameless age, when people readily revealed their most intimate secrets for the world to see, perhaps it was easy to imagine how the need for concealment might be forgotten.

Domenica remembered how, some years previously, she had been invited for a picnic by some people who had quite casually mentioned that the rug upon which they were sitting had been lifted from an airline. It had astonished her to think that these people imagined that she would not be shocked, or at least disapproving. She had wanted to say: "But that's theft!" but had lacked the courage to do that and had simply said: "Please pass me another sandwich."

Later, when she had thought about it further, it occurred to her that the reason why they had been so open about their act of thievery was simply this: they did not consider it dishonest to steal from a large organisation. She remembered reading that people were only too willing to make false or exaggerated claims on insurance companies, on the grounds that they were big and would never notice it, nor were they slow to massage the figures of their expenses claims. All of this was simply theft, or its moral equivalent, and yet many of those who did it would probably never dream of stealing a wallet from somebody's pocket, or slipping their hand into a shopkeeper's till. What weighed with such people, it seemed to Domenica, was the extent to which the taking was personal.

Well, if that was the case—and it appeared to be so, in spite of the indefensibility of making such a distinction—then one would have thought that stealing one's friend's blue-and-white Spode cup was a supremely personal taking, especially when one's friend had let one stay in her flat for virtually nothing. That was the act of a true psychopath— one with no conscience whatsoever.

"Yes, synaesthesia," said Antonia, pouring herself a cup of coffee into a plain white mug. "You know Edvard Munch's famous picture *The Scream*? That's a good example of the condition. Munch said that he was taking a walk one evening and saw a very intense bloodred sky. He then had an overpowering feeling that all of nature was screaming—one great, big, natural howl of pain.

"Now, as to my father," Antonia went on. "His case is very simple. He thinks that numbers have colours. When you ask him what colour the number three is, without a moment's hesitation he says: 'Why it's red, of course.' And ten, he says, is a shade of melancholy blue."

Domenica thought for a moment. "But blue is often melancholy, isn't it? Or that's what I've always thought. Does that make me a synaes-thetic?"

Antonia hesitated briefly before replying: "No, I don't think so. I think that is more a question of conditioning. We're told that blue is melancholy and so we associate that emotion with it. Just as Christmas is red, and white, being the colour of snow and ice, is cold. In my father's case, I suspect that when he was learning to read as a boy, he had a book which had the letters and numbers in dif-ferent colours. The figure three was probably painted in red, and that association was made and stuck. Our minds are like that, aren't they? Things stick.

"The association between blue and melancholy," Antonia continued, "is a cultural one. Somebody, a long time ago, a genuine synaesthetic perhaps, said: 'I'm feeling blue,' and the expression caught on."

"The birth of the blues," said Domenica.

"Precisely," agreed Antonia. She took a sip of her coffee. "Of course there are so many associations in our minds that it's not surprising that some get mixed up—wires get crossed. Whenever I hear cer-tain pieces of music, I think of places, people, times. That's only natural.

"People are always doing that with popular music. They remember where they were when they listened to something that made an impression on them."

"If you're going to San Francisco," said Domenica suddenly, "be sure to wear some flowers in your hair . . ."

Antonia stared at her.

"A song," explained Domenica. "Round about the late sixties, 1967, maybe. It makes me think not of San Francisco, but Orkney, because that's where I was when I listened to it. I loved it. And I can see Stromness, with its little streets, and the house I was staying in over the summer while I worked part-time in the hotel there. I was a student, and there was another student working there, a boy, and I suppose I was in love with him, although he never knew."

Antonia was silent. She looked at Domenica. She had never thought of Domenica having a love life, but she must have, because we all fall in love, and some of us are sentenced to unrequited love, talking about it over cups of coffee in flats like this, with friends just like this, oddly comforted by the process.

17. A Restoration in Prospect— and a New Suspicion

Domenica looked about her. Antonia's flat was a mirror image of hers in the arrangement of its rooms. But whereas the original features of her flat had been largely preserved, Antonia's had suffered a bad 1970s experience. The original panelled doors, examples of which survived in Domenica's flat, had either been taken down in Antonia's and replaced with unpleasant frosted-glass doors—for what conceivable purpose? Domenica wondered—or their panels had been tacked over with plywood to produce an unrelieved surface. That, one assumed, was the same aesthetic sense which had produced the St James Centre, a crude cluster of grey blocks at the end of the sadly mutilated Princes Street, or, at a slightly earlier stage, had sought the turning of Princes Street into an urban motorway and the conversion of the Princes Street Gardens into a car park.

One might not be surprised when some of these things were done by those with neither artistic sense nor training, but both the St James Centre and the plan to slice the city in two with a motorway had been the work of architects and planners. At a domestic level, these were the very same people who put in glass doors and took out old fireplaces.

"Yes," said Antonia. "I will have to do something about all this."

Domenica pretended surprise for a moment, but Antonia had intercepted her glances and knew what she was thinking.

"Don't imagine for a moment that this is my taste," Antonia warned. "I'm every bit as Georgian as you are."

It was an amusing way of putting it, and they

both laughed. Not everyone in the New Town lived a Georgian lifestyle, but some did. And of course Antonia and Domenica would find such people amusing with their insistence on period authenticity in their houses, although they themselves were equally inclined to much the same aesthetic.

Domenica waved a hand about her. "What are you going to do?"

"Just about everything," said Antonia. "Those doors over there. The plywood will come off. Panels back. I'll free the shutters. Free the shutters—that's a rallying call in these parts, you know."

Domenica looked at her friend. But her own shutters had indeed been freed, she had to admit.

"And then I'm going to take all the light fittings out," Antonia went on. "All this . . . this stuff." She pointed up at the spiky, angular light that was hanging from the ceiling. "And the fireplaces, of course. I shall go to the architectural salvage yard and see what they have."

"You'll need a builder," said Domenica, adding, with a smile, "We are mere women, you know."

"Oh, I'm ready for that. You know, people are so worried about builders. They seem to have such bad experiences with them."

"Perhaps it's that problem that builders have with their trousers," Domenica mused. "You know that issue of . . ."

Antonia was dismissive of that. "Low trousers

have never been a problem for me," she said. *"Nihil humanum alienum mihi est.** Although it is interesting—isn't it?—how trousers are getting lower each year. Or is it our age?"

Domenica thought for a moment. "You mean on young men? Young men's trousers?"

"Yes," said Antonia. "It's now mandatory for them to show the top of their underpants above the trouser waist. And the trousers get lower and lower."

As an anthropologist, there was little for Domenica to puzzle about in this. Male adornment occurred in all societies, although it took different forms. It was perfectly natural, she thought, for young men to display; the only question of interest was what limits society would put on it. And could one talk about society anymore when it came to clothing? T-shirts proclaimed the most intimate messages and nobody batted an eyelid. There were, she reflected, simply no arbiters.

Domenica decided that the issue of trousers had been explored enough. "And these builders," she said. "Where will you get them?"

"My friend Clifford Reed is a builder," Antonia said. "And a very good one, too. He'll help me out. He said he will. He has a Pole he's going to send over to take a look at what needs to be done, and then to do it. There are lots of Poles in Edinburgh

*Lit: nothing about humanity is alien to me; a common Edinburgh way of saying: I've seen it all.

now. All these builders and hotel porters and the like. All very hardworking. Staunch Catholics. Very reliable people."

Domenica thought for a moment. "You'll have to get a large mug to serve your Pole his tea in," she said. "None of this Spode for him. He'll want something more substantial."

She watched Antonia as she spoke. It was a somewhat obvious thing for her to say, she thought, a bit unsubtle, in fact. But she watched to see its effect on Antonia. Of course the true psychopath would be unmoved; such people were quite capable of telling the coldest of lies, of remaining cool in the face of the most damning accusations. That was why they were psychopaths—they simply did not care; they were untouched.

"Of course not," said Antonia flatly. "I keep my Spode for special occasions."

Domenica was completely taken aback by this remark and was not sure how to take it. I keep my Spode for special occasions. This could mean that she kept her Spode (as opposed to stolen Spode) for such occasions, or that her own visit was such an occasion and merited the bringing out of the Spode. It must be the latter, she told herself. It must be.

Their conversation continued in a desultory fashion for a further half hour. There was some talk of the early Scottish saints—Antonia's novel on the subject was not progressing well, Domenica was told—and there was a brief exchange of views about the latest special exhibition at the Scottish National Portrait Gallery. Then Domenica looked at her watch and excused herself.

She rose to her feet and began to walk towards the door. As she did so, something lying at the foot of the kitchen dresser caught her eye. It was a slipper, a slipper embroidered in red, and it was remarkably similar to one that she had. She glanced at it quickly and then looked away. What were the odds that two people living on the same stair in Scotland Street would both have identical pairs of red Chinese slippers? Astronomically small, she thought.

18. Bruce Finds a Place to Stay— *Just Perfect*

Since he had returned to Edinburgh, Bruce had been staying with friends in Comely Bank. These people were a couple whom he had known in his earlier days in Edinburgh; Neil had been at school with him at Morrison's Academy in Crieff, and he had known Caroline slightly before she met Neil. Both Neil and Caroline were keen skiers who had met on a skiing trip to Austria. Not all romances which start in the chalet or on the ski slopes survive the descent to sea level, but this one did. Now they were married and living in Comely Bank in a Victorian tenement halfway up the hill towards the heights of the west New Town. "Not quite Eton Terrace," Bruce had observed. "Nor St Bernard's Crescent, for that matter. But nice enough. If you like that sort of thing." Comely Bank was comfortable and was only a fifteen-minute walk from the West End and Neil's office, but, in Bruce's words again, it was "hardly the centre of the known universe."

In fact, even as he passed these somewhat dismissive comments, Bruce was trying to remember a poem he had heard about a man who died and who had "the Lord to thank / For sending him straight to Heaven from Comely Bank." Or something along those lines. Bruce smirked at the thought. Comely Bank was fine for Neil and Caroline, but not for him. He still wanted some fun, and in his view all the fun was to be found in the New Town in places like . . . well, in places like Julia Donald's flat, for instance.

Julia had quickly agreed to his suggestion that he might move in with her for a while.

"But of course you're welcome, Brucie," she had said. "I was going to suggest it, anyway. In fact, I'll probably stick around for a while. London can wait. You know what? I think Edinburgh's where it's at. I really do."

Bruce had smiled at her. It's where I'm at, he thought, which perhaps amounted to the same thing. He looked at her. Nice girl, he thought. Not a feminist, thank God. More interested in . . . well, not to put too crude a point on it, interested in men. And why not? Why should girls not be interested in men? You could talk to girls who were interested in men; they liked to listen; they appreciated you. Those others, those feminists, were always trying to prove something, he thought, trying to make up for something that was missing in their lives. Well, he knew what was missing, and he could show them if they liked! What a thought! Thank heavens for girls like Julia and for her offer of a room in her flat.

"That's really great, Julia," he said. "Can you show me the room?" He winked.

She led him to a room at the back of the flat. "This is the guest room, Brucie," she said. "You can keep your stuff in that cupboard over there— it's empty. And I'm right next door." She gestured at a door behind them. "When you need me."

Bruce clicked his tongue appreciatively and gave her a playful pinch. "Good girl," he said. "This is going to be fun."

Julia gave a little laugh. "You bet. When do you want to move in?"

"Tomorrow?"

"Suits me fine."

"And in the meantime," said Bruce. "Let's go somewhere this evening. A wine bar? A meal after-wards?"

This suited Julia very well, and they made their arrangements to meet. Bruce then left and went out into the street. He smiled. This was perfect, just perfect. He had found himself somewhere to stay—somewhere where he would not have Neil and Caroline cooing away in the background. Really, what a pair of lovebirds—gazing into one another's eyes for hours on end and going to bed early, pretending to be tired. Sickening, really, and if that was what marriage was like, then he counted himself lucky still to be single. Of course, if he wanted to get married, then he could do so—any day. All he would have to do would be to click his fingers—like that—and the girls would be lining up. But there would be plenty of time for that.

He walked down Northumberland Street and turned into Dundas Street. It was good, he thought, to be back in this familiar part of town, amongst his old haunts. A few blocks down the hill was the Cumberland Bar, where he had spent so many good evenings, and just beyond that Scotland Street itself. When he went down to London, he imagined that he had put all that behind him; it was almost as if he had wanted to forget it all. But now that he was back in Edinburgh, his memories of that period of his life were flooding back, and it had not been a bad time in his life, not at all. He thought of the girls he had known—that American girl, the one he met in the Cumberland; she was a stunner, but then she had proved rather unreliable in the long run. He frowned. And of course there was Pat herself, his little flatmate as he called her. She fell for me in a big way, he thought, poor girl. But she would have been inexperienced and emotionally demanding, and she would have clung to me if I had started anything. Nothing worse than that—a girl who clings. That can get difficult.

He continued to walk down Dundas Street. He realised that he was close to the gallery that she worked in, the gallery owned by the rather wet Matthew. He was one person he could do without seeing again, and yet he would probably still be hanging about the Cumberland Bar hoping for something to turn up. Sad.

He glanced towards the gallery window, and at that moment Pat looked out. Bruce stopped. She was staring at him and he could hardly just ignore her. He could wave and continue down the street, which would give her a very clear message, or he could go in and have a word with the poor girl.

He looked at his watch. There was no point in going back to Comely Bank and sitting in Neil and Caroline's kitchen until it was time to go out to dinner. So why not?

He pushed open the gallery door and went in.

19. Bruce Enjoys Telling His London Story

"London," said Pat. Bruce winked at her. "Fantastic place. London's just great. You should go there some time, Pat. Move on."

Pat looked at Bruce. He had not changed at all,

she decided. There was the same slightly superior look—a knowing expression, one might call it—and the hair . . . yes, it was the same gel, giving forth the same faint smell of cloves.

"How was the job down there?" she asked. "What did you do?"

Bruce ran a hand through his hair; cloves released. "Two jobs, actually. I left the first one after a week. The second one was more . . . how should I put it? More to my taste."

She was interested in this. Bruce would never admit to being fired, but if he left the job after a week, then that must have been what happened. "Oh. What went wrong?" she asked.

Bruce began to smile. "You really want to know?"

Pat nodded. She did want to know.

"All right," said Bruce. "I went for an interview for a job handling the commissioning of a portfolio of service flats. Not just any service flats—these were high-end places, Bayswater and so on. Diplomats—ones from serious countries, not Tonga, you know. Saudi, Brunei, places like that. Big Arabs. Fancy Japs. Eurotrash. Serious money.

"This firm was doing the decorating, installing the bits and pieces—everything, really. And money was going to be no object. Persian rugs—large ones—all the stuff you put in these places, you know—busts of Roman emperors, Hockney drawings, and so on. We were going to do the whole thing."

Pat raised an eyebrow. "But you're not a decorator, Bruce. You're . . ."

He did not let her finish. "Questioning my versatility, Patsy-girl? I've got an eye, you know."

Pat shrugged. Bruce had known nothing about wine, but that seemed not to have stopped him being a success in the wine business. So perhaps it was confidence that counted, and he was definitely not short of that.

Bruce sat down on Pat's desk. He adjusted the crease in his trousers. Chinos, Pat thought.

"So anyway," he continued, "I went for the interview with this guy. You should have seen him. Mr Colour Co-ordination himself. He knew how to match his trousers with his jacket. He was very nice. He asked me how I thought I could contribute, and I told him that I had managed properties in Edinburgh. Then he showed me a picture of an empty room and asked me what I'd put into it. He fished out this catalogue full of antiques and said I should pick something from there. I did, but I had a feeling there was something else going on. He was looking at me, you see. Like this."

Bruce turned sideways to Pat, glanced at her with widened eyes, and then looked away.

"Oh," said Pat.

Bruce smiled. "See what I mean? What do you think a look like that means? Well, you'll find out. The next thing he says is this: 'Let me guess,

Bruce—you're Aries, aren't you?' Just like that. Coming on hard."

Pat thought for a moment. She remembered Bruce's birthday, and it was true. He was an Aries.

"He got it right," she said.

"Yes. He got it right. But then he said: 'Do you like cooking?' Cooking! And that made it even clearer. So you know what I did? I knew that there were three or four people after this job—I'd seen them outside—and so I decided that I'd play along with all this. If that's what it took to get the job, I was ready. So I said: 'Cooking? I adore it!' Yes, I did! And he brightened up and said: 'That's great, just great. I love being in the kitchen.' Or something like that. Then he looked at his watch and said: 'If you want the job, Bruce, it's yours.' And so we got it all tied up there and then and I started at the beginning of the following week."

Pat looked down. She did not like this, and she did not want to hear anymore. But Bruce continued.

"It was a great job. I was meant to source the things we needed for the flats and to chase up the painters and plumbers and whatnot. I made up the spreadsheets for the projects with timelines and completion dates and stuff like that. It was great. But then Rick—that was his name—invited me to a dinner party at his place. Boy! You should have seen it. Furniture to die for. Big paintings—none of this Victorian junk you sell here. Big splashes of colour. And there was Rick in a caftan. Yes! I look around and think: where are the other guests? Surprise, surprise! No other guests.

" 'Unfortunately, the others cancelled,' said Rick. 'So inconsiderate of them!' He turns on the music."

Pat listened to Bruce with growing horror. I can't stand him, she thought. I can't stand him. He led that poor man on just to get the job. I can't stand him.

Bruce grinned. "So you know what I did? I said: 'Rick, I'm terribly sorry. I'm just developing this terrible headache. Really bad.' And I started to leave. So he says: 'But Bruce, you haven't had a thing to eat, not a thing! I can't let you set off with a headache and an empty stomach.' So I said that I wasn't really hungry and that maybe another day, and so he says: 'Tomorrow, Bruce? Same time?' And that was it, really. I phoned him at the office next day and left a message that I wouldn't be coming back. So that was the end of the job."

Pat looked away. There was nothing worse, in her view, than talking about something like that, a private encounter in which one person misunderstands another and is made to look pathetic. And Bruce was responsible for the whole misunderstanding by pretending to be gay. She turned back to him. "That's really horrible," she said. "Really horrible."

"I know," said Bruce, smiling broadly. "But I don't hold it against him. Not really."

Pat drew in her breath. It seemed impossible to dent his self-satisfaction, his utter self-assuredness. She wanted to hit him, because that, she thought, might be the only way of telling him what she felt. But she would not have had the chance, even if she had summoned up the courage, as Bruce now slid off the desk, patted her on the arm, and moved towards the door.

"*À bientôt*," he said. "Which, translated into the patois of these parts, means: see yous!"

20. *Miss Harmony Has News for the Children*

"Now listen, everybody," said Miss Harmony, clapping her hands to get attention. "We have some very interesting news." She looked out over the class, seated in a circle round the room. They were always somewhat excited at the beginning of a new term and usually took a few days to settle down, especially if there were any new members. As it happened, there were not, and indeed the class was one member down with the departure of Merlin. He had been withdrawn by his parents, who had decided to homeschool him for a trial period. Miss Harmony had not thought that a good idea, as she believed in the socialisation value of the classroom experience, particularly when the parents themselves were so odd. And she had the gravest doubts as to what Merlin's mother could actually teach her son. There was something very disconcerting about that woman, Miss Harmony thought, her vague, mystical pronouncements, her interest in crystals, and her slightly fey appearance did not inspire confidence. But it was her choice, and it would be respected, although when she thought about it hard enough, she wondered exactly why one should respect the choices of others when those choices were so patently bad ones. That would require further thought, she decided.

Looking around the class, there were various other pupils whom she would quite happily have seen withdrawn for homeschooling. Larch was one, with his aggressive outlook and his . . . well, she did not like to blame a child for his appearance, but there was no escaping the fact that Larch looked like a pugilist on day-release from Polmont Young Offenders' Institution. He was rather frightening, actually, and he really did spoil the class photographs.

These thoughts, though, were not really very charitable and Miss Harmony accepted that she should put them firmly from her mind, but not before she had allowed herself a final reflection on how Hiawatha, too, might also benefit from homeschooling, which would remove the constant problem of his socks and their somewhat unpleasant odour. Would a letter to his mother be in order? she wondered. It was difficult to imagine how one might put the matter tactfully; parents were so sensitive about such things.

"Yes," said Miss Harmony. "A lot has happened! First of all, you will notice that Merlin is no longer with us. We have said farewell to him, as he is going to be studying at home this year."

This announcement was greeted with silence, as the children looked at one another. Then Olive put up her hand.

"He won't be studying, Miss Harmony," she said. "He told me. He said that his mother wanted him to help her with her weaving. He said that he was going to be getting paid for it."

"Now, Olive," said Miss Harmony. "We mustn't always believe what others tell us, must we? Especially when they are having a little joke, as I am sure Merlin was. We all know that Merlin will be working very hard in his little home classroom and that his head will soon be bursting with knowledge." She stared hard at Olive. "Yes, Olive, bursting with knowledge."

Tofu now joined in. "I saw something about this on television," he said. "It was about carpet factories in India. The children all worked in the factories and made rugs."

Miss Harmony laughed. "That's child labour, Tofu, dear. And it is no longer allowed in this country. Certainly it used to be—chimney sweeps would make little boys—like you—go up the chimney for them. Charles Dickens wrote about that sort of thing. But now we do not allow that anymore." She paused. "Merlin will not be a child labourer, I assure you."

She gave Tofu a discouraging look. "Now then," she said. "The news that Merlin has left us is very sad news for us, of course. But there has also been some happy news. And I'm going to ask Bertie to tell us himself."

All eyes swung round to Bertie, who blushed.

"Come on, Bertie," said Miss Harmony. "You tell us about the little event which happened in your house over the holidays."

Bertie bit his lip. He had not been sure at first what Miss Harmony was alluding to, but now he knew.

"My mother had a baby," he muttered.

"Now, now, Bertie," encouraged Miss Harmony. "Good news must be given loud and clear."

"A baby," said Bertie. "My mother had a baby."

"See!" said Miss Harmony. "That's good news, isn't it everybody? Bertie now has a little brother. And what's his name, Bertie?"

Bertie looked down at the top of his desk. There was no escape, or at least one that he could identify. "Ulysses," he said.

Tofu, who had been staring at Bertie, now looked away and sniggered.

"Tofu," said Miss Harmony. "Ulysses is a very fine name."

Tofu said nothing.

"Yes," said Miss Harmony. "And we don't laugh at the names of others, do we, Tofu? Especially . . ." She hesitated. It was so tempting, impossible to resist, in fact. "Especially if we are called Tofu ourselves."

"Tofu's a stupid name," volunteered Olive. "It's that horrid white stuff that cranky people eat. It's a stupid name. I'd far rather be called Ulysses than Tofu, any day of the week. And anyway, Tofu, it's nice to hear that Miss Harmony thinks your name is stupid too."

"That is not what I said, Olive," said Miss Harmony quickly. "And let's move on, boys and girls. We are all very pleased, I'm sure, to hear about Bertie's new baby brother and we look forward to meeting him some day soon. I'm sure that Bertie is very proud of him and will bring him to the school to introduce us all. But in the meantime, boys and girls, we are going to start today with sums, just to see whether we've remembered what we learned last term!"

Much had been forgotten, and the rest of the morning was devoted to the reinstallation of vanished knowledge. Bertie worked quietly, but he noticed Olive looking at him from time to time and the observation made him feel uneasy. Bertie was wary of Olive on several counts, but principally because she laboured under the delusion that she was his girlfriend. And at the end of the day, his doubts proved to be well-founded.

"I'm really looking forward to seeing your new baby brother," said Olive, as they left the classroom. "I'm coming to see him soon."

Bertie frowned. "Who said?" he asked.

"My mother has spoken to your mother," Olive answered. "And your mother says that I can come to play at your house once a week if I like. So I will."

"But I didn't ask you," said Bertie.

"No," said Olive. "But that makes no difference. Your mummy did—and that's what counts." She paused. "And we're going to play house."

21. Pat Experiences a Moment of Brutal Honesty

Bruce had been gone a good hour, but Pat was still smarting from her encounter with her newly returned former flatmate. Much of her anger focused on the fact that she had not responded adequately to his unpleasant story of his London experiences; didn't-kiss-and-still-told was in her mind every bit as bad as kiss-and-tell. There was so much she could have said which would have indicated her disgust over his insensitive behaviour, so much, but, as was so often the case, the really pithy comments, those brilliant *mots justes* that might have deflated him, only occurred to her after he had left.

And then she wondered whether anything could ever deflate Bruce, such was the sheer Zeppelinscale volume of his self-satisfaction. At least their brief meeting had convinced her—if conviction were needed—that she disliked him intensely, and yet, and yet . . . when he had perched on her desk, uninvited, she found herself unable to ignore the brute fact of his extreme attractiveness. Bruce was, quite simply, devastatingly good-looking, an Adonis sent down to live among us. And the fact that she even noticed this worried her. She had already had a narrow escape with Wolf, who had similarly daz-zled her, and here she was looking at Bruce again in that way. Am I, she wondered, one of those people who fall for the physically desirable, irrespective of what they are like as people? In a moment of brutal honesty, she realised that the answer was probably: yes, I am. It was a bleak conclusion.

She thought of Matthew, solid, dependable, pre-dictable Matthew. These three epithets said it all, but they were words which had no excitement in them, no thrill. And yet when one compared Matthew with Bruce, Matthew's merits were over-whelming. But then again, there was the distressed-oatmeal, the crushed-strawberry factor . . .

The door of the gallery opened and Pat turned round. A man had entered the gallery, a largish man of rather elegant bearing, wearing grey slacks and a blazer, no tie, but a red silk bandanna tied around his neck. He sported a jaunty mustache. He smiled at Pat and gestured in the direction of the paintings. "Do you mind? May I?"

"Of course. Please."

He nodded to her in a friendly way and made his way across the gallery to stand in front of one of Matthew's recently acquired MacTaggart seascapes. Pat watched him from her desk. Some people who came into the gallery were merely passing the time, with no intention of buying anything; this man, though, with his urbane manner, had a different air about him.

He moved closer to one of the MacTaggarts and peered at a section of the large canvas. Two children were sitting on the edge of a wide, windswept beach. The children were windswept too, their hair ruffled. They were playing with the sand, which streamed away from their hands, caught in the breeze, in thin lines of gold.

The man turned round and addressed Pat across the floor. "Can you tell me anything about this?"

Pat rose from her desk and walked across to join him. "It's a MacTaggart," she said. "Do you know about him?"

"Not much," said the man. "But I do know a little. I like his work. There's a strange air about it. Something rather windblown, don't you think?"

Pat agreed. "It reminds me of places like Tantallon," she said. "Or Gullane beach, perhaps. That could be Fife on the other side of the water. Just there. There's some land, you see."

The man turned and smiled at her. "It probably

doesn't matter much," he said. "Just Scotland. Quite some time ago now."

"Yes." She waited for him to say something else, but his gaze had shifted. Now he was looking at Angus Lordie's painting. He moved forward and stared at the label beneath it; then he stood back and stared at it, his head slightly to one side.

Pat watched him. She was about to say something, to tell him that this was not entirely serious, but he had now turned to face her.

"Do you know 'Four minutes thirty-three seconds'?" he asked. "That piece by what's his name? John Cage? Complete silence. That's all it is—complete silence."

"Nothing?"

"Yes, nothing at all. Often done on the piano, but an orchestra can play it too. The conductor stands there, turning pages of the score, but nobody plays a note. And that's it."

"You've heard it?"

The man nodded. "I suppose you might say that we've all heard it. I heard it in New York. But if any of us has ever listened to four minutes of silence, anywhere, then I suppose you could say that we've heard what the composer wanted us to hear. But then, we don't listen to silence, do we? We're too preoccupied."

Pat looked at Angus Lordie's painting. "Well . . ." she began.

It was as if the man had not heard her. "That performance in New York was extraordinary. The moment the orchestra had stopped, there was confusion in the audience. Some of them knew the piece, of course, and applauded. They understood. Some laughed. Others were silent, not really knowing what to do."

"This painting is a bit like that," he said. "I like it, you know."

Pat stood quite still. One part of her wanted to tell him that it was absurd, that Matthew's joke had gone far enough; the other imagined Matthew's pleasure if she actually sold it. It was the sort of thing that would amuse him greatly, and, of course, there was Angus to think about. He was miserable over Cyril's plight and he would appreciate some good news.

"I don't suppose you want to buy it," Pat said. She was hesitant. I'm not trying to persuade him, she thought. I'm really not. And the painting was so absurdly pricey—for what it was—that only somebody who did not have to worry about money would buy it. Such people, surely, could look after themselves.

The man turned his head sideways to look at the painting from a slightly different angle. "Why not? My walls are a bit cluttered, you know. The usual stuff. I could do with a bit of minimalism. So, why not?"

Pat waited. "Yes?"

"Yes," he said. "Bung a red sticker under it. My name's Johannesburg. Here's my card."

113

He handed her his card. *The Duke of Johannesburg*, it read. *Single-Malt House*. And under that: *Clubs: Scottish Arts (Edinburgh)*; *Savile (London)*; *Gitchigumi (Duluth)*.

22. A Little Argument Develops Over . . . Guess What?

Matthew did not like it when people said "guess what?" to him, which is the very expression with which Pat greeted him when he returned to the gallery. Being asked to guess what had happened struck him as pointless—one could never guess accurately in such circumstances, which was precisely why one was asked to do so.

"I don't see why I should try to guess," he said peevishly. "If I did, I would be completely wrong and you would just revel in your advantage over me. So I'm not going to guess."

Pat looked at him with surprise. He had been in a good mood when he left for his appointment; something must have gone wrong with that meeting to produce this irritable response. "I was only asking," she said.

Matthew tossed the file that he was carrying down on the desk. "You weren't asking," he said. "Asking me to guess isn't really asking anything. You just want to show me that I don't know what's happened. That's all."

Pat was not sure how to react to this. It seemed

to her a completely unimportant matter—an argument over nothing. She had said "guess what?" but she was not really expecting him to try to guess. In fact, she had intended merely to point to the red sticker which now adorned Angus Lordie's painting. It was good news, after all, not bad. Aggrieved, she decided that she would defend herself. "I don't know why you're so ratty," she said. "Lots of people say 'guess what?' when they have some news to give somebody else. It's just a thing they say. They don't really expect you to guess."

"Well, I'm not guessing," said Matthew.

Pat looked away. "Then I'm not going to tell you," she said. She would not tell him; she would not.

For a moment there was silence. Then Matthew spoke. "You have to," he said. "You can't say something like that and then not tell me."

"Not if you're going to be so rude," said Pat.

Matthew raised his voice. "You're the one who was being rude. Not me. You're the one who wanted to expose my ignorance of whatever it is you know and I don't. That's hardly very friendly, is it?"

Pat was still seated at the desk and now she looked up at Matthew. "You're the one who's not being friendly," she said. "All I was trying to do was to give you some good news and you bit my head off. Just like that."

Matthew's expression remained impassive. "You sold a painting."

Pat had not expected this. "Maybe," she muttered.

"There!" crowed Matthew. "I guessed! Now, don't say anything. No, let me guess."

"You said you didn't want to guess," snapped Pat. "Now you're saying you do. You should make up your mind, you know."

"I'm guessing because I've decided I want to guess," said Matthew. "That's very different from being made to guess when you don't want to. You should have said: 'Would you like me to tell you something or would you prefer to guess?' That would have been much more polite." He paused. "Now, let me think. You've sold a painting. Right. So which painting would it be? One of the MacTaggarts? No, I don't think so. It's not the sort of day on which one sells a MacTaggart. No. So, let's see."

Pat decided to put an end to this. If Matthew had been unprepared to guess when she had very politely offered him the chance, then she did not see why he should now have the privilege of guessing. "I'm going to tell you. It's . . ."

"No!" interjected Matthew. "Don't spoil it. You can't get somebody guessing and then stop them. Come on, Pat—I'm going to guess. Let's think. All right—you sold Angus Lordie's painting. Yes! You sold the totally white one."

116

"You saw the sticker," said Pat. "That wasn't a proper guess."

Matthew was injured innocence itself. "I did not see the sticker! I did not!"

"You must have. You saw it when you came in and then you pretended not to. Well, I think that's just pathetic, I really do."

"I did not see the sticker," shouted Matthew. "Who knows better what I saw or didn't see? You or me? No, don't look like that, just tell me? Who knows what I saw? You or me?"

Pat recalled what her father had said about the mind and its tricks of perception. It was likely that Matthew had in fact seen the sticker when he came in, even if he did not know that he had seen it.

"You don't always know what you've seen," she said. "The mind registers things at a subconscious level. You may not know that you've seen something, but you have. The mind knows it subconsciously."

Matthew stared at her. "Look," he said, "let's not fight. I'm sorry if I went on about guessing. I suppose I'm just a bit . . . Well, I don't know, I'm just a bit."

She held out her hand and touched him briefly. "All right. Sorry too."

"I can hardly believe that you sold that painting," he said, adding, "If you can call it a painting. How did they pay?"

Pat reached for the card she had been given.

117

"Well, he hasn't paid yet. But he did ask for a red sticker to be put up."

She handed him the card. He examined it and frowned. "The Duke of where?"

"Johannesburg," said Pat. "He was a man with a mustache. About your height. He was wearing a red bandanna."

Matthew stared at the card. "I've never heard of him," he said. "Are you sure he exists? Are you sure this isn't some sort of joke?"

Pat felt defensive. She had begun to doubt herself now, and she wondered whether she should simply have taken the man's card and put up a sticker. It did seem a bit trusting, but if one couldn't trust dukes, then whom could one trust?

"He seemed . . ." She trailed off.

Matthew looked doubtful. "It seems a bit unlikely," he said. "Why would Johannesburg have a duke? And what's all this about these clubs? Where's the Gitchigumi Club for heaven's sake?"

"Duluth," said Pat. "That's what it says there. Duluth."

"And where exactly is that?" asked Matthew.

"Duluth?"

"Yes. Where's Duluth?"

Pat thought for a moment. "Guess," she said. She had no idea, and could only guess herself. Minnesota?

23. An Embarrassing Trip on the Bus for Bertie

When classes were over for the day and the children spilled out, Irene met Bertie at the school gate. This was not an ideal situation from Bertie's point of view as it gave his mother the opportunity to make the sort of arrangement which had caused him such concern—of which the proposed visit, or series of visits, by Olive was a prime example. He had suggested that they meet further up the road, at the junction of Spylaw Road and Ettrick Road, well away from the eyes of his classmates, but this proposal had been greeted by Irene with an understanding smile.

"Now, Bertie," she said, "Mummy knows that you're ashamed of her! And you mustn't feel ashamed of feeling ashamed. All children are embarrassed by their parents—it's a perfectly normal stage through which you go. Melanie Klein . . ." She paused. She could not recall precisely what Melanie Klein had written on the subject, but she was sure that there was something. It had to do with idealisation of the female parental figure, or mother, to use the vernacular. Or it was related to the need of the child to establish a socially visible persona which was defined in isolation from the mother's personality. By distancing himself from her, Bertie thought that he might grow in stature in relation to those boys who were still under maternal skirts. Well, that was understandable enough, but the development of the young ego could still be assisted by saying it does not matter. In that way, the child would transcend the awkward stage of parental/infant uncoupling and develop a more integrated, self-sufficient ego.

"It doesn't matter, Bertie," Irene said. "It really doesn't."

Bertie looked at his mother. It was difficult sometimes to make out what she was trying to say, and this was one of those occasions. "What doesn't matter?" he asked.

Irene reached out and took his hand. They were travelling home on the 23 bus, with Bertie's baby brother, Ulysses, fitted snugly round Irene's front in a sling. Bertie liked to travel on the upper deck, but they were not there now as the concentration of germs there was greater, Irene said, than below, and Ulysses's immune system was not yet as strong as it might be. Bertie tried to slip his hand out of his mother's, but her grip was tight. He looked around him furtively to see if anybody from school might see him holding hands with his mother on the bus; fortunately, there was nobody.

"It doesn't matter that you feel embarrassed about being seen with me at the school gate," she said. "Those feelings are natural. But it also doesn't matter what other people think of you, Bertie. It really doesn't."

Bertie's face flushed. He looked down at the floor. "I'm not embarrassed, Mummy," he said.

"Oh yes, you are!" said Irene, her voice rising playfully. "Mummy can tell! *Roberto è un poco imbarazzato!*"

"*Non è vero*," mumbled Bertie. He glanced out of the window; they were barely at Tollcross, which meant it was at least another ten minutes before they reached Dundas Street, ten minutes of agony. Ulysses, at least, was asleep, which meant that he was doing little to draw anybody's attention, but then he suddenly made a loud, embarrassing noise. On the other side of the bus, a boy only a few years older than Bertie, a boy travelling by himself, glanced at Bertie and smirked. Bertie looked away.

"You see, Bertie," Irene went on, "Mummy understands. And all I want is that you should be able to rise above the terrors of being your age. I know what it's like. You think I don't, because all children think that grown-ups know nothing. Well we know a lot—we really do. I know what it's like to be small and to be worried about what other children are thinking. All I want is for you to be free of that, to be able to be yourself. Do you understand what I'm saying?"

Bertie thought quickly. He found that one of the best strategies with his mother was to distract her in some way, to change the subject, and this is what he now did.

"Olive said that she was going to come to my house," he said.

"Our house," corrected Irene. "Bertie lives there with Mummy and Daddy and, of course, dear little Ulysses. And yes, *è vero*, I have invited Olive. I spoke to her mummy at the school gate and suggested that Olive should come down to Scotland Street one afternoon a week. This will suit her mummy, who is doing a degree course at the university, you see. And it will be nice to have somebody for you to play with. You'll have a lot of fun."

Bertie stared at his mother. "I don't want to play with Olive, Mummy. She's very bossy."

Irene laughed. "Bossy? Olive? Come now, Bertie, she's a charming little girl. You two will get on like a house on fire."

"I want to play with other boys," said Bertie.

Irene patted him on the shoulder. "There'll be time for that later on, Bertie. You'll find that Olive is plenty of fun to play with—more fun, in fact, than boys. And, anyway, we have agreed and we can hardly uninvite Olive, can we?"

Bertie said nothing. Long experience of his mother—all six years of it—had taught him that there was no point in arguing. He looked at Ulysses, who had now woken up and had opened his eyes. The baby was staring at Bertie with that steady, intense stare that only babies can manage. Bertie looked back at his little brother. Poor little boy, he thought. Just you wait. Just you wait until she starts on you. Mozart. Yoga. Melanie Klein . . .

Ulysses's gaze drifted away from Bertie and up towards Irene. Immediately, he began to cry.

"He's hungry," said Irene. And with that she loosened the sling and began to unbutton her blouse.

"Can't he wait, Mummy?" whispered Bertie. "Please let him wait."

"Babies can't," said Irene, now exposing her breast. "Here, darling. Mummy's ready."

Bertie froze. He dared not look across the aisle to where that boy was sitting, but then he snatched a quick glance and saw the boy staring at the scene, his face full of disgust. Bertie looked away quickly. I want to die, he thought suddenly. I just don't want to be here.

Ulysses was making guzzling sounds, and then burped.

24. Angus Meets the Expert on Mistake-Making

Angus Lordie, of course, did not yet know of his apparent good fortune. Had he known, his mood might have lifted, but then again it might not: Cyril was still detained, and life without Cyril was proving hard.

Cyril had been a constant presence in his life for the last six years. When he was working in his studio, Cyril would be there, lying in the basket provided for him in a corner, watching Angus with half an eye, ready to respond to the slightest sign that it was time for a walk. And when he went down to the Cumberland Bar to sit at his usual table and pass the time in conversation, Cyril would accompany him, lying under the table, guarding the small dish of beer which was his ration for the night. Cyril did not disagree with anything that Angus said or did; Cyril would wait for hours for the slightest acknowledgement of his presence by his master, wagging his tail with undisguised enthusiasm whenever his name was uttered. Cyril never complained, never indicated that he wanted things to be otherwise than they were as disposed by Angus. And now that Cyril was gone, there was a great yawning void in Angus Lordie's life.

Ever since Cyril's arrest, on suspicion of biting, Angus had done his utmost for him. He had immediately contacted his lawyer, who had been extremely supportive.

"We'll get him out," the lawyer had said. "They need proof that he's the one who did the biting. And I don't see what proof they have."

"Find an advocate," said Angus. "Get the best. I don't care what it costs."

The lawyer nodded. "If that's what you want."

It was, and now Angus was preparing for a consultation with the advocate who had been engaged to represent Cyril. They were to meet that morning, in the premises of the Faculty of Advocates, to discuss the case and the strategy that would be adopted. As Angus trudged up the Mound to attend this meeting, his mind was full of foreboding. He had seen an item in *The Scotsman* that morning about a sheepdog that had been ordered to be destroyed after it had herded a group of Japanese tourists into the waters of Loch Lomond. Would a similar order be made in respect of Cyril? Could dogs effectively be executed these days? Surely that was too cruel a punishment, even if a dog had bitten somebody. And that sheepdog was just doing what it thought was its duty.

He walked across Parliament Square, past the front of St Giles', the High Kirk, that scene of so many of Edinburgh's dramas. The streets here were steeped in history: here traitors, criminals, simple heretics had been dragged on their last journey; here the Edinburgh mob had howled its protests against its masters; here Charles Edward Stuart himself had ridden past in his vain attempt at the regaining of a kingdom; here Hume had walked with his friends. And now here was he in his private misery, going to the seat of justice to plead for the life of a dog whom he loved, who was his friend.

He walked into Parliament Hall and watched as lawyers strolled up and down the hall, deep in conversation with one another, going over their pleadings, strategies, possible settlements. He was early for the consultation—he had at least half an hour in hand—and he decided to sit down on a bench at the side. He looked up at the high hammer-beam roof with its great arches of Scandinavian oak and at the portraits which surrounded the hall; such dignity, such grandeur, and yet behind it all were the ordinary, stubborn facts of human existence—grinding labour, power, vanity. We dressed our affairs in splendour, but they remained at root grubby little mixtures of hope and tragedy and failure; while round about the foundations of this human world ran the dogs, enthusiasts all, pursuing their own doggy lives in the shadow of their masters, free, but only until they collided with human aims. And then the dogs were smacked or locked up, or, if they overstepped a mark they knew nothing about, given a sharp little injection that put an end to it all for them.

He was still looking up at the ceiling when he became aware of the fact that somebody had sat down on the bench beside him. Angus glanced at his neighbour—a man a bit younger than himself, wearing a suit and tie, and looking at that moment at his wristwatch.

Angus decided to strike up a conversation; anything was better than thinking about Cyril and durance vile. "You're giving evidence?" he asked.

"Yes. I'm a so-called expert." The other man laughed. "Actually, I suppose I am an expert—it's just that I never call myself that. I'm a psychologist, you see. I specialise in how people do things, in particular how they make mistakes."

Angus was interested. "So what's going on today?"

"Oh, it's the usual thing," said the psychologist. "Somebody made a mistake over something. They've called me to give evidence on how the mistake was made. They want to find out who's responsible. That's what they do up here."

"Whose fault?"

The psychologist smiled. "Well, yes. But what these people," he indicated the lawyers, "what they don't understand is that mistakes, human error, may have nothing to do with fault. We all make mistakes—however careful we are."

"Yes," mused Angus. "This morning I put tea in the coffee pot . . ."

"But of course you would!" said the psychologist. "That's exactly the sort of mistake that people make. We call it a slip/lapse error. We do that sort of thing mostly when we're doing things that we are very used to doing. We're wearing our glasses and we look for them. Or we dial one familiar number when we mean to dial another. I know somebody who thought he had dialled his lover and had dialled his wife. He launched straight into the conversation and said: 'I can't see you tonight—she's invited people to dinner.' And his wife said: 'Good. So you've remembered.'"

Angus laughed, although the story, he thought, was a sad one.

"And you?" asked the psychologist. "Why are you here?"

"Because of my god," Angus replied.

The psychologist frowned. Then his expression lightened. "You mean dog! Another slip/lapse error! The transposing of *g* and *d*." He paused. "Mind you," he said, "if one were a theist, your statement would be correct. Unless, of course, one removed the space between *a* and *theist,* in which case it would be incorrect."

"Oh," said Angus.

25. The Advocate Takes a Look at the Case of Cyril

The advocate instructed by Angus Lordie's lawyer was in his late thirties, a man with fine, rather aquiline features. As a portrait painter, Angus was sensitive to such matters, and he approved of this man's face. He liked people, and particularly faces, to suit occupations and often found himself feeling vaguely disappointed when face and profession were not in harmony. He had occasionally attended stock sales with a farming friend and had been struck by the faces of the Border farmers, by the ruddy complexions, by the features that gave every impression of having been left out overnight in the rain. One man, he thought, had looked like a haystack, with his hair sticking out in all directions—his skin the colour of well-dried hay, too, he observed; another, with a thick neck and heavy shoulders, looked to all intents and purposes like an Aberdeen Angus bull. These men were gifts to the portrait painter, he told himself, as was the face of the librarian who occasionally came into the Cumberland Bar, a man whose skin was like parchment, whose scholarly eyes looked out at the world from behind the lenses of small unframed spectacles—perfect.

And now here was this advocate, in his strippit breeks, with his sharp, legal face that would not have been out of place in an eighteenth-century engraving, a John Kay miniature—though Kay preferred his subjects wirlie, and this man would take a good twenty years to become truly wirlie.

"This is a very sad affair," said the advocate, looking down at the file of papers before him. "Your agent here tells me that you're very fond of your dog, Mr Lordie."

Angus looked at his lawyer, who smiled at him, a smile of sympathy, of regret.

"Yes, I am," he said. "I am. And I simply can't believe that I find myself . . . that my dog finds himself in this position."

The advocate sighed. "I suppose that even the best-behaved of dogs have their . . . their—how should one put it?—atavistic moments."

Angus stared at the lawyer, noticing the slight touch of redness that was beginning to colour the side of the aquiline nose. That was the effect of claret, he thought, an occupational hazard for Edinburgh lawyers. The observation distracted him for a moment, but he soon remembered where he was and what the advocate had just said. Cyril was not atavistic; he had not bitten anybody. But the advocate had implied that he was guilty—on what grounds? The mere assumption that any dog was capable of biting?

"That might apply to other dogs," he said. "But it certainly does not apply to mine. My dog is innocent."

Silence descended on the room. In the background, a large wall clock could be heard ticking.

"How can you be so sure?" asked the advocate.

"Because I know him well," said Angus. "One knows one's dog. He is not a biter."

The advocate looked down at his papers. "I see here that your dog has a gold tooth," he said. "May I ask: how did that come about? How did he lose the original tooth?"

"He bit another . . ." Angus stopped. The two lawyers were looking at him.

"Please go on," said the advocate. "He bit another . . . person?"

"He bit another dog," said Angus hotly. "And the fight in question was certainly not his fault."

"Yet he did bite, didn't he?" pressed the advocate. "You see, Mr Lordie, the situation looks a bit bleak. Your dog has bitten . . ."

Angus did not allow him to continue. "Excuse me," he said. "Perhaps I misunderstand the situation. I assumed that we had engaged you to help us establish Cyril's innocence. Aren't you meant to believe in that? Aren't you meant to argue that?"

The advocate sighed. "There is a difference between what I believe, Mr Lordie," he said, "and what I know to be the case. I can believe a large number of things which have yet to be established, either to my satisfaction or to the satisfaction of others."

Angus felt his neck getting warm. There was some truth in the expression getting hot under the collar; he was. "What if you know that somebody you're defending is guilty?" he began. "Can you defend him?"

The advocate looked unperturbed by the question. "It all depends on how I know that," he answered. "If I know that he's guilty because he's suddenly told me so in a consultation and because he wants me to put him in the box so that he can lie to the court—as sometimes happens—then I must ask him to get somebody else to defend him. I cannot stand up in court and let him lie. But if I just think he's guilty, then it's a different matter. He's entitled to have his story put before the court, whatever my personal suspicions may be."

Angus frowned. "But Cyril can't talk," he said. "He's a dog."

Again there was silence. Then the advocate spoke. "That is something that we can all agree we know to be the case."

"And since he can't give any story at all—because of his . . ."

"His canine condition," supplied the advocate.

Angus nodded. "Yes, because of his canine condition, then surely we must give him the benefit of the doubt."

"Of course we must," the advocate conceded. He gestured at the papers in front of him. "Except for the fact that there is rather a lot of evidence against him. This is why I believe we might be better to accept that he did it—that he bit these unfortunate people—and concentrate on how we can ensure that the outcome for him is the best one. In other words, we should think about making recommendations as to his supervision that the sheriff will see as reasonable. And it will be a sheriff court matter."

"Evidence?" Angus asked nervously.

"Yes," said the advocate. "Your solicitor has obtained various statements, Mr Lordie, and it seems that there are three people who say that they recognised your dog as the biter. They each say that they knew it was your dog because they had seen him with you in . . ." He looked down at a piece of paper. "In the Cumberland Bar. Drinking, I might add." He paused, and looked searchingly at Angus. "Do you think your dog might have been drunk when he bit these people, Mr Lordie?"

Angus did not reply. He was looking up at the ceiling. Cyril is going to be put down, he thought. This is the end.

26. Bertie Plucks Up Courage and Asks the Big Question

On several occasions, Bertie had asked his mother whether he might stop psychotherapy, but the answer had always been the same—he could not.

"I don't need to see Dr Fairbairn," he said to Irene. "You could still see him, though, Mummy. You could go up there and I could sit in the waiting room and read *Scottish Field*. You know that magazine. I could even look after Ulysses while you went in to see Dr Fairbairn. Ulysses could look at *Scottish Field* with me."

Irene laughed. "Dear Bertie," she said. "Why should I want to see Dr Fairbairn? It's you who are his patient, not Mummy."

"But you like him, don't you?" said Bertie. "You like him a lot, Mummy. I know you do."

Irene laughed again—slightly more nervously this time. "Well, it's true that I don't mind Dr Fairbairn. I certainly don't dislike him. Mummy doesn't dislike many people, Bertie. Mummy is what we call tolerant."

Bertie thought about this for a moment. It seemed to him that much of what his mother said was simply not true. And yet she was always telling him that it was wrong to tell fibs—which of course he never did. She was the one who was fibbing now, he thought. "But there are lots of people you don't like, Mummy," he protested. "There's that lady at the advanced kindergarten, Mrs Macfadzean. You didn't like her."

"Miss Macfadzean," Irene corrected. "She was Miss Macfadzean because no man in his right mind would ever have married her, poor woman."

"But you didn't like her, did you, Mummy?" Bertie asked again.

"It was not a question of disliking her, Bertie," said Irene. "It was more a question of feeling sorry for her. Those are two different things, you know. Mummy felt pity for Miss Macfadzean because of her limited vision. That's all. And her conservative outlook. But that's quite different from disliking her. Quite different."

Bertie thought about this. It had seemed very much like dislike to him, but then adults, he noticed, had a way of making subtle distinctions in the meaning of words. But even if his mother claimed not to have disliked Miss Macfadzean, then there were still other people whom he was sure she did not like at all. One of these was Tofu, Bertie's friend—of sorts—from school.

"What about Tofu?" he asked. "You don't like him, Mummy. You hate him, don't you?"

Irene gasped. "But Bertie, you mustn't ever say things like that! Mummy certainly does not hate Tofu. Mummy just thinks . . ." She trailed off.

"Thinks what, Mummy?" Bertie asked.

"I think that Tofu is just a little bit aggressive,"

Irene said. "I don't want you to grow up being aggressive, Bertie. I want you to grow up to be the sort of person who is aware of the feelings of others. The sort of boy who knows about the pain of other people. I want you to be *simpatico*, Bertie. That's what I want."

Bertie looked thoughtful. "And you don't like Hiawatha," he said. "That other boy in my class. You said you didn't like him. You told me so yourself, Mummy."

Irene glanced away. "Bertie," she said, "you really mustn't put words into my mouth. I did not say that I disliked Hiawatha. All I said was that I didn't like the way Hiawatha . . . well, not to beat about the bush, I didn't like the way that Hiawatha smelled. He really is a rather unsavoury little boy."

"But if you don't like somebody's smell," said Bertie, "doesn't that mean that you don't like them?"

"Not at all," countered Irene. "You can dislike the way a person smells without disliking them, in their essence." She paused. "And anyway, Bertie, I really don't think that this conversation is getting us anywhere. We were really meant to be talking about Dr Fairbairn. I was giving you an answer to the question that you asked about stopping your psychotherapy. And the answer, Bertie, is that you must keep up with it until Dr Fairbairn tells us that there's no longer any need for you to see him. He has not done that yet."

Bertie looked down at his shoes, thinking of how the answer was always no. Well, if his mother wanted to talk about Dr Fairbairn, then there was something that had been preying on his mind.

"Mummy," he began. "Don't you think that Ulysses looks a lot like Dr Fairbairn? Haven't you noticed?"

Irene was quite still. "Oh?" she said. "What do you mean by that, Bertie?"

"I mean that Ulysses has the same sort of face as Dr Fairbairn. You know how they both look. This bit here . . ." He gestured to his forehead.

Irene laughed. "But everybody has a forehead, Bertie! And I suspect if you compared Ulysses's forehead with lots of other people's, then you would reach the same conclusion."

"And his ears," went on Bertie. "Dr Fairbairn's ears go like that—and so do Ulysses's."

"Nonsense," said Irene abruptly.

"Do you think that Dr Fairbairn could be Ulysses's daddy?" asked Bertie.

He waited for his mother to respond. It had just occurred to Bertie that if Ulysses were to be Dr Fairbairn's son, then that could mean that he would go and live with him, and Bertie would no longer have the inconvenience of having a smaller brother in the house. He was not sure how Ulysses could be the psychotherapist's son, but it was, he assumed, possible. Bertie had only the haziest idea of how babies came about, but he did know that it was

136

something to do with adults having a conversation with one another. His mother and Dr Fairbairn had certainly talked to one another enough—enough to result in a baby, Bertie thought.

Irene was looking at her fingernails. "Bertie," she said. "There are some questions we never ask, and that is one of them. You never ask if somebody is a baby's real daddy! That's very rude indeed! It's the person whom the baby calls Daddy who is the daddy. We just have to accept that, even if sometimes we wonder whether it's not true. And of course it's not true in this case—I mean, it's not true that there's another daddy. Daddy is Ulysses's daddy. And that's that."

Bertie listened attentively. He wondered if there was a chance that Irene was not his real mother, and he would have loved to have asked about that, but this was not the right time, Bertie sensed.

27. It's Never Rude to Say Things to a Doctor

Now, sitting in Dr Fairbairn's waiting room, Bertie paged though an old issue of *Scottish Field*. His mother was closeted in the consulting room with the psychotherapist, and Bertie knew that they were discussing him, as they always did at the beginning of one of his sessions. He did not like this, but he knew that there was nothing he could do about it. It was hard enough to tackle his mother by herself; when she teamed up with Dr Fairbairn, it seemed to Bertie that he was up against impossible odds.

Bertie liked reading *Scottish Field*, and his regular encounters with the magazine helped to make the visits to Dr Fairbairn at least bearable. He wondered if it would be possible to take the magazine in with him to read during the psychotherapy session itself, as it seemed to him that Dr Fairbairn was quite content to do all the talking and it would make no difference if he was reading at the time. But he decided that this request would have little hope of being met; adults were so difficult over things like that.

He turned to the back of the magazine. After looking at the advertisements for fishing jackets and Aga cookers, which he liked, he turned to the social pages, which were his particular favourite. There were photographs there of people all over Scotland going to parties and events, and in every photograph everybody seemed to be smiling. Bertie had not been to many children's parties, but at those to which he had been there had always been one or two people who burst into tears over something or other. It seemed that this did not happen at grown-ups' parties, where there was just all this smiling. Bertie thought that this might have something to do with the fact that many of the people in the photographs were holding glasses of wine and were therefore probably drunk. If you were drunk, he had heard, you smiled and laughed.

He examined the photographs of a party which had been held at a very couthie place called Ramsay Garden. Somebody who lived there, it said, was giving drinks to his friends, who were all standing around laughing. That's nice, thought Bertie. One or two of the friends looked a bit drunk, in Bertie's view, but at least they were still standing, which was also nice. And there was a photograph of a man playing the kind-looking host's piano. His hands were raised over the keyboard and he was smiling at the camera, which Bertie thought was very clever, as it was hard to get your fingers on the right notes if you were not looking. Underneath the photograph there was a line which said: *Eric von Ibler accompanies the singing, while David Todd turns the pages*. Bertie wondered what the guests had been singing. He had once walked with his father past a pub where everybody was singing "Cod Liver Oil and the Orange Juice," which was a very strange song, thought Bertie. Was that what they were singing at the Ramsay Garden party? he wondered. Perhaps.

Bertie sighed and turned the page. There was a lot of fun being had in Scotland, mostly by grown-ups, and he wondered if he would ever be able to join in. He looked at the new spread of photographs and his eye was caught by some familiar faces. Yes, there was Mr Roddy Martine whom Bertie had seen in a previous copy of the magazine months ago. Mr Martine was very lucky, thought Bertie. All these invitations! And this was a party to launch his book about Rosslyn Chapel, and there was a photograph of Mr Charlie Maclean, balancing a glass of whisky on his nose. *Mr Charlie Maclean entertains the guests,* the caption read, *while Mr Bryan Johnston and Mr Humphrey Holmes look on.* That was very clever, thought Bertie. They must have had such fun at that party.

"Bertie?"

He looked up from *Scottish Field* and all the colour, all the warmth of the world of those pages seemed to drain away. Now he was back in monochrome. Dr Fairbairn.

Irene came from behind Dr Fairbairn and took a seat in the waiting room. Ulysses was strapped to her front in his tartan sling. She glanced with disapproval at *Scottish Field* and picked up, instead, a copy of *The Economist.*

"Dr Fairbairn's ready to see you now, Bertie," she said. "Just half an hour today."

Bertie went into the consulting room and sat in his usual seat. Outside, he could see the tops of the trees in Queen Street Gardens. They were moving in the breeze. It would be a good place to fly a kite, he thought, if he had one, which he did not.

"Now, Bertie," said Dr Fairbairn. "You've had a very big change in your life, haven't you? Your younger brother. Wee Ulysses. That's a big change."

"Yes," said Bertie. Ulysses had brought many changes, especially a lot of mess and noise.

"Having a new brother or sister is a major event in our lives, Bertie," said Dr Fairbairn. "And we must express our feelings about it."

Bertie said nothing. He was staring at Dr Fairbairn's forehead. Just above his eyebrows, on either side, there was a sort of bump, or ridge. And it was just like the bump he had seen on Ulysses's brow, whatever his mother said. Other people did not have that, Bertie was sure of that—just Dr Fairbairn and Ulysses.

"Yes," Dr Fairbairn went on. "Perhaps you would like to tell me what you're thinking about Ulysses. Then we can look at these feelings. We can talk about them. We can get them out in the open."

Bertie thought for a moment. Was this really what Dr Fairbairn wanted? "Are you sure?" he asked. "You won't think I'm being rude?"

Dr Fairbairn laughed. "Being rude? My goodness me, no, Bertie. It's not rude to articulate these feelings to a therapist!"

Bertie took a deep breath. The leaves outside the window were moving more energetically now. A kite would fly so well out there, so high. "Am I allowed to?" he asked. "Mummy said it was rude . . ."

"Of course you're allowed to, Bertie! Remember that I'm a sort of doctor. It's never rude to say things to a doctor. Doctors have heard hundreds and hundreds of rude things in their job. That's what doctors are for. They're there to tell rude things to. You can't shock a doctor, Bertie!"

Bertie looked out of the window again. Very well.

"Are you really Ulysses's daddy, Dr Fairbairn?" he asked.

28. So Who Exactly Is the New Man in Big Lou's Life?

Big Lou's customers could be divided into two groups. During the earlier part of the morning, between eight and ten, there were always the same twenty or so people who came in for a morning coffee on the way to work. These were people whom Big Lou described as her "hard workers," in contrast to those who came in after ten—Matthew and Angus and the like—whose day was only just starting when the hard workers had already put in an hour or two at the office.

Coming from Arbroath, as she did, and from an agricultural background, Big Lou knew all about hard work. Indeed, unremitting labour had been Big Lou's lot from childhood. It had been natural for her to help as a child on the farm, dealing with lambs that needed attention—a pleasant job which she enjoyed—or helping to muck out the byre— not such a pleasant job, but one which she had always performed with good grace. And then there had been kitchen work, which again she had been raised to, and scrubbing floors, and dusting shelves, and carrying trays of tea to bed-bound elderly relatives. Big Lou had done it all.

"You don't know you're born," she once said to Matthew.

Matthew smiled. "I'm not sure how to interpret that remark, Lou," he replied. "At one level—the literal—it's patently absurd. Of course I know I'm born. I'm aware of my existence. But if you're suggesting . . ."

"You ken fine what I'm suggesting," interjected Big Lou. "I'm suggesting you haven't got a clue."

Matthew smiled again. "About what, Lou? You know, you really shouldn't be so opaque."

"I mean that you don't know what hard work's all about." Big Lou spoke slowly, as if explaining something to a particularly slow child.

"Ah," said Matthew. "Now your meaning becomes clearer, Lou. We're on to that one again. Well, you're the one who needs a bit of a reality check. Work patterns have changed, Lou. Or they've changed in countries like this. We don't make things anymore, you may have noticed. Things are made in China. So we're doing different sorts of work. It's all changed. Different work patterns."

Big Lou looked at him coolly. "China?"

"Yes. Everything—or virtually everything. Take a look at the label—it'll tell you. Made in China. Clothes. Shoes too now. All the electronic

143

thingamabobs. Everything. Except for cars, which are made by the Japanese and occasionally by the Germans. That's it."

Big Lou moved her polishing cloth across the bar. "A second industrial revolution. Just like the first. All the plants, all the equipment are set up in one country and that's where everything's made." She paused. "And us? What's left for us to do?"

"We'll design things," said Matthew. "We'll produce the intellectual property. That's the theory, anyway."

Big Lou looked thoughtful. "But can't they do that just as well in the East? In India, for example?"

Matthew shrugged. "They have to leave something for us to do."

"Do they?"

Big Lou waited for an answer to her question, but none was forthcoming. So she decided to ask another one. "Matthew, what do you think a fool's paradise looks like?"

Matthew looked about him. Then he turned to Lou. "Let's change the subject, Lou. Who's your new man?"

Lou stopped polishing for a moment. She stared at Matthew. "New man?"

"Come on, Lou," said Matthew. "You know how news gets around. I've heard that you've got a new man. Robert? Angus told me. That's his name, isn't it?"

Big Lou hesitated for a moment. Then she resumed her polishing. "My affairs are my business, Matthew."

Matthew smiled. "So you're not denying that there's somebody?"

"There might be."

"In other words, there is."

Big Lou said nothing. She had been embarrassed by the public way in which her break-up with Eddie had happened; she felt humiliated by that. And if anything similar were to happen with Robert, she did not want people to know about it. Nobody likes to be seen to be rejected, and Big Lou was no exception to that rule.

Matthew lifted his coffee cup and drained it. "I hope it works out this time, Lou," he said. "You deserve it."

She raised her eyes and looked at him. He meant it, she decided. "Thank you, Matthew. He's a nice man. I'll tell him to come in one morning so that you can meet him."

"What does he do?" asked Matthew.

"Ceilings," said Lou. "Robert does ceilings. You know, when you want to replace cornicing, you need moulds. Robert does that. And he makes new cornices. He's quite an artist."

"Sounds good," said Matthew. This was better, he thought, than Eddie, with his Rootsie-Tootsie Club and his teenage girls.

"Yes," Big Lou went on. "He's very good at that.

Architects use him. Historic Scotland. People like that. But his real passion is history. That's how I met him. I went to a lecture at the museum and I found myself sitting next to him. That's how it happened. It was a lecture by Paul Scott on the Act of Union. Robert was there."

"Nice," said Matthew. He knew this sounded trite, but he could not think of anything else to say. And it was nice, he thought, to picture Big Lou going to a lecture on the Act of Union and finding a man. There were undoubtedly many women who went to lectures at the museum and did not find a man.

Then Matthew thought of something else to say. He was fond of Big Lou; an almost brotherly affection, he felt, and brothers should on occasion sound a warning note. "You'll be careful, won't you, Lou?" he said quietly. "There are some men who . . . Well, I don't want to remind you of Eddie, Lou, but remember what happened there. I don't want your heart to be broken again, Lou."

She reached out and put a hand on Matthew's forearm. They had never touched before; this was the first time. "I'll be careful," she said. "And thank you for saying that."

Matthew lifted up his cup. It was completely empty, without even any froth around the rim to lick off. He looked at the bottom of the cup, where there was a small mark and some printing. *China,* it said.

"Look," he said to Big Lou. "See."

Lou took the cup from Matthew and looked at its base. "But that's what it is," she said.

29. *That Chap Over There— Know Who That Is?*

That evening, Matthew went to the Cumberland Bar. He was due to meet Pat at eight and had promised to take her somewhere exciting for dinner. That promise was beginning to worry him—not because he was unwilling to take her out, rather it was the difficulty of choosing somewhere which she would consider exciting. In one interpretation, exciting was synonymous with plush and expensive; in which case they could go to the Witchery or even Prestonfield House. But that, he thought, was not what Pat had in mind. An exciting restaurant for her probably meant a place where both the décor and the people were unusual, the sort of place where celebrities went. But where were these places, and were there any celebrities in Edinburgh anyway? And if there were, then who were they? The Lord Provost? Sir Timothy Clifford? Ian Rankin? Possibly. But where did these people go for dinner? Ian Rankin went to the Oxford Bar, of course, but you wouldn't get much to eat there. And the Lord Provost had her own dining room in the City Chambers. She probably had dinner there, looking out over the top of Princes Street, reading council minutes, wondering which streets could be dug up next.

Angus Lordie was in the bar, sitting morosely at his table, the place at his feet where Cyril normally sat deserted now. Matthew joined him.

"Where's your young friend?" Angus asked.

"She's got a name," said Matthew. "Pat."

"That's the one. Where is she?"

Matthew took a sip of his beer. "I'm meeting her later on. We're going out for dinner."

Angus nodded at this information. He did not seem particularly interested, and indeed it was very uninteresting information, Matthew thought. That's my trouble, he said to himself—I'm not exciting.

"I haven't decided where to take her yet," said Matthew. He looked at Angus quizzically. "Tell me, Angus, do you know any exciting restaurants?"

Angus shook his head. "Exciting restaurants? Not me, I'm afraid. I never go out for a meal, except for lunch at the Scottish Arts Club. Of course, I had a meal down in Canonmills once, but that place closed. And there's a nice Italian place round the corner, but the proprietor went back to Italy. Lucca, I think." He paused. "Has that been any help?"

"Not really," said Matthew. "Although I suppose it closes off certain possibilities."

"Mind you," said Angus, "there used to be some exciting restaurants in Edinburgh. There was the

Armenian Restaurant, of course, which used to be down in that old steamie opposite the Academy. You won't remember it, but I used to go there from time to time. Then he moved up to that old place near Holyrood. He may still be there—I don't know. Very exotic place that—exciting too, if the proprietor got on to the subject of Armenian history."

Angus looked down at Cyril's empty place. It was at this very table that, some time ago, he had been reunited with Cyril after he had escaped his captors. He looked up at the door through which Cyril had been led by his rescuer, the man who worked for the Royal Bank of Scotland. If only he would come back through that door again, with Cyril on a lead; idle thought, impossible thought; the state was a much more efficient kidnapper of dogs, and Cyril would be firmly under lock and key, conditions that would require a Houdini Terrier—if there was such a breed—to enable escape.

He looked up. "Why not make her dinner at your place? Candlelight. A nice bottle of something. That's what I would do if . . ." He broke off, his attention suddenly attracted by something he had seen on the other side of the room. "Interesting."

"What?"

"That chap over there," said Angus, inclining his head to the far side of the bar. "That one, with the grey jacket. Yes, him. You know who that is?"

149

Matthew looked at the person indicated by Angus. He was a man somewhere in his late thirties or early forties, neatly dressed, with dark hair. He was engaged in conversation with a couple of other men seated at his table. One of them was leaning forward to listen to him, while the other sat back and looked up at the ceiling, as if weighing up what was being said.

Matthew turned back to Angus. "Never seen him," he said. "Who is he?"

Angus leant forward conspiratorially. "That, Matthew my friend, is Rabbie Cromach—Big Lou's new friend. That's who he is!"

Matthew turned back to stare at the man. "I see," he said. "Well, that's interesting."

"Yes," said Angus. "But what's more interesting is the company he's in."

Matthew's heart sank. It seemed that Big Lou was destined to choose unsuitable men—men who bordered on the criminal. Was she doing it again? He hardly dared ask. "Bad company?" he said finally.

Angus smiled. "Depends on your view of a number of things," he said. "The Act of Settlement for one thing. The Hanoverians. General Wade. The list could go on."

"I'm not with you," said Matthew.

Angus leant forward again. "Sorry to be obscure, but you'll soon see what I mean. That man directly opposite Rabbie—the one with the blue jacket—him, yes him. He's an eighty-four-horsepower fruitcake, if I may mix my metaphors. Always writing to the papers. Got chucked out of the public gallery at the General Assembly a few years ago and out of the Scottish Parliament too. Shouting his heid off about Hanoverian usurpers. Get my drift?"

Matthew looked in fascination. "Jacobites?"

"Yes," said Angus. "Those two—I forget the other one's name, but he's in it up to here—those two are well-known Jacobites—the real McCoy. They actually believe in the whole thing. King over the Water toasts and all that."

Matthew looked at the three men in fascination. It struck him as odd that people could harbour a historical grudge so long—to the point of disturbing the succession to the throne. But then, the whole story was such a romantic one that people just forgot what the Stuarts, or many of them, were actually like. Of course they thought that the Hanoverians were German—and they were right.

Through Matthew's mind there suddenly ran a snatch of song, half-remembered, but strangely familiar. "Noo a big prince cam to Edinburgh-toon / And he was just a wee bit German lairdie / For a far better man than ever he was / Lay oot in the heather wi' his tartan plaidie!"

One could get caught up in sentiments like that. Perhaps it was not as ridiculous as it seemed.

Angus now patted Matthew on the forearm. "Matthew," he said. "I want to tell you a story. About those characters. Interested?"

151

30. Things Behind Things in the Circular City

Matthew was interested. Angus Lordie's views on the world were often rather quirky—off-centre, in an unexpected way—but he had an extraordinary knowledge of things that were out of the experience of most people. This came in part from his unconventional background, and in part from his interest in what he termed "things behind things."

On another occasion, when they had been talking to one another in the Cumberland Bar, Matthew had asked him: "And what exactly do you mean by 'things behind things'?" To which Angus had replied: "It's all about what people really mean. Most people, you see, act on two levels—the public and the private. They have a public life, which anybody can see, and then they have a private life, which is what really counts. So take politicians, for instance; they all say more or less the same thing—utter the same slogans about improving services and so on—but what really counts is the private understandings they have with one another, with their backers. So things are not necessarily what they seem to be on the surface. You have to look at the networks."

He had expanded. "And this city is a good example. It's full of understandings, connections, networks. Some of these are fairly open.

Everybody knows who's in which political party and who their friends will be. So when a public job comes up, the rhetoric will be about who's best for the post and so on. But we all know that that is just rhetoric. What really counts is who knows the people in power. Which shouldn't surprise anybody, I suppose. That's how most places are run, isn't it? We like our friends; we trust them; we reward them.

"But if you think that it's all that open, then you need to think again. It's the connections beneath the surface that can be really important. If you go to some grand function or other, what do you find? I'll tell you, Matthew: everybody there knows one another, except you! Isn't that interesting? When I was on the Artists' Benevolent Committee, I would be thrown a few scraps of invitations to some of these official parties—receptions and so on—and what do you think I found? Everybody who came in the door immediately went off and chatted with somebody or other. Nobody stood around and looked spare. They all knew one another.

"Now, I'm not one of these people who imagine conspiracies, Matthew, but I'm not blind. And I'm also quite interested in what makes things tick, and so I had to ask myself: how did they all know one another? And what do you think the reason is?"

Matthew looked vague. He was thinking of how many people he knew, and he had decided that it was not very many. He was intrigued, though, and he wondered if Angus knew of some secret cabal. Was his father involved? he asked himself. His father seemed to know an awful lot of people, and Matthew had always assumed that this was because he was a Watsonian and had played rugby. But was there something more to it than that? He looked at Angus. "Are there . . . are there circles?"

For a moment, Angus appeared puzzled by the question. Then he leant forward and whispered: "Yes. There are circles." And with that he had made a circular movement with a finger.

Matthew was not sure how to take this. So he simply repeated: "Circles."

Angus nodded gravely. "Lots of them."

"But what proof do you have?" Matthew asked.

"Look at the architecture," said Angus. "And I don't just mean Rosslyn Chapel, although that's very interesting. Look at Moray Place. Start walking at one point and carry on, and where do you end up? Where you started! It's a circle, you see.

"And then there's Muirfield Golf Course, where the Honourable Company of Edinburgh Golfers has its seat. What happens if you start on the first tee? You walk all over the place, but you end up more or less where you started—back at the club-house. Circular."

"So what does all this mean?" asked Matthew.

"I would have thought it's pretty obvious," replied Angus. "This is a city which is built on the circular. So if you want to understand it, you have to get into that circular frame of mind. And that frame of mind is everywhere. Look at an Eightsome Reel. How do people arrange themselves? In a circle. And that's a metaphor, Matthew, for the whole process. You get in a circle, and you work from there. You refer to others in the same circle. You don't think outside the circle."

"You mean outside the box," Matthew corrected him.

"No, I said circle," insisted Angus. "And that's what I mean."

And then Angus had become silent. Matthew wanted him to say more, but he had not, and he had been left with the uncomfortable conclusion that Angus was either slightly mad or . . . , and this was a distinct possibility, slightly circular. But the conversation had remained with him, and now, sitting again in the Cumberland Bar, again with Angus, he had reason to recollect it as they looked across the room at the small circle of men at the other table . . . circle . . .

"That," said Angus quietly, "is a Jacobite circle. The one in the blue jacket is called Michael somebody-or-other and he's the one I've met before. I was in a pub over the other side of town, the Captain's Bar, in South College Street, near the university. It's a funny wee place, very narrow, with a bunch of crabbit regulars and a smattering of students. Not the sort of place one would have gone in the old days if one objected to being kippered in smoke. I was there with an old friend from art college days who liked to drink there. Anyway, there we were when in came that fellow over there, Michael, and another couple of people—a lang-nebbit woman wearing a sort of Paisley shawl and a man in a brown tweed coat. Jimmy, my friend from art college, knew the woman in the shawl, and so we ended up standing next to one another and a conversation started. It was pleasant enough, I suppose, and we bought each other a round of drinks. Then Michael looked at his watch and said that they had to go, but that we were welcome to go along with them if we had nothing better to do. Jimmy said: 'I suppose you're off to one of your meetings.' And Michael laughed and said that they were, but that we would be welcome too. There would be something to eat, they said, and since we were both feeling hungry, we agreed to go.

"And that," said Angus, "is how I became aware of that particular circle of Jacobites, and their strange interest in things Stuart. Would you like to hear about what they get up to? Will you believe me if I tell you?"

Matthew nodded. "I would like to hear, and yes, I will believe you. You don't embroider the truth do you, Angus?"

Angus smiled. "It depends," he said.

31. Edinburgh Is Full of All Sorts of Clubs

"We went off with these three," said Angus. "Michael, the woman in the shawl and the man in the brown tweed coat. A motley crew, I must admit.

"I asked Jimmy what sort of meeting we were heading for, but he didn't answer directly. 'Edinburgh's full of all sorts of clubs,' was all he said. Which was true, of course. We all know that Edinburgh's riddled with these things, and always has been. Back in the eighteenth century, there were scores of them. The Rankenian Club, for example—Hume was a member of that. That was intellectually respectable, of course, but some of the clubs were pretty much the opposite of that. You've heard of the Dirty Club, perhaps, where no member was allowed to appear in clean linen. Or the Odd Fellows, where the members wrote their names upside down. And there was even something called the Sweating Club, the members of which would enjoy themselves in a tavern and then rush out to chase whomsoever they came across and tear his wig off, if he was wearing one. The idea was to make the poor victim sweat. Very strange.

"Burns belonged to a club, you know. He joined the Crochallan Fencibles, as poor Robert Fergusson had joined the Cape Club before him. He so enjoyed that—Fergusson did—and his life was to be so brief. I still weep, you know, when I see his grave down in the Canongate Kirkyard. He could have been as great a poet as Burns, don't you think? Burns certainly did.

"Speaking of the eighteenth century, there were some clubs which would never have survived into Victorian Scotland because of the onset of prudery. There's the famous Beggar's Benison club, which started in Fife, of all places—not a place we immediately associate with licentiousness. I really can't say too much about that club, Matthew; decency prevents my describing their rituals, but initiation into the membership was really shocking (if one is shocked by things like that). What is it about men in groups that makes them do that sort of thing, Matthew? Of course they felt that London was trying to take away all the fun—the English had imposed a new monarchy, and a Union to boot. What was there left for Scotland to do but to turn to the older, phallic gods?

"So there have always been these clubs, and of course old habits die hard. There are still bags of these clubs in Edinburgh, but nobody ever talks about them. And why do you think that is, Matthew? Well, I'll tell you. It's because there are too many people who want to stop us having fun. That's the reason. They've always been with us. And if it's a group of males having fun together, then look out!

"So the Edinburgh clubs went more or less

underground. How many people, for instance, know about the Monks of St Giles?"

Matthew looked blank. "I don't."

Angus lowered his voice. "The Monks of St Giles is a club. It still exists—still meets. They give themselves Latin names and they meet and compose poetry. They even have a clubhouse, but I'm not going to tell you where it is. Some very influential people are members. And it sounds terrific fun, since they wear robes, but there'd be such a fuss if word got out. Can you imagine the prying, humourless journalists who would love to have a go at them? I can. Composing poetry in private! Not the sort of thing we want in an inclusive Scotland, where everybody will have to be able to read everybody else's poetry!

"Have you seen the Archers? That's another club. They've got a clubhouse too. Over near the Meadows. They call it their Hall, which is rather a nice name for a clubhouse. They're frightfully grand, and I'd like to know how you become a member. Can you apply? If not, why not? But we shouldn't really ask that sort of question. Why can't these people get on with their private fantasies without being taken to task for being elitist or whatever the charge would be? Or for not having female monks, or whatever? Women are fully entitled to their secret societies, Matthew, and have them, in this very city. Have you heard of the Sisters of Portia, which is for women lawyers?

Virtually all the women lawyers in Edinburgh belong to that, but they don't let on, and they certainly wouldn't let men have a men-only legal club. Can you imagine the fuss? Of course, some of them say that men used to have a male-only club called the Law Society of Scotland, but I don't think that's funny, Matthew. Do you? The Sisters of Portia are every bit as fishy as the Freemasons, if you ask me. They give one another a professional leg-up and they close ranks at the drop of the hat. Or the Red Garter, which is a club that meets every month in the Balmoral Hotel. That's for women in politics, except for Conservatives, who aren't allowed. And most of the women politicians are in it, but nobody lets on, and they even deny it exists if you ask.

"I haven't mentioned the most secretive one of all. That's a strictly women's club called the Ravelston Dykes. They meet every other week in Ravelston. But let's not even think of them, Matthew. They're fully entitled to exist and have a bit of fun. If only they'd extend us the same courtesy.

"And then there's another society which is said to have survived from the eighteenth century and which meets by candlelight on Wednesday evenings. The thing about that one, Matthew, is that it doesn't actually exist! Every so often, people make a fuss about it, but the truth of the matter is that it's entirely fictional! But I'm not concerned with apocryphal clubs like that one; I want to tell you about the club that we ended up going to that night. And it was far from apocryphal!"

Matthew looked encouragingly at Angus. He enjoyed listening to these strange accounts of Edinburgh institutions, but he was keen for Angus to get on to the point of the story. What sort of club was it that he and his friend were taken to that night? Was it a reincarnation of the Beggar's Benison? Surely not something so lewd as that. Edinburgh, after all, was a respectable city, and whatever the eighteenth century had been like, the twenty-first was certainly quite different.

He looked at Angus. Such an unreconstructed man, he thought; it's surprising that he hasn't been taken to task, or even fined, for the things he says.

32. Some Relative Warmth for the Ice Man

Angus continued the story of his meeting with Big Lou's friend and his friends in the Captain's Bar.

"As we went out into the night," he said, "the woman in the Paisley shawl introduced herself to me and we walked along together. She was called Heather McDowall, she told me, and she was something or other in the Health Board—an administrator, I think. She then explained that she had a Gaelic name as well, and she pointed out that I could call her Mhic dhu ghaill, if I wished.

"We were walking along South College Street

when she said this. The others were slightly ahead, engaged in conversation of their own, while la McDowall and I trailed a bit behind. It had rained, and the stone setts paving the road glistened in the street lights. I felt exhilarated by the operatic beauty of our surroundings: the dark bulk of the Old College to our left, the high, rather dingy tenement to our right. At any moment, I thought, a window might open in the tenement above and a *basso profondo* lean out and break into song. That might happen in Naples, I suppose, but not Edinburgh; still, one might dream.

"La McDowall then launched into an explanation of the name McDowall and her ancestry. Have you noticed how these people are often obsessed with their ancestry? What does it matter? We're most of us cousins in Scotland, if you go far enough back, and if you go even farther back, don't we all come from five ur-women in Western Europe somewhere? Isn't that what Professor Sykes says in his book?

"Talking of Professor Sykes, do you know that I met him, Matthew? No, you don't. Well, I did. I happened to be friendly with a fellow of All Souls in Oxford. Wonderful place, that. Free lunch and dinner for life—the best job there is. Anyway, this friend of mine is an economic historian down there—Scottish historians, you may have noticed, have taken over from Scottish missionaries in carrying the light to those parts. And we've got some jolly good historians, Matthew—Ted Cowan, Hew Strachan, Sandy Fenton, with his old ploughs and historic brose, Rosalind Marshall, who's just written this book about Mary's female pals, Hugh Cheape, who knows all about old bagpipes and suchlike, and any number of others. Anyway, I knew this chap when he was so-high, running around Perthshire in funny breeks like Wee Eck's. He invited me down for a feast, as they call it, and I decided to go out of curiosity. I was put up in a guest room in All Souls itself—no bathroom for miles, of course, and an ancient retainer who brought in a jug of water and said something which I just couldn't make out. Some strange English dialect; you know how they mutilate the language down there.

"The feast was quite extraordinary, and it reaffirmed my conviction that the English are half mad when they think nobody's looking. They're a charming people—very tolerant and decent at heart—but they have this distinct streak of insanity which comes out in places like Oxford and in some of the London clubs. It's harmless, of course, but it takes some getting used to, I can tell you.

"We had roast beef and all the trimmings—roast tatties, big crumbling hunks of Stilton, and ancient port. They did us proud. There were a couple of speeches in Latin, I think, and of course we kicked off with an interminable grace which, among other things, called down the Lord's fury on the college's enemies. That one was in English, just in case the Lord didn't get the point. This brought lots of enthusiastic amens, and I realised that these people must be feeling the pressure a bit, what with all this talk of relevance and inclusiveness and all those things. And I couldn't help feeling a bit sorry for them, you know, Matthew. Imagine if you had fixed yourself up with a number like that and then suddenly the winds of change start blowing and people want to stop you having feasts and eating Stilton. It can't be easy.

"Of course, it's foolishness of a high order to destroy these things. The Americans would sell their souls just to get something vaguely approximating to All Souls—they really would. It's such a pity, because they would have such fun in places like that. The Canadians, of course, have got something like it. I know somebody who visited it once—a place called Massey College in Toronto. It was presided over by Robertson Davies, you know—that wonderful novelist. He was the Master. Now they've got somebody of the same great stripe, an agreeable character called John Fraser, who has a highly developed talent for hospitality, as it happens. Thank God for the Canadians.

"Well, at the feast, I ended up sitting next to none other than Professor Sykes, the genetics man, and he told me the most extraordinary story. I know it has nothing to do with anything, Matthew, but I must tell you. You may remember that he was the person who did the DNA tests on the Ice Man, that poor fellow they dug out of a glacier in France. He'd kicked the bucket five thousand years ago, but was in pretty good condition and so they were able to conduct a postmortem and look at the DNA while they were about it. Anyway, Sykes decided to ask for a random volunteer down in England somewhere and see if this person was connected in any way to the Ice Man. Some woman stepped up to the block and he nicked off a bit of her nose, or whatever it is that these people do, and—lo and behold!—she shares a bit of DNA with the old Ice Man. Which just goes to prove what Sykes had been saying for years—that we're all pretty closely related, even if some of us shrugged off this mortal coil five millennia ago.

"But then, Matthew, it gets even more peculiar. When this woman from Dorset or wherever it was got wind of the fact that she was related to the Ice Man, do you know what she started to do? She began to behave like a relative, and started to ask for a decent burial for the Ice Man!

"Which just goes to show, Matthew, that when expectations are created, people rise to the occasion. They always do. Always." Angus paused. "What do you think of that, Matthew?"

"I think she did the right thing," said Matthew.

33. Old Injustices Have Their Resonances

Angus Lordie stared at Matthew incredulously. "Did I understand you correctly?" he asked. "Did you say that this woman did the right thing? That she should have asked for a decent burial for the Ice Man?"

Matthew thought for a moment. He had answered the question impulsively, and he wondered if he was right. But now, on reflection, even if brief, he decided that he was.

"Yes," he said evenly. "I think that this was probably the right thing. Look, Angus, would you like to be put on display in a museum or wherever, even if you were not around to object? If you went tomorrow, what would you think if I put you on display in, say, a glass case in Big Lou's café? You'd not want that, I assume. And nor, I imagine, would the Ice Man have wanted to be displayed. He might have had beliefs about spirits not getting released until burial, or something of that sort. We just don't know what his beliefs were. But we can imagine that he probably would not like to be stared at."

Angus frowned. "No, maybe not. But then, even if we presume that he wouldn't want that, do we really have to respect the wishes of people who lived that long ago—five thousand years? Do we owe them anything at all? And, come to think of it, can you actually harm the dead? Can you do them a wrong?"

Matthew thought that you could. "Yes," he said. "Why not? Let's say I name you executor in my will. I ask you to do something or other, and you don't do it. Don't you think that people would say that you've done me a wrong, even though I'm not around to protest?"

Matthew was warming to the theme. The argument, he thought, was a strong one. Yes, it was wrong to ignore the wishes of the dead. "And what about this?" he continued. "What if you snuffed it tomorrow, Angus, and I told people things about you that damaged your reputation—that you were a plagiarist, for instance? That your paintings were copies of somebody else's. Wouldn't you say that I had harmed you? Wouldn't people be entitled to say: 'He's done Angus Lordie a great wrong'?"

Angus looked doubtful. "Not really," he said. "There'll be no more Lordie. I'll be beyond harm. Nothing can harm me then. That's the great thing about being dead. You don't mind the weather at all."

"But you could say: 'He's harmed his reputation'? You could say that, couldn't you?"

"Yes," said Angus. "You could say that, because I shall still have a reputation—I hope—for a short time after I go. But the Ice Man's another matter altogether. As is Julius Caesar or Napoleon Bonaparte. You can say whatever you like about them because . . . because they're no longer part of the human community." Angus looked pleased with the phrase. "Yes, that's it—that's the distinction. Those who have recently left us are still part of the human community—and have some rights, if you will—whereas those who left us a long time ago don't have those rights."

Something was bothering Matthew. "What about these posthumous pardons? What about the men who were shot for cowardice in the First World War? Aren't they being pardoned now? What do you think of that, Angus? With your argument, surely they would be too long dead to have any claim to this?"

Angus took a sip of his beer. "I'm not sure about that," he said. "They still have relatives—descendants perhaps, who want to clear their names. They feel strongly enough and they're still very much with us. So the duty is to the living rather than to people who no longer exist."

"But what if their descendants knew nothing about it?" asked Matthew. "What if there weren't any families asking for pardons? Would we have any duty to them then? A simple, human duty to recognise that they were people . . . people just like us?"

Angus was beginning to look uncomfortable. He had argued himself into a position in which he appeared to be careless of the human bonds which united us one to another, quick and dead. Matthew, he thought, was right. Feeling concerned for the Ice Man was a simple recognition of human hopes, whenever they had been entertained. Ancient feelings were feelings nonetheless; old injustices, like the shooting of those poor, shell-shocked men, had their resonances, even today. And the government, he thought, was probably quite right to pardon the lot of them on the grounds that you couldn't distinguish between cases at this distance.

"You're right," Angus said. "You win."

"Oh," said Matthew. "I didn't think you'd agree."

"Well, I do," said Angus. "But let's get back to la McDowall. Where were we?"

"You were walking down South College Street. She was telling you about McDowalls in general."

"Oh yes," said Angus. "Well, she suddenly turned to me, la McDowall did, and said: 'We go back a very long way, you know, my family.' Of course I refrained from pointing out to her that we all went back as far as each other, and so she continued. 'Yes,' she said. 'I can trace things back quite a way, you know. I happen to be descended from Duegald de Galloway, younger grandson of Prince Fergus de Galloway, and his forebears can be traced back to Rolf the Dane, who died back in 927 AD.'

"That was pretty rich, but I let her go on. It's best not to interrupt these people once they get going— they can easily blow a valve. So she said: 'Oh yes. And if we go back from Rolf we eventually get back to Dowal himself, who lived in Galloway in 232 BC.'

"I ask you, Matthew! What nonsense. And here was this otherwise perfectly rational woman, who went each day into an office somewhere in Edinburgh and made administrative decisions or whatever, claiming that she went back to 232 BC!" He shook his head. "Personally, I blame the Lord Lyon, you know. He has the authority to stamp that sort of thing out, but what does he do? Nothing. He should tell these McDowalls that their claims are outrageous and that they shouldn't mislead people with all this nonsense."

"But I've heard he's a very nice man," said Matthew. "Perhaps he just feels that people like that are harmless. And if he started to engage with the McDowalls, he'd have all those Campbells and MacDonalds and people like that on to him. Scotland's full of this stuff. It's what keeps half the population going."

The earlier consensus between them disappeared, immediately. "That sort of thing is very important," said Angus. "I happen to believe that clan reunions, clan gatherings and so on—these are important. They remind us who we are."

"Oh well," said Matthew. "I know who I am. But let's not disagree. If you don't mind, tell me what happened."

34. Miss Harmony Has a Word in Bertie's Ear

On the day that Olive was due to come to visit Scotland Street, Bertie went to school with a heavy heart. He had pleaded with his mother to cancel the invitation, but his imprecations had been rejected, as they always seemed to be.

"But Bertie, *carissimo*," said Irene. "One cannot cancel an invitation! *Pacta sunt servanda*! You can't uninvite people once you've invited them! That's not the way adults behave."

"I'm not an adult, Mummy," said Bertie. "I think that boys are allowed to uninvite people. I promise you, Mummy; they are. Tofu invited me to his house once and cancelled the invitation ten minutes later. He does that all the time."

"What Tofu does or does not do is of no concern to us, Bertie," said Irene. "As you well know, I have reservations about Tofu."

Bertie thought he might try another tack. "But I've read about invitations being cancelled by grown-ups," he said. "The Turks invited the Pope to see them and then some of them said that he shouldn't come, didn't they?"

Irene sighed. "I'm sure that the Turks didn't mean to be rude," she said. "And I'm sure that the Pope would have understood that. I'm also one hundred per cent sure that if the Pope invites you to the Vatican, the invitation is never cancelled. So we cannot possibly uninvite Olive. And we don't want to, anyway! It's going to be tremendous fun."

Bertie had abandoned his attempt to persuade his mother. But in a last, desperate throw of the dice, on the morning of the visit, using a red ballpoint pen, he applied several spots to his right forearm and presented this with concern to his mother.

"I don't think that Olive will be able to come to play, Mummy," he said, trying to appear regretful. "It looks like I've got measles, again."

Irene had inspected the spots and then laughed. "Dear Bertie," she said. "Have no fear. Red ballpoint ink is not infectious. Messy, perhaps, but not infectious."

At school that morning, it was not long before Olive had an opportunity to make her plans known.

"I'm going to Bertie's house this afternoon," she volunteered, adding, "by invitation."

"How nice!" said Miss Harmony. "It is very encouraging, children, when we see you all getting on together so well. We are one big, happy family here, and it is good to see the girls playing nicely with the boys, and vice versa."

Bertie said nothing.

"I don't think Bertie wants her to go," said Tofu. "Look at his face, Miss Harmony."

Miss Harmony glanced at Bertie. "I'm sure that you're mistaken, Tofu. Bertie is a very polite boy, unlike some boys." She tried not to look at Tofu when she said this, but her eyes just seemed to slide inexorably in his direction.

"No, I'm not mistaken," said Tofu. "Bertie hates Olive. Everybody knows that. It's because she's so bossy."

Olive spun round and glared at Tofu. "Bertie doesn't hate me," she said. "Otherwise, why would he invite me to his house? Answer me that, Tofu!"

Bertie opened his mouth to say something, but Miss Harmony, sensing complications, immediately changed the subject, and the class resumed its reading exercise. But later, when everybody was involved in private work, she bent down and whispered in Bertie's ear. "Is it true, Bertie? Did you invite Olive to play?"

"No," whispered Bertie. "I didn't, Miss Harmony. It's my mother. She invited her. I don't want to play with Olive, I really don't. I want to play with other boys. I want to have fun."

Miss Harmony slipped her arm over his shoulder. "I'm sure that you must have some fun, Bertie. I'm sure you do."

"Not really, Miss Harmony," said Bertie. "You see my mother thinks . . ." He broke off. He was not sure what his mother thought. It was all too complicated.

The teacher crouched beside him. Bertie could smell the scent that she used, the scent that he had always liked. It was lavender, he thought, or something like that. In his mind it was the smell of kindness.

"Bertie," whispered Miss Harmony. "Sometimes mummies make it hard for their boys. They don't mean to do it, but they do. And the boy feels that the world is all wrong, that nothing works the way he wants it to work. And he looks around and sees other people having fun and he wonders whether he'll ever have any fun himself. Well, Bertie, the truth of the matter is that things tend to work out all right. Boys in that position eventually get a little bit of freedom and are able to do the things they really want to do. That happens, you know. But the important thing is that you should try to remember that Mummy is doing what she thinks is her best for you. So if you can just grin and bear it for a while, that's probably best."

Bertie listened attentively. This was a teacher speaking; this was the voice of ultimate authority. And what was that voice saying to him? It was hard to decide.

"So just try to be nice to Olive," went on Miss Harmony. "Try to look at things from her point of view."

"She wants to play house," whispered Bertie. "I don't want to do that."

Miss Harmony smiled. "Girls love playing house." And she thought: genetics—the bane of nonsexist theories of childrearing. Stubborn, inescapable genetics.

174

Bertie was silent. Miss Harmony stayed with him for a moment longer, but she was now beginning to attract curious stares from Tofu and Olive, and so she gave him a final pat on the shoulder and straightened up.

"Do try to pay attention to your own work, Tofu," she said. "It's always best that way. And you, Olive, should do so too."

Bertie kept his eyes down on his desk. He had been encouraged by what Miss Harmony had said to him—a bit—and he would make the effort to be civil to Olive. And he was cheered, too, by the prospect of liberation that the teacher had held out to him. She must have met people like his mother before, and boys like him too, and if she had seen things go well for them, then perhaps there was a chance for him. But the way ahead seemed so long, so cluttered with yoga and psychotherapy and Italian *conversazioni*, that it was as much as he could do to believe in any future at all, any prospect of happiness.

"You'll enjoy playing house," said Olive to Bertie as they travelled back on the bus with Irene. "I'll be the mummy and you, Bertie . . ." She paused for a moment. "And you will be the mummy's boyfriend."

35. Bedrooms Are the Place for Playing House

"Now, where would you two like to play?" asked Irene as she unlocked the door to the Pollock flat in 44 Scotland Street.

"In the bedroom, please," said Olive confidently. "We're going to play house, Mrs Pollock, and that's the best place."

Bertie caught his breath. He had been hoping to keep Olive out of his bedroom, because if she saw it she could hardly fail to notice that it was painted pink. And that, he feared, would give her a potent bit of information which she would undoubtedly use as a bargaining chip. All she would have to do would be to threaten to reveal to Tofu and the other boys at school that his room was pink unless he complied with whatever schemes she had in mind. It would be a hopeless situation, thought Bertie; he would be completely in her power and unable to stand up for himself, which, he suspected, was exactly what Olive had in mind.

"If you don't mind," said Bertie, "we could play in the sitting room. There are some very comfortable chairs there, and it will be just right for playing house in. Don't you agree, Mummy?"

He looked imploringly at his mother, willing her to agree with him.

"I don't think so," said Irene. "House is best

played in bedrooms. And I'm planning to write some letters in the sitting room. You won't want me interfering with your game of house, will you, Olive?"

"No, thank you," said Olive. "Although you could always be the granny."

Irene glanced at Olive. She raised an eyebrow. "Oh, I see."

"You could pretend to be the granny who has to stay in bed, and we could feed you soup from a cup," Olive went on. "And you could pretend to forget everything we said to you."

"I don't think so, Olive," said Irene coldly. "But thank you anyway. You two just go off and play in Bertie's room. At half past four, I'll make you some juice and scones. I'll be putting Ulysses down for a sleep shortly and he will be ready to wake up then."

"He's a very nice baby, Mrs Pollock," said Olive. "My mummy says that you're lucky to have him."

Irene smiled. "Well, thank you, Olive," she said. "We're all very lucky to have Ulysses come into our lives."

"Yes," Olive continued. "Mummy said that she thought you were too old to have another baby. She said that wonders will never cease."

Irene was silent for a few moments. "I think that you should go and play now," she said, tight-lipped. "Off you go!"

"Where's your room, Bertie?" asked Olive. "Can you show me the way, please?"

Bertie cast his eyes about in desperation. There seemed to be no escape, or was there?

"It's at the end of this corridor," he said, pointing in the direction of the dining room. "That's the door over there."

Olive walked over to the door and opened it. She looked inside, at the table and chairs, and the small bureau where Stuart sometimes did the work that he brought home with him. "Is this it?" she asked. "Is this your room, Bertie?"

Bertie nodded.

"Where's your bed?" asked Olive. "Don't tell me you sleep on the table."

Bertie gave a forced laugh. "Oh no," he said. "I don't sleep on the table. I sleep over there, in that corner. We have some cushions and a sleeping bag. We put them over there each night before I go to bed. It's healthier, you see."

"So you don't even have a proper bed?" asked Olive.

"No," said Bertie. "But that's quite common these days. Didn't you know that?"

Olive did not wish to appear uninformed, and so she nodded in a superior way. "You don't have to tell me that," she said. "I know about these things." She paused, looking around at the sparsely furnished room. "But where do you keep your clothes?"

Bertie glanced at the sideboard. "In those drawers over there," he said.

Olive turned her head and looked in the direction of the sideboard. Then, without giving any warning, she took a few steps across the room and opened the top drawer.

"You mustn't," protested Bertie. "That's private. You can't go and look in other people's drawers. What if they keep their pants in them?"

"There are no pants here," said Olive scornfully. "All there is, are these mats. What are these table mats doing in your drawer, Bertie?"

"I collect them," said Bertie. "It's my hobby."

"A pretty stupid hobby," said Olive. She slammed the drawer shut and then immediately bent down and opened the drawer beneath it.

"And there aren't even any clothes in this one either," she said. "Look. Just candles and some knives and forks. Why do you keep knives and forks in your bedroom, Bertie? What's wrong with you?"

Bertie sat down on the floor. "I'm very ill," he said. "You're going to have to go home, Olive. I'm too ill to play house. I'm sorry."

Olive looked at him for a moment. "You don't look ill," she said. "But anyway, you can still play house when you're ill. I'll just put you to bed and nurse you. Then you can get up when you're better. Come, Bertie, let's find a better room for that."

Bertie tried to resist, but Olive had seized his hand and had dragged him to his feet. She was surprisingly strong for a girl, he thought.

Half-pulled, half-pushed, Bertie was propelled down the corridor by Olive. His bedroom door was slightly ajar, and she now pushed this open and saw the bed within. And she saw Bertie's construction set, which was on the floor, and his spare pair of shoes at the bottom of the bed.

"So this is your real room!" she exclaimed, with the satisfaction of one who has discovered an important secret. "And it's pink."

"No, it isn't," said Bertie weakly. "You mustn't say it's pink. It's crushed strawberry."

"Crushed strawberries are a pink colour," Olive retorted, pushing Bertie towards the bed. "This is a very nice room, Bertie! But quick, you must get into bed since you're so ill. I'm the nurse now. Come along, darling, into bed you go. That's better. Now, you're very lucky that I brought my nurse kit with me."

Bertie watched in mute horror as Olive took a small plastic box from her school bag. It had a red cross on the lid, and when she opened it he saw a tiny plastic hammer, some wooden spatulas, and a few small bottles. But Olive was interested in none of these. She had taken out a disposable syringe, complete with a long, entirely real needle.

"You're going to have to give a blood sample, Bertie," Olive said. "It'll only hurt a little, but you'll feel much better afterwards, I promise you. Now where do you want me to take it from?"

36. What Exactly Is the Problem with Caroline?

It had been a very satisfactory day for Bruce. His flat-hunting, which had taken less than three hours, had resulted in his finding a very comfortable room in Julia Donald's flat in Howe Street. There had been no mention of rent—not once in the conversation—and Bruce saw no reason why the subject should ever come up. From his point of view, he was going to be staying with her as a friend, a close friend probably, and it was inappropriate for friends to pay one another rent, especially when the friend who owned the flat had no mortgage to pay. So that was a major advantage to the arrangement, he thought. And even if Julia should become a little bit trying—and she was a bit inclined to gush, Bruce thought—he was still confident that he could handle her firmly, but tactfully. Bruce knew how to deal with women; he knew that he had only to look at them with the look—and they were putty in his hands. It was extraordinary: the slightest smoulder from Bruce, just the slightest, seemed to make them go weak at the knees, and in the head too. Bruce smiled. It's so very easy, he thought—so very easy.

Before he went out that evening, Bruce took a shower in Neil and Caroline's flat in Comely Bank. There were minor irritations involved in this, as he did not like the multiple bottles of shampoo and conditioner which Caroline insisted on arranging on the small shelf in the shower. Bruce moved these every time he used the shower, shifting them to a place on top of the bathroom cupboard, but he noticed that they always migrated back to their position within the shower cubicle. He thought of saying something to Caroline about this, but refrained from doing so, as he was not absolutely sure if she appreciated him as much as most women did. He had tried giving her the look, but she had returned it with a blank stare, which thoroughly unsettled him. Normally, he would have put such a response down to a lack of interest based on lesbianism, but the fact that Caroline was happily married to Neil made that judgement unlikely. So what exactly is her problem? Bruce asked himself. Was it something to do with rent? He saw no reason why he should pay them anything when he was going to be there for such a short time, and they had, after all, invited him to stay, or almost. No, there was something more complicated at work here, he decided.

And then it occurred to him exactly what this was. Bruce decided that Caroline was jealous of him. That must be it! Neil, her husband, was such a weedy specimen in comparison with Bruce, that it must be hard for Caroline to have somebody in the house who was so clearly at the opposite end of the spectrum from him. So rather than resenting her husband for being puny, she was transferring her dissatisfaction onto Bruce himself.

This insight made Bruce feel almost sorry for Caroline, and as a result of this he had said something to her in an attempt to make things easier.

"Don't judge Neil too harshly," he remarked one evening when he found himself alone in the kitchen with her.

She had looked at him in astonishment. "What on earth do you mean? Judge Neil harshly? Why would I do that?"

Bruce had smiled. "Well, you know. Some men are a bit more . . . how shall I put it? Impressive. Yes, that's it. Impressive."

She stared at him. "I have no idea what you're talking about."

He winked. "Don't you . . . ?"

She had continued to stare at him. "I really have no idea what you're going on about, Bruce," she had said. "And, by the way, do you mind not moving my conditioner bottles from the shower? You know that little shelf in there? That's where I like them to be. That's where I put them."

Bruce smiled. "Come and show me," he said. "Show me when I'm in the shower."

She did not appreciate that, he decided, which was typical of somebody like her. There was a sense-of-humour failure there, he thought. A serious one. And she did not take well either to his next remark, which took the form of a good-natured question.

"Are you interested in other women, Caroline?" he asked. "I just want to know."

"What do you mean?"

Bruce sighed. "I'm really having to spell it out," he said. "I mean: are you, you know, interested in other women? Don't look so cross. Lots of people are a little bit that way, you know, now and then. It's perfectly understandable, you know . . ."

"How dare you!" Caroline screamed. "I'm going to tell Neil when he comes back. I just can't believe it. I can't believe that I'm being talked to like this in my own kitchen."

"Temper! Temper!" said Bruce. "Most people these days don't get all uptight about these things. We live in a very enlightened age, you know. I mean, hello!"

Now, standing in the shower, Bruce poured on a bit of Caroline's conditioner and rubbed it into his hair. His conversation with his hostess had not been an edifying one, and it was probably just as well that he was going out for dinner with Julia Donald that evening. He might even move out that very evening, which would give Caroline something to think about, but any decision could wait. For the moment, he had the sheer pleasure of the shower ahead of him; a shower first, then decisions, said Bruce to himself. That's a good one, he thought. Just like Bertolt Brecht with his *Grub* first, then ethics.

He turned his head slightly and caught sight of

his reflection in the glass wall of the shower cubicle. His profile, he thought, was the real strength of his face, that straight nose, in perfect proportion to the rest of the features—spot-on. It was amazing, he thought, how nature gets it just right. And the cleft in his chin—how many women had put the tip of their little finger in there?—it was almost as if they could not resist it, a Venus fly-trap, perhaps.

He pouted. "Drop-dead gorgeous," he whispered, through the sound of the shower.

37. A Little Bit of Bottle Bother at the Tower

Bruce had suggested to Julia that they should meet in the Tower Restaurant, above the Museum. He had been there once before when a client of Macauley Holmes Richardson Black had invited him to discuss over lunch the purchase of a piece of land near Peebles. Bruce had made a mental note to return for a more leisurely meal, but then he had become occupied with his wine business—a "semi-success" as he called it—and that had been followed by his removal to London. Eating out in London, of course, was ruinously expensive and, unless invited, he had avoided it as far as possible. Now, back in Edinburgh, he contemplated, with pleasure, the variety of restaurants he would be able to explore with Julia. She was the sort of girl who would pay the bill without complaint, although he would reach into his own pocket from time to time if pressed; Bruce was not mean.

The Tower Restaurant was above the new part of the National Museum of Scotland. As a boy, Bruce had been taken to the museum on several occasions, on school trips from Crieff, and had enjoyed pressing the buttons of the machines kept on display in great, ancient cases. The cavernous hall of the museum, with its vast glass roof, had been etched into the memory of those days, and could still impress him, but now it was the business of dinner that needed to be attended to.

He was early. Perched on one of the bar stools, he nursed a martini in front of him while waiting for Julia. Bruce did not normally drink martinis, but tonight's date justified one, he thought; and the effect, he noted, was as intended—the gin, barely diluted by vermouth, indeed possibly unacquainted with it, was quickly lifting his spirits even further. How had Churchill made martinis? he asked himself. He smiled as he remembered the snippet he had read in *The Decanter* or somewhere like that— Churchill had poured the gin on one side of the room while nodding in the direction of the vermouth bottle on the other side. What a man, thought Bruce, a bit like me in some ways.

Julia arrived ten minutes late.

"Perfect timing," said Bruce, rising from the bar stool to plant a kiss on her cheek. "For a woman, that is. And you look so stunning too. That dress . . ."

186

Julia beamed. "Oh, thank you, Brucie! It's ancient—prehistoric, actually. I bought it from Armstrongs down in the Grassmarket. You know that place that has all those old clothes. *Très* retro!"

Bruce touched the small trim of ostrich feathers around the neck of the dress. "It's a flapper dress, isn't it?"

Julia was not sure what a flapper dress was, but it sounded right. "Yes," she said. "It's good for flapping in."

"Very funny!" said Bruce.

They both laughed.

"Let's go to our table," said Bruce. "That's the maître d' over there. I'll catch his eye."

"You can catch anybody's eye, Brucie," said Julia playfully. "You're eye candy."

"Eye toffee," said Bruce, taking hold of her forearm. "I stick to people." He smiled as he remembered something. "You know, we had a dog up in Crieff and he had a sweet tooth. I gave him a toffee once and he started to chew it and got his teeth completely stuck together. It was seriously funny."

Julia laughed. "When I was at Glenalmond, we gave our housemistress a piece of cake with toffee hidden in the middle. It stuck her false teeth together and she had to take them out to get rid of it!"

"The things one does when young," said Bruce.

"A scream," said Julia.

They moved to the table. "You must let me treat you," said Bruce as they were handed the menu.

"Oh, please let me," said Julia.

"All right," said Bruce quickly. "Thanks. What are you going to have?"

If Julia was taken aback, it was only momentarily. "I love oysters," she said. "I'm going to start with those."

"Make sure that you put a bit of Tabasco in," said Bruce. "And lemon. Delicious."

"What about you?" asked Julia.

"Lobster," said Bruce, examining the menu. "Market price. That's helpful, isn't it? Everything is market price if you come to think of it. Anyway, I'll start with lobster, then . . ." he examined the menu. "Which do you think would win in a fight? A lobster or an oyster?"

Julia looked out of the window. "That's a very interesting question, Brucie. I've never thought about that, you know."

"The lobster would have the advantage of mobility," said Bruce. "But the oyster has pretty good defences, I would have thought. It would probably be a stand-off."

"Yes," agreed Julia. "Interesting."

The waiter came and took their order. "And wine?" he asked.

Bruce looked at the list. "You know, I was in the wine trade for a while," he said to Julia, but loud enough for the waiter to hear.

"I'll fetch the sommelier," said the waiter.

"No need . . ." Bruce began. But the waiter had moved off and was whispering something into the ear of a colleague. The sommelier nodded and came over to Bruce and Julia's table.

"So, sir," he said. "Have you any ideas?"

Bruce looked at the wine list. "Bit thin," he said. "No offence, of course. No Brunello, for instance." He smiled at Julia as he spoke. She made a face as if to mourn the absence of Brunello.

"Oh, but I think there is, sir," said the sommelier. "Perhaps you did not register the name of the producers. Look, over there, for example. Banfi. We don't always feel it's necessary to describe exactly where a wine comes from. We assume that in many cases people know . . ."

"Where?" snapped Bruce. "Oh, yes, Banfi. Wrong side, of course."

"Of what, sir?"

"The river," said Bruce.

"But there isn't a river in Montalcino," said the sommelier gently. "Perhaps you're thinking of somewhere else. The Arno perhaps?"

Bruce did not respond to this; he was peering at the list. "What about a Chianti?" he said. "What about this one here?"

The sommelier peered over his shoulder. "Mmm," he said. "I find that a bit unexciting, personally."

"Well, why do you have it on the list, then?"

Bruce said. His tone was now defensive, rattled.

"Well," said the sommelier, smiling, "we like to have one or two—how shall I put it?—pedestrian wines for some of our diners who have . . . well, not very sophisticated tastes. We don't actually carry Blue Nun, but that's pretty much for the diner who would go for a bottle of Blue Nun. I would have thought that you might be interested in something much more . . . much more complex."

Bruce kept his eyes on the list. "We'll have a bottle of this," he said, pointing wildly.

"Oh, a very good choice," said the sommelier. "And well worth the extra money. I always say that when you pay that much, you're on safe ground. Well chosen, sir."

38. Anyway, What Are You Going to Do, Brucie?

Bruce ate his lobster with gusto, watched by Julia, whose oysters had slipped down with alacrity. He offered her a claw, but she declined, a small appetite for one so curvaceous, Bruce thought.

"I prefer really small courses," she said. "We went to a restaurant in New York once, you know the one near the new modern art thingy. Mummy, or whatever it's called."

"MoMA," muttered Bruce, wiping mayonnaise from the side of his mouth.

"That's the place. Strange name."

Bruce reached out and patted her gently on the wrist. "Nothing to do with mother," he said. "It stands for the Museum of Modern Art."

Julia thought for a moment. "I don't get it. Anyway, this place, you wouldn't know that it's a restaurant, as there's nothing on the door. Just a glass door. It's really cool."

Bruce nodded. "That's to keep the wrong sort out," he said. "They have to do that. It's the same in London. There are no signs outside the really good clubs. Nothing to tell you they're there. You could spend weeks in London and not see any of the really good places because you just wouldn't know."

Julia looked at Bruce. She was studying his chin, which had a cleft that she found quite fascinating. She watched that and she noticed, too, how when he smiled the smallest dimple appeared in each of his cheeks. It was unfair, she thought, it really was that a man should have a skin like that and not have to worry about moisturisers and all the expensive things that she had to use. Unfair, just unfair. He put something on his hair, though, something with a rather strange smell. What was it? Cloves? Perhaps she should ask him. Would he mind? Or she could find out by going through his things in the bathroom, that would be easy, and interesting. Julia liked going through men's things in the bathroom; it was a sort of hobby, really.

She brought herself back to the present. "Yes,"

she said. "That restaurant in New York served tiny portions. Tiny. This size." She made a tight circle with her thumb and forefinger.

Bruce speared a piece of lobster meat. "Really?"

"Yes. I filled up on olive bread and Daddy asked for a banana. Everything cost thirty-six dollars. Except for the banana, which was free."

"There you are," said Bruce. "Every cloud . . ."

Julia interrupted him. "Anyway, Brucie, what are you going to do, now that you're back?"

Bruce, the lobster finished, pushed his plate to one side. "Well, I'm not going back to being a surveyor. Been there, done that, got the T-shirt. *Pas plus de ça pour moi.* So I've been thinking and I've had one or two ideas."

"Such as?"

Bruce sat back in his chair. "Personal training," he said. "I think I'll be a personal trainer."

A shadow of disappointment crossed Julia's face. She had not envisaged settling down with a personal trainer. "You mean one of those types you see in the gym?" she said. "The ones who hold their stopwatches and tell you how long to spend on the treadmill?"

It was clear to Bruce that she did not think much of his plan. He would have to explain; Julia was a bit—how might one put it?—limited in her outlook, poor girl. Rich, but limited.

"Personal trainers do much more than that," he said. "Getting people fit is one part of it, but there's

192

much more to it. Lifestyle advice, for example. Telling people how to dress, how to deal with anxiety, stress and all the rest. Sorting out relationships. That sort of thing."

Julia's reservations evaporated. "Brilliant!" she said. "I'm sure that there'll be a demand for that sort of thing. Lifestyle coach. Style guru. That sort of thing." She paused. "And personal shopper?"

Bruce looked doubtful. "I've heard of them. But I'm not sure what a personal shopper does."

Julia knew. "They usually have them in big shops," she said. "If you go somewhere like Harrods or Harvey Nicks, they have these people who will get you what you need. You tell them your general requirements and they find it for you. But one could do it as a freelance. Then you could shop all over the place."

"I don't know if I could do that," said Bruce. "I don't know enough about shopping."

"I do," said Julia quickly. "I've done a lot of shopping."

Bruce smiled. He had no doubt about that; Julia was certainly a shopper. Then a possibility came to him. He and Julia could enter into a . . .

"Partnership?" said Julia. "Do you think it would work, Brucie? You do the personal thingy and I'll do the personal shopping. We can offer a complete service."

Bruce nodded. "There are start-up costs," he said. "There always are."

Julia waved a hand dismissively. "How much?"

It was a fine calculation for Bruce. It was always difficult to decide just how much to ask for. The trick, he had read, was to try to put oneself in the shoes of the person with the funds and work out how much they would think reasonable. In this case, the start-up costs would be quite small—a few advertisements, a brochure, perhaps a press launch. But then there would be a salary for him, for, say, six months.

"Thirty thousand," he said. "Give or take a couple of thousand."

He watched her face. "Thirty thousand?" She hesitated. "All right. We're in business."

She looked down at her plate. I'm buying him for thirty thousand, she thought. But if that's what it costs to get a husband, then that's what it costs. And her father, she knew, would not quibble over a small sum like that. He had been hoping that she would settle down with a suitable man, and he would certainly approve of Bruce. Dear Daddy! He had said to her once, when she was twenty or so: "When you eventually decide to settle down with somebody, darling, don't for God's sake go for some dreadful spiv or intellectual. Go for good stock. You know what I mean by that? Do you? Do I have to spell it out to you?"

He would like Bruce, she knew it. And that would complete her happiness. A husband, a contented father, and before too long a couple of children. For that's what her father had meant, and she had known it. Good breeding stock. And Bruce was definitely that. Just look at him.

She looked at Bruce and smiled. And as she did so, she thought: maybe I should just forget to be careful. It's so easily done, particularly if you want to forget.

39. The Builders Who Began with a Bow

Antonia Collie sat in her flat in Scotland Street, a set of architect's drawings on the table before her; to her side, in a Spode blue and white cup, possibly stolen from Domenica Macdonald's family—or removed by mistake—the Earl Grey tea she so appreciated. Antonia was engrossed in the drawings and in their complexity; what seemed to her to be a simple business of extracting old kitchen units and inserting new ones, of removing an old and uncomfortable bath and installing a modern and inviting one, and of doing one or other minor improvements to the flat, had been translated into page after page of detailed drawings by her friend Alex Philip, the architect. These were all executed in black ink with careful instructions to the builders as to the thickness of materials, the positioning of screws and wiring, about plaster and skirting-boards and tiles. A copy of the plans had been given to Antonia by Alex, and it was these that she was now trying to understand.

Antonia understood about the inconvenience which building work brought in its wake. In Perthshire, they had attempted an enlargement of their farm kitchen, a small project that had taken almost eighteen months to complete owing to the builder's disappearance halfway through the work.

"They all disappear," a friend had comforted her. "But they come back. The important thing to do is not to abandon belief in your builders. It's rather like believing in fairies in *Peter Pan*; if you don't believe in builders, their light goes out."

There were more stories of this nature. Another friend narrated the tale of a builder he had engaged for a house in France; this builder had been arrested for murder some time into the contract, and had been replaced by his son, who had then been shot by the relatives of his father's victim; passions ran deep in the French countryside, it seemed. But her position was different—she had the best builder in the business on her side.

Now, at her table, Antonia heard the bell ring and realised that the two men sent to begin work had arrived. Their rubbish skip, a giant, elongated bucket, had preceded them by a day or two and stood on the roadside, ready to receive the detritus from Antonia's flat. In time-honoured Edinburgh fashion, though, the neighbours had sneaked out at night and deposited unwanted property in the skip: several large pieces of wood, a pile of flattened cardboard boxes, an old tricycle missing its chain and a wheel—the abandoned property, Antonia decided, of that strange little boy downstairs . . . Bertie, or whatever he was called. And there was also a pile of old editions of *Mankind Quarterly*, which could only have been put there by Domenica. Really! thought Antonia. I'm paying for that skip, every single cubic foot of it, and yet people think that they have the right . . .

Antonia went to the front door and opened it to the men standing outside. It was obvious enough from their outfits that they were the builders, but she asked them nonetheless who they were.

"I take it that you're from Hutton and Read?" she said. "Clifford's men?"

The taller of the two men, a man in his early thirties with a rather good-looking face, nodded enthusiastically. "Clifford!" he said, and then added for emphasis "Clifford!"

Antonia gestured for the two men to enter. They turned round and each picked up a small chest of tools that they had put down on the landing behind them.

"I don't know where you want to start," said Antonia. "I suggest that you just begin wherever you want to. Don't mind me."

She looked at the two men, who returned her stare. The tall man smiled and nodded. "Brick," he said.

Antonia frowned. "Brick?"

"Brick," said the man.

"I don't know about that," said Antonia. "I assume that you use brick in your internal walls. But I really don't know. I take it that you've seen the architect's plans, have you?"

"Brick," said the builder. He had now put down the tool chest in the hall and was struggling with the catch that secured its lid.

"I really don't see the point of saying brick," said Antonia, somewhat tetchily. "What I really want to know is where you want to start."

"Poland," said the tall man.

Antonia looked at him. It had taken a few minutes, but at least now it was clear. "Poland?" she asked.

The tall man smiled. "Poland," he replied, pointing out of the window vaguely in the direction of Cumberland Street.

Antonia shook her head. "No," she said. "That's west. Poland is over there. There." She pointed in the direction of London Street and the Mansfield Traquair Church.

The builder looked concerned and glanced at his colleague, as if for reassurance.

"Poland," said the second man, staring intensely at Antonia.

"Well, I do get the point," said Antonia. "And I don't think we need worry too much about the exact location of Poland. I think that you make your point clearly enough. You're Polish. And you're here to work on my flat. But I take it that you understand nothing of what I have just said."

"Poland," said the tall man and held out his hands, palms up, in a gesture of resignation.

Antonia nodded, and pointed to the kitchen. "Go and look," she said. "Kitchen."

The senior Pole bowed to her and moved towards the kitchen with his friend. Scottish builders did not bow, thought Antonia, but then they did not carry on their shoulders quite such a history of defeat and invasion and dashed hopes. She watched the Poles as they entered the kitchen and set down their cases of tools. What was it like, she wondered, to be so far from home, in a country where one could not speak the language, without one's family? These men knew the answer to that, she assumed, but they could not tell her.

She went through to the kitchen, put on the kettle, and made tea. The Poles, in between the unpacking of their tool chests, watched her. And when she poured them each a mug of tea, they took it gravely, as if it were a precious gift, and cradled the mug in their hands, tenderly. She saw that these hands were rough and whitened, as if they had been handling plaster.

The tall man watched her and smiled. His eyes, she thought, had that strange blueness which one sometimes sees in those who come from northern places, as if they could see long distances, faraway things that others could not see.

Antonia raised her mug to them, as if in toast.

The tall man returned the gesture. As he did so, he mouthed something, and smiled. Antonia, who had hardly looked at a man over the previous year, looked at him.

40. A Significant Revelation on the Stair

While Antonia was busy communicating, albeit to a very small degree, with her new Polish builders, Angus Lordie was making his way up the stair of No. 44. He was coming to visit Domenica, not Antonia; indeed, it was the cause of some anxiety on his part that Antonia could, theoretically, be met on the way up to Domenica's house. Angus was in some awe of Antonia.

There was to be a meeting on the stair that morning, but not between Angus and Antonia. Halfway up, as he turned a corner, Angus came across a small boy sitting disconsolately on one of the stone steps. It was Bertie.

"Ah!" said Angus, peering down and inspecting Bertie. "The young man who plays the saxophone, I believe. The very same young man who exchanged warm words with my dog . . ."

The mention of Cyril had slipped out, and it revived the pain that seemed to be always there, just below the surface, as the mention of the names of those we have lost can do.

"He's a very nice dog," said Bertie. "I wish I had a dog."

"Oh, do you?" said Angus. "Well, every boy should have a dog, in my view. Having a dog goes with being a boy."

"I'm not allowed to have one," said Bertie. "My mother . . ."

"Ah, yes," said Angus. "Your mother." He knew exactly who Irene was, and Bertie had his unreserved sympathy. "Well," he went on, "don't worry. I'm sure that you'll get a dog one of these days."

There was a brief moment of silence. There's something wrong, thought Angus. This little boy is feeling miserable. Is it something to do with that mother of his? I would certainly feel miserable if I were her son, poor little boy.

"Are you unhappy?" Angus asked.

Bertie, still seated on the stone stair, hugging his knees in front of him, lowered his head. "Yes," he said. His voice was small, defeated, and Angus felt a surge of feeling for him. He, too, had endured periods of unhappiness as a boy—when he had been bullied—and he remembered what it was like. Unhappiness in childhood was worse than the unhappiness one encountered in later life; it was so complete, so seemingly without end.

"I'm sorry to hear that," Angus said. "It's rotten being unhappy, isn't it?" He paused. "I'm a bit unhappy myself at the moment. But you tell me why you're unhappy and then I'll tell you why I'm feeling the same way. Maybe we could help one another."

"It's because of Olive," said Bertie. "She's a girl at school. She came to play today and she pretended to be a nurse. She took some of my blood."

Angus's eyes widened. "Took some of your blood?"

"Yes," said Bertie. "She had a syringe which she found in her bathroom cupboard. It had a proper needle and everything."

"My goodness," said Angus. "Did she actually . . . actually . . . ?"

"Yes," said Bertie. "She stuck the needle into my arm—there, just about there—and then she squirted the blood into a little bottle. She said she was going to do some tests on it and would let me know the result."

"Well, I'm sorry to hear about that," said Angus. "She shouldn't have been playing with needles."

"She said that the needle was a clean one," said Bertie. "It was all wrapped up in plastic and she had to take it out."

"Well, that's a relief," said Angus. "But why did you let her do this? I wouldn't."

"I thought that she was just pretending," said Bertie. "So I closed my eyes. Then the next thing I knew she had the needle in my arm and was telling me not to move or it would go all the way through to the other side."

Angus extracted a handkerchief from his pocket and mopped his brow. "How very unpleasant for you, Bertie," he said. "Did you tell your mother about this?"

"Yes," said Bertie. "I ran through and told her, but I don't think she heard me. She just started to talk to Olive, who was pretending that nothing had happened. She's very cunning that way."

"I can imagine that," said Angus. "Well, Bertie, I don't know what to say, other than to suggest that you give Olive a wide berth in the future. But I suppose that's difficult. And I certainly won't say to you that you should cheer yourself up by thinking of how many other people are worse off than you are yourself. The contemplation of the toothache of another does very little to help one's own toothache, you know."

Bertie nodded. "Daddy sometimes says: worse things happen at sea. But when I ask him what these worse things are, he can't tell me. Do you know what they are, Mr Lordie?"

Angus thought for a moment. Terrible things undoubtedly happened at sea, but he did not think it appropriate to tell Bertie about them. "Oh, this and that, Bertie," he said. "It's best not to talk about these things."

Bertie appeared to accept this. He looked up at Angus and asked: "Mr Lordie, you said that you were unhappy too. Why are you unhappy?"

"My dog," said Angus. "He's in the pound. He's been accused of biting people in Northumberland Street."

Bertie thought for a moment. "That's another dog," he said eventually. "It looks like your dog, but it's another one. I've seen it."

Angus hardly dared speak. "Are you sure?" he whispered.

"Of course," said Bertie. "There's a dog who lives in a basement flat in Northumberland Street. They let him wander about. And he's a very bad dog—he tried to bite me once in Drummond Place Gardens, but I ran away in time."

Angus could barely contain his excitement. "Bertie!" he said. "Would you be able to help me find that dog? Would you?"

"Of course," said Bertie. "I can show you where he lives. But you'll have to ask my mother if I'm allowed."

"I most certainly shall," said Angus. "Oh, Bertie, you excellent boy! You have no idea what this means to me."

"That's all right, Mr Lordie," said Bertie. "And I'm glad that you're happy again."

"Happy?" exclaimed Angus. "I'm ecstatic!"

41. A Powerful Ally in the Campaign to Free Cyril

"I've just had the most extraordinary conversation," said Angus, as he entered Domenica's flat. "I met that funny little boy from down below. He was sitting on one of the stairs, like Christopher

Robin, his head bowed, looking utterly miserable."

"It's his mother," said Domenica. "She's a frightful woman. That poor little boy has the most terrible time at her hands. She's always banging on about Melanie Klein and the like, while all that poor wee Bertie wants to do is to have a normal boyhood. He's mad keen on trains, I believe, but she, of course, thinks that his time is better spent in yoga lessons. Yoga lessons! I ask you, Angus. What six-year-old boy wants to do yoga?"

"There might be some," mused Angus. "In these ashrams, or whatever. Some of the monks are tiny—young boys, really."

"Those are Buddhists," said Domenica. "You really should get your facts right, Angus. Buddhists meditate—there are some Buddhist schools of yoga, but generally the Buddhists don't turn themselves inside out."

"Well, be that as it may," said Angus. "I had a conversation with young Bertie, and he came up with an extraordinary story about some game of doctors and nurses that he had been involved in. But then . . ." he paused for effect; Domenica was watching him closely. "But then he revealed that he knew the dog who had done the biting with which Cyril is charged. And he says that he can show me where he lives!"

Domenica clapped her hands together. "What a relief! You've been like a bear with a sore head since Cyril was arrested, Angus. It will be a great relief to have you back with us again."

"And what about Cyril's feelings?" asked Angus peevishly. "Aren't you pleased for his sake?"

"Of course I am," said Domenica soothingly. "Nobody wants the innocent to suffer."

"So all we have to do is to explain to the police that it was this other dog—whoever he is—who did it, and they'll release Cyril."

Domenica frowned. It would not necessarily be so simple, she thought. One could hardly get the fiscal to drop proceedings just because somebody—and an interested party at that—explains that he thinks that another dog is to blame. No, they would have to be more convincing than that.

"We'll need to think about this," she said to Angus. "We can't just barge in and expect to get Cyril out. We must marshal our facts. We must prepare our case, and then, at the right moment, we produce the real culprit from a hat—metaphorically speaking, of course."

Angus nodded his agreement to this. He was convinced now that Cyril would be exculpated, and he did not mind if the process required some planning and thought. In fact, he was quite willing to leave all this to Domenica; she was so forceful, he thought, she would be a very powerful ally for Cyril in the campaign to establish his innocence.

"Whatever you say, Domenica," Angus said.

"Cyril and I are quite content to leave our fate in your hands."

They moved through to the kitchen, where Domenica prepared a cup of coffee for them both. Then she turned and addressed Angus with the air of one about to make an important statement. "Angus," she began, "don't you find that there are times when everything seems to be happening at once? When, for some reason, life seems speeded up?"

"Most certainly," said Angus. "And do you think we are in such a time right now?"

"It seems a little bit like that to me," said Domenica. "Here I am, back from the Malacca Straits. No sooner have I returned than Antonia announces her intention of becoming my neighbour on a permanent basis. Not that she asked me, mind you. I've always thought that one should ask one's neighbours before one gets too firmly settled in."

"Impossible," said Angus. "Neighbours are given to us on the same basis as we are given our families. There is no element of choice involved—none at all."

"Is there not?" asked Domenica. "Well what about Ann Street? I was under the impression that the people who live in Ann Street will buy up any house that comes on the market in order to make sure that it doesn't end up in the wrong hands."

"Nonsense," said Angus. "That really is an

ancient canard, Domenica. People have been saying that about Ann Street for years. But it's complete nonsense. It's a very inclusive street. Anybody who's got a million pounds to spend on a house is in. They're terrifically accepting."

"Then all these stories about Edinburgh being full of icy types are false?"

"Absolutely," said Angus frostily.

Domenica was not convinced, but she did not want to get involved at that moment in a discussion about the mores of Edinburgh; she had other news to impart to Angus.

"Yes," she said. "Developments seem to be occurring at a frightening rate. And here am I with somebody else coming to live with me. No sooner have I dispatched Antonia, than I hear from my aunt that she would like to come and spend a few months in Edinburgh with me."

"How nice for you," said Angus. "Company, and so on."

"Yes," said Domenica. "I don't begrudge her the visit. It's just that she belongs to a generation that was used to paying rather long visits. We think in terms of three days; they thought nothing of descending on people for three months." She paused. "And she's virtually one hundred years old; ninety-six I think. But remarkably sprightly."

"Then she will have a great deal to talk about," said Angus. "A lot will have happened in those ninety-six years."

"Indeed," said Domenica. "We can expect to hear a great deal about it."

"Do I detect a certain lack of enthusiasm?" asked Angus.

"Well . . ."

"Because I would love to have somebody like that stay with me," said Angus. "You should be more appreciative, Domenica."

Domenica thought for a moment. "All right," she said. "She can stay with you, Angus. Thank you for the offer."

Angus looked flustered. "But I'm not sure that she would approve of my lifestyle," he said. "You know . . ."

"My aunt is very tolerant," said Domenica. "So thank you, Angus, it really is very kind of you."

"No, Domenica. Sorry. She's your responsibility. Blood is thicker than whisky."

"Whisky?"

"Why, thank you," said Angus.

42. A Dinner Date with Pat . . . and a Surprise

After leaving the Cumberland Bar, where he had been regaled by Angus Lordie with all the details of that extraordinary evening with the Jacobites, Matthew had returned to his flat in India Street to prepare for his dinner outing with Pat. Angus had not been much help in recommending restaurants, and so he had consulted a guide and chosen a small place, Le Bistrôt des Arts, at the Morningside end of Colinton Road, convenient for Pat—it was ten minutes' walk from the Grange—and well-reviewed by a normally picky critic.

He was at the table when she arrived. He appeared to be studying one of the spoons, but he was really looking at his reflection in the silver. The concave shape distorted him, but even taking that into account, Matthew felt that it captured the essential him. And the problem with that was that the essential him, he thought, was nothing special. I really have nothing to offer this girl, he told himself; me, with my distressed-oatmeal sweater—a failure—and my crushed-strawberry trousers—another failure—and my Macgregor tartan underpants. I just don't have it.

She slipped out of her coat. "You've been waiting for ages? I'm sorry."

"No," he said. "Five minutes. If that." He stood up to greet her, and she kissed him on the cheek. She did not always do that, and he flushed with pleasure. Matthew wanted this to work; he thought that it would not, but he wanted it.

"I'm going to order champagne," he said impulsively. He might be a failure, but he was a failure with more than four million three hundred thousand pounds (the market was doing well). "Would you like that?"

She swept the hair back from her forehead, and

he saw that there were small drops of rain on her skin. "What's the occasion?" she asked.

He smiled. "Meeting you here. Being with you."

He stopped. Did that sound corny? Nobody said that sort of thing, he thought. But he had said it spontaneously; he had meant it, and now, to his relief, he saw her return his smile.

"That's a very sweet thing to say, Matthew. Thank you."

He felt emboldened. "Well, I meant it. I like being with you. I like you so much, you see. So much."

She looked down at the table. I've embarrassed her, he thought. I should not have said that. She doesn't want to be liked by me.

"I like you too, Matthew."

Well, he thought, that's something. But how much did she like him? As much as he liked her? As much as she had liked Wolf? Or Bruce for that matter? Or was that a different sort of liking? Wolf and Bruce were sexy; they dripped with sexual appeal, if one can drip with such a thing. Dripping came into it somewhere, but Matthew was not sure where and did not like to think about it really, about the things that he did not have.

For a few moments there was silence. Then he said: "Do you think there's much of a future for us?"

Pat raised her eyes to meet his. "What do you mean?"

211

"A future. You know. Are we going to carry on going out together?"

She seemed to relax—quite visibly—and it occurred to him that she might have misinterpreted him. He imagined that she had thought that he was proposing to her, and the thought appalled him. It was not that he would not like to marry Pat, but he had never thought of marriage to anybody. She would do fine, of course, if he did; but he hadn't . . .

"I'd like to carry on seeing you," she said, reaching for the menu. "So let's not talk about it anymore. Let's just carry on."

She reached across the table and took his hand, gave it a squeeze, released it. He thought: she might do that with a brother—take his hand, squeeze it, and let go. If he had been Wolf, would she not have taken his hand, squeezed it, and then clung on?

"All right," he said.

"Now let's choose something to eat," she said.

Matthew turned round to catch the proprietor's eye. "I'm going to order that champagne," he said. "Bollinger."

She glanced at the menu. It looked expensive, and she could not tell the difference between champagnes. "A bit extravagant."

He shrugged. "Why not?"

She said: "Have you forgiven me?"

He was puzzled. "For what? What have I got to forgive you for?"

"For that business over Angus Lordie's painting. For selling it to . . ."

"To that man with the mustache? The Duke of . . ."

"Johannesburg. Yes. For doing all that. Because, anyway, I've sorted it all out."

He looked puzzled. "Has he paid?"

He had not. But she had felt guilty about it and been in touch with him. He had said that he would pay, she explained. "He was very nice about it," she said. "He said that he had been meaning to get in touch and that he was glad that I had phoned. And he's asked us to a party."

"Hold on," said Matthew. "He—the Duke, that is—has asked us—you and me, that is—to a party?"

"Yes," said Pat. "Tonight. Any time before twelve. He said that things get a bit slower at midnight."

Matthew shook his head. "I can't believe this! You went off and set all this up—why didn't you ask me? What if I had been going to do something else?"

"But you wouldn't," Pat said. "You never do . . ." She left the sentence unfinished, as well she might—she had not intended even to begin it. It was true, of course; Matthew never did anything, never went out. His life, when one came to think of it, was remarkably empty, not that she had meant to tell him that.

But he had heard. "I never do what?" There was

213

an edge to his voice, disclosing, perhaps, a sense of having been misjudged.

"You never do anything on a Tuesday night," Pat said quickly.

"It's Wednesday."

"Same difference," she said. "Anyway, the point is this: the Duke has invited us and I think we should go. And he said that he'd give us the cheque there. So we have to go."

"All right," said Matthew. But he did not think that it was all right; it was all wrong in his view. He was so passive, so useless, that she had to make the decisions. He looked down at his new pair of mid-brown, handmade shoes that had arrived from John Lobb that morning. She had not noticed them; she never would.

43. *Like a Couple of Boxers, Waiting to Land a Blow*

After dinner, Matthew and Pat took a taxi out to Single-Malt House, on the southern extremes of the city. Matthew had cheered up during the course of the meal, and they had both laughed to the brink of tears when a garlic-buttered snail had slipped off Matthew's fork and disappeared down his shirt front.

"You're so sweet," Pat had said suddenly. "With your snails and . . ."

Matthew was not sure whether it was a good thing

to be called sweet. Being called cute was a different matter; that was a compliment, and one did not have to be in short trousers to receive it. But most men, he thought, would object to being called sweet. Indeed, the Scots term sweetie-wife was commonly used, in a pejorative sense, for a man who liked to gossip with women. Matthew, for his part, saw nothing wrong in gossiping with women, which he rather enjoyed when he had the chance. He liked talking to Big Lou; he liked talking to Pat; in fact, he liked talking to any woman who was prepared to talk to him. At the heart of Scots culture, though, was an awful interdiction of such emotional close-ness between men and women; a terrible separation inflicted by a distorted football-obsessed emotional tyranny, such a deep injury of the soul.

Yet it was not an evening to take offence at what was undoubtedly intended as a compliment, and so Matthew said nothing, but merely nodded in acknowledgement. "And you're sweet too," he said, adding, "in a different way."

The conversation moved on.

"Who was in the Cumberland Bar this evening?" asked Pat.

"The usual crowd," said Matthew. "But I only spoke to Angus Lordie. You've heard about Cyril?"

"I have," said Pat. "And it's awful. My father says that they'll have him put down, for sure. He said that he has a patient whose dog was put down for biting. My father said that the owner experienced

215

real grief and suffered from depression for a long time. You'd think that they'd take that into account before they order dogs to be destroyed. Those dogs are members of somebody's family."

"Exactly," said Matthew. "And Angus is really upset, as you can imagine. Anyway, he told me about Big Lou's new boyfriend, Robert something-or-other. It's one of those very Scottish surnames—Crolloch or something like that. Crumblie, maybe. Robert Crumblie? No, I don't think so."

"Smellie? That's a common name."

Matthew laughed. "Yes, it is. I knew a boy called Smellie at school. The family came from Fife, where they often have these interesting names. There are people called McSporran up there, which is fine, but you have to admit it is a pretty striking name. Like Smellie."

Pat was intrigued. "What was Smellie like?"

Matthew thought for a moment. He was trying to remember what Smellie's first name was. Archie MacPherson Smellie. That was it. And then he smiled at the memory.

"Archie," he said. "Archie Smellie. He was a great betting man, or, I suppose, betting boy. He had a numbers racket at school, which we all paid into. You would choose a number between one and fifty and Archie would write it down in his book. Then, each week, Archie would announce which number he was going to pay up on, and you'd get fifteen times your stake if it was your number."

"How did he choose the number?"

Matthew laughed. "That's the point. Archie never told us that, and sometimes there were weeks in which he said no number came up and he pocketed the whole proceeds. You'd think that we would have seen through it, but we didn't. I suppose we were very trusting."

"And what became of him?"

"He became an accountant," said Matthew. "I saw him the other day in Great King Street. He was walking along in the opposite direction. I stopped him and said: 'Hello, Smellie,' and he stared at me for a moment. Then I think he vaguely recognised me and muttered: 'Actually, it's Smiley these days.'"

"That's sad that he felt that he had to change his name."

Matthew agreed, but said that he understood. "Your name defines you," he said. "And I don't see why you should go through life being called something that embarrasses you. Mind you, some people make a point of sticking to an embarrassing name. They more or less challenge you to laugh. People like that show great courage, I think."

Pat tried to think of people she knew who had shown courage in the face of an embarrassing name. She could not think of anybody.

But Matthew could. "I know somebody called Winterpoo," he said. "Martin Winterpoo. Poor chap. But he's stuck to his name, which shows great qualities, in my view." He paused. "Would you like to be called something different, Pat?"

Pat hesitated before answering. The truth of the matter was that she would. Pat was such a brief name, so without character. It said nothing about its bearer. And it was androgynous.

She looked at Matthew. "You think I should be called something else? Is that what you think?"

"No, I didn't say that. I just asked you. There's nothing wrong with being called Pat."

Pat looked down at the tablecloth. "And what about your own name, Matthew? What about that? If I'm Pat, then you're Matt."

Reaching for the champagne, Matthew topped up Pat's glass. We're arguing again, he thought. It seems to happen rather too often recently. We're like two boxers dancing around one another in the ring, waiting to land a blow. This thought depressed him, and he did not want to be depressed; not tonight, with the Bollinger on the table and the prospect of a party at the Duke's house. He decided to change the subject.

"What should we call the Duke?" he asked. "Your Grace?"

"No," said Pat. "That's far too formal. I think that we should probably just call him Johannesburg."

"Is that what dukes are called by their friends?"

Pat shrugged. "No, they use their first names. Harry, or Jim, or whatever. But he called himself Johannesburg."

"I see," said Matthew. He paused. "Do you think that he's a real duke, Pat? I looked him up in *Who's Who in Scotland*, and he wasn't there. He wasn't there under Johannesburg or Duke. Nothing."

"I think he's a fraud," said Pat. "His real name is probably Smellie, or something like that."

"We'll find out," said Matthew.

"Will we?"

"Maybe not." Then he asked: "I wonder who else will be there, Pat? *Le tout Edimbourg*?"

44. Dukes Don't All Live in Grand Houses

Single-Malt House was a comfortable, rather rambling farmhouse on the very edge of town. It stood on the lower slopes of the Pentland Hills, those misty presences that provide the southern backdrop to Edinburgh. To the east, dropping slowly towards the North Sea, lay the rich farmland of East Lothian, broken here and there by pocket glens sheltering the remnants of old coal mines—the villages of miners' cottages, the occasional tower, the scars that coal can leave on a landscape.

The house itself was not large, but was flanked by a byre, behind which a garden sloped up to a stand of oaks, and beyond the oaks, the steeper parts of the hillside itself, pines, scree, the sky.

"I've driven past this place hundreds of times," said Matthew, as he and Pat alighted from the taxi in the driveway. "And never noticed it. That's the

Biggar road out there. We used to go out to Flotterstone Inn when I was a boy. We'd have sandwiches and cakes from one of those three-tiered plate things and then go for a walk up to the Glencorse Reservoir."

"So did we," said Pat. "And there were always crows in those trees near the reservoir wall. Remember them? Crows in the trees, and sheep always on the wrong side of the dyke."

They stood for a moment under the night sky, the taxi reversing down the drive behind them. Matthew reached out and put his arm around Pat's waist. "We could walk over there now," he said. "We could go over the top of the hill, then down past the firing ranges." He wanted to be alone with her, away from distraction, to have her full attention, which he thought he never had.

She shivered. "Too cold," she said. "And we've been invited to a party."

They looked up at the house behind them. There was clearly a party going on inside, as lights spilled out of the front windows and the murmur of many conversations could be heard coming from within.

"Somehow, I don't imagine him living here," said Matthew. "I don't know why. I just don't."

"They don't all live in grand houses," Pat said. "Some dukes are probably pretty hard-up these days."

Matthew raised an eyebrow. "But this one paid thirty-two thousand for a plain white canvas. That doesn't sound like penury." He paused. "Of course, he hasn't paid yet."

They walked to the front door and Matthew pulled at the old-fashioned bell tug.

"They'll never hear that inside," said Pat. "Let's just go in."

Matthew was reluctant. "Should we?"

"Why not? Look, nobody's answered. We can't just stand here."

They pushed the door open and entered a narrow hall. At the side of this hall was an umbrella and walking-stick stand of the sort which is always to be seen in country houses—a jumble of cromachs, a couple of golf umbrellas, and to the side, along with a boot scraper, mud-encrusted Wellingtons, a pair of hiking boots for a child, a tossed-aside dog collar and lead.

The hall became a corridor which ran off towards the back of the house. The sound of conversation was louder now—laughter, a tap being run some-where in the background—and then, from a door to their right, a man emerged. He was wearing a crumpled linen suit and a forest green shirt, open at the neck.

"So, there you are," said the Duke of Johannesburg. "Hoped for, but not entirely expected." He came up to Pat and kissed her lightly on each cheek—a delicate gesture for a large man. Then he turned to Matthew and extended his hand.

Matthew, flustered, said, "Your Grace."

"Please!" protested the Duke. "Just call me Johannesburg. We're all very New Labour round here." He turned to Pat as he said this and winked. "Hardly," he added.

Pat smiled at the Duke. "Where exactly is Johannesburg?" she asked.

The Duke looked at her in surprise. "Over there," he said, waving his hand out of the window. "A long way away, thank God." He paused. "Do I shock you? I think I do. That's the problem these days—nobody speaks their mind. No, don't smile. They really don't. We've been browbeaten into conformity by all sorts of people who tell us what we can and cannot say. Haven't you noticed it? The tyranny of political correctness. Don't pass any judgement on anything. Don't open your trap in case you offend somebody or other."

He led them through the door into the room from which he had just emerged.

"Everybody knows," he went on, "that there are some places which are, quite frankly, awful, but nobody says that out loud. Except some bravely spoken journalists now and then. Do let me get you a drink."

He reached for a couple of glasses from a library shelf to his side. "Some years ago," he continued, "*The Oldie* ran a series called Great Dumps of the World—a brilliant idea. They got a rather clever friend of mine, Lance Butler, to write about Monaco, and he did a brilliant job. What a dump that place is! All those rich people busy not wanting to pay tax and living in chi-chi little apartments above glove and perfume shops. Disgusting place! And their funny wee monarchy with its clockwork soldiers and the princess who took up with a lion tamer—can you believe it? What a dump! But they didn't like it at all. There was an awful fuss. These people take themselves so seriously.

"Come to think of it," the Duke continued, "Johannesburg isn't all that bad. Once they get crime under control, it'll be rather nice, in fact. That beautiful, invigorating highveld air. Marvellous. And nice people. They put up with an awful lot in the bad old days—oppression, cruelty etc.—but they came out smiling, which says a lot for them. So I hope things turn out well."

He handed Pat and Matthew their glasses. "You may be wondering why I'm the Duke of Johannesburg. Well, the reason is that my grandfather gave an awful lot of money to a political party a long time ago on the express understanding that they would make him a duke. He had visited Jo'burg years before when he was in the Scots Greys and he rather liked the place, so he chose that as his title. And then they went and ratted on their agreement and said they didn't go in for creating dukedoms anymore and would he be satisfied with an ordinary peerage? He said no and used the moniker thereafter, as did my old man, on the grounds that he was morally entitled to it. So that's how it came about. There are some pedants who claim that I shouldn't call myself what I do, but I ignore them. Pedants!"

He raised his glass. "*Slàinte!*"

45. Minimalism Is Not Confined to the Canvas

But there were others in the room. Matthew and Pat had hardly noticed them, so engaged had they been by the flow of their host's conversation. So that was the reason why there was no mention of a Duke of Johannesburg in *Who's Who in Scotland*—there was no such duke, at least not in the sense that one would be recognised by the Lord Lyon. Yet what did such recognition amount to? Matthew asked himself. All that it did was give a stamp of purely conventional authenticity, conventional in the sense of agreed, or settled, and ultimately that was merely a question of arbitrary social arrangements. There was no real difference between this duke and any other better-known duke, just as there was no real difference between a real duke and any one of Jock Tamson's bairns. We were all just people who chose to call ourselves by curious things known as names, and the only significant difference between any of us lay in what we did with our lives.

Matthew found himself drawn to the Duke of

Johannesburg, with his easy-going conviviality and his cheerful demeanour. This was a man, he thought, who dared and, like most men, Matthew admired men who dared. He himself did not exactly dare, but he would like to dare, if he dared.

"Yes," said the Duke, looking around the room. "There are a couple of other guests. And I'm ignoring my social responsibilities by not introducing you. I shouldn't go on about these old and irrelevant matters. Nobody's interested in any of that."

"Oh, but we are!" said a man standing near the fireplace. "That's where you're mistaken, Johannesburg. We all like to hear about these things."

"That's my Greek chorus over there," said the Duke, nodding in the direction of the man by the fireplace. "You must meet him."

The Duke drew Matthew and Pat over to the other guest and made introductions.

"Humphrey Holmes," said the Duke.

Matthew looked at Humphrey. He had seen him before—and heard of him—but he had never actually met him. He was a dapper man, wearing a black velvet jacket and bow tie.

"I hear you sold Johannesburg a painting," said Humphrey. "He was telling me about it. Something very minimalist, I gather."

Matthew laughed. "Very." He glanced around the room, at the pictures on the walls. There were several family portraits—a picture of three boys in kilts, in almost sepia tones, from a long time ago; one looked a bit like the Duke, but it was hard to tell. Then there was a powerful James Howie landscape, one of those glowing pictures that the artist scraped away at for years in order to get the light just as he wanted it to be. Matthew knew his work and sold it occasionally, when Howie, a perfectionist, could be persuaded to part with a painting.

"I was surprised when he said he'd bought something minimalist," remarked Humphrey. "As you can see, this isn't exactly a minimalist room."

"Perhaps he'll hang it somewhere else," said Pat.

Humphrey turned to her and smiled politely. "Perhaps. Perhaps there are minimalist things here already—it's just that we can't see them. But, tell me, do you like minimalism in music?"

Matthew looked down at his feet. "Well, I'm not sure . . ."

"You mean people like Glass and Adams?" Pat interjected.

"Yes," said Humphrey. "Some people are very sniffy about them. I heard somebody say the other day that it's amazing how people like Adams make so much out of three notes. Which isn't exactly fair. There's quite a lot there, you know, if you start to look at Pärt and people like that."

"I like Pärt," said Pat.

"Oh, so do I," said Humphrey.

"And then there's Max Richter," said Pat. "Do

you know that he lives in Edinburgh? His music's wonderful. Really haunting."

"I shall look out for him," said Humphrey. "Johannesburg wouldn't be interested, of course. He listens to the pipes mostly. And some nineteenth-century stuff. Italian operas and so on. One of his boys is shaping up to be quite a good piper. That's him coming in now."

They looked in the direction of a boy who had entered the room, holding a plate of smoked salmon on small squares of bread. From behind a blond fringe, the boy looked back at them.

"Will you play for us, East Lothian?" asked Humphrey.

"Yes," answered the boy. "Later."

"Good boy," said Humphrey. "Johannesburg has three boys, you know. That lad's East Lothian. Then there's West Lothian and Midlothian. Real boys. And he's taught them to do things that boys used to know how to do. How to make a sporran out of a badger you find run over on the road. How to repair a lobster creel. Things like that. I think . . ."

He was interrupted by the return of the Duke, who had gone out of the room once he had made the introductions.

"I have my cheque book," said the Duke, holding up a rectangular green leather wallet. "If I don't pay for the painting now, I shall forget. So . . ." He unfolded the wallet, and leaning it on Humphrey's back, scribbled out a cheque, which he handed to Matthew with a flourish.

Matthew looked at the cheque. The Duke's handwriting was firm and clear—strong, masculine downstrokes. Three hundred and twenty pounds.

Matthew's expression gave it away.

"Something wrong?" asked the Duke. There was concern in his voice.

"I . . ." Matthew began.

Pat took the cheque from him and glanced at it. "Actually, the painting was thirty-two thousand pounds," she said.

"Good heavens!" said the Duke. "I thought . . . Well I must have assumed that there was a decimal point before the last two zeros. Thirty-two thousand pounds! Sorry. The exchequer can't rise to that."

"This'll do," said Pat firmly. "Our mistake. This'll do fine, won't it, Matthew?"

Matthew glanced at Humphrey, who was smiling benignly. Elsewhere in the room, there was silence, as other guests had realised what was going on. It was easy to imagine a mistake of this nature being made. And three hundred and twenty pounds was quite enough for that particular painting, far too much, really.

"I shall be more careful in my labelling in future," Matthew said magnanimously. "Of course that's all right."

The tension which had suffused the room now dissipated. People began to talk again freely, and the Duke reached for a bottle of wine to refill glasses.

"That was good of you," murmured Humphrey.

"It was nothing," said Matthew. "It really was."

"But it wasn't," protested Humphrey.

"I meant the painting was nothing," said Matthew, which was true.

46. *He Wanted Her Only to Answer His Question*

Later in the evening, Matthew, wanting, he said, to get some air, suggested that they go out into the garden. Pat nodded and followed him out through the hall. She had gone out into gardens with boys before this and knew what it meant. Boys were usually not very interested in gardens, except at night, when their interest sharpened. Outside, the evening was unusually warm for the time of the year, almost balmy; the air was still, the branches of the oak trees farther up the steeply sloping garden were motionless.

For a few moments, they stood on the driveway. Matthew reached for Pat's hand. "Look at that," he said, gesturing up at the sky. "We don't often see that in town, do we? All that?"

The sky was a dark, black velvet, rich and deep, studded here and there with small points of starlight, one or two of which seemed to burn with great intensity.

229

"No," she said. "All those yellow streetlights. Light pollution."

Matthew squeezed her hand. This time, she returned the pressure, did not let go of his hand.

"Whenever I look up there," he said, "I think the same thing. I think of how small we are and how all our concerns, our anxieties and all the rest of it, are so irrelevant, so tiny. Not that we think they are—but they are, aren't they?"

She looked at him. "I suppose they are."

"And I also think of how we make one another miserable by worrying about these small things, when we should really just hug one another and say thank you to somebody, to something, for the great privilege of being alive—when everything up there"—he nodded in the direction of the sky—"when everything up there is cold and dead. Dead stars. Collapsing stars. Suns that are going out, dying."

She was silent. She wanted to say to him: "I think so too." But she did not.

He began to walk over towards the byre, leading her gently by the hand. "You know, a long time ago, when I had just left school, I had a friendship with another boy. It was the most intense friend-ship I ever had. I really loved my friend. And why not? It was pure—it really was. Nothing happened. It was completely innocent. Do you understand about that?"

"Of course I do," she replied. "Women are much

easier about loving their friends. It's only men who have difficulty with that."

"Yes. Anyway, we were in Perthshire once, fishing, and we sat down on the rocks beside the river and I looked up at the sky, which was completely empty, and I suddenly had the feeling that I wasn't alone anymore. I can't explain it in any other way. I suppose it was one of those moments that people sometimes call mystical. A moment of insight. And I never forgot it. I still think of it."

They were outside the byre now. It had been converted and appeared to be used as some sort of office. A French window, framed by creepers, was open, and they could see into the room on the other side of the window.

"Come," said Matthew. "Come on, I don't think they'll mind."

They pushed open one of the French windows and stepped inside the room. Through a large window in the roof there was enough light coming in from outside, from the glow that spilled out from the main house, from the light of the sky itself, to reveal a cluttered desk, a wall of bookshelves, and a sofa. In the far corner of the room, a squat, dark shape revealed the presence of a wood-burning stove. There was, about the room, an air of wood-smoke that had settled, a reassuring, comfortable smell that had also been present in the house, with its open fires.

"This looks like his study," said Matthew. His

voice was lowered, almost to a sepulchral whisper, although there was nobody about.

"It's so quiet after the din back there," Pat said.

They sat down on the sofa. Matthew felt his heart beating within him and knew that even if he had not made up his mind in a conscious sense, at the level of the subconscious there was certainty.

"I wanted to talk to you," he whispered. "Just us. Without anybody else around. I wanted to ask you . . . to ask you whether you thought that we could . . . well, whether we could get engaged."

He had said it, but he had said it in such a clumsy fashion. Nobody said that anymore, he said to himself; nobody asks anybody else if they would like to be engaged. Like everything I do, he thought, it sounds awkward and old-fashioned.

For a few moments, Pat said nothing, and Matthew wondered if she had heard him. They were seated so close together that she must have been able to sense the agitated beating of his heart and must have known. At least she knew her presence excited him, made him catch his breath, made his heart go like that; one could not fake those symptoms of affection.

Then a square of light fell onto the driveway and lighted, too, the byre's interior. The front door had been opened and somebody came out, footfall upon gravel.

She said: "Somebody's coming."

The steps came nearer and reached the French

windows, a figure moving in the darkness, a shadow. Matthew wanted her only to answer his question—gauche though it may have been, it expressed everything that he now felt. Because I'm fed up, he thought, with being lonely and out of place and seeing everybody else in the company of somebody they love. That was why he wanted an answer to his question.

"Please tell me," he said. "Please just think about it."

She did not have the time to answer, or if she answered he could not hear. Young East Lothian, his pipes under his arm, was inflating the bag, his drones were beginning to wail; that protest of the pipes before they wrought their magic. He had gone out there to warm up, and now he began to play.

" 'Mist-covered Mountains,' " said Matthew. "Do you know it?"

"Yes," said Pat. And then: "That question you just asked . . ."

"You don't have to answer," said Matthew. "I'm sorry."

"But I want to . . ." she said, and his heart gave a great leap, then descent: "I want to think about it. Give me . . . give me a few weeks."

"Of course."

Outside, the "Mist-covered Mountains" continued; such a tune, expressing all the longing, the love, that we feel for country and place, and for people.

47. The Statistical Lady Is Not for Smiling at

Stuart Pollock, statistician in the Scottish Executive (with special responsibility for the adjustment of forecasts), husband of Irene Pollock, father of Bertie (six) and Ulysses (four months); co-proprietor of the second flat (right) in 44 Scotland Street, Edinburgh; all of this is what Stuart was, and all of these descriptors he now mulled over as he walked home early, making his way down Waterloo Place after a long and tedious meeting in the neo-Stalinist St Andrew's House.

A life might be summed up within such short compass, thought Stuart. He saw actuaries do it in their assessments in which we were all so reduced to become, for instance, a single female, aged thirty-two, nonsmoker, resident of the Central Belt—so truncated a description of what that person probably was, about her life and its saliences, but useful for the purposes for which they made these abridgements. Such a person had an allotted span, which the actuaries might reel off in much the same way as a fairground fortune-teller might do from the lines of the hand or on the turn of the Tarot card. You have thirty years before the environmental risk of living in the Central Belt becomes significant. The fortune-teller was not so direct, and certainly less clinical, but it amounted to the same advice: beware.

It had been a long-drawn-out meeting, and a frustrating one, in which Stuart, together with four other colleagues and a couple of parliamentarians, had been looking at health statistics. The news from Scotland was bad, and the Executive was looking for ways of making it sound just a little bit better. Nobody liked to pick on Glasgow, a vigorous and entertaining city, but the inescapable fact was that everybody knew that it had the worst diet in Western Europe and the highest rate of heart disease. Was there any way in which this information might be presented to the world in a slightly more positive way? "Such as?" Stuart had asked.

This question had not gone down well. The politicians had looked at one another, and then at Stuart. Did one have to restrict the area in question to Western Europe? Could one not compare the Glaswegian diet with, say, diets in countries where there was a similar penchant for high-fat, high-sodium, high-risk food? Such as parts of the United States, particularly those parts with the highest obesity rates? Yes, but although the United States has a similar fondness for pizza, they don't actually fry it, as they do in Scotland. There's a difference there.

Very well, but what exactly was Western Europe anyway? If one took Turkey into account, and Turkey was almost in Western Europe—particularly if one overlooked the fact that most of it was in Asia and perhaps somewhat far to the east—did it change the picture? Might Glasgow not be compared with Istanbul, and, if one did that, how did the comparison look? Still bad, alas: the Turks did not eat so many fats and sweet things, and they were really rather good about consuming their greens. So were there not other places somewhere, anywhere, where everybody smoked like chimneys, drank to excess, and fried everything . . . ? No, not really.

Stuart smiled as he negotiated the corner at the end of Waterloo Place and began to walk towards Picardy Place. As a statistician, he thought, I'm a messenger; that's what I do. And, like all messengers, some people would prefer to shoot me.

He looked down the street at the people walking towards him, young, old, in-between. After that day's meeting, it was taking some time for him to move back from the professional to the personal. Here, approaching him, was a sixty-year-old woman, with two point four children, twenty-three years to go, with a weekly income of . . . and so on. Now there were carbon footprints to consider, too, and that was fun. This woman was walking, but had probably taken a bus. She did not go on holiday to distant destinations, Spain at the most, and so she used little aviation fuel. Her carbon footprint was probably not too bad, particularly by comparison with . . . with those who went to international conferences on carbon footprints. The thought amused him, and he smiled again.

"You laughing at me, son?"

The woman had stopped in front of him.

Stuart was startled. "What? Laughing at you? No, not at all."

"Because I dinnae like being laughed at," said the woman, shaking a finger at him.

"Of course not."

She gave him a scowl and then moved on. Chastened, Stuart continued his walk. The trouble with allowing one's thoughts to wander was that people might misunderstand. So he put statistics out of his mind and began to think of what lay ahead of him. Bertie had to be taken to his saxophone lesson, and he would do that, as Irene had her hands full with Ulysses. That suited Stuart rather well, as he found that the late afternoon was a difficult time for Ulysses, who tended to girn until he had his bath and his evening feed. Stuart had rather forgotten Bertie's infancy, what it was like, and the presence of a young baby in the flat was proving trying. At least going off to the lesson would give him the chance to get out with Bertie, which he wanted to do more often.

They had once gone through to Glasgow together on the train and that had been such a success, or at least the journey itself had been. The meeting in Glasgow with that dreadful Lard O'Connor had been a bit of a nightmare, Stuart recalled, but they had emerged unscathed, and Irene and Bertie's subsequent encounter with Lard, when he had shown up unannounced in Scotland Street, had been mercifully brief. It was important that Bertie should know that such people as Lard O'Connor and his henchmen existed, that he should not think that the whole world was like Edinburgh. There were people who did assume that, and who were rudely surprised when they travelled furth of the city; going to London, for example, could be a terrible shock for people from Edinburgh.

Stuart wanted to spend more time with Bertie and—the awkward thought came unbidden—less time with Irene. That was a terrible thought, and he suppressed it immediately. He loved and admired Irene, even if she was sometimes a bit outspoken in her convictions. Then another awkward thought intruded: if he wanted to spend less time with Irene, Bertie probably wanted exactly the same thing. But should I, a father, he asked himself, try to save my son from his mother? Was there a general answer to that, he wondered, an answer for all fathers and all sons, or did it depend on the mother?

48. He Wanted So Much to Be the Average Boy

"Ask Lewis Morrison when he thinks Bertie will be ready for his Grade Eight exam," said Irene, as Stuart helped Bertie into his coat.

"But he's just done his Grade Seven," Stuart

pointed out. "Two months ago." He looked down at Bertie and patted him on the shoulder. "And we got a distinction, didn't we, my boy?"

"The sight reading was a very easy piece," said Bertie modestly. "Even Ulysses could have played it. If his fingers were long enough."

"There you are," said Irene. "Bertie's obviously ready for the next hurdle."

Bertie listened to this solemnly, but said nothing. He did not mind doing music exams, which for the most part he found very easy, but he wished that he had slightly fewer of them. He had thought that Grade Eight of the Associated Board of the Royal Schools of Music was the highest examination available, and he had been dismayed when Irene had pointed out that it was possible to do examinations beyond that—in particular the Licentiate. Perhaps the best thing to do would be to fail Grade Eight deliberately and continue to fail it at every resitting. But he had tried that technique with his audition for the Edinburgh Teenage Orchestra and had only succeeded in getting himself accepted into the orchestra immediately. He looked up at his father. "Why all these hurdles, Daddy?" he whispered.

"What was that, Bertie?" his father asked.

Bertie glanced at Irene. She was watching him.

"He said he enjoys hurdles," said Irene. "So just ask Lewis for the details—set pieces and all the rest. Then Bertie can get cracking."

"People who do Grade Eight are usually much older," said Bertie. "Sixteen, at least."

Irene reached forward and ruffled his hair fondly. "But you're exceptional, Bertie," she said. "You're very lucky. I don't wish to swell your little head, Bertie, but you are not the average boy."

Bertie swallowed hard. He wanted so much to be the average boy, but he knew that this would forever be beyond his reach. The average boy, he knew, had the average mother, and his mother was not that.

They left the flat with the issue of Grade Eight unresolved. As they went downstairs, Bertie asked his father if they were going to go to the lesson by bus or car. Bertie loved going in their car and rarely had the chance to do so, as Irene believed in using the bus whenever possible.

"You'd like to go in the car, wouldn't you?" said Stuart.

Bertie nodded his head vigorously.

"Well, in that case," said Stuart, "let's go in the car, Bertie! And then afterwards—after your lesson—we could take a spin out into the Pentlands, perhaps, or down to Musselburgh. Would you like that?"

Bertie squealed with pleasure. "Yes, Daddy," he said. "Or we could drive round Arthur's Seat, all the way round."

"That's another possibility," said Stuart. "The whole world—or at least that bit of it within twenty miles or so of Edinburgh—is our oyster, Bertie. We can go wherever we like!"

Bertie, who was holding his father's hand as they walked downstairs, gave the hand a squeeze of encouragement.

"Thank you, Daddy! Thank you so much!"

Stuart smiled. Bertie was so easy to please, he found; all that he wanted was a bit of company, a bit of time. Now they stepped out into the street and Bertie looked about him.

"Where's our car, Daddy? Is it far away?"

Stuart hesitated. He looked up Scotland Street, up one side, and then down the other. There was no sign of the car.

"Has Mummy used it today?" he asked.

Bertie shook his head. "No, Daddy. You were the last one to use it. Last week. You came in and said that you had parked the car and you put the keys down on the kitchen table. I saw you, Daddy."

Stuart scratched his head. "You know, Bertie, I think that you're right. But I just can't for the life of me remember where I parked it. Did I say anything about where I'd parked it?"

Bertie thought for a moment. "No, I don't think so, Daddy. Can't you just try to remember?"

Stuart glanced at his watch. "I'm sorry, Bertie, I can't. And time's getting on a bit. If we don't leave now we'll be late for Lewis Morrison, and Mummy will be cross. So we're just going to have to go and catch a bus on Dundas Street."

Bertie knew that what his father said was true. It was a bitter disappointment to him, though; his parents were always forgetting where they parked the car, and it often meant that outings were delayed or cancelled altogether. His mother was always telling him that people who lost or otherwise did not look after their things did not deserve to have them in the first place. Well, if that was the case, he wondered if his parents deserved to have a car, or if it should be taken away from them and given to somebody who deserved it. It was so disappointing. Other boys had cars which were never mislaid; and most of these cars were rather more impressive than the Pollocks' old red Volvo. Even Tofu, whose father had converted their car to run on vegetable oil, had a better car than Bertie had, and one that collected him every afternoon at the school gate, its motor purring away as contentedly as if it were running on ordinary petrol. That was Tofu. And then there was Hiawatha, whose mother had a small open BMW sports car in which she would collect him from school each afternoon. Olive had expressed the view that Hiawatha's family needed to have an open-topped car because of the way that Hiawatha's socks smelled, but Bertie had ignored this uncharitable suggestion, even if it had the ring of truth about it.

Bertie walked in silence to the bus stop with his father. There would be no run out to the Pentlands or Musselburgh. There would be no circumnavigation of Arthur's Seat. There would just be a saxophone lesson and a return to Scotland Street to his mother and Ulysses with all his girning.

Stuart understood his son's silence. "Bertie," he said, "I promised you an outing, and you will have one. When we come back, we'll go to that little café in Dundas Street. We might find something really unhealthy to eat. Would you like that?"

Bertie said that he would, Scottish genes.

49. This Is a Very Nice Place— Is It a Nightclub?

With Bertie's saxophone lesson over, he and Stuart made their way back across town by bus. The lesson had gone well; Lewis Morrison had been pleased with Bertie's performance of Boccherini's Adagio and Moszkowski's Spanish Dance. There had been some technical issues with his interpretation of Harvey's Rue Maurice-Berteau, but these had quickly been sorted out, and had Bertie himself not drawn attention to them they might even have passed unnoticed.

They got off the bus shortly after the junction of Dundas Street and Heriot Row. It was now just early evening, but Big Lou's Coffee Bar was still open; Lou did not like to leave before six-thirty, even if there were no customers. She had never stopped work before then when she was in

Arbroath or Aberdeen, and the habit had remained.

Stuart, who was carrying the saxophone case in his right hand, gave Bertie his left as they crossed the road.

"The café's still open, Daddy," said Bertie excitedly, pointing over the road. "I can see the lights."

"Good," said Stuart. "And I do hope that Big Lou has some really nice cake for us. She often does, you know."

"One with cream?" asked Bertie.

"Possibly. Or maybe a piece of millionaire's shortbread. Have you ever had that?"

"No," said Bertie. "But Tofu had a piece at school once. He let me look at it, and have just one lick, on approval, and then he tried to sell it to me."

"Quite the little entrepreneur, your friend Tofu," said Stuart, laughing. "You didn't buy it?"

"No," said Bertie. "But I might buy the X-ray specs that he says he'll sell me. I'd like those."

Stuart smiled. X-ray specs! What boy has not yearned for a pair of X-ray specs, as advertised in the faded pages of half-forgotten comics, complete with illustrations of the fortunate possessor of a pair of such specs looking through the clothing of passers-by, to the manifest envy of his friends! An irresistible advertisement, at any age.

They made their way down the steep steps that led to Big Lou's. As they descended, they caught a glimpse of Big Lou inside, at the counter, polishing cloth in hand, talking to a man in a black overcoat.

"Yes," said Stuart, winking at Bertie. "We're in business, Bertie!"

Bertie pushed open the door and they entered the coffee bar. Big Lou looked up as they went in. She smiled. She knew Stuart slightly as one of her occasional customers, and although she had never met Bertie before, she had seen him once or twice. From conversations with Angus and Matthew, she also knew that Bertie's life was not an easy one, at least from the maternal point of view. Big Lou remembered the incident in which, under severe provocation, Cyril had sunk his teeth into Irene's ankle. Although this incident was not talked about during Cyril's current legal difficulties, it had been remembered in the area and had indeed passed into local legend.

"Well, young man," said Big Lou, smiling at Bertie. "I see that you've brought your father in for a treat. That's kind of you."

Stuart nodded to the other man standing at the counter, the man who had been talking to Big Lou when they had entered. Then he asked Big Lou if she had something large and sweet for Bertie to eat. She replied that, as it happened, there was a Dundee cake which she had baked herself and which tasted rather good with copious quantities of sweetened cream ladled on the top. This went rather well with Irn-Bru, she said, and what would Bertie's views be on that?

With the order placed, Bertie and his father sat down at one of the nearby tables.

"This is a very nice place, Daddy," said Bertie politely, swinging his legs backwards and forwards under the table. "Is it a nightclub?"

"No," said Stuart. "Nightclubs are a bit different, Bertie." He thought for a moment. He wondered if he had ever been in a nightclub before and concluded that he had not. And if there were nightclubs in Edinburgh, where were they? He looked at Bertie. "Where did you hear about nightclubs?"

"From Tofu," said Bertie. "He says that he goes to nightclubs sometimes."

Stuart suppressed a smile. "Quite the lad, Tofu," he said.

Bertie nodded. "Most of the time he tells fibs," he said. "So I don't really believe him."

"Rather wise," said Stuart.

They sat in companionable silence for a few minutes while Big Lou prepared the order, which she then brought across. Bertie stared appreciatively at the large glass of orange-coloured fizzy drink that was placed before him and the sizeable chunk of rich Dundee cake under its mantle of whipped cream. He looked up at Big Lou and smiled. "Thank you," he said.

"Aye, well, that's the stuff that a boy needs," she said. "Especially after a music lesson." She nodded in the direction of the saxophone case. "Is that your trumpet, Bertie?"

"It's a saxophone," said Bertie. "The saxophone was invented by Adolf Sax, who was a Belgian . . ." He did not finish his explanation. The man who had been talking to Big Lou, and who was still standing at the bar, now turned round. "A sax?" he said. "And you play it?"

Bertie looked at his interlocutor. "Yes," he said. "I can play jazz, and some other things. I used to play 'As Time Goes By' a lot, but now I've got a new piece from Mr Morrison."

Big Lou, who was standing nearby, thought it time to effect introductions. "This is my old friend Alan Steadman," she said. "His cousin married my cousin, up in Kirriemuir. He runs a jazz show on Radio Tay. And a club too. Near Arbroath."

"Arbroath?" said Stuart. "Is there jazz up there?"

Big Lou rounded on him. "What do you mean, is there jazz up there? Of course there's jazz in Arbroath."

"Hospitalfield, actually," said Alan. "Do you know it? It's an art college these days, but, as it happens, we do have a monthly jazz club there. There are lots of people round about who like to listen to jazz. We get great players going up there, you know. Brian Kellock's coming up in a few weeks' time. He's based here in Edinburgh, but comes up to Arbroath now and then. Great pianist."

"Aye, he's that," joined in Big Lou. "He did a great Fats Waller tribute some time ago. I heard it."

"You should come up and listen," said Alan.

247

"You and your dad. You'd be very welcome, you know."

"Aye," said Big Lou. "I'll come along with you. It's about time somebody went up to Arbroath."

Stuart smiled. Why should he and Bertie not go up to Arbroath with Big Lou and listen to jazz together? He would have to find the car first, of course, but after that . . . Well, why not?

"Thanks," he said. "We'll come." He looked at Bertie, who was busy drinking his Irn-Bru through a straw.

"Great stuff, that," said Alan Steadman. "Made from girders."

And sugar, thought Stuart.

50. Bertie's Words Stop Stuart in His Tracks

They walked back to Scotland Street, hand in hand, Stuart and Bertie, father and son. The visit to Big Lou's had been an unqualified success—in every respect. Two generous pieces of Dundee cake had been followed by three large squares of vanilla tablet, and the whole thing had been washed down with a couple of brimming glasses of Barr's Irn-Bru. That had been Bertie's portion. For his part, Stuart had restricted himself to a large cup of café latte and a dovetail-shaped piece of Big Lou's home-baked shortbread; more modest fare than that of his son, but for both of them it had been perfect.

The invitation extended by Big Lou's friend, Alan Steadman, had been an agreeable bonus. They would all three of them—Stuart, Big Lou, and Bertie—travel up to Arbroath for the next jazz evening at Hospitalfield. Alan wrote out the details on a piece of paper, along with the directions, and scribbled down his telephone number in case they should need to contact him. Everything was satisfactorily arranged. And if they left early enough on the Saturday afternoon, Big Lou promised, they would be able to call in at her cousin's farm, and Bertie could look at the two retired Clydesdale horses who lived there. That was also agreed, and duly planned for.

"What will Mummy do while we're up in Arbroath?" asked Bertie, as they made their way back round Drummond Place.

Stuart thought for a moment. "She'll stay and look after Ulysses," he answered. "Ulysses, you see, is too young to appreciate jazz. Pity about that, but there we are."

Bertie nodded. It would be best to leave his mother behind, he thought, as he could not imagine her in a jazz club in Arbroath. He hoped that she would agree.

As they walked down Scotland Street, Stuart fell silent.

"Are you all right, Daddy?" asked Bertie. "You didn't eat too much, did you?"

Stuart looked down at Bertie and laughed. But

there was a nervous edge to his laugh. "No, I didn't," he said. "I'm just thinking. That's all."

"About statistics?" asked Bertie.

It would have been easy for Stuart to answer yes to that, as he had been thinking about his chances, which appeared to be diminishing the nearer they approached the front door of 44 Scotland Street. To begin with, before any other charges were considered, he and Bertie were late. They had spent rather longer than he had intended at Big Lou's, and the meal which Irene would have prepared for them would have been ready a good twenty minutes earlier. That would undoubtedly be an issue. But then there was the question of the trip to Arbroath. He was reluctant to ask Bertie not to mention it, as that would suggest that something was being kept from Irene, but if Bertie mentioned it before he, Stuart, had the chance to do so, then the whole outing might not be presented in quite the right light. Irene could hardly be expected to agree to Bertie's going to a club of any sort; there had been that unseemly row over his attending Tofu's birthday party at the bowling alley in Fountainbridge, and a jazz club was surely even one step beyond that. It would be far better, Stuart thought, if they could present the occasion as a concert. To say that one was going to Arbroath for a concert sounded much better than saying that one was going to a jazz club in Arbroath—that was clear.

He broached the subject with Bertie as they

climbed the stairs to their front door. "Bertie," he began, "let me tell Mummy about that concert we're going to. I think that might be best."

"What concert?" asked Bertie. "Do you mean the jazz club?"

"Well, yes, I suppose I do. It's just that there are ways of explaining things to other people. Mummy is not a great aficionado of jazz, is she? She doesn't know about jazz clubs, but she does know about concerts. I think it might be better for us to say that we're going to a concert—which is true, of course. It will be a sort of a concert, won't it?"

Bertie nodded. He was relieved that his father seemed willing to take on the task of persuading Irene. "Of course, Daddy," he said. "And Mummy is your wife, isn't she? You know her better than I do, even if Ulysses might not be your baby."

Stuart stopped. He stood quite still. They were halfway up the stairs, and he stopped there, one foot on one stair and one on another, as if caught mid-motion by some calamity, as at Pompeii. Bertie stood beside him, holding his hand, looking rather surprised that his father had come to this abrupt halt.

"Now, Bertie," said Stuart, his voice barely above a whisper. "That's a very odd thing to say. Why do you think Ulysses might not be my baby? Whatever gave you that idea?"

"He doesn't look like you, Daddy," said Bertie. "At least, I don't think he does."

Stuart's relief was palpable. "Oh, I see. Is that all it is?" He laughed and patted Bertie on the shoulder. "Babies often don't look like anybody in particular, Bertie. Except Winston Churchill, of course. All babies look like Winston Churchill. But you can't draw any conclusions from that!"

"But Ulysses does look like somebody, Daddy," said Bertie. "He looks like Dr Fairbairn. You should look at Dr Fairbairn's ears, and his forehead too. Ulysses has this little bump, you see . . ."

Bertie became aware that something was amiss. Stuart was leaning back against the banister, staring at him.

"Are you feeling all right, Daddy?" asked Bertie, the concern rising in his voice. "Are you sure that you didn't have too much shortbread?"

"No, I'm all right, Bertie," Stuart stuttered. He leaned forward so that his face was close to Bertie's. On the little boy's breath he could smell the Irn-Bru, an odour of sugar, and violent orange, an odour of a whole Scotland that would disappear one day, along with the Broons and Oor Wullie, a whole culture, things so loved, so taken for granted.

He recovered, but only to the extent of being able to say to Bertie: "I don't think that you should talk about that, Bertie. That sort of thing is a bit sensitive. People are funny about it."

"I know," said Bertie. "You should have seen how Dr Fairbairn looked when I asked him."

51. So Many Books Unread and Bikes Uncycled

The following morning, Domenica Macdonald took slightly longer over her breakfast than usual. This was not because there was more to eat—her breakfasts were always the same: a bowl of porridge, made from the cut oats she obtained from the real-food shop in Broughton Street and two slices of toast, one spread thinly with Marmite and one with marmalade. This breakfast never varied, at least when she was at home, and it was accompanied by whatever reading was current at the time—*Mankind Quarterly*, with its earnest anthropological papers, rubbed shoulders with the toast as easily as did the daily newspaper or an interesting letter set aside for leisurely perusal. Not that there were many of those: Domenica still wrote letters, by hand, but received few back, so depleted had the ranks of letter-writers become.

She had read somewhere that the vast majority of boxes of notelets that were sold in stationery shops were never used. They were bought with good intentions, or given as presents in the same spirit, but they remained in their boxes. But that, she reflected that morning, was a common fate for so many objects which we make and give to one another. Exercise bicycles, for example, were not designed to go anywhere, but the wheels, at least, were meant to go round, which they rarely did. Exercise bicycles in gyms might be used, but this did not apply to those—the majority—bought for use in the home. They stood there, in mute affront to their owners, quite idle, before being moved to a spare room and ultimately to an attic. Then they were recycled, which did not mean, in this case, that they had been cycled in the first place.

She poured herself a cup of coffee and stared out of the window. And then, she thought, there were those books bought and not read. Somewhere there might be those who read each and every book they acquire—read them with attention and gravity and then put them carefully on a shelf, alongside other books that had received the same treatment. But for many books, being placed on the shelf was the full extent of their encounter with their owner. She smiled at this thought, remembering the anecdote about the late King George VI—she thought, or V perhaps, or even Edward VII—who was presented with a book by its author and said: "Thank you, Mr So-and-So, I shall put it on the shelf with all the other books." This was not meant to be a put-down to the author—it was, by contrast, a polite and entirely honest account of what would be done. And one could not expect one who was, after all, an emperor, to read every book given to him, or indeed any. Although—and this thought came to Domenica as she took a first sip of her coffee— even those whose office makes them too busy to read are never too busy to write their book when they leave office—a book which, by its very nature, will be most likely to appeal to those in similar office, who will be too busy to read it.

Some books, of course, were destined not to be read, largely because of their unintelligibility to all except a very small number of people. Domenica could think of several examples of this, including the remarkable books of her friend Andrew Ranicki, a professor of mathematics at the university. She had once asked him how many people in the world would understand his highly regarded but very obscure books from cover to cover, and he had replied, with very little hesitation: "Forty-five." He had said this not with an air of resigned acceptance, as might be shown by an author reporting on the public's failure of taste, but with the air of one who knows from the beginning that he is writing for forty-five people. And surely it is better that forty-five should buy the book and actually read it, than should many thousands, indeed millions, buy it and put it on their shelves, like George VI (or V, or Edward VII, or possibly somebody else altogether). That, she remembered, had been the fate of Professor Hawking's *Brief History of Time*. That was a book that had been bought by many millions, but had been demonstrated to have been read by only a minute proportion of those who had acquired it. For do we not all have a copy of that on our shelves, and who amongst us can claim to have read beyond the first page, in spite of the pellucid prose of its author and his evident desire to share with us his knowledge of . . . of whatever it is that the book is about?

And then, she thought, there were those novels that went on forever. Readers in a more leisurely age may have stayed the course, but not now. Domenica herself had tried to read Vikram Seth's *A Suitable Boy* four times, but on each occasion had got only as far as page eighty. This was not because of any lack of merit in the novel—it was very fine—but because of its sheer scale. Such a fat book, she thought, in her defence, so many pages and marriages and family relationships. Almost like Proust, whom she had never finished, and whom she accepted she now never would. *À la recherche du temps perdu* was on her shelves—and in a prominent position—and every so often she would dip into it and wander away into a world of dreamy reminiscence, but she would never finish it; she knew that. The sentences were too long. Modern sentences are short. In Proust, we encounter sentences which appear interminable, meandering on and on in a way which suggests that the author had no desire to bring a satisfying or intriguing line of thought to any form of conclusion, wishing rather to prolong the pleasure, as one might wish if one were an author like Proust, who spent most of his time languishing in bed—he was a chronic hypochondriac—rather than experiencing life—an approach which encouraged him to produce sentences of remarkable length, the longest one being that sentence which, if printed out in standard-size type, would wind round a wine bottle seventeen and a half times, or so we are told by Alain de Boton in his *How Proust Can Change Your Life*, a book which has surely been read by most of those who have bought it, so light and amusing it is.

Domenica stopped. She had been gazing out of the window, allowing her thoughts to wander. But there were things to be done that day, and Proustian reverie would not help. One of these things was to remind Antonia that it would be her turn to sweep the common stair next week, not an onerous duty perhaps, but one of those small things upon which the larger civilisation in which we live is undoubtedly based.

52. It Was a Pity That Things Had Come to This

When Domenica went out of her flat onto the landing, she noticed immediately that the pot plant which grew beside the banister had been damaged. It was a large split-leaf philodendron, which she had bought some years before and which she had nurtured to its current considerable size. In this task she had received, she observed, very little support. When Bruce had occupied the other flat on the landing, he had professed an interest in the plant's welfare, but had rarely, if ever, raised a finger in support. Such a narcissistic young man, Domenica thought; had the leaves developed reflective surfaces, of course, it might have been different. Pat, who had at that point shared the flat with Bruce, had been more conscientious and helpfully had washed the leaves from time to time, something which the plant appeared to appreciate and which it rewarded with fresh sprouts of growth. But Antonia, in spite of having been very specifically asked to ensure that the plant was well-watered while Domenica was in the Far East, had proved to be an indifferent guardian at best, and Domenica was convinced that it was only as a result of Angus having come in to water it discreetly that the plant had survived her absence.

Now something had ripped the plant's largest leaf and something else had broken one of the stems, leaving a leaf hanging by no more than a few sinews. Domenica stared in dismay at the damage that had been done: two years' growth, she thought, had been casually destroyed in a few moments of carelessness.

She looked up and saw that Antonia's front door was ajar. It was as if a detective had arrived on the scene of the crime and seen the culprit's footprint etched clearly into the ground. It was now obvious to her what had happened—Antonia had been carrying something into the flat, swinging her bag perhaps, and had brushed against the plant, thus causing this damage. And rather than attend to it—to break off the damaged leaf—and rather than knock on Domenica's door and offer some sort of apology, she had merely disregarded what had happened. Well! That showed gratitude. That showed how much she appreciated everything that Domenica had done for her—offering her flat for the full period of her absence for nothing, and indeed getting nothing in return other than this cavalier conduct towards the local flora.

And then there had been the incident of the blue Spode teacup, which Domenica had found Antonia using in her flat, having obviously removed it from her own kitchen. Remove was a charitable term in this context; steal might be more accurate. That was business that had yet to be resolved, and it was difficult to see how this could be done. It is a major step to accuse one's neighbour of theft; it implies a complete breakdown in relations and leads one into a position from which there is no easy retreat. It is quite possible, though, to make a remark that falls short of an outright accusation, but yet which makes a clear implication of negligence at the very least.

Domenica had given some thought to the Spode issue and had decided that she would raise the matter by saying: "I wonder if you've forgotten, perhaps, to return the cup you borrowed." That would indicate to Antonia that she knew that the cup was there, that she had not got away with it, but at the same time it did not amount to a direct accusation of theft.

It was a pity that things had come to this, she thought. Antonia had been a friend, and she had not imagined that there would be any breach in relations. But it had occurred, or was about to occur, and this, Domenica thought, demonstrated the wisdom of those who said that you never really knew your friends until you had lived in close proximity with them for some time. Going on holiday with friends was a good way of testing a friendship. In some cases, this worked well, and served to cement the relationship; in others, it revealed the fault lines in that relationship as accurately as any seismograph will reveal the movement between plates.

Domenica had welcomed Antonia to Scotland Street even though she thought that it was slightly tactless of Antonia to have moved into the next-door flat without consulting her. She had wondered whether she was being excessively sensitive about this, as strictly speaking it was none of her business which flat Antonia should choose to buy. There was an open market in housing, and Scotland Street was part of that market. But then she thought that Antonia's purchase of the neighbouring flat meant that she who had come as a guest to the larger address—44 Scotland Street—would not be leaving, but remaining. And that, Domenica decided, constituted a unilateral extension of a relationship that had been entered into on the understanding that it would be temporary. Or that is how an anthropologist might put it, which was what Domenica was.

As she stood there, peering at Antonia's half-open door, there crossed Domenica's mind the idea that one way of signalling displeasure to another would be to write an academic paper expressing this displeasure, but couched in general terms and, of course, without mentioning the specific *casus belli*. So, in this case, she might write a paper which she would ask Antonia to read before she sent it off to *Mankind Quarterly*, or *Cultural Anthropology*. The title would be something like "Residential Property Exchanges and Expectations of Continuing Neighbourhood Relationships," and it would purport to deal with the issue of social expectations in circumstances where one party (Antonia, obviously, but just not so described) accepts a time-limited gift of another's house (Domenica's flat in Scotland Street, but again not described). That would set the scene, and there would then follow a discussion of how important it is for social harmony that the party accepting the gift should understand that he or she should not presume to transform the host/guest relationship into something quite different, namely, a neighbour/neighbour relationship.

Antonia was a perceptive person, thought

Domenica, and she would get the point of that. But there was a further challenge, and that was more difficult: how would one incorporate into such a paper some mention of a blue Spode teacup? After all, one did not want to be too obvious.

53. She Could See the Attraction—
It Was the Eyes

Domenica peered round Antonia's door into the hall. She would normally have knocked, but her sense of grievance over the ruined philodendron made her feel disinclined to extend to Antonia that courtesy; wanton destroyers of philodendra must expect some consequences. The hall light was on, and a portable workbench had been set up, with pieces of timber stacked against it; there was sawdust on the floor and the smell of cut wood. A large metal box lay open beside the bench, with various tools displayed—a power saw, a jumble of cable, clamps.

Domenica cleared her throat. "Antonia?"

She waited a few seconds for a reply and then called out again. It now occurred to her that Antonia was out and that the door had been left open by the workmen. More than that, the workmen appeared to have left the flat unattended for some reason, as there was no response from them. She realised now that she had jumped to conclusions: the damage to the plant would not have been Antonia's doing, but must have been caused by the builders. Manipulating a piece of timber around a small landing would not be easy, and any philodendron that should find itself in the way was bound to be damaged. She sighed. It would have been easy for somebody to have spoken to her about this in advance and to have suggested that the plant be stored in her flat until the work was over. That would have been so simple and straightforward, but nobody had thought of that—including herself, she concluded, which gave a different complexion to the whole matter. It was an accident, she decided; Antonia, I forgive you.

She moved further into the hall. A light was coming from the bathroom, and she looked into that. The floorboards were up, revealing the joists and copper piping below. The sides of the bath enclosure had been removed too, and everything was covered with a layer of dust. She moved away. Dust, or at least dust in such quantities as that, made Domenica's eyes water—an allergy with which she had struggled when she had lived in India, where the dust had settled every day, no matter how assiduously the house servants had swept and polished.

"Domenica?"

She spun round. Antonia had emerged from a door on the other side of the hall and was standing there, her hair slightly ruffled.

"Oh." It was all that Domenica could manage

initially, but then, after a few seconds of hesitation, she added, "I knocked."

She had not intended to say that, because she had not knocked, but it came out nonetheless.

"I didn't hear you," said Antonia. "I was . . . I was busy."

"Of course. I'm sorry. I didn't mean to barge in like this." She paused. It did not seem to her that Antonia was angry over the intrusion; in fact, it seemed to her that her neighbour looked defensive, as if it was she who had been discovered in the other's flat.

Domenica continued. "It's just that I noticed that the plant outside," she gestured in the direction of the landing. "The plant was damaged. It must have been the workmen. Easily done, of course, with all this stuff being brought in."

She stopped. A man had appeared in the doorway behind Antonia, a tall man wearing jeans and a checked shirt. He glanced at Domenica, and then looked at Antonia, as if expecting an explanation.

"This is Markus," said Antonia. "Markus. Domenica."

The man took a few steps across the hall and shook hands with Domenica. She felt his hand, which was warm, and roughened by work.

"Markus is Polish," said Antonia, straightening her hair with her right hand. "He's my builder, as you see. We've been looking at the plans. That's why I didn't hear you."

Domenica knew immediately that this was a lie, and she knew immediately what had been happening. She was amused. That was why Antonia had been almost defensive at the beginning; she had been caught in the arms of her builder. Of course, there was nothing wrong with that, she thought. One might fall in love with a Polish builder as readily as one might fall in love with anybody else, but it all seemed a bit sudden. Building work had only started a day or two ago; one would have thought that one might wait . . . what, a week? . . . before one fell in love with the builder.

She turned to Markus. "So, Markus," she said brightly. "Are you enjoying living in Scotland?"

Markus looked at her gravely. "Brick," he replied.

"Markus doesn't have much English yet," said Antonia. "I'm sure that he'll be learning it, but at the moment . . ."

Domenica nodded. She turned back towards Markus and, speaking very slowly and articulating each word with great care, she said: "Where are you from in Poland, Markus?"

The builder looked at her again, and Domenica noticed his eyes. She could understand why Antonia had fallen; it was the eyes.

"Brick."

Domenica turned to Antonia. "Markus says brick a lot, doesn't he?"

Antonia waved a hand in the air. "It's all he says," she answered. "But then, how many words of Polish do we know? Could we even say brick in Polish?"

Markus now bowed slightly to Domenica. "Poland," he said.

"Ah yes," said Domenica. "Poland."

There followed a silence. Then Markus bowed his head again slightly in Domenica's direction and walked over to the toolbox from which he extracted an electric drill.

"Well," said Antonia breezily, "work must get on. How about a cup of tea, Domenica?" She paused, and then added, "Since you're here."

Domenica had not intended to stay, but she felt that in the circumstances she could not very well leave, and so she accepted. They moved through to the kitchen.

"A nice man," said Domenica.

"Very."

Domenica waited for Antonia to say something else, but she did not. The electric kettle, switched on without an adequate amount of water inside it, began to hiss in protest. "Will you teach him English, do you think?" she asked.

"Perhaps," said Antonia. "I suspect that he will prove a quick learner."

"Well, he's already learned brick," said Domenica. "That's a start."

"Yes."

"And the novel?" asked Domenica. "Are you managing to write with all this building going on? Surely it's a bit difficult to get yourself back into the minds of those Scottish saints of yours while there are electric drills whining away in the background."

Antonia looked out of the window.

"Their own times were noisy enough," she said. "I imagine that they had to contend with all the noises that humanity makes when it's in close proximity with itself. Crying babies. People groaning because they were in pain. That sort of thing. Remember that people didn't have much domestic room in those days. Our flats would have been considered palaces. They lived in hovels, really."

She turned and fixed Domenica with a stare—as if in reproach.

54. It Did Not Do to Think About Sex on Heriot Row

Domenica felt unsettled when she went out into Scotland Street. The encounter with Antonia had been unsatisfactory from her point of view: she had entered the flat in a spirit of righteous indignation over the damage to the philodendron. She had expected that Antonia would at least make some attempt at an excuse, even if she did not actually apologise, but none of that had been forthcoming.

Indeed, after Domenica had broached the subject, nothing more had been said about the plant, as Markus had appeared in the hall in highly suggestive circumstances. This had completely thrown Domenica; after that, it had been impossible to raise the issue of the plant, which she would now simply have to move into her own flat for a while in protest at her neighbour's attitude towards its safety. Not that Antonia would necessarily notice, but at least it would be a gesture.

She was not sure how to take Markus. The question of having an affair with somebody with whom one could not communicate in language was an interesting one, and as she walked up Scotland Street, she turned this over in her mind. If one could not say anything to the other, and he could say nothing to you, what remained? All close relationships between people—unless they were purely instrumental—were based on some feeling for the other. That feeling required that one should know something about that person and that one should be able to share experiences. If one could say nothing about the world to one another, then what precisely was the shared experience upon which the relationship was founded? Only the carnal, surely; or could there be spiritual and emotional sharing without language? Human vulnerability, human tenderness—the understanding of these required no words, but could be achieved through gestures, through looking, through mute empathy; a bit boring, though, Domenica thought, once the initial excitement of the physical side of the relationship wore off; if it was to wear off, and sometimes the pulse remained quickened, she understood, for years . . .

But that was another question altogether which she would have to come back to, as she had now reached the corner of Heriot Row, and it did not do to think about sex on Heriot Row. She smiled at the thought. It was another Barbara Pym moment. Of course, one could think about sex while walking along Heriot Row—these days. That tickled her, although not everybody, she thought, would be amused about that: the words "these days" did a lot of work there. It all depended on an understanding of Edinburgh as a city of cultivated, outward respectability beneath which there lay of world of priapic indulgence. But was that still the reality? Perhaps it was. One had only to look at Moray Place, that most respectable of addresses and reflect on how many nudists lived there. That was very strange: Jekyll clothed, and then, after a quick disrobing, there was Hyde unclothed!

Domenica had agreed to meet her friend James Holloway for coffee at the Scottish National Portrait Gallery, where he was the director. By the time she arrived at the Gothic Revival sandstone building on Queen Street, she had put out of her mind all thought of Antonia's torrid affair—at least she assumed it was torrid and, anyway, she wondered if there was any point in having an affair which was not torrid. Now, as she sat in the coffee room, waiting for James to come down from his office upstairs, she looked up at the Bellany portraits on the wall above her table. Sean Connery looked out of one of them rather forbiddingly, but then he was perhaps a touch disapproving, which was why people in Scotland were so proud of him. Scots heroes were not meant to be benign in their outlook; they needed to be at least a little bit cross about something, preferably an injustice committed against them, individually or nationally, some time ago. Sean Connery certainly looked rather cross about something. Perhaps he was cross at having his portrait painted, in the way in which such people often looked cross at having their photographs taken. Perhaps, thought Domenica, there were paparazzi portraitists, who lurked with their easels outside hotels and fashionable night-clubs and painted quick likenesses of well-known people as they left the building—absurd thought.

James arrived and fetched the coffee. "I need your advice," he said as he sat down. "We've been offered an exhibition of the photographs of famous anthropologists. Pitt Rivers, Mead, and the like. I'd like to show you the names. Some of them are unfamiliar to me. There's one who spent some time among head-hunters in the Philippines . . ."

"Probably R.F. Barton," interjected Domenica. "He spent some time with head-hunting tribes there back in the nineteen-thirties, although there was an anthropologist who lived among headhunters as late as the late nineteen-sixties. That was Renato Rosaldo, if I remember correctly."

"Did they come back?" asked James, adding, "In one piece?"

"Oh yes," said Domenica. "The headhunters were usually very good hosts. They tended to go for heads belonging to their enemies, not their friends. Friends' heads were left in situ, so to speak."

James looked thoughtful. "I see," he said. "I suppose this very gallery is full of heads. Pictures, of course, but heads nonetheless. Does that make us headhunters?"

"Virtual," said Domenica. "Virtual headhunters. But enough of that, James, what about your travels?"

"Since I last saw you," said James, "there's been India. Again."

"On your motorcycle?"

"Not my Ducati," said James. "That stayed in Scotland. But I got hold of a very nice hired bike. A Royal Enfield Bullet, 650cc. Made in Madras. I went up to the Himalayas and down into Rajasthan."

Domenica frowned. "Is Madras still Madras? Isn't it . . . ?"

"Chennai," supplied James. "For some people it may be, and that's fine, but we're talking English, aren't we? And we have English words for certain places. Those words exist irrespective of what the people who live in the place in question may call it. So why change the name?"

He paused. "Take Florence," he said. "Would you ever say I'm off to Firenze? You would not, unless you were extremely pretentious, which you aren't. Or Milan. Who goes to Milano? And the French have Édimbourg and Londres. Would you insist on their using Edinburgh and London? No, you wouldn't. In fact, one can't insist that the French do anything—everybody knows that.

"So I go to Bombay," he continued, "rather than to Mumbai, and I must say that when I'm there I find that most people I talk to say Bombay rather than Mumbai."

Domenica thought for a moment. There was a scrap of a poem coming back to her. What was it? Yes, that was it.

"Under Mr de Valera," she ventured inconsequentially, "Ireland changed herself to Eire / England didn't change her name / And is still called England just the same."

"What odd things one remembers," said James.

55. What Can Be the Secret of the Tiny Stars?

"But don't you think that it's a question of respect?" asked Domenica. "We went round the world giving names to places that already had their own names. This is a gesture—a sign that we respect the real identity of the places we named incorrectly."

James Holloway shook his head. "I don't think it reveals any lack of respect to call Naples Naples rather than Napoli."

Domenica looked up at the ceiling. There was a difference, she thought, but what exactly was it? "But we didn't impose Naples on the Italians. The name Naples was for our use, not theirs. We imposed Bombay on India. Now we are saying: we'll call you what you want us to call you. That's a rather different attitude, I think."

James picked up his coffee cup. "Of course, the names of whole peoples have been changed too. Remember the Hottentots? They've become the Khoi now, which means that the Germans will have to retire that wonderful word of theirs, *Hottentotenpotentatenstantenattentäter*, which means, as you know, one who attacks the aunt of a Hottentot potentate." He paused. "But I'm uncomfortable with the deliberate manipulation of the language. I think that we have to be careful about

273

that. It's rather like rewriting history. We can't go back and sanitise things."

The subject now had to be changed. James wanted to show Domenica the list of anthropologists, and that would entail going up to his office above the coffee room. He suggested that they do this, and they left.

"Such a nice smell of cooking," observed Domenica as they made their way up the small staircase that led to the director's office.

James laughed. "They're doing something with coriander today. I suspect that this is the only gallery in the world where the director works immediately above the kitchen," he said. "A great privilege."

They sat at the large conference table in James's office. There were two other members of the gallery staff there—Anne Backhouse, who extracted the list of anthropologists from a large file marked *Anthropologists,* and Nicola Kalinsky, the chief curator, who had been waiting to see James about another matter.

"Nicola knows all about Jacobite glass," said James as he introduced Domenica. "And Gainsborough, of course. She's been putting things together for the Drambuie collection which we're showing."

Domenica looked at a large photograph which Nicola had on the table in front of her. A wine glass, long-stemmed and elegant, stood against a dark background. The glass was engraved with a rose, intertwined with leaves, behind which there was what looked like a field of stars.

"That dates from about seventeen fifty," said Nicola. "Not too long after the Forty-Five. I suppose that whoever had it then might be drowning his sorrows over the fate of Bonnie Prince Charlie and the attempt at the Stuart restoration. The rose is a Jacobite symbol, as you know. And this is a particularly attractive one."

Domenica picked up the photograph. "I'm always surprised that old glass survives," she said. "You'd think that over a couple of centuries somebody might fumble and drop it."

"Ah, but these Jacobite glasses were special," said James. "And special things have a way of surviving. These glasses were tucked away for use in secret—they would not have been everyday ware."

"I don't have a particularly high opinion of the Stuarts," said Domenica. "Apart from Mary, Queen of Scots, of course, who had such a difficult cousin, after all. And Charles II, of course, had what we might today call an enlightened arts policy. . . . But as for Charlie . . . well, that was a narrow escape for Scotland, if you ask me."

She examined the photograph more closely. "Those stars are so delicately engraved," she said. "Look at them all."

"Yes," said James. "But that's the extraordinary thing. That glass is part of a set of six—or it looks like a set. Usually, one comes across only one or two together, but there are six with that design. Very strange, wouldn't you agree, Nicola?"

Nicola nodded. "There's something very unusual about it. Normally, one finds only one star on these glasses, if there is a star at all. But here we have hundreds of little stars—it's very strange."

"And you have no idea of the meaning?" asked Domenica.

"None, I'm afraid," said Nicola. "I've looked through the literature on the subject—and there's quite a bit on Jacobite glass—but these particular glasses seem to be completely unusual. We just don't know what the stars mean."

For a few moments the room became silent; outside in Queen Street, the vague hum of traffic; light slanted in through a window, pure, thin, northern light. Domenica felt the presence of the gallery around her; the repository of a nation's memory, now distilled into this precious object depicted in the photograph—a moment of contact between the hands that had made the glass and engraved it so finely, and her.

James broke the silence. "There seems to us to be some pattern to the stars," he said. "Look. Here and here. And again here. They're in clusters. Shapes."

"I wondered if they could make a coded message of some sort," said Anne from her desk at the side of the room.

Domenica looked at the photograph. She would

mention it to Angus, who had said something about Jacobites to her recently—what was it? She could not remember, but it was something about modern Jacobites sounding off even now about the Stuarts, still wanting them back.

"Of course, there are modern sympathisers of the cause, are there not?" asked Domenica.

"Oh yes," said James. "They have their pretender, Francis II, who lives in Bavaria, I believe. Not that he has ever made any claim to the throne. But there are one or two people who still claim that he is the real King of Scotland."

"How colourful," said Domenica. She was still trying to remember what Angus had said. She had not been paying particular attention, but it involved Big Lou for some reason. What possible connection could Big Lou have with Prince Charlie and Francis II and the whole arcane Stuart dynasty?

James tapped the photograph with his finger. "If there were a coded message on the glasses, it would be rather interesting to find out what it is," he said. "Perhaps we could get Bletchley Park, or whoever cracks codes these days, to work out what it says."

Domenica laughed. "Let's not let our imaginations run away with us," she said. "Codes only occur in ridiculous novels. The real world is much more prosaic."

The photograph was slipped back into a large

envelope and Domenica turned her attention to the list of anthropologists.

Fifteen minutes later, James Holloway escorted her to the front door of the gallery and said goodbye to her there. They would see one another again soon, he said; Domenica suggested lunch with their mutual friend, Dilly Emslie, and James agreed. Then she walked down the hill towards Drummond Place and Scotland Street. As she passed Queen Street Gardens, the wind moved the branches of the trees against the sky, gently, almost imperceptibly. This city is so beautiful, she thought, so intriguing. If one had it, the city, as one's lover, that would be almost enough, almost enough.

56. So Many Moves— Time to Make the Next One

Moving, thought Bruce, had become rather familiar. Within the space of a year there had been his move from Edinburgh to London, where there were several moves, and then the move back to Edinburgh. His first flat in London had been a shared one in Fulham. He had liked that and would have been prepared to stay there longer, but had been unable to resist an offer he had received to move in with friends in Notting Hill. That had suited him perfectly; the flat was a couple of doors from an Italian restaurant and a small set of film studios. The film people often ate in the restaurant, along with other creative types, and this appealed greatly to Bruce. They had been stand-offish, though, and had not welcomed an overture which Bruce had once made, when he had offered their table an olive from a plate of olives on his own table. Bruce had thought this rude; there was something symbolic about rejecting an olive—or was the symbolism attached purely to whole olive branches? In spite of that, he still felt that by living there, and eating from time to time in that particular restaurant, he was at the heart of this fashionable and vibrant part of London. *Je suis arrivé*, he said to himself and reflected on how unimportant and faraway Scotland now seemed.

But things in London had not worked out quite as Bruce had planned. The flat in Notting Hill was expensive, even when the rent was divided three ways, and Bruce soon found that the money he had brought with him—most of it from that highly lucrative Chateau Petrus deal—soon haemorrhaged away, as money has a habit of doing in London. There was no shortage of work there, of course, but not all of it was the sort of work that Bruce wanted to do, and he began to think with a degree of regret of the job with Macauley Holmes Richardson Black, the Edinburgh surveyors. It had been time to move on from that, of course, and he could not imagine himself doing that sort of work for the rest of his life, but it had been steady and reasonably well paid, and often involved free tickets to Murrayfield for the rugby, even for the popular game against England, for which tickets were always in such short supply.

It was all the fault of that awful Todd woman, thought Bruce. She had accosted him—yes, accosted—in that bookshop in George Street and virtually forced him to take her to lunch at the Café St Honoré. Of course I should have been on my guard, he thought: Edinburgh was full of women like that who were itching for an affair with a younger man, particularly somebody like me, and I should have shown a little bit more savvy. But what made it all so unjust was that nothing had happened, and it was only because her husband had come into the restaurant at the precise moment that this rapacious woman had seized his hand that the situation had become awkward.

Nothing like that had happened in London, of course, but over the months it had become apparent to Bruce that the reality of life in London was one of struggle; people worked hard, put up with cramped conditions, and had to travel miles to conduct their social lives—they struggled. With the inherent good nature of the English, they generally remained remarkably cheerful about all this, but such hardships began to wear Bruce down. He looked back with longing to the days when he had been able to walk to work—even to go home for lunch or for a quick dalliance with a girlfriend if he so desired; that was impossible in London. He remembered how he could walk from the Cumberland Bar to Murrayfield Stadium in half an hour, with his friends, and then walk with them to a dinner and a party thereafter. And he remembered those friends: Gordon, Hamish, Iain, Simon, Fergus . . . and he found that he missed them.

So there had been the move back to Edinburgh and into the flat in Comely Bank owned by his friend Neil. Now there was the move out of that flat and into the flat in Howe Street owned by Julia Donald. So many moves . . . He zipped up his suit-case and moved it off the bed and onto the floor. Caroline, Neil's wife, was standing in the doorway, watching him, and Bruce turned round to face her.

"Well," he said. "That's more or less it. I hope I haven't left anything. If I have, give it to the Oxfam shop." He paused. He did not like the way that Caroline watched him; it was distinctly discon-certing, and he wondered if she did it to Neil too. I could never put up with being married to some-body like her, thought Bruce; poor Neil.

"Neil said that I should offer to drive you over there," Caroline said. "Would you like me to do that?"

Bruce considered the offer for a moment. It was significant, he thought, that she had said that Neil had made the suggestion. She was not making the offer, her husband was. "No thanks," he said. "I wouldn't want to put you out. I'll phone for a cab."

She nodded. "Do you want to leave anything for the phone?" she said.

"Sorry?"

"For your phone calls," she said. "Sometimes when one stays somewhere one leaves money for one's share of the phone bill. That sometimes happens."

Bruce blushed. This woman was the end. She was *le fin*, he thought.

"I haven't kept a note," he said. "Sorry. Maybe I should have noted down the length of the calls. You know, something like: Edinburgh to Glasgow, two minutes ten seconds. That sort of thing." His lip curled as he spoke; she would hardly understand sarcasm, he thought; such people rarely do.

"Yes," she said. "Maybe you should have."

Bruce looked down at his suitcase. "You've got a problem, Caroline," he said. "You've got a big problem. Maybe with phones, but also with men, I'd say, and I'm sorry about that, because there are lots of men about, you know."

Caroline's reply came quickly. "Not with all men," she said. "Just some."

Bruce shrugged. "Whatever," he said. He picked up his suitcase; there was no point in prolonging this. "You've been very kind," he said. "Thanks for everything."

Caroline did not move from the doorway. "My conditioner," she said, between clenched teeth.

"Put it back in the shower! You've moved it again, and I told you, I told you. I want it in the shower, on that little shelf. That's where it lives. That conditioner lives there."

57. He Felt a Wave of Contentment Come Over Him

"It's amazing how petty some people are," said Bruce. "They get really, really upset about tiny things. You know, really tiny things." Julia Donald looked at him adoringly. "Such as?" she asked.

Bruce leaned back in his chair. "Well, Caroline was one of these OCD-types—you know, obsessive-compulsive disorder. She used to line the conditioner bottles up in the shower just like this, plonk plonk plonk, and she would go absolutely mental if you touched any of them. And of course you have to have a bit of room to move in a shower . . ." At this, he winked at Julia. "Ideally, showers should have enough room for two. Saves energy."

Julia giggled. "And it's somehow more . . . more friendly."

"Precisely," said Bruce, glancing for a finely timed moment in the direction of the bathroom, which lay behind him in Julia's flat. "Anyway, Caroline would go through the roof if any of her stupid conditioner bottles was moved. Ballistic. Stupid woman."

"You'd think that she'd have better things to do," said Julia. "I can't bear obsessively tidy people."

Bruce glanced around her sitting room—their sitting room now. In the New Town, of course, he knew it would be called a drawing room, depending on how one defined oneself. As a surveyor, he had prided himself on being able to tell exactly when a living room would be described as such, or as a lounge (never), or when it would be a drawing room. It was not always easy, but there were many clues. A drawing room was genteel, and there were many drawing rooms in Edinburgh; this, he was sure, was one.

"It's so comfortable," he said, smiling at Julia. "It's so comfortable, sitting here in the . . . in the . . ."

"Drawing room," she supplied.

Well, thought Bruce, that settles that. There were few surprises in life if one had fine social antennae, which, he thought, I have. He looked at Julia. She was very attractive—in a slightly outdoorsy way, and by that he did not mean rustic, or agricultural, but more . . . well, grouse-moorish. There was a breed of women who frequented grouse moors, standing around outside Land Rovers while their husbands and boyfriends peppered birds with lead-shot, an activity which, in an atavistic, tribal way appeared to give them pleasure. Some of these women themselves actually shot—ladies who shoot their lunch, as *Country Life* had so wittily put it. These women wore green down-filled jackets and green Wellingtons and liked dogs—although they only seemed to have one breed of dog, which was a Labrador. They liked Labradors and Aga cookers, thought Bruce, and smiled at the thought. That was Julia.

And Julia, looking at Bruce, thought: he is so gorgeous, so hunkalato. It's his shape, really—the whole shape of him. And that cleft in his chin. Do men have plastic surgery to put clefts in? Why not? Silly thought. I can just see him standing in his dressing gown in front of the Aga, cup of coffee in his hand, hair still wet from the shower, and mine, all mine! But who's going to make the first move? He will, of course. Or he'd better. He won't wait long.

And what if he says to me: are you, you know . . . What should I say? No, it's not wrong, not really. If I don't get him, then some girl is going to get her claws into him and he may not be as happy with her as he is with me. I'll make him happy—of course I will. He'll be really happy with me, and the baby. Baby! A real little baby! Mine. Mr and Mrs Bruce Anderson. Or, rather, Bruce and Julia Anderson. And little Rory Anderson? Charlotte Anderson? And we can still have lots of fun because we'll get somebody to help. A Swedish girl, maybe. No. Not a Swede. They're pretty and we want somebody homely. So it'll have to be a girl from . . . (and here she mentally named a town in Scotland, known for its homely girls).

Bruce stretched out his arms. "Yes, it's really great being here, Julia. Thanks a lot." He glanced at his watch. "I thought that I might have a shower, and then how about I cook some pasta?"

"Great," said Julia. "Fab idea."

Bruce rose to his feet. "Where's the shower?" he asked.

Julia gestured to the corridor. "Along there." She paused. "It's a bit temperamental," she said. "I need to get the plumber to come and take a look at it. But there's a trick to working it. You have to turn the lever all the way to the right and then a little bit to the left. I can show you how to do it."

Bruce smiled. "But won't you get wet? Unless . . ."

She smiled encouragingly. "Unless what, Brucie?"

"Unless . . ."

She rose to her feet, kicking off her shoes as she did so. "You go," she said. "I'll just be a sec."

Bruce went through to his bedroom and stood for a moment in front of his window. Julia was all right, he supposed, but it was clear to him that she would keep him occupied. There were some women who were simply high maintenance, in his terms, and she, he imagined, was one of them. That could be managed, he thought, but it could become difficult if they started to cling. That was the point at which one had to make it clear to them that men were not there to be used, and that they should not be tied down too much. And that, thought Bruce, was the problem. Women get hold of a man and then they think they own him. That would not happen to him, and if Julia had ideas along those lines, then she would have to be disabused of them. He was happy to keep Julia happy, but he was not going to be tied down. That would have to be made quite clear—a little bit later.

He gazed out of the window, which overlooked Howe Street, a street that sloped down sharply to sweep round into the elegant crescents of Royal Circus. It was one of Bruce's favourite streets in that part of Edinburgh, and he felt a wave of contentment come over him. Here I am, he thought, exactly where I want to be. I have a place to live. I have a woman who is wild keen on me. I have no rent to pay and probably no electricity bills, etc., etc. And I even have a job, financed by Julia, bless her. Perfection.

He moved away from the window. In the background, down the corridor, he could hear the shower being run. Duty calls, he said to himself.

58. Patriotism and the Jacobite Connection

While Bruce was entertaining Julia in her flat in Howe Street, Big Lou was busy with one of her periodic cleanings of the coffeehouse in Dundas Street. It was a Saturday, and Saturdays were always quieter than weekdays, with many of the usual customers—office people—at home in places such as Barnton or Corstorphine, contemplating their gardens or their dirty cars and resolving to do something about both of them, but perhaps tomorrow rather than today. Dundas Street itself was reasonably busy, but for some reason many of the people in the street had things other than coffee on their minds, and this left Big Lou the time to do her cleaning.

Big Lou came from a background of cleanliness. The east coast of Scotland may at times be a cold, even a harsh place to live, but it was a well-scrubbed and self-respecting part of the world. In Arbroath, where Big Lou hailed from, kitchens were almost always spotless, and even the most modest of houses would make some attempt at a formal front room. You just did not leave things lying about, just as you did not waste things, nor spend money profligately. There was an idea of order there, forged in a tradition of stewardship and careful use of what resources the land, and the sea, provided. And what, thought Big Lou, is wrong with that? If the rest of Scotland followed the rules of places such as Arbroath or Carnoustie, then life would be better for all, of that Big Lou was quite convinced.

That Saturday, as Big Lou polished the inner windowsills of the coffeehouse, she saw her new boyfriend, Robbie Cromach, descending the steps that led down from the street. Big Lou straightened up and tucked her duster into her pocket. She liked to look her best for Robbie, who was something of a natty dresser himself, and here she was in her working clothes, hair all over the place, and no lipstick to speak of.

"Noo den," said Robbie, as he came in the door. "What's up with you, Lou?"

It was rather a strange greeting, but it was one which he used whenever he saw her, and she had become used to it. "Noo den," she understood, was Shetlandic for now then; Robbie's mother was from Shetland, and he liked to use the occasional bit of dialect. But noo den? Big Lou had been told that one might say, in reply: "Aye, aye boy, foo is du?" but she had decided that this sounded too like "you're fu'," which was, of course, an accusation of drunkenness.

"Nothing much, Robbie," said Big Lou. "Just cleaning up."

Robbie crossed the room and gave Big Lou a kiss on the cheek. He looked at his watch. "I've arranged with some of the lads to meet here," he said. "Can you do us a few cups of coffee?"

"Of course." Big Lou paused. "The lads? The usual . . ."

Robbie nodded. "Aye. Michael, Jimmy, Heather. That's all. Maybe Willie will turn up, but I don't think so."

Big Lou moved to her counter, took four cups off the shelf, and lined them up in a row. She looked at Robbie. She did not like these friends of his—she

289

had tried—but there was something about them that she just did not take to. Michael, she supposed, was not too bad, but that Heather woman—Heather McDowall—she was, well, away with the fairies if you asked Lou, and Jimmy, she thought, was just rather pathetic, a train-spotting type who seemed to have latched onto Michael and who followed him round as if waiting for some priceless pearl of wisdom to fall from the older man's lips.

Robbie, of course, was a different matter. He was immensely attractive in Big Lou's eyes, and in the eyes of others too—Big Lou knew that. Women can tell when the heads of other women are turned; they see it—the heads turn, ever so slightly, but they turn, as an attractive man walks by. And he was good company, and gentle, which was something that Big Lou admired in a man, but had seen so rarely.

"This is a meeting?" asked Big Lou. "Or purely social?"

Robbie, leaning against the counter, looked about him quickly, as if searching for those who might overhear. "I wanted to have a word with you about that, Lou," he said. "You know how I feel about . . . about historical matters."

Lou nodded. "You've told me, Robbie," she said. "You're a Scottish patriot. That's fine by me. I'm not really political myself, you know. But it's fine by me that you should be."

Robbie appeared pleased with this. "Good," he

290

said. "But there's a particular angle here, Lou. Some of us feel very strongly about the monarchy."

"I know that, Robbie," Big Lou said. "And I support the monarchy too. Look at the Queen, at all the hard work she does. And Prince Charles too—not that many people give him credit for it. They're always sniping at him and in the meantime he's dashing around doing these things for other people."

"Yes, yes," said Robbie, a note of impatience in his voice. "I'm not denying any of that. They do a fine job. But there's still a problem, Lou. We had our own line of kings in Scotland, you know, and they took the throne away from us and gave it to the Germans. The Germans! To a line of wee German lairdies! Did they ask us? Did they ask the permission of our parliament?" Robbie was now becoming flushed. "They did not ask us, Lou! They did not. And we don't accept it." He shook his head. "We just won't accept it, Lou!"

Big Lou stood there. She said nothing.

"So," said Robbie. "There are some of us who will not let this pass. Not while we have breath in our bodies."

He looked at Big Lou, waiting for a response.

"I'm not sure," she began. What else could she say? she wondered. Big Lou remembered something that an aunt of hers had once said: "A man needs a hobby, Lou—remember that and you can't go far wrong. Always let your man have a hobby and he won't stray."

"I suppose it's all right with me, Robbie," she said.

Robbie relaxed. "Well, that's good, Lou. I'm pleased that we can count you in on this."

On what? thought Big Lou.

Robbie provided the answer. "We're Jacobites, you see, Lou. And we like to talk about the cause. And we like to remind people from time to time who is the real king of Scotland."

"Oh," said Big Lou. "Where does he live, this real king?"

"Germany," replied Robbie.

59. A Visitor from Belgium Is Expected

Only a few minutes elapsed between Big Lou's conversation with Robbie about the Jacobite cause and the arrival in her coffeehouse of the Jacobites in person. Big Lou, her back turned to the door, did not see them come in, and turned round to find Michael, Jimmy, and Heather, now seated at a table with Robbie. They sneaked in, she thought, behind my back, furtively.

She made coffee and took it over on a tray. Michael looked up and smiled at her. "Thank you, Lou," he said. "Won't you join us?"

Big Lou looked at Robbie, who nodded his encouragement. "Why not, Lou?"

Big Lou sat down. Jimmy was on one side of her, Heather McDowall on the other.

"I love your coffee," said Heather. "Mmm. Smell that, folks. Gorgeous."

"It's just coffee," said Big Lou. "That's all."

"But it's the way you make it," enthused Heather. "That's where the skill lies. Oh yes."

Big Lou said nothing. She did not like this woman, with her gushing ways, and as for Jimmy, sitting there, his eyes fixed on Michael, he's like an adoring dog, thought Big Lou; it's unhealthy.

Michael cleared his throat. "Is Lou . . . ?" he began tentatively. "Is Lou . . . on board?"

Robbie glanced at Lou. "You're a sympathiser, aren't you, Lou?" he asked. There was an eagerness in his tone which made Big Lou realise that it was important to him that she should agree with him on this issue. That was a problem, she thought, but it was a problem that many women had, and husbands too, come to think of it. Could one be out of political sympathy with one's spouse? There were probably plenty of couples who voted different ways in the privacy of the polling booth, but that probably only applied when the spouses concerned were not particularly political. It was rare—if not almost unheard of—for the wives or husbands of active politicians to take a different political view from that of their spouses. It was implicit, thought Big Lou, that the wife of the prime minister did not support the Opposition, although there were cases—and she had heard of one or two—where the wives or husbands of ministers of religion were less than enthusiastic about religion. But she was in no doubt of the fact that Robbie wanted her support, and she was similarly in no doubt that she wanted Robbie.

"Well," began Big Lou, "I see nothing wrong in taking an interest in . . . in historical matters. If it makes you happy. After all . . ." She was on the point of saying it makes absolutely no difference, but decided not to, even if it was perfectly obvious that nothing that these people believed in relation to the succession to the crown would have the slightest impact on anything.

"That's fine, then," said Michael. "Welcome to the movement, Lou."

Lou inclined her head graciously. "Thank you." She was not sure if she was expected to say anything more than that, but it became apparent that she was not, as Michael immediately moved the conversation on.

"Now, friends," he said. "Heather has some very interesting news to report." He turned to Heather, who was sitting back in her chair, arms folded in the satisfied manner of one who is harbouring information that others do not have.

"Extremely interesting," Heather said. "News from Belgium."

Big Lou watched her, repelled, yet fascinated, by the air of triumph. There's something wrong with this woman, she thought.

Heather lowered her voice. "Our visitor," she

said, "has confirmed that he is coming. He will arrive. It's confirmed."

For a few moments, there was complete silence. Jimmy was staring at Michael, waiting for his response; Robbie had clasped his hands together and glanced at Big Lou, as if to gauge her reaction; Michael had reached out across the table to grip Heather's forearm.

When Michael spoke, his voice was barely above a whisper. "When?" he asked.

Heather leaned forward. "Just over three weeks from now," she whispered. "Three weeks on Friday."

Again, a silence descended. The Jacobites looked at one another, to all intents and purposes, thought Big Lou, like children who had just heard of an impending treat. They were to receive a visitor from Belgium; obviously somebody of importance in their movement, a historian perhaps or . . . No, that was highly unlikely; in fact it was absurd.

"Who exactly . . . ?" Big Lou began to ask.

Michael interrupted her, raising a finger in the air in warning. "One minute," he said. "Before further details are revealed, I must ask you, Lou, to give your word that this conversation will be kept confidential. It's absolutely imperative that . . ."

Robbie now interrupted Michael. "You will, won't you, Lou? You won't speak about this, will you?"

Big Lou shrugged. "I don't like secrets very

much," she said. "But then I don't talk about things it's no business of mine to talk about."

"That's fine, then," said Robbie, turning to Michael. "Lou's fine on that."

Michael looked doubtful for a moment, but Robbie held his gaze and eventually he nodded. "All right, this is it. We're receiving a visit from a member of the Stuart family. He's coming to Scotland. A direct descendant of Charles Edward Stuart, or Bonnie Prince Charlie as you may know him, Lou."

Jimmy, who had been hanging on Michael's every word, now turned and looked at Big Lou. She noticed, as he did so, a trace of milk from his cappuccino making a thin line around his weak, immature mouth. "See," he said. "Just like Charlie himself. A Young Pretender."

Big Lou stared at him. "Really?" she said. "Coming to Scotland to claim his kingdom?"

"Well, not exactly," said Michael, glancing discouragingly at Jimmy. "What Jimmy means is that there are parallels. As you know, Charles Edward Stuart came to incite an uprising against the usurpers. Conditions are different today. This is more of a consciousness-raising exercise. This member of the Stuart family is not exactly acting on behalf of His Majesty King Francis, whom we recognise as the rightful king, even if he's never made that claim himself and doesn't use that title. His Majesty keeps himself out of all of this. He's very dignified. This young man's a descendant of Charles through a subsidiary line. He's coming for a few weeks to assist us in our endeavours."

"So this is not the Forty-Five all over again?" asked Big Lou.

Michael laughed, waving a hand in the air. "Hardly! No, this is more of a courtesy call by a member of the family to those in this country who have kept alive the claims of the Stuarts. That's all."

"Yes," said Jimmy, slightly aggressively. "That's all. We're not bampots, you know."

Big Lou looked at him. "Have you finished with that coffee cup?" she asked.

60. Does Scotland Need All This Nonsense?

Robbie stayed with Big Lou for half an hour or so after the rest of the Jacobites had left. She had hoped that he would stay for longer, that he would keep her company while she continued with her cleaning, but he had seemed nervous, as if he was uneasy about something, and had kept looking at his watch.

"You're awful fiddly," she said at one point. "Looking at your watch like that. Is there something . . . ?"

Robbie cut her short. "Nothing," he said. "It's nothing."

Big Lou shook her head. "Well, it's nothing that's

worrying you then," she said. "And what is this nothing?"

"I said . . ."

Big Lou sighed. "Robbie. I'm no wet aboot the ears. It's those folks, isn't it? Your friends."

Robbie was defensive. "What about them? Have you got a problem with them, Lou?"

Big Lou hesitated. The truthful answer was that she did have a problem with them—with all of them, but most of all with Heather McDowall and Michael's acolyte, Jimmy. But Lou was tactful, and melancholy experience had taught her that men sometimes did not respond well to direct criticism, particularly the sort of men with whom she found herself ending up.

"Don't get me wrong, Robbie," she began. "I'm not the sort of person who likes to find fault. I'm sure that there are lots of things about your friends that are very good, very positive." She tried to think of these qualities, but they seemed to elude her for the moment.

"But?" asked Robbie. "There's a but, isn't there?"

"Well," said Big Lou, "there is a small but. Just a small one. This Jacobite business. This character who's coming over. Isn't that a bit . . . ?"

"A bit what?"

She took a breath. What she wanted to say was that it was bizarre—ridiculous, even, that people should want to open such obviously finished business. But then she realised that there were many people who were interested in precisely that—old business. People lived in the past, fought old quarrels, clung to the horrors of decades . . . centuries ago. But the futility of this had always struck Big Lou forcibly. There were plenty of old quarrels that she could keep alive if she wished, nursing her wrath to keep it warm—like Tam O'Shanter's wife—but she found she had no desire to do this, nor the energy.

"Well," she began, "I think it's a good idea to let go. Scotland used to have Stuarts—now it doesn't. And the Hanoverians used to be Germans, now they aren't. They're British. So what's the point of looking for some ridiculous Pretender? Haven't your friends got anything better to do?"

Robbie shook his head in dismay. "You're talking about people who are prepared to do anything for Scotland," he said. "To die, even."

Big Lou dropped her dusting cloth. "To die? Are you serious, Robbie?"

Robbie looked straight back at her. "Aye, Lou. Dead serious."

She laughed. "That wee boy, Jimmy. He's drinking all this in from Michael, with his posh voice and his fancy clothes. Die for the cause? Does Scotland need all this nonsense, or does it need something done about its real problems? About teenage binge drinking? About all those folk who get by on next to nothing? About that sort of thing?"

Robbie reached out to touch Big Lou on the arm, but she withdrew. "Answer my question, Robbie Cromach," she snapped.

Lou's man looked at his hands. The hands of a plasterer, they were cracked from exposure to lime and grit. "All right," he said. "I'll answer you, Lou." He looked up at her, and she saw the features that had attracted her so much, the high cheek-bones, the boyish vulnerability.

"I know that there's a lot wrong with this country of ours," he said. "I know fine that there are folk who can't earn a decent wage, no matter how hard they work. I know that there's a very rich company in this city, for instance, that pays its cleaners a pittance while it rakes in the profits big-time. Shame on them. Shame on them. I know that there are places where the kids are all fuelled up on Buckie and pills and where the fathers are not there or are drunk or otherwise out of it. I know that we've got a wee parliament that makes lots and lots of grand-sounding bodies and is full of high heid-yins and tsars. I know all that, Lou. But all of this goes back, you see. It goes back to things not being right with ourselves. And until we get that right—until we take back what was taken away from us right back there when they took our kings away from us, then the rest is going to be wrong. That's what I believe, Lou. God's truth—that's what I believe."

Robbie stopped. He looked at Big Lou almost

imploringly, as if he was willing her to see the situation as he saw it.

"I understand all that, Robbie," she said quietly. "It's just that I think that sounding off about something as old as that is not very helpful. It was all very romantic—I give you that—when Charlie landed and when it looked like he was going to get his kingdom back. But for what? What sort of rulers had those people been? And anyway, it makes no difference, surely. It's old, old business, Robbie. Surely you can see that?"

Big Lou waited for Robbie's response. It was slow, but at last he said something: "No. I don't see that, Lou. Sorry, I don't."

Big Lou sighed. Why was it her lot in life, she wondered, to find men who had something odd about them? Every time, every single time, she had been involved with a man, there had been something strange about him. There had been that man in Aberdeen who had been obsessed with billiards and who had spent all his spare time watching replays of classic games; that had been very trying. Then there had been Eddie, with his thing about teenage girls; that had been intolerable. And now here was Robbie, who was, of all things, a Jacobite! She had to smile, she really had to. Teenage girls or obscure Jacobite shenanigans? Which was worse?

There was no doubt in Big Lou's mind. "Oh well, Robbie," she said at last. "Whatever makes you happy."

Robbie leaned forward and kissed Big Lou on the cheek. "You're a trouper, Lou," he said. "One of the best. Just like Flora MacDonald."

61. *"Middle-Class" Used as a Term of Abuse*

It was rare for the Pollock family to go on an outing together. This was not through any lack of inclination to do so, but it was rather because of the crowded timetable which Irene prepared for Bertie. Not only was there a saxophone lesson each week—complemented by a daily practice session of at least half an hour (scales, arpeggios, and set pieces)—but there was also Bertie's yoga in Stockbridge, which took at least two hours, and Italian structured *conversazione* at the Italian Cultural Institute in Nicolson Street. On top of that, of course, there was psychotherapy, which, although it might take only an hour, seemed to occupy much more time, what with Bertie's writing up of dreams in the dream notebook and the walk up to Queen Street for the actual session.

It was an extremely full life for a little boy, and there was more to come: Irene had planned a book group for Bertie, in which five or six children from the New Town would meet regularly in each other's flats and discuss a book that they had read.

The model for this was, in Irene's mind, her own Kleinian book group, which had flourished for several months before it had been sabotaged by one of the members. This still rankled with Irene, who had resisted this other member's attempts to introduce works of fiction into the group's programme. This had effectively split the group and left such a sour taste in the mouths of Irene and her allies that the group's meetings had fizzled out and never restarted.

"The whole point about our group," Irene had complained to a friend, "is that we are not one of those awful groups of middle-class ladies who meet and talk about the latest vapid imaginings of some novelist. That we are not."

The friend had nodded her agreement. "Thank heavens for that," she said. "Those people are so earnest. So self-consciously serious. All trying to outdo one another in the depth of their comments. It's quite funny when you come to think of it."

This conversation had taken place in the Pollocks' flat in Scotland Street and had been over-heard by Stuart. He wondered what was wrong with book groups, which he thought were a rather good idea. Indeed, Stuart would have liked to have been in a book group himself and had almost joined one organised by a colleague in the office—a book group for men—but Irene had poured cold water on the idea.

"Join it if you wish," she had said disparagingly. "But it's sad, don't you think? Rather sad to think of these middle-class men all sitting around talking about some novel they've tried to finish in time for the meeting."

Stuart had said nothing. He had never understood Irene's prejudice against people whom she called middle-class; indeed, he had never comprehended why the term middle-class should be considered a term of abuse. To begin with, he thought that they themselves were middle-class; not that he dared say that to his wife, but surely it was true. In income terms, they were about the middle, and they lived in a street where just about everybody else was in roughly the same position. And Edinburgh, of course, was itself mostly middle-class, whatever some people liked to think. As a statistician, Stuart knew the figures: 60 per cent of the population of the city was in highly skilled jobs and was therefore middle-class. So why should Irene speak so scornfully about the middle-class when the middle-class was all about her; and if you took the middle-class away, the city would die . . . just as it would if you took away the people who did the hard, thankless jobs, the manual work that was just as important in keeping things going. That, thought Stuart, was why class talk was so utterly pointless: everybody counted.

And now, overhearing this attack on book groups, Stuart pondered this again. It might be true that middle-class ladies belonged to book groups, but what was wrong with that? It seemed to him to be an entirely reasonable and interesting thing to do. It was fun to discuss books with others—to share the pleasure of reading—and one might learn from the views of one's fellow members, even if they were middle-class.

Irene was an enigma to him. He admired her, and there was a bit of him that loved her—just—but he could not understand her contempt for others and her desire to be something that she was not. Stuart was a reasonable person, who saw the good and the bad in others without reference to where they stood politically. He would read any newspaper he found lying about in the office and find something of interest in it. And if he did not agree with what was written, he would nonetheless reflect on the arguments put forward and weigh them up. Irene did not do that. There was one newspaper she read, and one alone, and she would barely look at anything else. On occasion, Stuart came back from the office with another paper, and this would trigger a firm response from Irene.

"Stuart, I don't think it's wise to bring the *Daily Telegraph* into the house," she said. "Just think for a moment. What if Bertie read it? You know how he picks things up and reads them."

Stuart had shrugged. "He's got to learn what the world's like sooner or later," he said. He wondered if he should add: "He's got to learn that there are Conservatives . . ." but a look from Irene discouraged him.

"That, if I may say so," she said, "is utterly and

completely irresponsible. Do you want his mind to be poisoned? It'll be the *Daily Mail* next. Or the *Sun*. For heaven's sake, Stuart! And what if somebody saw you carrying that paper? What would they think?"

That argument had not gone any further, for Stuart had capitulated, as he always seemed to do, and had agreed that inappropriate newspapers would not be brought into the house in the future. But, as they set off on their walk that Saturday morning, he thought about it and wondered why he had not defended freedom of thought.

"Where are we going?" asked Bertie, as Stuart and Irene jointly manipulated Ulysses's baby buggy down the common stair to the front door.

"Valvona & Crolla," replied Irene. "It'll be a nice walk." Bertie was pleased to hear this. He liked the delicatessen, with its high shelves of Italian produce. For the most part, they bought olive oil there and sun-dried tomatoes and packets of pasta. But there were other delights there too, such as Panforte di Siena, and Bertie, with all his soul, loved Panforte di Siena.

62. It Seemed the World Was Full of Killing

They walked around Drummond Place, the four of them—Irene, Stuart, Bertie, and Ulysses, who did not walk, of course, but was pushed in his new MobileBaby baby buggy, of which Bertie was inordinately proud. Their car might be old, but their baby buggy, at least, was brand-new. In fact, as they rounded the corner into London Street, Bertie saw their car, parked on the other side of the road.

"There's our car!" he exclaimed. "Look, Daddy. There it is."

"So I see, Bertie," said Stuart. "That's where Mummy must have parked it."

Irene reacted sharply. "I beg your pardon. You parked it there, Stuart. I very rarely park in this street."

Stuart looked down at the pavement. He was sure that he had not parked the car there, but he understood that there was no point in arguing about it. Irene seemed to win any argument that they had, particularly in relation to their car, often by the simple technique of staring at Stuart until he became silent. It was a powerful method of overcoming opposition, and Stuart had come across one or two politicians who used it to great effect. These were generally the same ones who refused to answer any questions, usually by giving a response which bore no relation to the actual question which was asked. In fact, when he came to think of it, Irene would make a good politician—but for which party? Would Jack McConnell have her in the Labour Party, he wondered, or would she simply stare at him until he became uncomfortable? Irene would not join the Conservatives, and they, quite understandably, would not want her. Which left the

Liberal Democrats, the Scottish National Party, and the Greens. The Greens! There was an idea. Stuart knew Robin Harper, their leader, and liked him, but wondered if even Robin Harper, the leader of the Greens, could continue to smile if he found himself faced with Irene. No, Irene should perhaps remain out of politics after all.

"Well, at least we know where our car is," said Bertie. "That's something."

They continued down London Street, with Bertie throwing the occasional glance over his shoulder at the car. Now they went up the hill, up Broughton Street and into Union Street, in the direction of Leith Walk. A dog walking along Union Street with its owner made Bertie think of Cyril and the plight in which the dog found himself.

"Tofu says that they'll cut Cyril's tail off as a punishment for biting," he ventured. "Tofu said that's what happens to dogs that bite."

"That's absolute nonsense," said Irene. "Your friend Tofu is full of ridiculous notions. It would be much better, Bertie, if you had nothing to do with him."

Bertie was relieved to hear that Tofu, as usual, was wrong. "So they won't do anything cruel like that?"

"Of course not," said Irene.

"Then what will they do?" asked Bertie. "If they find him guilty?"

There was an awkward silence.

"Well?" said Stuart, looking at Irene. "Will you answer, or shall I?" He waited a moment and then turned to his son. "I'm afraid that they'll put Cyril down, Bertie. Sorry to have to tell you that."

Bertie looked puzzled. "Put him down where?" he asked.

There was another silence. Then Irene took charge of the situation. She remembered Cyril as the dog who had bitten her—quite without provocation—in Dundas Street. He was a nasty, smelly creature in her view, and she still had a slight scar, a redness, on her ankle where his gold tooth had penetrated the skin.

"Put down is a euphemism, Bertie," she said. "You'll remember that Mummy told you about euphemisms. They're words which sound nicer than . . . than other words."

Bertie remembered their conversation about euphemisms, but he could not remember any examples that his mother had given. In fact, he had pressed his mother for examples and she had been strangely reluctant to give any. "Such as, Mummy?"

"Well . . ." said Irene. She trailed off.

"Putting down for . . . for killing," said Stuart.

Bertie stopped in his tracks, causing them all to come to a halt. He looked up at his father, who immediately regretted what he had said.

"You mean that they're going to kill Cyril?" asked Bertie, his voice faltering.

309

"I'm afraid so," said Stuart. "But they'll do it humanely, Bertie. They won't shoot him or anything like that."

"Will they put him in an electric kennel?" asked Bertie. "Just like an electric chair?"

Stuart reached for Bertie's hand. "Of course not, Bertie!" he said. "What an idea!"

Holding his father's hand was a comfort for Bertie, but it was not enough. As he stood there on the pavement in Union Street, his eyes began to fill with tears. He could not believe that anybody would wish to kill Cyril, or any dog, really. Nor could he believe that anybody would want to kill anything, for that matter, and yet it seemed that the world was filled with killing. People killed seals and deer and birds. They killed elephants and rhinoceroses and buffalo. The Japanese even killed whales, when just about everybody else had recognised that as wrong; those great, intelligent, friendly creatures—they killed them. And then people killed other people with equal, if not more, gusto: Bertie had seen pictures in the newspaper of a war that somebody was fighting somewhere, and had seen a soldier firing a gun at somebody who was firing back at him. That seemed utterly absurd to him. People should play with one another, he thought, not fight. But then obviously there were people who disagreed with that, who wanted to fight; people such as Larch, for example, who loved to punch people and kick them too, if he had the chance. Larch had pinned a sign saying KICK ME on Tofu's back and had then kicked him hard in the seat of the pants. That had brought whoops of delight from Olive, who had witnessed the event and who had run over to try to kick Tofu while the offer still stood, only to have her hair pulled by an enraged Tofu. That sort of violence solved nothing, thought Bertie. But that, it seemed to him, was what the world was like. People kicked one another and pulled each other's hair and wept at the result. Why?

"There, there, Bertie," said his father. "I'm sure that everything will turn out well in the end."

Irene shook her head. "It'll do no good your telling Bertie that, Stuart," she said. "It won't. You know it. I know it. It won't."

63. Panforte for Bertie and a Shock for Stuart

In the delicious caverns of Valvona & Crolla, Mary Contini, author of *Dear Olivia*, was busy adjusting jars of truffle oil on a shelf when the Pollock family entered. She turned round and saw Irene, and for a moment her heart sank. She knew Irene slightly, and their relationship had not been easy. Irene had strong views on olive oil and was only too ready to share these with the staff of the delicatessen, even when, as was often the case, she was on shaky ground. Mary listened patiently and refrained from correcting or contradicting Irene, but it was not easy. And that poor little boy of hers, she thought. And the husband! Look at him. There's a hearth from which freedom has been excluded, if ever there was one. And now there was another baby, who would no doubt have to face the same awful battle that poor little Bertie had faced. Poor child!

Irene smiled at Mary. She had read her books and enjoyed them, but it did remind her that she herself could have written a number of books, and that these books would undoubtedly have been very successful; indeed, they would have been seminal books. But she had not actually got round to doing this yet, although it was, she felt, merely a question of time. The books would certainly come, and she would handle the resulting success very much better than many authors did. Of that she was certain.

"Can we get some Panforte di Siena, Mummy?" asked Bertie. "I know where they keep it."

"Very well, Bertie," said Irene. "But not a large one. Just one of those small ones. In Italy, boys eat small pieces of Panforte di Siena."

Bertie led his mother to the shelf where the panforte was stacked, resplendent in its box with its Renaissance picture. He picked up a small box and showed it to his mother, who nodded her approval. Then they all went on to the sun-dried tomato section and, after that, to the counter where the salami and cold meats were served.

312

Once their purchases were complete, Stuart looked at his watch. "I think I'm going to walk over to the Fruitmarket Gallery," he said.

Irene agreed to this. She would go home with Bertie, she said: he had saxophone practice to do in view of his impending examination. Bertie was not pleased by this, but his mind was now on the panforte, and he was wondering if he could persuade his mother to allow him to eat it all in one sitting. This was unlikely, he thought, but he could always try. Irene believed in rationing pleasures, and Bertie was never allowed more than a small square of chocolate or a spoonful or so of ice cream. And some pleasures—such as Irn-Bru—were completely banned; it was only when Stuart was in charge that they slipped through the protective net.

Irene and Bertie walked back together. It was a fine morning, and Drummond Place was filled with light. In Scotland Street, they saw Domenica walking up the opposite side of the road, and she waved cheerfully to them. Bertie returned the wave.

"Poor woman," said Irene quietly.

Bertie said nothing. He did not understand why his mother should call Domenica poor woman; it seemed to him that Domenica was quite contented with life, as well she might be, he thought, with her large, custard-coloured Mercedes-Benz. But then Bertie realised that his mother had views on just about all the neighbours, with whom there was, in her view, always something wrong.

Inside the flat, Bertie was allowed to eat half the panforte, with a promise that he could eat the remainder the following day, provided he did his music practice.

"Mr Morrison is counting on you to do well in the examination," said Irene. "So don't let him down."

"I won't," said Bertie, licking the white dusting of icing sugar from his lips. Panforte was Italy's greatest invention, he thought. His mother went on about Italian culture, about Dante and Botticelli and all the rest, but in Bertie's mind it was Panforte di Siena which was Italy's greatest gift to the world. That, and ice cream.

Bertie's practice was finished by the time that Stuart returned from the Fruitmarket Gallery. He let himself into the flat and sauntered into the kitchen, where Irene was standing at the stove, stirring a pot of soup, and Bertie was sitting at the table, reading.

Irene turned round to greet Stuart. "Interesting exhibition?" she asked.

"Very," said Stuart. "All sorts of marvellous artists—Crosbie, Houston, McClure. And I saw that chap Duncan Macmillan there. You know, he's the one who has been poking such fun at the Turner Prize recently. And he's right, in my opinion."

Irene was not particularly interested in this. The Turner Prize was, in her view, a progressive prize, and it was nothing new to have people attack progressiveness. She put down her spoon. "Where's Ulysses?" she asked. "Is he in the hall?"

Stuart, who was standing in the doorway leading into the kitchen, seemed to sway. "Ulysses?" he asked. His voice suddenly sounded strained.

"Yes," said Irene sarcastically. "Your other son."

Stuart reached for the door handle and gripped it hard, his knuckles showing white under the pressure of his grip.

"Oh no . . ." he began.

Irene let out a scream. "Stuart! What have you . . . ?"

"I thought you had him," said Stuart. "You parked the baby buggy . . ."

He did not finish. "I did not park it anywhere," shouted Irene. "You were meant to take him to the Fruitmarket Gallery. You were pushing him at Valvona & Crolla. You're the one who parked him somewhere. Where is he? Where have you parked Ulysses?"

Stuart threw himself across the room to the table on which the telephone stood. "I'll phone them right away," he said. "Quick, Bertie, get me the telephone directory. Quick."

Bertie ran through to the hall and returned with the telephone directory. But then, noticing a Valvona & Crolla packet, he said, "We don't need to look it up, Daddy," he said. "The number's there on the packet. Look."

With fumbling fingers, Stuart dialled the number. It was a moment or two before the telephone was answered at the other end. "Our baby," he shouted into the receiver. "Have you found a baby in the shop, or outside?"

"No," said a voice at the other end. "No babies. An umbrella, yes. But no babies."

64. You Mean You Lost a Tiny Baby?

In the storm that followed, three voices were raised, each offering different suggestions. Irene, her face flushed with rage, insisted that Stuart go immediately to Valvona & Crolla and personally search the shop for any sign of Ulysses. Stuart disagreed, and tried to make his voice heard above the screech of his wife's. There was no point in going back to the shop if they reported that there was no trace of a lost baby.

"Lost?" raged Irene. "You mean abandoned. Lost is when you . . . when you forget where you put something. Abandoned is when you simply walk away from something. Ulysses was abandoned."

"It takes two to tango," Stuart stuttered. "You were jointly in charge."

"What's a tango?" asked Bertie.

Stuart looked down at his son. "It's an Argentinian dance," he began to explain. "The Argentinians were very keen on dancing back in the . . ."

"Stuart!" shouted Irene. "We are discussing Ulysses. Every second may be vital, and there you are talking about Argentina."

Stuart blushed. "I thought you were going to take him when I said that I was going to the Fruitmarket Gallery," he said mildly. "I really did."

"Well you had no reason to think that," snapped Irene. "I distinctly remember saying to you that you should take him. We were standing outside the shop and I . . ."

"So he wasn't in the shop at all," said Stuart. "Well, that's something. Now we know that we have to look for him in the street, rather than in the delicatessen." He paused. Irene had sunk her head in her hands and appeared to be crying.

Bertie moved forward to comfort her. "Don't cry, Mummy," he said. "Ulysses will be all right, I'm sure he will. Even if somebody's stolen him by now, they'll give him a nice home. He'll be very happy somewhere."

For a moment, Bertie reflected on the opportunities that might have opened up for Ulysses. He might have been taken by a supporter of Hearts Football Club, for example, and these new parents might even buy him one of those baby outfits in the football team's wine-red colours that Bertie had seen in the newspaper. Ulysses would like that, and when he grew up in that Hearts-supporting home, he could go to Tynecastle with his new father and watch the games. Ulysses would never have had that opportunity if he had remained in Scotland Street. And the new parents might have a better car too, thought Bertie, a Jaguar perhaps, and they might send him to a boarding school, somewhere where there would be midnight feasts in the dorm and proper friends who were quite unlike Tofu and Larch. All of that was possible now.

Bertie's attempt to reassure his mother did not have the desired effect. Irene now rose to her feet and grabbed Stuart's arm. "We must go to Leith Walk right now," she said. "We must look for . . . look for . . ." Her voice broke. It was impossible for her to utter Ulysses's name, and so it was left for Bertie to say it for her.

"Ulysses," he said.

Stuart rose to his feet. "I'll call a taxi," he said. "It'll be quicker."

By the time the taxi arrived, Irene, Stuart, and Bertie were standing at the front door of 44 Scotland Street. Stuart gave directions to the driver that he was to take them to Valvona & Crolla and that they were then to drive slowly down Leith Walk while they looked for something they had lost.

"What have you lost?" he asked. "A bicycle? There's lots of bicycles go missing in Leith Walk, I can tell you. My brother's boy had a . . ."

Stuart interrupted him. "Not a bicycle," he said. "A child."

"Oh," said the driver. "Bairns tend to come back of their own accord. Don't worry too much. By the time he feels like he wants his tea, he'll come strolling in the door."

"He can't stroll," said Bertie. "In fact, he can't walk at all. He's only a baby, you see."

The taxi driver looked in his mirror. "You mean you lost a tiny baby?" he asked.

"It would seem so," said Stuart. "He was left in his baby buggy outside Valvona & Crolla. A mistake, you know."

The taxi driver whistled. "Well, if you ask me, we should go straight to the council child protection nursery. You know the place? It's where they take babies who've been taken into care. Emergency cases. Things like that."

Stuart thought for a moment. "If the police had been called," he asked, "would they take the baby straight there?"

"Yes," said the taxi driver. "They wouldn't take the baby to the police station. They'd go straight to the nursery. That's likely where your baby will be right now."

"Then we'll go there," snapped Irene. "And please hurry."

It took less than fifteen minutes to reach the emergency nursery, a converted Victorian house on the other side of Duddingston. Slamming the door of the cab behind her, Irene ran up the path, leaving Stuart to pay the fare and bring Bertie to the front door. This door was locked, but she rattled at the handle and rang the bell aggressively until a woman appeared and opened up.

"My baby," said Irene. "My husband left him

319

outside Valvona & Crolla. Just for a few minutes, you'll understand, and it was all a misunderstanding. But when we went back . . ."

The woman gestured for Irene to enter. "And this is your husband here?" she asked, nodding in the direction of Stuart, who smiled at her, but was rebuffed with a scowl.

"Our baby," said Irene. "Has he been . . . handed in?"

"Well we've just had a baby brought round," said the woman. "But we obviously can't let him go to the first person who turns up. Can you describe the baby buggy he came in? And what he was wearing?"

Irene closed her eyes and gave the description. The woman's attitude irritated her, but she was astute enough to realise where power lay in these circumstances.

When Irene had finished, the woman nodded her head. "Close enough," she said.

"So can we have him back?" asked Irene.

"Yes," said the woman. "He's in the nursery. We've given him a change and he's sleeping very peacefully with the three other babies we've got in at the moment. If you would come with me?"

They followed the woman down a corridor into the house. "You wait outside," she said. "I'll bring the baby out to you. We don't want too many germs in there, if you don't mind."

She opened a door off the corridor and went into

a side-room. A few minutes later, she came out again and handed over Ulysses, who was now heavily swaddled in a rough, white shawl.

"Here we are," she said, as she passed Ulysses over to Irene. "Your baby. Safe and sound." And then she added: "None the worse for the neglect."

65. It Was Almost Too Terrible to Describe

In the taxi on the way back to Scotland Street, Irene was unusually quiet. With Ulysses sleeping in her arms, she sat there, tight-lipped, deliberately making no eye contact with Stuart, who perched nervously opposite her on the jump seat, his hands clasped around his knees. He looked at Irene, and then looked away again; he understood her perfectly. It was his fault that Ulysses had been misplaced, and he knew that he would be reminded of it for a long time to come. But anyone, he thought, could have done what he had done, could have misunderstood who was in charge of the baby. It was all very well for Irene to heap the blame upon him, but had she never made a mistake herself? Of course she had, not that she liked to admit it. Irene was always right.

Bertie could sense that his father was miserable, and his heart went out to him. He did not blame Stuart for what had happened to Ulysses, and the important thing, he thought, was that Ulysses was unharmed and back with his family—not that

Bertie was entirely pleased with that; he would have been quite happy for Ulysses to have found somewhere else to live, but he knew that this was not the way in which adults looked on the matter, and he did not express this view.

"There's Arthur's Seat," he said, in an attempt to cheer his father up. "Look, Daddy. There it is."

Stuart looked out of the window at the green bulk of the hill, outlined like a crouching lion against the sky. He nodded to Bertie. "Yes," he said, glancing at Irene. "That's right, Bertie. There it is."

"Have you ever climbed Arthur's Seat, Mummy?" asked Bertie. "Right up to the top?"

Irene pursed her lips. "No," she said. "I haven't, Bertie. There's no need to climb Arthur's Seat."

There was silence. Then, quite suddenly, Irene looked up and addressed Stuart. "The humiliation," she began. "The sheer humiliation of it all. That woman. Did you hear what she said to me, Stuart? Did you?"

Stuart looked out of the window. "I wouldn't worry too much about that," he said mildly. "Often people mutter things that don't really mean very much. I find that with my minister sometimes. You just have to let it flow over you. And then they forget that they ever said it. And you do, too. The other day, for example, the minister said that we needed a policy review of the statistical process. I was there with my immediate boss, and we both just said something about a pigeon that had landed on the windowsill—you know, one of those grey, Edinburgh City Council pigeons—and the minister plain forgot what he had just said and . . ."

"Nonsense!" said Irene. "That woman in the nursery knew exactly what she was saying. She chose her words very carefully indeed."

Bertie had been following this exchange between his parents. Now he intervened. "What did she say, Mummy?"

Irene's answer was directed at Stuart, at whom she was now glaring. "She said that Ulysses was none the worse for the neglect. Neglect! That's what she accused me of. And I had to stand there and take it, because otherwise she probably wouldn't have given Ulysses back without all sorts of forms and waiting and heaven-knows-what. I felt so humiliated.

"That sort of woman," went on Irene, "relishes every bit of authority she has. I know the type. And what does she know about me and how I bring up Ulysses? Nothing. And then she goes and accuses me of neglect."

Stuart shrugged. "People say things," he muttered. "Just forget it. The important thing is that we've got Ulysses back."

"Sticks and stones may break my bones," Bertie quoted, "but words will never hurt me. Have you heard that poem, Mummy? That's what Tofu said to Larch."

"Oh?" said Stuart. "And then what happened?"

"Larch hit him," said Bertie. "He hit him and walked away."

"The point is," said Irene, resuming control of the conversation. "The point is that if there was any neglect, it was not on my part."

This was greeted by silence.

"I'm going to get in touch with our councillor," said Irene. "And I'm going to complain about that woman. I'm going to insist on an apology."

Nothing much more was said during the rest of the journey. Ulysses was still asleep, and although he opened his eyes briefly when being carried up the stairs, he merely smiled, and went back to sleep.

"He's had such a traumatic experience, poor little thing," said Irene pointedly. "Imagine being left outside Valvona & Crolla in your baby buggy!"

"He wouldn't have minded, Mummy," said Bertie. "Ulysses doesn't really know where he is."

"Exactly," said Stuart.

Ulysses was placed in his cot, and the family returned to the kitchen, where Irene heated up the soup she had been making and served out three bowls.

"Such a relief," said Stuart. "I'm so sorry."

"Daddy's sorry," said Bertie.

Irene nodded. "I heard him, Bertie."

It was at this point that Ulysses started to cry. Bertie, eager to promote concord, decided that he would offer to change him; he had been instructed in this task, which he disliked intensely, but he felt that such an offer would mollify his mother.

"Thank you, Bertie," she said. "And call us if you need any help. We'll give Ulysses a bath later on, and then he can have his tea."

Bertie went through to the room at the end of the corridor. He picked up Ulysses, and laid him down on the changing mat. Then he began to remove the blanket in which he had been wrapped. Underneath was a romper suit, which Bertie carefully peeled off. And then . . .

Bertie stood quite still. Ulysses was very different. Something awful had happened; something almost too terrible to describe.

"Mummy!" Bertie shouted. "Come quickly. Come quickly. Something's happened to Ulysses! His . . . His . . . It's dropped off! Quick, Mummy! Quick!"

There was the noise of a chair being knocked over in the kitchen and Irene came rushing into the room, followed by Stuart. She pushed Bertie aside and looked at Ulysses, who was lying contentedly on the changing mat.

"Oh! Oh!"

It was all she could say. Ulysses was not Ulysses at all. This was a girl.

"The wrong baby!" Stuart stuttered. "They've given us the wrong baby!"

Bertie stared intently at the baby, who smiled back at him.

"Do you think we can keep this one, Mummy?" he asked.

66. *Speculation on What Might Have Been*

While the unsettling discovery was being made in the Pollock household that the wrong baby had been handed over at the council holding nursery, Matthew was hanging his BACK IN TWENTY MIN- UTES sign in the doorway of his gallery. This sign, as had been pointed out by numerous people, including Pat, was ambiguous and men- dacious. In the first place, it did not reveal when the twenty minutes began, so that the person reading it would not know whether it had been placed there nineteen minutes earlier, or just one minute before. Then, anybody who knew Matthew's habits would be aware of the fact that he rarely spent less than forty minutes over coffee in Big Lou's coffee bar, and that anybody choosing to wait on the doorstep of the gallery until his return could face a much longer wait than they anticipated.

It was Angus Lordie who had suggested a dif- ferent sign, one that said, quite simply: OUT. That would have the merit of clarity and would raise no false hopes. "There are occasions," he said, "when the simple word is best. And that reminds me of the story told by George Mackay Brown, I think it was, about the Orcadian who completely disappeared for eight years. When he returned, simply walking into his house, he was asked by his astonished family where he had been. He gave a one-word answer: 'Oot.' "

Matthew had found this very amusing. "Funny," he said. "That's really funny."

"Yes," mused Angus. "It's funny to us. But, you know, I'm not sure if that would be all that funny outside Scotland. There are some things which are made funny because of a very specific cultural context."

"Oh, I think that would be funny anywhere," said Matthew.

Angus smiled. "Maybe. But here's something which is only funny in Scotland. It was told to me by a teacher. Do you want to hear it?"

"Only if it's funny," said Matthew.

"It is," said Angus. "It's funny here, as I said. A teacher noticed that a boy called Jimmy wasn't eating fish when it was served in the school lunch. After a while, she decided to take up the matter with the boy's mother and wrote a note to her to this effect. Back came a letter from the mother which said: See me? See my husband? See Jimmy? See fish? We dinnae eat it."

There was only a moment's silence before Matthew burst out laughing. "That's very funny indeed," he said.

Angus nodded. "Of course it is. But you could tell that story down in London and they'd look very puzzled. So why do we find it so amusing?"

Matthew pondered this. There was the habit of

saying "see" before any observation; that was a common way of raising a subject, but in itself was not all that amusing. Was it the way in which the mother developed her response, step by step, in the manner of a syllogism? That was it! It was a peculiar variant of syllogistic reasoning, perhaps, and its expression in the demotic seemed surprising and out of place. But there was something more. It was the conflict between two worlds: the world of the teacher and the world of the mother. When two very different worlds come into contact, we are amused.

Angus might have read Matthew's mind. "It's the desire to deflate officialdom," he said. "There's a strong streak of that in Scottish humour, and that's what's going on here, don't you think?"

Matthew nodded, and thought: and there's something funny about Angus.

That day, which was Saturday, was usually a busy day for Matthew, and he might have felt reluctant to leave the gallery unattended, but by the time that ten o'clock came round he was feeling distinctly edgy, and thought that one of Big Lou's double espressos might help.

When he entered the café, Big Lou was by herself, standing at the bar, reading a book. She looked up at Matthew when he came in, slipped a bookmark between the pages of the book, and closed the cover.

"Don't let me disturb you, Lou," said Matthew,

glancing at the title of the book. "Eric Linklater. *The . . .*"

"*The Prince in the Heather*," Big Lou said. "Robbie gave it to me. It's quite a book. All about Bonnie Prince Charlie being chased through the Highlands."

Matthew reached over and took the book from Lou. He opened it at random; a picture of a wild coast, a map, the prince himself draped in tartan. "Quite a story, isn't it?" he mused. "It seems like a game from this distance."

"It was no game at the time," said Big Lou.

Matthew sensed that he was being judged for levity. "No," he said. "Of course not. But there's something that interests me, Lou. What would have happened if Charlie had pushed on just a bit more? Weren't things rather disorganised in London? What if he had huffed and puffed a bit more and blown their house right down?"

Big Lou's answer came quickly. One did not engage in such idle speculation in Arbroath. "No point thinking about that," she said. "It didn't happen."

"But it could have," said Matthew. "It could easily have happened. Look at how far he actually got. And anyway, there's nothing wrong in asking these 'what if' questions. I saw a whole book on them the other day. What would have happened if the American planes had been on a different deck at the critical moment in the Battle of Midway? What would have happened if the wind had been coming from the other direction when the Spanish fleet took on the English? We'd be speaking Spanish now, Lou, as would the Americans if the wind had shifted just a few degrees. You know that, Lou?"

Big Lou shrugged. "Well, Prince Charlie didn't get there," she said.

"If he had," mused Matthew. "We'd have had more bishops."

Big Lou looked thoughtful. "Robbie . . ." she began.

"I know," said Matthew. "He's got this thing about them, hasn't he? He's a Jacobite, I gather. I suppose that it's a harmless enough bit of historical enthusiasm. Like those people who reenact battles. What do they call themselves? The Sealed Knot Society or something. You know, Lou, I was going for a walk in the hills above Dollar once and suddenly a whole horde of people came screaming down the slope. And suddenly I saw this chap in front of me dressed in sacking and wielding a claymore. And do you know who it was? It was an Edinburgh lawyer! Very strange. That's how he spent his Sundays, apparently."

67. We All Need to Believe in Something

Big Lou stepped back from the counter and started to fiddle with her coffee machine. "Men need hobbies," she began. "Women are usually far too busy with looking after the bairns and running the home and so on. Men have to find some outlet—now that they no longer need to hunt in packs."

Matthew smiled. "So dressing up in sackcloth and pretending to be some ancient clan warrior is entirely healthy?"

"Well, it's not unhealthy," said Big Lou. "It's odd, I suppose. But it's male play, isn't it? There are all sorts of male play, Matthew."

"Such as?"

Big Lou ladled coffee into a small conical container and pressed the grounds down with an inverted spoon. "Golf clubs," she said. "Car rallies. Football. The Masons. The list goes on and on."

"And don't women play?" asked Matthew.

Big Lou switched on the machine, stood back, and wiped her hands. "Not so much, you know. We women are much more practical. We just don't feel the need."

"Very interesting," said Matthew. "But to get back to Robbie and his friends. Is it play, do you think, or are they serious?"

Big Lou looked up at the ceiling. She was not sure that it was that simple. Play involved a suspension of disbelief, but once that step was taken, then one might imagine that everything was very serious. "Do you go to the theatre?" she asked. "Or the cinema?"

"Yes," said Matthew, and he thought: But I don't really go to anything these days.

"Well, when you're in the cinema, you believe in

what's happening on the screen, don't you? You engage with the actors and with what's happening to them. You believe in it, although you know it's not real."

"I suppose I do," said Matthew. "Everyone does. Everyone wants the men in the white hats to sort out the men in the black hats. Or they used to. Maybe it's different now."

"I don't know about hats," said Big Lou. "But the point is this. Robbie and his friends know that there are not many of them. They know that there'll never be a restitution of the Stuarts. But they act as if it's possible because . . ." She trailed off.

For Matthew, this was the most interesting part. How could people hold on to so evidently a lost cause and expect to be taken seriously? "Well, Lou," he pressed. "Why?"

The coffee machine was beginning to hiss, and Lou reached out to operate a small lever that released steam into the jug of milk she had placed below it. "Because we need to believe in something," she said. "Otherwise our lives are empty. You can believe in anything, you know, Matthew. Art. Music. God. As long as you have something."

Matthew knew that this was true. He would not have expressed the idea in that way, but he knew that what Big Lou said was true. And it was as true of him as it was of Robbie. Robbie believed in something while he, Matthew, believed in nothing, and that made a major difference. If I believed in something, thought Matthew, then my life would have some meaning. I wouldn't be drifting, as I am now, I would have some sense of purpose.

Could he become a Jacobite, or even an ardent nationalist? Could he find his personal salvation by becoming enthusiastic about Scotland's cause? He did not think so. He did not think it was that simple. What about becoming a Catholic—converting—and sinking deeply into a whole community of belief? If you became a Catholic, then at least you had a strong sense of identity. Catholics knew who their fellow Catholics were. They belonged. For a moment, he thought: it would solve everything; I'd become a Catholic and then I'd meet a Catholic girl who would appreciate me. But then he thought: no, I can't make that particular leap. It's different if you're born to something like that. It's part of you, part of your aesthetic. But it's not part of me.

And yet all that—all that embracing of a whole raft of rituals—was attractive. Matthew had met somebody who had become Jewish, not for reasons of marriage, but out of spiritual conviction. The rabbis had been surprised, of course, because they didn't seek to convert people, but he had found them, and the spirituality that they had, and had gone down to London to a rabbinical court and been accepted. And then he had never looked back. A whole world opened to him: a culture, a cuisine, a way of dressing, if one wanted that. He had been very content.

I would like something, thought Matthew, but I haven't got it. He looked at Big Lou, whose back was turned to him, and suddenly he felt a sense of her human frailty, her preciousness. For the most part, we treat others in a matter-of-fact way; we have to, in order to get on with our lives. But every so often, in a moment of insight that can be very nearly mystical in its intensity, we see others in their real humanity, in a way which makes us want to cherish them as joint pilgrims, almost, on a perilous journey. That is how Matthew felt. He felt sympathy for Big Lou—sympathy for everything: for the hard childhood she had had; for her struggle to improve herself with her reading; for her desire to be loved; for what she represented—a whole country, a whole Scotland of hard work and common decency. Oh Lou, he thought, I understand, I do, I understand.

Big Lou turned round. "Here's your coffee, Matthew."

He took it from her and took a sip of it, scalding hot though it was.

"Careful," said Big Lou. "I had somebody in the other day who burned his tongue. You have to let coffee cool down. Those machines heat it up something dreadful."

Matthew nodded. "I'll let it cool down." He paused. "I'm not wasting your time, am I, Lou?" he asked. "I come over here and blether away with you. And it never occurs to me to ask if I'm wasting your time."

"Of course you're not," said Big Lou.

"Good," said Matthew. And it was good, because he felt better about everything now, and he had a strong feeling that something was about to happen—something positive.

Big Lou looked at him. "You'll find somebody, Matthew," she said. "I know you've got somebody already. I know about Pat. But . . ."

"But she's not for me," said Matthew. "Is that what you think, Lou?"

Lou nodded. "Best to tell the truth," she said.

68. How Do You Tell Someone "It's Over"?

And Lou was right, thought Matthew, as he crossed the street to return to the gallery. She had told him nothing that he did not already know—deep within him; that was often the case with that which purported to be a disclosure: we knew it already. He had somehow convinced himself that he would be happy with Pat, but in his heart he knew that this was not so. Now the thought that he had even gone so far as to propose to her at that party made him feel extremely uncomfortable. She had asked for time to consider and had mentioned a few weeks. What if she decided to accept? If he wanted to avoid that embarrassment, then he would need to speak to her soon and tell her that it was over.

Now, it might have been simple for some young men to drop a girlfriend, but it was not easy for

Matthew. There were two reasons for this. One was that Matthew had never done this before; he had always been the one who had been discouraged or disposed of, and he had no idea how one should let the other person know. The other reason was that he was kind by nature, and the thought of causing distress to another was quite alien to him. That is, of course, if Pat would be distressed, and it occurred to him that there was a strong possibility that she would not be. In fact, there was even the possibility that she would be relieved. She had never been unduly demonstrative towards Matthew—indeed, there had been many occasions on which Matthew had thought that she was quite indifferent to him. Well, if that was the case, then it could be a release for both of them.

Matthew felt quite cheered by this thought as he completed his crossing of Dundas Street and approached the door of the gallery. He now noticed that there was somebody standing outside peering into his display window. It was a woman, not as young as Pat, but about Matthew's age, or perhaps a year or two older. Twenty-eight or twenty-nine, thought Matthew as he drew nearer.

"I'm about to open up again," said Matthew, as he reached for his keys. "If there's anything you'd like to look at more closely, please come in."

The woman seemed flustered. "Oh no," she said. "I'm not really thinking of buying a painting. I was just looking at that picture over there. That little one in the window. It's so . . . Well, it's so beautiful."

Matthew looked over her shoulder at the painting behind the glass. It was a small Cowie oil that he had acquired recently at an auction—the front of a building with a girl sitting on stone steps. And beyond this a sweep of rolling countryside, fields, the dark green of trees.

"That's by James Cowie," he said. "He was a very fine painter. You may know that big painting of his in the modern art gallery. Do you? That big one of the people sitting in front of a wide stretch of countryside with a curtain behind them and a man on a horse? It's one of my absolute favourites."

She shook her head. "I'm not sure if I've seen it," she said. "I'll go, though. I'll go and look for it."

Matthew watched her as she spoke. She has a lovely face, he thought, lovely, like one of those Italian madonnas, smooth skin. And I like her eyes. I just like them.

"Come in and look at it," he pressed. "Most people who go into galleries have no intention of buying a painting. Please."

She hesitated for a moment and then agreed. "I've been shopping," she said, gesturing to a small bag she was carrying. "I've spent enough money."

Matthew ushered her into the gallery. "Shopping for things you need?" he asked. "Or for things you don't need?"

She laughed. "The latter, I'm afraid. You've got such a nice antiques shop just down the road. The Thrie Estaits. Do you know it?"

"Of course," said Matthew. "I know Peter Powell. He's got a very good eye. Everything in his shop is very beautiful."

"Yes," said woman. "And this is what I bought. Look."

She reached into the bag and took out a small vase, chalice-shaped, made of streaky, opaque glass. "It's called slag-ware," she said. "He told me that the glassmakers put something into the glass to make it look like this." She traced a pattern along the side of the vase, following a whorl of purple. "Isn't it lovely? He had three or four of these. I chose this one. It's a present to myself. I know that sounds awful, but I really wanted it."

"It's very attractive," said Matthew. "May I take a closer look?"

She handed him the vase and he took it over towards the window to look at it in the light. "The colours are really wonderful," said Matthew. "Look at these different shades of purple. And that lovely creamy white."

Then he dropped it. He had been holding it firmly enough—or so he thought—but the vase suddenly slipped through his hands and tumbled downwards. Matthew gave a shout—a strangled cry of alarm—and the glass broke, shattering into fragments which went shooting across the floor.

Matthew stared at the floor for a few moments. Then he looked up at the young woman. She was gazing at the broken vase, her eyes wide with shock.

"Oh," said Matthew. "Look what I've done. I'm so sorry. I'm so, so sorry."

He bent down to start picking up the pieces, and held two together, as if working out whether the vase could be put together again somehow. But it was far beyond repair; some of the pieces were tiny, little more than fragments.

"It's all right," she said. "These things happen. Please don't worry."

"But it's broken," said Matthew. "I don't know what to say. I feel so stupid. It somehow . . . well, it seemed to jump out of my hands. I . . ."

"Please don't worry," she said. "I'm always breaking things. Everybody does."

Matthew stood up, looking at his hands, to which a few tiny fragments of glass had stuck.

"You must be careful," she said. "You must get those off without cutting yourself."

She reached out for Matthew's right hand and carefully brushed at it with a handkerchief. Her touch was very light, very gentle.

69. A Replacement— and an Extra Little Present

She tried to stop him, but he would have none of her objections. "I insist," Matthew said. "I broke it, and I'm going to replace it."

"It was an accident," the woman said. "Anybody can drop things. You mustn't think twice about it. It's not the end of the world."

Matthew shook his head. "Of course it's not the end of the world," he said. "But that's not the point. The point is that I stupidly dropped your beautiful slag-ware vase. That was my fault and my fault alone. Fortunately, you happened to mention that Peter has others, and so I'm going to go down the road and get you one to replace the one I broke. And that's that."

He moved towards the door. "You stay and look after the gallery for five, ten minutes at the most. Just stay. I'll be back with the replacement."

She sighed. "You're very insistent," she said.

"Yes," said Matthew, although he thought: nobody's ever called me insistent before. Nor decisive. But that is what I'm going to be. He looked at her. I've decided, he thought. I've decided.

He turned and walked out onto the street, looking back briefly to see the woman standing in the gallery, watching him. He waved to her cheerfully, and she smiled at him. It was, he thought, a smile of concession.

Down the road, at The Thrie Estaits, Peter Powell welcomed him from behind his desk. In front of him, half on the desk and half resting on an upturned leather suitcase, was a Benin bronze of a leopard, teeth bared in a smile. A stuffed spaniel in a case stood on guard beside the desk, while on the wall behind Peter's head, a large gilded sconce hung at a slightly drunken angle.

"Slag-ware, Peter," said Matthew. "A slag-ware vase, to be precise."

Peter smiled. "As it happens, I have three," he said. "And I've just sold another. What is it about slag-ware that makes it suddenly so popular?"

"I've just broken the one you sold," said Matthew. "And I want to replace it. I'll take the best of the three."

Peter rose to his feet and went to a small cupboard. Matthew saw the three vases within and noticed, with relief, that they looked identical to the one which he had just shattered. Peter examined the price ticket.

"They're not too expensive," he said. "But then they're not all that cheap. Are you sure that you want the most expensive one?"

"Yes," said Matthew. "I'm sure."

"And what about a small Indian puppet theatre?" Peter asked. "Or a bottle with a sand picture of Naples in it?"

341

Matthew laughed. "No thanks." He paused. "That woman who came in to buy the vase," he said. "Did she like anything else? Did she express an interest in anything other than the vase?"

Peter thought for a moment. "Well, yes, she did, as it happens. She was very taken with that Meissen figure over there. You see, that one, the figure of the girl. She liked that. But it's rather too expensive, I'm afraid. It's very rare, you see, and quite an early example."

"How much?" asked Matthew.

Peter picked up the delicate figure of the girl and looked underneath it. "Prepare yourself for a shock," he said. "Sixteen hundred pounds."

Matthew did not blink. "That's fine," he said. "I'll take that too."

Peter knew about Matthew's more-than-comfortable financial situation; Big Lou had told him, discreetly of course. "If you're sure . . ."

"I am," said Matthew. "I've never been surer in my life."

With his purchases cosseted in bubble wrap, Matthew left the Thrie Estaits and walked briskly back up the road. Inside the gallery, she looked at him reproachfully, but he noticed that she was struggling not to smile. "You're very bad," she said. "You shouldn't have done that."

"Well, I have," said Matthew. "And here you are. Here's your replacement. As good as the last one, I'm told."

She took the package and unwrapped it. "Thank you," she said. "I didn't expect that. But thank you."

Matthew blushed. His heart was racing now, but he felt a curious elation. "And I bought you an extra little present to make up for my clumsiness," he said. "Here."

He thrust the parcelled-up Meissen figure into her hands and waited for her to unwrap it.

"But you can't!" she protested. "You really can't. The vase was one thing, this is . . ."

"Please," said Matthew. "Please just unwrap it. Go on."

She removed the bubble wrap carefully. When the figure was half-exposed, she stopped, and looked up at Matthew. "I really can't accept this," she said. "You're very kind, but I can't."

Matthew held up his hands. "But why not? Why?"

She looked down at the figure and removed the last of the wrapping. "Because I know what this cost," she said quietly. "And I can't accept a present like this from somebody I don't even know."

Matthew looked down at the floor in sheer, bitter frustration. It was such a familiar experience for him; every time he tried to get close to somebody, it ended this way—with a rebuff. He knew that buying this present was an extravagant gesture, an unusual thing to do, but he thought that perhaps this one time it would work. But now he could see her recoiling, embarrassed, eager to end their brief acquaintance.

He thought quickly. He would be decisive; he had nothing to lose.

"I understand," he said. "It's just that I wanted to get you something." He paused. He would speak. "You see, the moment I saw you, the very first moment, I . . . well, I fell for you. I know it sounds corny, and I'm sorry if that embarrasses you, but there it is. Nothing like this has ever happened to me before. Nothing."

She cradled the Meissen figure. "I don't know what to think," she said. "I'm sorry." But then she looked up at him. "You've been very honest," she said. "You really have. So I should be honest too. When I saw you, I felt I rather liked you. But . . . But we don't even know each other's names."

"I'm Matthew," Matthew blurted out.

"And I'm Elspeth," she said. "Elspeth Harmony."

Matthew reached out to take the Meissen figure from her. "Let's put this down somewhere," he said. Then he asked: "What do you do, Elspeth?"

"I'm a teacher," she said. "At the Rudolf Steiner School."

Matthew thought of Bertie. "There's a little boy called Bertie," he began. "He lives near here. In Scotland Street."

"One of mine!" said Miss Harmony.

70. She Could Not Help but Hear the Conversation

Domenica Macdonald was aware that something was happening downstairs. One of the great glories of 44 Scotland Street, she had always felt, was the fact that noise did not travel—with the exception of Bertie's saxophone practice—and that, as a result, one heard little of the neighbours' private lives. This was thanks to Edinburgh architecture, and the generosity of construction methods which prevailed during the building of the great Georgian and Victorian sweeps of Edinburgh. In Scotland Street, the walls were a good two feet thick, of which solid stone formed the greatest part.

Used to this as she was, Domenica was always astonished to see the sheer flimsiness of walls in other places, particularly in postwar British construction, with its mean proportions (oppressive, low ceilings) and its weak structures (paper-thin walls). She had noticed how different things were on the Continent, where even very modest houses in countries such as France or Germany seemed so much more solid. But that was part of a larger problem—the problem of the meanness and cheapness which had crept into British life. And there was an impermanence too, which reached its height in the building of that great and silly edifice, the Millennium Dome, a "muckle great tent," as

Angus Lordie had described it. "That could have been a cathedral or a great museum," said Angus, "but don't expect anything as morally serious as that these days. Smoke and mirrors. Big tents."

Edinburgh at least could be grateful that it was, to a very large extent, made of stone, and that this gave a degree of privacy to domestic life. But in a tenement, if there was noise on the common stair, that could carry. As in the cave of Dionysius in Syracuse, a whisper at the bottom of the stair might be heard with some clarity at the top. And similarly, each door that gave onto the landing might be an ear as to what was said directly outside, with the result that remarks about neighbours had to be limited to the charitable or the complimentary until one was inside one's own flat; at that point, true opinions might be voiced—might be shouted even, if that helped—without any danger that the object of the opinion might hear.

Domenica had heard none of the discussion that preceded the dreadful discovery below that the wrong baby had been picked up at the council emergency nursery. Nor had she heard the cries of alarm that accompanied the actual discovery. But what she had heard that day was a great banging of doors and hurried footfall on the stairs as the Pollock family headed off to the nursery in search of the missing Ulysses. This had caused her to look out of the window and to see Irene, Stuart, and Bertie piling into a waiting taxi and racing off in the direction of Drummond Place. Where, she wondered, was the baby?

Then, a couple of hours later, she had heard them talking on the stairs as they returned. She had cautiously opened her door and peered down from the landing to see that all was well. What she saw was Irene holding Ulysses as she waited for Stuart to open the door. Bertie was there too, and he seemed cheerful enough, so she had gone back into the flat, reassured that all was well.

What she heard next was more slamming of doors. When she looked out of the window this time, she saw the entire Pollock family, including what she thought was Ulysses, again getting into a taxi and again racing off up the road at some speed. This time, it was not much more than an hour before she heard the door at the bottom of the stair close with a bang and the sound of Irene's voice drifting upwards.

Domenica could not help but hear, even had she not been standing close to her front door, which was held open very slightly.

"Humiliation!" said Irene. "Sheer, utter humiliation! How dare she say that we should have checked the baby first to see that it was the right one! Isn't that her job? Isn't she meant to make sure that she's handing over a boy rather than a girl? It's easy enough, for heaven's sake!"

Stuart muttered something which Domenica did not quite catch. But she did catch Irene's reply.

"Nonsense! Complete nonsense! Your trouble, Stuart, is that you're a bureaucrat and you're too willing to forgive the crass ineptitude of your fellow bureaucrats. What if Ulysses had been given to somebody else . . . ?"

The door slammed, and the conversation was cut off. Domenica smiled. It sounded as if there had been some sort of mix-up over babies. But she was not sure how this could have occurred, and it had obviously been sorted out in the end. Her curiosity satisfied, she was about to close her door when she noticed that Antonia's door on the other side of the landing was open. For a moment, she thought that her neighbour had perhaps been doing exactly what she was doing—listening to the conversation below, and she felt a flush of shame. It was a most ignoble thing to do, to listen in to the conversation of others, but there were occasions when it was, quite frankly, irresistible. And if we can't be ignoble from time to time, then we are simply failing to be human.

For a moment or two, Domenica hesitated. There were no sounds coming from Antonia's flat, so the builders were probably not there. But if they were not there, then who, if anybody, was? Had Antonia perhaps left the door open by mistake when she went out on some errand? If that were the case, then it was Domenica's duty, she felt, to check up that all was well and then close the door for her.

Domenica crossed the landing and pushed

Antonia's door wide open. "Antonia?" she called out.

There was silence, apart from the ticking of a clock somewhere inside the flat. She went in, peering through the hall and into the kitchen beyond. There was no sign of anybody.

"Antonia?"

Again there was only silence. Then, quite suddenly—so suddenly, in fact, that Domenica emitted a gasp—a man appeared from a door off the hall. It was Markus, the builder.

"You gave me a fright," Domenica said.

Markus looked at her. He was frowning.

"Where's Antonia?" she asked. There was something about his manner which worried her. It was something strange, almost threatening.

"Where is she?" Domenica repeated.

Markus said nothing as he moved behind Domenica and closed the front door.

71. For a Moment, Domenica Felt Real Alarm

Anthropologists, of course, are no strangers to danger. Although relations between them and their hosts are usually warm, developing in some cases into lifelong friendships, there are still circumstances in which the distance which the anthropologist must maintain reminds the host of the fact that the anthropologist does not, in fact, belong.

This may not matter if one is studying a group of people not known for their violent propensities, but it may matter a great deal if one is, for instance, taking an interest in organisation and command structures within the Shining Path in Peru. Or looking at gift-exchange patterns among *narco-traficantes* in Colombia: here, at any moment, misunderstandings may occur, with awkward consequences for the anthropologist. Indeed, awareness of this problem prompted the American Anthropological Association to publish a report entitled "Surviving Fieldwork," which revealed that anthropology is one of the most dangerous professions in the world, with risks ranging from military attack (2 per cent) to suspicion of spying (13 per cent) and being bitten by animals (17 per cent).

Domenica had experienced her fair share of these dangers in the course of her career and had discovered that physical peril had a curiously calming effect on her. While some of us may panic, or at least feel intense fear, Domenica found that danger merely focused her mind on the exigencies of the moment and on the question of how best to deal with them. Now, trapped in Antonia's flat—or so it appeared, once Markus had closed the front door and was standing, solidly, between the door and her—Domenica quickly began to consider why it was that she should feel threatened.

The closing of the door may have been a perfectly natural thing for Markus to do; a builder working within a house would not normally leave the front door open. And, of course, the Poles would not be affected by the paranoia and distrust which have affected those countries where it is considered unwise for a man to be in a room with a woman unless the door is left open. That ghastly custom, insulting to all concerned, would not yet have reached the less politically correct shores of Poland, thank heavens, and long may they be preserved from such inanity, thought Domenica.

She found her voice. "Now, Markus," she said. "I know that you don't speak English, and I, alas, do not speak Polish. But my question is a simple one: Antonia?" As she pronounced her neighbour's name, Domenica made a gesture which, she thought, would unambiguously convey the sense of what she was trying to say—a sort of tentative pointing gesture, ending in a whirl of a hand to signify its interrogative nature.

Markus looked at her in puzzlement. "Brick?"

Domenica sighed. "Brick! Brick! I'm sorry, we've really said everything there is to be said about bricks. Antonia? Antonia?"

Markus shook his head sorrowfully and muttered something under his breath. For a moment, Domenica felt real alarm—not for herself, now, but for Antonia. Had something happened? She took a few steps forward so that she was standing right before him. She repeated her sign. Surely he could understand that, at least.

As she gestured, Domenica found herself remembering one of the most curious books in her library, Jean and Thomas Sebeok's *Monastic Sign Languages*. She had come across this book years ago in Atticus Books in Toronto and had been astonished that anybody should have made a detailed study of such a subject. But there it was, complete with page after page of photographs of Cistercian monks, bound by their rule of silence, making expressive signs to one another to convey sometimes quite complex messages. She had toyed with buying it, but had been put off by its price of one hundred and forty Canadian dollars. This had been a bad decision: we always regret impulsive purchases not made, and no sooner had she returned to Scotland than she thought how much pleasure she would have obtained from the book.

Years later, finding herself again in Toronto for an anthropological conference, Domenica had returned to Atticus Books and innocently asked: "Do you by any chance have a book on monastic sign language?"

The proprietor of the bookshop concealed his delight. "As it happens," he said . . .

But now, standing before Markus, she found herself desperately trying to recall the Cistercian sign for where is, a simple enough phrase and presumably a commonly used sign—but not one she could remember. Instead, she remembered the sign for cat, which involved the twisting of an imaginary mustache on both sides of the upper lip with the tips of the thumbs and forefingers.

That was no good, of course, but the need now passed, as Markus appeared to have grasped the gist of her inquiry and was smiling and nodding his head. "Antonia," he said enthusiastically and pointed downstairs. Then he tapped his watch and held up five fingers. That, thought Domenica signified five minutes, or possibly five hours. Among some North American Indians, it might even have meant five moons. Five minutes, she decided, was the most likely meaning.

It was not even that. A few moments after communication had been established between Domenica and Markus, the front door of the flat was pushed open and Antonia appeared, carrying a bulging shopping bag. She gave a start of surprise at seeing Domenica in the flat, and then she cast a glance in the direction of Markus. But that was all it was—a glance. It was not a lingering look of the sort that Domenica had seen her give him before: this was a dismissive glance.

"I wish he would get on with his work rather than standing about," she muttered to Domenica. "Polish builders are meant to be hard-working."

This remark, taken together with the glance, was enough to inform Domenica immediately that the affair between Antonia and Markus was over. She was not surprised, of course, as she had wondered how a relationship which must, by linguistic necessity, have been uncommunicative, could last. The answer was now apparent: a week or so.

She looked at Antonia, who had placed the shopping bag on the ground and was beginning to unbutton her coat.

"You clearly need a cup of tea," she said. "Or something stronger. How about . . . a glass of Crabbie's Green Ginger Wine? Come to my flat."

Crabbie's Green Ginger Wine, those wonderful evocative words, balm to the troubled Edinburgh soul, metaphorical oil upon metaphorically troubled waters! And redolent of everything quintessentially Edinburgh: slightly sharp, slightly disapproving, slightly superior.

"Tea, please," said Antonia.

72. "I've let myself down," she said. "Badly."

Domenica ushered Antonia into her flat and closed the door behind her. "You'll forgive me if I have a glass of Crabbie's," she said. "I shall make tea for you. Earl Grey?"

"Oh, anything will do," said Antonia. She looked up at her neighbour. "This is very kind of you."

"Not at all," said Domenica. "I sense that . . . Well, I might as well be frank. Things are fraught next door, I take it?"

Antonia looked down at her shoes. "A bit." There

was a short silence, and then she added, "Very fraught, actually."

"Markus?"

Antonia sighed. "Yes. I must confess that I have been having a little fling with him."

"I could tell that," said Domenica, adding, hastily, "Not that it's any business of mine. But one notices."

"I don't care if anybody knows," said Antonia. "But it's over now, and it's not very easy having one's ex working in the house. You'll understand that, won't you?"

"Of course," said Domenica. "I had a boyfriend once in the field, years ago. He was a young man from Princeton, a heartbreaker—unintentionally, of course. When it didn't work out, we found that we still had three months of one another's company in the field. We were in New Guinea and we could hardly get away from one another. Sharing a tiny hut which the local tribe had thoughtfully built for visiting anthropologists. It was very trying for both of us, I think."

Antonia nodded. "It must have been. It's not quite that bad for me, but I still feel a bit raw over the whole thing."

Domenica poured the boiling water into the teapot. "I take it that it was a comprehension problem. After all, he seems to have only one word of English. I suppose one can put a lot of expression into one word, but the whole thing can't have been easy."

"Oh, we communicated quite well," said Antonia. "It's amazing how much one can say without actually saying anything."

"Cistercian monks . . ." began Domenica, but the look on Antonia's face made her trail off.

"He's married," said Antonia abruptly. "He showed me a picture of his wife and children."

Domenica said nothing for a moment. Of the problems that she had foreseen with this relationship, this was not one of them, and beside this, issues of communication seemed to fade into insignificance. "I'm very sorry," she said. It sounded trite, she knew, but it was what she felt—she was sorry.

"It's my own fault," said Antonia. "What else can one expect if one takes up with somebody who's virtually a complete stranger?"

Domenica tried to console her. "We all make mistakes when it comes to matters of the heart," she said. "It's part of the human condition. I've certainly made mistakes."

Antonia shook her head. "One makes such mistakes in one's twenties, perhaps," she said. "But not later. No, there's no excuse for me. None at all."

It seemed to Domenica that Antonia was berating herself unnecessarily. It had been foolish of her, perhaps, to get involved so quickly, but she had no reason to apologise for that. Antonia was the victim here and so had no need to look for excuses. She thought this as she went to the kitchen cupboard to get the bottle of green ginger wine. As Domenica poured herself a small glass, Antonia continued to speak. "I've been such a fool. I really have."

"You haven't," said Domenica. "You've been human—that's all."

"And he's been human too?"

Domenica looked up at the ceiling. "Men take comfort where they can find it," she said. "And all the evidence is, is it not, that they are genetically designed to take up with as many women as they can. It's something to do with genetic survival." She paused. "But lest you believe that I'm condoning this sort of thing, I must say that we're designed to do exactly the opposite. We have to raise children, who take a lot of time. So we're designed to keep men under control and in the home, providing for everybody. That's the way it's meant to work."

Antonia took a sip of her Earl Grey tea. It was all very well talking about genetic destiny, she thought, but she felt let down, both by herself and by Markus. "I've let myself down," she said. "Badly."

Domenica did not agree. "How can one let oneself down?" she said. "Unless one is going to be intensely dualistic?"

Antonia ignored the question. "Anyway," she said. "I've learned my lesson. From now on, I shall look for a very different sort of man."

"One to whom you can talk?" Domenica

regretted saying this the moment she spoke, but Antonia appeared not to have taken offence.

"You know that I'm writing a novel about the early Scottish saints?" she said. "Well, I shall look for a man who is the modern equivalent of the hero of my book."

Domenica picked up her glass of green ginger wine and glanced at Antonia over the rim. "Are we being practical?" she asked. "Are there any saints out there?"

Antonia met her gaze. "I'm sure there are. It's only a question of finding them."

"And it will have to be an unmarried saint."

Antonia nodded. "Naturally."

"But where exactly will you find a contemporary saint?" said Domenica. "It's hard enough to meet any half-decent man these days, let alone somebody saintly."

Antonia thought for a moment. Then she said: "Saintly men presumably go to church. I shall find one at St Giles' perhaps, or the Episcopal Cathedral over on Palmerston Place. I find Episcopalian men rather interesting, don't you?"

Domenica stared at her neighbour. She wondered if she was perhaps not quite feeling herself, if she needed to see somebody. First, there had been the ridiculous affair with Markus, and now there was this absurd notion that she would meet a man in church. It really was ridiculous, she thought, quite unrealistic, risible really.

"Are you quite serious?" she asked gently.

"Of course," said Antonia, setting her teacup down on the table. It was a Blue Spode teacup, the companion of the one which had appeared next door and which Domenica believed had been stolen.

"I've got a cup just like that," said Antonia casually.

Domenica drew in her breath sharply. Antonia was a dangerous, deluded woman—an unrepentant stealer of teacups, a siren to Polish builders, a predator really. She—Domenica—would have to proceed extremely carefully.

73. Julia Makes a Joyful Discovery

It was now almost two weeks since Bruce had moved into Julia's flat in Howe Street. It had been for both of them a blissful fortnight. For Bruce, it had been a period marked by the discovery of just how comfortable it was to have one's every whim catered for. Julia cooked for him and made just the dishes he liked—risotto, truffle oil salad, venison pie—while she also attended to his wardrobe, sewing buttons back on those shirts from which they had dropped, pressing his trousers, and generally making sure that he had everything that he wanted. She also drove Bruce about town in the small sports car which her father had given her for her last birthday, taking him to the gym and spa, to the squash club, and wherever else he needed to go.

For Bruce, the bargain was a good one. He was looked after in return for his company—not a bad arrangement, he felt, even if there were times when he found her a bit overbearing and perhaps just a little bit too anxious to please. Although he had his own room in the flat, it had rapidly become no more than a dressing room, where he kept his clothes and his supplies of hair gel and what he referred to as his *après-rasage*. He and Julia now shared her bedroom, which was dominated by a queen-size bed on which large red cushions were scattered. On each side of the bed, there was a small table stacked with magazines—*Vanity Fair*, *Harpers & Queen*, *Cosmopolitan* on her side, and on Bruce's, *Gentleman's Quarterly* and *High Performance Car*, all of them bought by Julia.

Julia liked to lie on top of the bed, paging through the magazines, a small plate of cashew and macadamia nuts beside her. "This is bliss," she said. "I'm so happy."

"Good," said Bruce. He wanted her to be happy—not too happy, perhaps, but happy enough. If she were to become too happy, then he feared that she might start talking about commitment and permanence, as women tended to do, and this was not on the agenda, as far as he was concerned.

Julia had a small diary in which she noted certain facts. On one page of this diary—a day which coincided with Bruce's moving into the flat, she had written, enigmatically, day fourteen. That was two weeks ago, and now, while Bruce sat watching television in the kitchen, she made her way through to the bathroom off the main bedroom. It was not very tidy, and there was a riot of shampoo bottles cluttering the shelf above the basin. But from a cupboard behind that—one of those flat medicine cupboards fronted with a mirror—she extracted a small box. From this she took a plastic tube. Her hands were shaking as she read the leaflet that came with this; the instructions were clear enough, but Julia read them through twice, just to be certain.

In the kitchen, Bruce rose from his chair and fetched a bottle of mineral water from the fridge. Pouring himself a glass, he downed it quickly and then wiped his mouth with the back of his hand. He noticed that the fridge was, as usual, almost completely full, and this gave him a particular pleasure. He could barely remember when he had last had to do any shopping for food, which he had never liked doing very much. And now here was a constantly refilling cornucopia, including that delicious sparkling mineral water tinged with the merest hint of lemon. He poured himself another glass of that, drank it, stretched his arms above him, and then flopped down on the chair in front of the television.

In the bathroom, Julia held the tube up to the light. A small marker tab inside would reveal the result, the leaflet had promised: a blue line would appear if the test were positive. She peered at the tab. Five seconds, ten seconds . . . a blue line! She closed her eyes and then looked again. This time, the blue line was even more clearly present.

She disposed of the tube carefully. Bruce would probably not know what it was, but she did not want to run the risk of his finding it and asking any awkward questions before she was ready to answer them. Then, standing in front of the mirror, she placed a hand gently against her stomach. "I'm pregnant," she whispered. I'm pregnant!

It had been very quick, and this was the very first day on which she could perform the test after that first passionate encounter when she had shown him how to use the shower. What a place for it to happen! But how lovely, she thought. If it were a girl—which she rather hoped it would be—then perhaps they could even call her Doccia, which was Italian for shower. It was a very nice-sounding name, she thought—Doccia Anderson; but no, it could be awkward for the poor child later on. One wouldn't want a child to know that she originated in a shower; one could never tell the effects of that.

Julia looked at her watch. Where would her father be now? Probably in his office in Melville Street, from which he ran the hotels and other businesses in which he dabbled. She picked up the telephone and dialled the number.

"Daddy?"

Her father chuckled. "Julia! And how is Daddy's girlie today? Working hard?"

362

"Of course. But I shouldn't overdo it. Not in my condition."

There was a silence at the other end of the line. Then her father spoke. "What did you say? What condition?"

"You're going to be a grandfather." She had rehearsed that in her mind, and it was what she thought would give him greatest pleasure.

Again there was silence for a few moments. Then he said: "Please say that once more. Slowly this time."

Julia repeated herself, but was then cut off by a whoop of joy from her father. She was now slightly concerned that she was being a bit premature in conveying the news, but her instinct had been right as to her father's likely reaction: he was evidently thrilled. But then a hesitant note crept into his voice. "Do you mind my asking," he said, "but who's the young man?"

"He's called Bruce, Daddy. And you'll love him."

"Has he asked you to marry him?" her father asked.

"Not quite. But I'm sure he will. With a little . . ."

"Yes, with a little what?"

"With a little help from you," said Julia. "And I know how good you are at getting people to do the things you want them to."

74. *Julia Decides to Test the Temperature*

When Julia went back into the kitchen, still light-headed from the discovery she had made in the bathroom—a discovery which she knew would change the course of her entire future—she found Bruce sitting with his feet up on the breakfast table. On the other side of the room, the small portable television set which she kept in the kitchen was disgorging some football match which appeared to interest Bruce greatly.

"They're rubbish," said Bruce, gesturing towards the television. "They can't play. They just can't play."

"Oh dear," said Julia. "That's bad."

Bruce grunted, and Julia crossed over to the fridge to pour herself a glass of milk. Calcium, she thought. I must get some calcium.

She turned to Bruce, the container of milk still in her hand. "Calcium, Brucie?"

Bruce looked up from the football match. "What?"

Julia blushed. The word calcium had slipped out unintentionally. "Milk?" she asked.

Bruce made a dismissive gesture. "No thanks. But if you're making coffee, I wouldn't mind."

Julia picked up the kettle and began to fill it with water. There is nothing she would have wished for more than to be able to tell him, to share her news with him, but she realised that it would be unwise to do so—just yet. There would be time enough for that in the future, when the moment was right, and when she would perhaps have the support of her father. For the moment, though, it might still be possible to test the temperature of the water by making one or two pertinent remarks. She suspected that Bruce would be a good father, and a willing husband, of course, but it might be an idea just to ascertain exactly where he stood.

Joining him at the table, she made a determined effort to ignore the fact that his feet were on the surface from which they ate. Men were like that, she reminded herself; they were really quite unsanitary in their habits.

"I bumped into an old friend this morning," she said casually.

Bruce did not take his eyes off the television set. "Oh yes," he said.

"Yes," said Julia. "I was at school with her. A girl called Catherine. We were actually very close friends at school."

"The best sort of friend," said Bruce. "As long as they don't change. Sometimes you find these people you knew a while ago have become all gross and domestic."

Julia caught her breath. Did he think that grossness and domesticity went together? "Well, she is married," she ventured. "But it hasn't really changed her. She's even happier than she used to be, in fact."

"*Chacun à son goût*," remarked Bruce. Then he added: "Glad to hear it."

Julia looked at her fingernails. "She told me she's pregnant."

"That happens," said Bruce. He was not interested in this sort of thing, women's gossip, he thought.

Julia persevered. "You couldn't tell yet, of course. But, anyway, she's really pleased about that. She and her husband have been hoping for this to happen."

"They may as well get some sleep now—while they can," said Bruce, reaching for his glass of sparkling water. "They won't get any for the next ten years."

"But sleep isn't everything, Brucie!" Julia teased. "And lots of babies sleep quite well, you know. They can be fun."

There was a silence. On the television set, in some unspecified distant place, a man kicked a ball into a goal. There was cheering and despair. Bruce raised a finger and shook it at the set. "There you are," he said. "That's what comes from having a cripple for a goalkeeper."

"Some babies you hardly even notice," Julia went on.

"These people are seriously useless," said Bruce. "Did you see that? They've just let the other side score a goal and now they're risking having somebody sent off. Incredible. Just incredible."

He rose to his feet and walked across to switch off the television set. "I can't bear anymore," he said. "I'm going to go and have a bath. Should we go out for dinner tonight? You choose."

Julia nodded vaguely, but her mind was elsewhere. This was not going to be easy, she thought. She watched Bruce as he left the kitchen, and she realised that, quite apart from anything else, quite apart from the baby—their baby!—she had to secure this man, this gorgeous, gorgeous man, as she thought of him. This Adonis—what exactly did that word mean?—this rock star—this husband!

Bruce went into the bathroom and slipped out of the moccasins he was wearing. He loved the bathroom floor, which was made of limestone, and had a cool, rough feel on the soles of the feet. And he liked the decor too, the stone-lined shower cubicle—even if the shower itself required special handling—the double basins with their designer bases, the entire glass shelf which Julia had cleared for the hair gels and shampoo she had seen him unpacking in his room. It was a bathroom for living in, Bruce had decided. One could move one's stuff in here and just live in it.

He bent over and started the bath running. There was a cube of bath salts on the edge of the bath, left there by Julia, and he picked this up and smelled it. Lily of the Valley. Well, not what he would exactly have chosen—he preferred sandalwood—but he liked the feel of these things and the way they made the water milky white. So he unwrapped it and broke it into the rapidly filling bath. Then he turned round and his eye caught the small leaflet which was lying on the floor at the end of the bath. He reached forward and picked it up. He became quite still.

For a few moments after he had finished reading the leaflet that came with Julia's pregnancy testing kit, Bruce did nothing. Then, quite slowly, he pivoted round and turned off the running water. Now there was silence in the bathroom.

Bruce looked at the leaflet again. She told me, he thought. I asked her and she told me. I very specifically, very considerately, asked her, and she reassured me. And now . . . What if the result had been positive? What if he was already responsible for . . . He suddenly remembered the conversation they had had in the kitchen. He had dismissed it, thought nothing of it. Women always talked about babies, but now he realised that there was a very good reason for Julia having raised the subject.

He looked at the bathwater. He would get in and do some serious thinking in the bath, thinking about his future, thinking about escape routes.

75. A Prayer from a Painter in Utter Despair

Angus Lordie had painted very little since the fateful day of Cyril's arrest. He had been finishing a portrait which had been commissioned by the board of a whisky company; the sittings were done, and he was now working from photographs, but his heart was not in it. It seemed to him that although Cyril was no longer lying at his feet, as he normally did, he was somehow insinuating himself into the very painting, somewhere in the background, a canine presence, a shadow. No, it was hopeless: a painter could not work when his muse lay somewhere in a cold pound, awaiting trial for something that he did not do.

On that morning, although Angus knew that he would have to force himself into his studio, he sat unhappily at his breakfast table, toying with his food; even a Pittenweem kipper seemed unappetising while he was in this frame of mind. Food was a problem. The previous evening, to tempt himself to eat, he had treated himself to several thick slices of the smoked salmon sent down to him from Argyll by his friend Archie Graham. Archie's salmon, which he steeped in rum and then smoked himself, was, in Angus Lordie's opinion, the finest smoked salmon in Scotland, but he had found that in his current mood he had little appetite even for that. Indeed, since Cyril's arrest, Angus had lost a considerable amount of weight. He now had to wear a belt with the trousers that had previously fitted him perfectly *ungebelt*, and his collars, normally slightly tight because of the age of his shirts, could now have two fingers inserted between them and his neck and waggled about without discomfort. If a dog could pine for a man, thought Angus, then a man could just as readily pine for a dog.

He lingered over his coffee, watching a shaft of sunlight creep slowly across the table to illuminate the cracks in the wooden surface, the ancient crumbs these contained. We are not worthy, he thought, so much as to gather up the crumbs under thy table . . . The familiar words of the Book of Common Prayer came back to him unbidden, from the liturgy of the Scottish Episcopal Church, in which he had been raised and to which, when he felt the need, he always went home; these phrases lodged in the mind, to surface at unexpected moments, such as this, and brought with them their particular form of consolation. Such language, such resonant, echoing phrases—man that is born of woman hath but a short time to live . . . Dearly Beloved we are gathered together here in the sight of God—this was the linguistic heritage bequeathed to the English-speaking peoples in the liturgy and in the Authorised Version by Cranmer and by Jamie Sext, James VI, a monarch with whom Angus had always felt a great affinity. And what had we done with it, with this language and all its dignity? Exchanged it for the banalities of the disc jockey, for the cheap coin of a debased English, for all the vulgarities and obscenities that had polluted broadcasting. And nobody taught children how to speak clearly anymore; nobody taught them to articulate, with the result that there were so many now who spoke from unopened mouths, their words all joined together in some indecipherable slur. You have taken away our language; you have betrayed us. Yes. Yes.

Our situation, he thought, is serious. Our nightmares are waking ones: global warming; the loss of control over our lives; a degenerate, irretrievably superficial popular culture; the arrival, with bands playing, of Orwell's Big Brother. He stared at his table in despair. Did he want to live through all this? Did he want to see the world he knew turned so utterly upside down?

He closed his eyes. Even then, he could feel the presence of the sun as it cast its light upon his table. It was there, a yellow glow, a patch of warmth. He lowered his head and brought his hands together on his lap; hands on which the smell of paint and turps seemed always to linger, the hands of one who made something, an artist. Suddenly, and with complete humility, he began to pray. At first, he felt self-conscious as he performed the forgotten act, last done how many years ago? But, after a moment, that went away, and he felt the onset of a proper humility, a glow. Because I am nothing, he thought, just an ordinary man, a tiny speck of consciousness on a half-burned-out star, precisely because of that I lower my head and pray. And it seemed to him at that moment that it did not matter if there was nobody listening; the very act of prayer was an acknowledgement of his humanity, a reminder of true scale.

"Oh Lord," he whispered, "who judges all men and to whom alone the secrets of the heart are known; forgive me my human failings, my manifold acts of wickedness. Open my heart to love. Turn thy healing gaze to me. Forgive me for that which I have not done which I ought to have done."

It was a hotch-potch of half-remembered phrases, taken out of context and patched together, but as he spoke them, uttered each one, he felt their transformative power. He saw a man beside a shore. He saw children at the feet of the man. What he saw was love and compassion; he was sure of that, utterly sure.

Angus opened his eyes and saw the sunlight upon the table. He moved his hands so that they lay in the square of warmth. He looked. The hairs on his hands were picked out by the light; there was a small fleck of white paint on one knuckle. He closed his eyes and concluded his prayer. "And I ask one final thing," he muttered. "I ask that you restore to me my dog."

He rose to his feet and looked about him. How

foolish, he thought, to imagine that words uttered by him could change the world in the slightest way, what a massive, sentimental delusion!

But then the telephone rang. Angus gave a start, and then crossed the room to answer. For a second or two, he imagined that his prayer had brought results and that the call would bring news of Cyril. But that, he knew, was not how the world worked. The world was one of chance, a biological lottery, not one ruled by eternal verities and design. Prayer was a wishful-thinking conversation with self; that's what he told himself. Of course he knew that.

He picked up the telephone. It was his lawyer, George More, on the other end. "Come round to the office," said the lawyer. "There's somebody here who's looking forward to seeing you again."

Angus frowned. Who could George have in the office? Then he heard, coming down the line, a bark.

76. All Hail Cyril as He Returns in Triumph

They had not expected it in the Cumberland Bar. There they were, the regulars—Jock, Sid, Harry, Maggie, Gerry, all sitting there, as they always did at six o'clock, waiting for somebody to say something memorable—which nobody ever did—and in walked Angus Lordie, with—*mirabile dictu*, as Harry, a classical scholar, was so fond of saying— Cyril behind him, gold tooth flashing, tongue hanging out of the side of his mouth as it always did. For a moment, nobody said anything, but all eyes were turned to them; and, a few moments later, before Angus had taken more than a few steps into the bar, the assembled company erupted.

Cyril barked once or twice, but for the most part accepted the fuss calmly and with dignity. Unfamiliar hands ruffled the fur on his head, stroked him, patted him vigorously on the back, all of which he took in his stride, for this is what humans do to dogs, and Cyril understood his place.

Angus, glowing with pleasure, ordered his drink from the bar and the dish of beer for Cyril. Then he went over to his table, where friends were ready to ply him with questions.

"He's been acquitted?"

"What happened at the trial?"

"Is he on probation?"

None of these questions were relevant, and Angus simply shook his head. Then he began to explain.

"I received a telephone call this morning," he said. "I must admit I was feeling somewhat low, and I almost didn't answer the phone. Thank heavens I did! There was George More on the line and he said . . ." He looked down at Cyril, who had finished his beer and was looking up at his master, his eyes damp with contentment.

"He said," Angus continued, "that he had acted on the information which we passed on—information about the real culprit, which that funny wee boy in Scotland Street . . ."

"Bertie," prompted Maggie. "The one with the . . ."

"With the mother," said Harry.

Angus nodded. "Anyway, George said to me that he had been in touch with the powers that be and told them that we intended to lodge a special defence of incrimination. Apparently, that's what you do when you say that it wasn't you, it was somebody else.

"Apparently, this caused disarray at the other end, because nobody has ever lodged that defence in a case involving a dog. And there was the additional issue of whether or not any of the defences normally available in a criminal trial would be able to be applied to a dog. Nobody at the Crown Office seemed to know!"

"So?" asked Maggie, reaching down to pat Cyril again.

"So the fiscal asked the police to go and see if they could find the dog in question. Which they did . . . with very convenient results. Convenient for us, that is."

Angus looked about him at the expressions of his friends.

"They found that dog all right," he went on. "They found him and the dog very obligingly bit one of the policemen on the shins. Not a bad bite—just a nip really, but enough to suggest that the finger was pointing in the right direction."

There were expressions of satisfaction all round. Most people in the Cumberland Bar had been convinced of Cyril's innocence, and this result merely confirmed what they had always believed. Now they crowded round Angus, sharing his manifest joy and relief.

"I can get back to work now," Angus said, smiling. "I haven't been able to paint a thing—not a thing."

His friends nodded in sympathy. And when, an hour or so later, Angus rose to go home, they raised their glasses to Cyril as he walked past, a triumph of sorts, a victory march. Cyril wagged his tail and his gold tooth flashed in the light. "He's a very great dog," said the barman. "Would you just look at him? One of the finest dogs of his generation."

As they made their way out onto Dundonald Street, Cyril raised his head and sniffed at the air. There were the familiar smells of Drummond Place, the smell of the gardens in the centre, the sharp smell of oil on the stone setts, a cooking smell from somewhere close by, the smell of damp. All of that was there, but there was something else, a smell so exciting that Cyril quivered in anticipation.

"What is it, boy?" Angus asked.

Cyril looked up at his master. Then he twisted his neck round and smelled the air again. He had to go where his nose took him; he simply had to.

"What's troubling you, old chap?" asked Angus. "Are you hungry?"

Cyril tugged at his lead. It was an insistent tug, an urgent one, and Angus decided to let him go where he wanted to go. So, with Cyril pulling at the leash, Angus followed him across the road, to the gardens in the centre of Drummond Place.

"So you want a run round?" asked Angus, when they reached the half-open gate of the gardens. "All right. But make it brief. I'm hungry."

He bent down to take the leash off Cyril's collar. The moment he did this, Cyril tore towards the centre of the gardens. Angus, bemused at Cyril's sudden, but totally understandable desire for a bit of freedom, followed behind his dog.

It was one of those generous summer evenings when the light persists, and it was quite bright enough for him to see exactly what was happening. A woman had been walking her dog, a large terrier of some sort, in the gardens, and now, to Angus Lordie's horror, Cyril rushed over to this dog and began what could only be interpreted as amatory advances. The woman shouted loudly and threw something at Cyril, missing him by some margin. Angus dashed forward, shouting his apologies as he did so. Cyril and the female dog were now in full embrace.

"Stop him!" shouted the woman. "Stop him!"

Angus struck at Cyril with his leash, using it as a whip, but he missed. He raised his arm again and struck once more. This time, the lead connected with Cyril, but the amorous dog seemed to be impervious to his master's displeasure. There was a growling sound, a warning.

Angus turned to the woman. "I'm terribly sorry," he said. "It appears that . . ."

The woman glared at him.

"Listen," said Angus testily. "You shouldn't take a dog out in that condition."

"How dare you!" snapped the woman.

Angus looked at Cyril reproachfully. New dogs, perhaps, behaved with greater sensitivity; Cyril, it seemed, was not a new dog.

77. Olive Has News of Bertie's Blood Test

Ever since Olive had come to play "house" in Scotland Street, Bertie had tried to avoid her at school. One reason for this was that he feared that if he talked to her she would try to arrange a further visit; another was that he was concerned that she might wish to give him the result of the blood test she had carried out.

Bertie remembered with a shudder the moment when Olive had cornered him in his room and insisted on plunging the needle of her syringe into his upper arm. It had hurt, even if not quite as much as he had feared, but what had terrified him was the sight of his blood rising so very easily in the barrel of the syringe. Olive herself had seemed to be slightly surprised at this and remarked, with some satisfaction: "I seem to have found a vein first time, Bertie! And look at all that blood. Look at it!"

That had been some days ago, and Bertie hoped that Olive had forgotten all about the test, whatever it was, that she was proposing to conduct. He wondered if he could ask for his blood back, and if it could be injected back into him—by a proper nurse this time. But he thought that it was probably too late for that, and this was confirmed when Olive eventually trapped him in the playground.

"No, don't go away, Bertie," she said. "I need to talk to you."

Bertie looked about him desperately. At the other side of the playground, Tofu and several other boys were engaged in some game; they had not noticed Bertie, and so no help would come from that quarter. Bertie decided to go on the attack.

"I want my blood back," he said.

Olive laughed. "Why? Why do you want it back?"

"I want it injected back in," said Bertie. "You didn't ask me properly before you took it."

Olive laughed, screwing up her eyes in amusement. "Oh, Bertie," she crowed, "you're so silly! Everybody knows that blood goes dry and hard after a while, especially your yucky sort of blood. You can't put it back in."

Bertie frowned. Every day on the bus he went past the Blood Transfusion Service in Lauriston Place. He had asked his mother about this, and it

379

had been explained to him that blood was taken there and stored until needed for transfusion. Olive, he thought, was clearly lying.

"What about blood transfusions, then?" he challenged. "Don't you know about those?"

Olive, who could not bear to be bettered in any discussion, took a moment or two to compose herself. "Those are different," she said. "I would have thought that you would have known how they do that."

Bertie waited for her to continue, but she did not.

"Well?" he said. "How are they different?"

Olive waved a hand airily. "I haven't got time to go into all that," she said. "I need to talk to you about the tests I did. I did some tests, you see, then I threw your blood away. Into the rubbish bin, in fact."

Bertie glared at her in anger. But he was experiencing another emotion too—anxiety. One part of him did not believe that Olive had been able to carry out any tests at all, but another remembered advertisements he had seen for various home-testing kits. It was just possible, perhaps, that Olive had got her hands on one of these and had subjected his blood sample to some procedure or other. He shuddered.

"Worried?" asked Olive. "Well, that's quite understandable, Bertie. It's not knowing that's the worst. That's what everybody says."

"Not knowing what?" asked Bertie. He tried to

sound strong and insouciant, but that was not how his voice came out.

"Not knowing the result of a test," said Olive calmly. "But you mustn't worry too much, Bertie—yet. I promise I'll tell you gently."

He gasped. He opened his mouth to say something, but Olive silenced him. "Not very good news, I'm afraid," she said. "You've tested positive for leprosy. Sorry about that, Bertie."

Bertie stared at Olive. He looked at her fingers, hoping that he would see them crossed—a sure sign that she was telling lies. But there was no sign of that. All he saw was Olive looking at him sympathetically, a concerned frown on her brow.

"Leprosy is a very serious disease," Olive went on. "It's quite rare these days, you know. There's hardly any at the school."

"What happens . . . ?" Bertie stuttered.

"Well," said Olive. "Your nose can fall off. And your fingers too. It's not very nice. That's why lepers are given a bell. They ring it to warn people to keep away."

Bertie reached up and felt his nose. It seemed to be fastened securely enough. He looked at his fingers again; these seemed unaffected.

"How do you catch it?" Bertie asked.

"I've been reading about it in the encyclopaedia," said Olive. "They say that it's very difficult to get. You have to have very close contact with somebody who has it."

"By shaking hands?" asked Bertie. If that was so, then Tofu would have it too. He and Bertie had shaken hands the previous day when they had agreed to swap comics. Would this mean that Tofu would have leprosy too?

As it happened, Tofu was now making his way across the playground to join them.

"What's going on here?" he asked.

"Olive says that I've got leprosy," said Bertie. And then he added, "And if I have, then you might have it too, Tofu. I shook hands with you yesterday, remember?"

Tofu looked at Olive, who stared back at him defiantly, as would one who had science on her side. "Oh yes?" he said. "And can you get it from the spit of somebody who's got it?"

"Of course," said Olive. "That's an easy way to get it."

Tofu smiled at Bertie, and then turned back to face Olive. "In that case," he said, "you've got it too!"

And with that, he spat at her.

Olive screamed. It was an extremely loud scream, high and painful on the ear, and although there was a certain amount of background noise in the playground, it carried.

Inside the building, Miss Harmony, who was enjoying a cup of tea in the staff room, leapt to her feet and looked out of the window before she hurried out to deal with the emergency.

"Olive!" she cried, as she ran towards the screaming girl. "What on earth's wrong?"

Olive opened her eyes. "These boys spat at me, Miss Harmony," she said. "I was just talking to them and they spat at me."

Miss Harmony sighed. Her task in life was every bit as difficult, she thought, as that taken on by the late Dr Livingstone.

78. Question Time for the Boys— and for Olive

Inside the classroom, while the rest of the class busied itself with an arithmetical exercise, Miss Harmony took Tofu and Bertie to one side.

"Now, I don't think I really need to say how disappointed I am," the teacher began. "Spitting at somebody is not only a very unkind thing to do, it's also very insanitary. You know that, don't you? Both of you know that you should never spit at another person."

"I didn't," said Tofu. "She's lying, Miss Harmony. Olive tells lies all the time. Everybody knows that."

Bertie drew in his breath. Tofu was telling a barefaced lie now, and he marvelled at his ability to do so. Surely Miss Harmony would know that he was lying or, worse than that, she might ask Bertie if it were true. That worried Bertie: it was one thing for Tofu to lie to Miss Harmony, quite another for him to do the same thing. In fact, he would never be able to do it.

"Now, Tofu," said Miss Harmony. "Why would Olive tell me that you boys had spat at her if you hadn't? And, anyway, I noticed that there was something on her face."

"That was slime," said Tofu. "That had nothing to do with me."

Miss Harmony turned to Bertie. "Now, Bertie," she said. "You're a truthful boy, aren't you? You tell me: did you spit at Olive?"

Bertie thought for a moment. He could answer this question quite truthfully. He had not spat at Olive, and he could tell Miss Harmony that. "No," he said, with some indignation. "I didn't spit at her, Miss Harmony. Cross my heart, I didn't."

"And Tofu, then?" asked the teacher. "Can you tell me, Bertie, did Tofu spit at Olive?"

Bertie looked at Tofu. The other boy had been looking away, but now he shot a glance at Bertie and made a quick throat-slitting gesture with his hand. He did it quickly, but not quickly enough for Miss Harmony not to notice it.

"I see," said the teacher. "Ignore that, please, Bertie. Tofu has just confirmed his guilt."

Tofu flushed. "It was her fault, Miss Harmony," he protested. "She told Bertie that he had leprosy."

Miss Harmony frowned. "Bertie, did Olive tell you that?"

Bertie nodded miserably. "Yes, Miss Harmony.

She took some blood of mine, you see, and did some tests."

"Blood!" exclaimed Miss Harmony. "Are you making this up, Bertie?"

Bertie shook his head and began to explain to Miss Harmony about what had happened. He told her of Olive's visit to Scotland Street and of the junior nurse's set. When he came to tell her of the syringe and the taking of the blood sample, Miss Harmony winced and shook her head in disbelief.

"She actually put the needle in, Bertie?" she asked.

"Yes," said Bertie. "Then she told me that she had done some tests and that I had leprosy. That's when Tofu came and . . ."

"Well, we can pass over that," said Miss Harmony hurriedly, adding, "in the circumstances. But first of all, Bertie, let me assure you: you do not have leprosy. You positively don't."

Bertie felt a great weight of anxiety lift off him. Instinctively, he felt his nose again: it seemed more firmly anchored than ever.

"So," went on Miss Harmony, "you should now forget all about that. Olive had no right to do any of that, and even if we cannot condone spitting . . ." and here she looked at Tofu, "there are some occasions in which a blind eye might properly be turned. And so I want you two boys to go and sit down and not to think anymore about all this. No more nonsense about leprosy! And no more spitting either!"

From the other side of the classroom, Olive had

been watching this carefully. Now she saw the two boys sitting down in their seats and she noticed, somewhat to her alarm, that they were smiling. And now, even more to her alarm, she saw Miss Harmony beckoning her over to her desk.

"Yes, Miss Harmony?" said Olive as she approached the teacher.

"Olive," said Miss Harmony. "I want a straight answer. No ifs, no buts. Just a straight answer. Did you take a blood sample from Bertie?"

Olive looked down at the floor. "Maybe," she said. And then she added, "I was only trying to help him, Miss Harmony."

Miss Harmony expelled breath from between her teeth. To Olive, it sounded alarmingly like a hiss.

"You silly, silly little girl," said the teacher. "Do you realise how dangerous it is to stick a needle into somebody? Do you realise that?"

Olive did not have time to answer before Miss Harmony continued. "And then you went and told him that he had leprosy! Of all the stupid, unkind things to do, that takes some beating. Do you even begin to understand how silly that is?"

Olive looked up at her teacher. She knew that her position was very difficult, but it was not in her nature to give up without a fight. "Please don't destroy my confidence, Miss Harmony," she said.

"What did you say?" hissed Miss Harmony. "Destroy your what?"

"My confidence," said Olive.

It was at this point that Miss Harmony felt her self-control evaporating. She was a graduate of Moray House, the beneficiary of a fine training in the Scots pedagogical tradition. She knew all the theory of how to maintain control in the classroom; she knew all the theory about reinforcing positive behaviour. She also knew that one should never use violence against children, no matter what the temptation. Yet here, faced with this infinitely irritating child, she felt an almost irresistible urge to do something physical.

She tried to collect her thoughts. "Olive," she said, "do you know the test that people used to see if somebody had leprosy? They would pinch them on the ear to see if they felt pain. The poor people with leprosy didn't, you see. Look, I'll show you."

She leaned forward and took Olive's right ear-lobe between her thumb and forefinger. "There," she said. "That's what they did."

She pinched extremely hard, and Olive gave a yelp of pain.

"Good," said Miss Harmony. "So you haven't got leprosy. That's a relief, isn't it?"

As Olive made her way back to her desk, Miss Harmony looked out of the window. She knew that the eyes of all the children were on her; they had heard Olive's yelp; they had seen what had happened. Yes, thought Miss Harmony. I have just abandoned everything I was ever taught, but, oh my goodness, it was satisfying!

79. A Confusion of Daddies
at the Dinner Table

Several days had passed since the evening on which Julia and Bruce had made their respective discoveries; or rather, since Julia had made her discovery and Bruce had discovered her discovery.

For Julia, it had been an exciting and positive moment; she wanted to secure Bruce, and she knew that this might be difficult without a certain amount of leverage. And what better leverage was there than the fact of a pregnancy? He might not like the idea at first, but, with a certain amount of help from her father, she thought that any slight objections that Bruce might have to marriage could be smoothed over. That was her strategy.

For Bruce, the finding of the instruction sheet for the home pregnancy test had been the cause of immediate panic. Fortunately, as he lay in the bath and reflected on what had happened, this panic subsided, and he began to work out the best approach to the problem. What he required was level-headedness; a careful appreciation of just where he stood and where the danger lay would be followed by a few cautious moves, and, with one bound, he would be free. Julia might think herself smart, but she was no match for Bruce, or so he thought. Indeed, as he reflected on it, he realised that he had never once been outsmarted by a woman. That's not at all bad, he said to himself. In all my years of playing the field, I've never once, on any single occasion, had any girl get the better of me. Hah! And I've known quite a few, he thought, who were considerably wilier than Julia Donald.

He felt reassured; the situation was awkward, yes, but no more than that. And Julia would get over him quickly enough, even if she decided to go ahead with having the baby. If she did that, of course, Bruce felt that it would be her own decision—and her own responsibility. The baby, no doubt, would be good-looking—just like me, he mused—and would keep her company, would give her something to do other than read those stupid magazines and have her hair styled. So getting her pregnant, really, was an act of kindness on his part, a gift.

Over the days that followed, Bruce was careful to give no indication that he had found out about Julia's pregnancy. And Julia, for her part, did nothing to indicate that her situation had changed. They were pleasant enough to one another and they talked about much the same things that they always talked about. They went to a party together and had some mutual friends round to the flat in Howe Street. Nothing was said, not a word, to suggest that anything had changed or would change in the future.

But then Julia announced to Bruce one morning

that she had invited her father for dinner that night and that he was looking forward to meeting her new flatmate.

"He likes you already," she said. "He told me that on the phone."

Bruce smiled. Of course her father would like him, but surely he should have the chance to meet him first. It was typical of Julia, he thought, half-fondly: she was enthusiastic about everything.

"But he hasn't met me yet," Bruce pointed out. "I'm not sure if one can like somebody without meeting him first."

Julia laughed. "But Daddy does," she said. "I tell him all the things you say, and he says: 'Seems pretty sound to me.' So, you see, he knows you quite well already."

"Oh well," said Bruce. "I look forward to meeting him too. He sounds a nice guy, your old man."

"Oh, he is," said Julia. "He's so kind too. He's always been kind."

Bruce was curious about Julia's mother. She had never mentioned her, as he could recall, and he wondered if there was some difficulty there.

"And your mother, Julia? Is she . . . ?"

Julia looked down at the floor. "She's dead, I'm afraid. Or we think she's dead."

Bruce was puzzled. "You don't know?"

"Well, it was fairly awful," said Julia. "They went to the Iguazu Falls in South America. They didn't take me—I was quite young then, and I was left with my aunt in Drymen. You know, right on Loch Lomond. And . . ."

"Nice place," said Bruce.

"Yes," said Julia. "But they were in Argentina, you see, and . . ." She broke off.

"Oh well," said Bruce.

Julia said nothing, and Bruce shifted in his chair. Something had obviously happened at the Iguazu Falls, but perhaps it was better not to go there, he thought, in the metaphorical sense, of course. One could always go to the Iguazu Falls but not . . .

Julia interrupted his train of thought. "I don't really like to talk about it," she said.

"No," said Bruce. "But I'm really looking forward to meeting your father. I really am."

"I'm so pleased, Brucie," she said. "Just the four of us."

Bruce looked up sharply. "Four?"

Julia's eyes widened. "Did I say four? Four? I meant three, of course. Daddy, me, daddy. That's three. That's what I meant."

Bruce frowned. "You counted your father twice," he said. "You mentioned two daddies. You did."

Julia was becoming flustered. "Oh, Brucie, you're getting me all mixed up. What I meant was you, me, and Daddy. That makes three."

"I see."

"And I'm going to cook something really nice," she said. "And you'll have the chance to chat with Daddy."

"About?" asked Bruce casually.

"Anything," said Julia. "Rugby. Business. Politics. Anything you like. He's very easy. In fact, you could talk to him about property things. You know a lot about that, being a surveyor and all. Daddy has quite a bit of commercial property."

Bruce hesitated a moment. "Commercial property?"

"Yes," said Julia. "You know those shops in Queensferry Street? He has quite a few there. And George Street too. He has some there."

"Interesting," said Bruce.

"Not to me," Julia said. "I find all that talk of square metres and rents and stuff like that really boring." She paused. "Anyway, I'm really glad that you and Daddy are going to get on so well. And now I'm going to go and start to get things ready."

She left Bruce and went into the kitchen. He stood up and walked to the window of the flat, looking down onto Howe Street. He was very comfortable here, and Julia was not all that bad; if she went on, one could simply turn off and let it all wash over. And she was certainly attractive in her dim, rather vacuous sort of way. In fact, she was a real head-turner, now that one came to think of it, and there would be no shame involved in walking into a wine bar with her. A wine bar . . .

There were wine bars in George Street, and she had said that her father had commercial property there. It would be interesting if it turned out that he owned a wine bar. Very interesting.

80. Julia's Father Comes Straight to the Point

Julia ushered her father into the flat. "Every time I come here," said Graeme Donald, "I find myself thinking—they really understood the need for space, those Georgians. I was in one of those new flats the other day—you know those ones down the road there. Tiny. And quite a price, too. Ridiculously expensive."

He was a tall, well-built man with an air of easy self-assurance about him. He kissed his daughter on the cheek, almost absentmindedly, and cast a glance towards the open door of the drawing room. "In there?" he whispered. "This young man of yours?"

Julia nodded. "Yes. And you will do what we discussed? Is that all right, Daddy?"

He looked at her. "Is that what you want? Are you sure he's the one? Because there'll be plenty of time to be sorry if . . ."

"Believe me, Daddy. We just click. He's lovely."

He closed his eyes briefly. "Anything that makes my girl happy. Anything."

Julia took him gently by the arm. "Just make sure that he won't say no," she said, her voice still low.

"Well, as long as he's reasonably well-disposed, then I think I can make things attractive enough for him."

"Good."

They entered the drawing room, where Bruce was sitting by the window. As they entered, he rose and crossed the floor to shake hands with Graeme.

"So you're Bruce." Graeme took Bruce's hand and shook it warmly.

"Sir."

"Please call me Graeme."

Julia moved to Bruce's side and linked her arm in his. "You two will have lots to talk about," she said, gazing at Bruce. "Daddy, Bruce used to be a surveyor."

"Macauley Holmes etc.," said Bruce.

Graeme nodded. "Good firm. I've had dealings with them. Nice chaps, the Todds."

"Yes," said Bruce, less than enthusiastically.

"Why did you leave?" asked Graeme.

Bruce's answer came readily. "Challenge," he said. "I needed to get my teeth into something new."

Graeme nodded appreciatively. "Always a good idea."

There was silence for a moment. Then Bruce spoke. "You're in commercial property yourself, Julia tells me."

"Yes," said Graeme. "Mostly here in Edinburgh. Shops. I prefer them to offices, you know. I felt that you're more at the mercy of the economy if you have office space on your hands. But if you have retail property in a good area, then there's always somebody prepared to take on a lease. Or that's

394

what I've found. The triumph of hope over commercial experience."

Bruce laughed. "George Street?" he asked. "Julia said something about George Street."

Graeme nodded. "I have a wine bar there," he said. "You may know it."

Bruce did know it. It was one of the more fashionable wine bars. He and Julia had been there together and she had said something about her father, but he had paid no attention.

"A great bar," said Bruce. "It must do very well."

"It could do better," said Graeme. "I need to get somebody to take it in hand. Somebody who . . ." He trailed off. He was watching Bruce, and he saw the slight movement of the brows. I can see what she sees in him, Graeme thought. And what a relief, with all that riff-raff around these days; at long last she's come up with a young man about whom I can be enthusiastic; somebody who shares my values. Bit dim, I suspect, but obviously capable of producing grandchildren, and nothing in the least artistic about him, thank heavens, unlike the last one: talk about barking up the wrong tree with him! No, she's quite right; this is more like it.

He looked at Bruce. "Would you mind if I had a frank talk with you?" he asked suddenly. "I've never been one to beat about the bush—I don't see the point. Man to man. Much better."

Bruce froze. She's told him, he thought. She's gone and told him.

"You see," said Graeme, "we're not a big family. I lost my wife, as you may know, some time ago."

Bruce thought of Julia's mother, lost at the Iguazu Falls. He nodded.

"And so I'm very close to Julia," Graeme went on. "And the one thing I want is her happiness. That means more to me than anything. Can you understand that?"

Bruce nodded. This was going to be very embarrassing.

"So if there's a young man who's keen to marry her," said Graeme, "then that young man . . ." he paused for a moment, fixing him with a direct stare, "whoever he might turn out to be, will find himself very . . . how should I put it? . . . very well provided for. In fact, he would find himself in the business, as a director. And Julia, of course, would end up with a very nice share of the business, too— the whole lot, eventually. For instance, that wine bar in George Street. The young man would probably rather like being the . . . being the owner of that. And there are two parking garages that go with it, you know. He would need somewhere to park the little run-about that would go with the job. Not that a Porsche needs all that much space, of course!"

For a few moments, there was complete silence, at least in the drawing room. In the kitchen, there was the sound of a mixer whirring and then a metal spoon scraping against the side of a pot.

Bruce had been taken aback by the directness of the approach, but at least Graeme had made his position clear. And why shouldn't he? Bruce asked himself. He was making an offer, and what point was there in making the offer less than clear?

Bruce did a rapid calculation. A wine bar in George Street would be worth well over a million. And that was without the other things that Graeme had hinted at. Life was a battle, Bruce thought, and here was he with nothing very much to show for the last six years. Look at Neil in that flat in Comely Bank, stuck there for the foreseeable future, struggling to make ends meet on what was probably a perfectly good salary. How long would that mortgage be? Twenty-five years? Anything would be better than that, anything.

He looked at Graeme, who was smiling at him nervously. "You . . . you've spelled it out," said Bruce. "Nobody could excuse you of . . ."

"Being oversubtle?" supplied Graeme.

"Well . . ." said Bruce.

Graeme raised a hand. "Julia seems very fond of you."

"And I'm fond of her," Bruce said, which he was, in a way. He was reasonably fond of her, for all her . . . all her empty-headedness. No. Time to call it quits. Every bachelor has to face it, he thought. And this was, after all, a magnificent landing.

"All right, if I have your permission," said Bruce, "I'd like to ask Julia to marry me."

"You have it," said Graeme quickly. He reached out for Bruce's hand and shook it. "I think she'll be very pleased."

"Good," said Bruce. "I'll . . ."

"Go through now," said Graeme. "Go and speak to her. I'll stay here. But you go and pop the question." He paused, rubbing his hands together. "And tell me, when's the happy day to be?"

"The wedding? Well, I don't know . . ."

"No, not that," said Graeme. "You know what I mean."

81. A Clean Break—
Not Without an Argument

On the day on which Bruce's situation became so dramatically better, Matthew, whose long-term prospects had improved markedly on his meeting with Miss Harmony, now faced short-term discomfort in his relationship with Pat. He had decided to make a clean break with Pat even before he had so fortuitously met Elspeth Harmony, so nobody could accuse him of trading one woman for another. But even if he had not been disloyal, he still felt uncomfortable about the actual process of ending the relationship. On several occasions, he had rehearsed what he would say, trying various scripts, fretting over the degree to which each might be thought either too heartless or too ambivalent. Nothing sounded quite right.

And when the time came, it sounded flat, sounded phoney. "Pat," he began. "You and I need to talk."

She looked up from a letter which she was in the process of opening. "Talk? All right. But about what?"

"Us," said Matthew. "That is, you. Me. Us, as a . . . a couple."

She saw that he was blushing, and this worried her. She had hoped that he would have forgotten what he had said that evening, at the Duke of Johannesburg's party, but he evidently had not. Oh dear, she thought, I'm going to have to hurt his feelings. Poor Matthew! And he's wearing his distressed-oatmeal sweater too.

"Yes," Matthew went on, averting his gaze. "I've been having a serious think about us, and I think that we need to go back to being friends. Just friends. You know that I'm very fond of you, you know that. But I think that we're in different places. We have different plans. I want to settle down and you . . . you, quite rightly, don't really want that, do you? You're younger. It's natural."

Pat listened attentively. Her reaction was one of immense relief, but she did not want Matthew to see that. She hoped that she sounded sufficiently concerned.

"Are you sure?" she asked.

"Yes, I think so."

She sighed. "You've been very kind to me, Matthew. And always thoughtful."

Matthew blushed.

"But you're probably right," Pat went on quickly. "You need something I can't give you."

"I'm glad you understand." He paused. "So you're not too upset?"

"No . . . I mean of course I'm sorry, but I'll get over it. And I really think it's for the best."

His relief was palpable. It had been far easier than he had imagined.

"And I hope that you find somebody else, Matthew. I really hope that. You deserve somebody nice, somebody who wants what you want." She looked at him. Poor Matthew. He would find it hard to get somebody else.

Matthew hesitated. He had not been sure whether he should mention Elspeth to her, but now it struck him that it would be almost dishonest not to do so, now that she had mentioned the possibility. "In actual fact," he ventured, "I've met somebody. Just a few days ago."

Pat gave a start. "You've met another girl?"

"Yes. She's a teacher. She came into the gallery, and, well, it just happened. We fell for each other."

Pat said nothing for a moment. For each other? Or was it more a case of Matthew doing the falling? The problem, she thought, was that nobody would fall for Matthew just like that. He was very kind; he was very gentle; but he was not the sort for whom women fell—they simply did not. The thought was a disloyal one, and she tried to put it out of her mind. So she asked Matthew who she was.

"She's older than you are," said Matthew. "She's about my age, or even a year or two older. I don't know exactly. And she's called Elspeth Harmony."

Pat nodded. "Go on."

"Well, I don't really know too much about her," Matthew continued. "Except that she likes china. I bought her a Meissen figure, in fact. From The Thrie Estaits down the road."

Pat stared at him. "You bought her a Meissen figure?"

"Yes. She loved it. And it was really special."

Pat's voice was now considerably quieter. "And me?" she asked. "What did you ever buy me?"

Matthew was taken aback by this question. "Look," he said, "I didn't know we counted presents."

"No, we don't," she said. "But if I did count . . . well, it wouldn't come to much. It would come to nothing, actually."

"Don't be ridiculous . . ."

"Oh, you think that's ridiculous?" There was new spirit in her voice. "I'm being ridiculous in thinking that it's a bit strange that you know her for—how long?—two days, and you buy her a Meissen figure. You know me for over a year, two years really, and you buy me nothing. Nothing.

When's my birthday, Matthew? Go on, tell me when my birthday is."

"You mean you've forgotten?"

"Don't try to be funny," she said, her voice now raised. "You can't pull it off, Matthew. Sitting there in that beige sweater, trying to be funny."

"It's not beige," said Matthew sharply. "It's distressed oatmeal."

"Distressed oatmeal!" Pat countered. "Distressed beige. That's your trouble, Matthew. I'm sorry, but your clothes . . ." she paused, seeming to search for the right term. "Your clothes, Matthew, are tragic, really tragic."

Matthew looked away. "You think I'm tragic, do you?"

Pat did not think about what she was saying. But she was smarting over the question of presents. "Yes, I do. And she must be really tragic, this Elspeth Meissen."

"She's not called Meissen," he said. "The figure was Meissen. And if I'm tragic, then what does that make you? The girlfriend of a tragedy?"

"That's really childish!"

Neither said anything. Both were surprised by the sudden exchange of insults. And both regretted it. Suddenly, Pat reached out and put her hand on Matthew's arm. "I'm sorry," she said. "We're being really silly about this. It's my fault."

Matthew turned and gave her hand an affectionate squeeze. "No, it's mine. And I'm sorry too."

Pat smiled. "I'll never say anything like that to you again. I promise."

"Me too," Matthew responded. "And I'd like to give you something to . . . to make up for my insensitivity."

He rose to his feet and looked about the gallery. On the wall opposite him was a painting that Pat had admired. He walked across the room and took it off the wall. He gave it to her.

She said, "This is far too expensive. You can't give this to me."

He shook his head. "Yes I can. I want you to have it."

She took the painting from him. It was heavier than she had imagined it would be—heavy in its expansive gilt frame. Guilt frame, she thought, his—or mine?

82. A Shopping Trip for a Special Dinner Date

When Matthew locked up the gallery and went out onto Dundas Street that evening, he felt almost light-headed with relief. He had dreaded the break-up with Pat. He had imagined that there would be recriminations, threats, tears, and there had been none of that, unless, of course, one counted the brief and really rather silly exchange over beige and distressed oatmeal. And one should not really make much of such an adolescent flare-up, in

403

which nothing really hurtful was said, and which led, anyway, to immediate apologies.

After Matthew had given Pat the painting—which was a rather nice little Stanley Spencer watercolour, a generous present by any standards—they had finished their conversation with what Matthew described as housekeeping matters.

Pat should not feel that she should give up her part-time job at the gallery; that position had nothing to do with their relationship, and he did not think it would be at all difficult for them to continue to see one another as colleagues and friends. Pat agreed, but thought that she would consider it anyway. Her university work was becoming more pressing, and she was not sure how much time she could devote to working in the gallery. But if she did find that she had to give the job up, or do fewer hours, she had a friend in the same degree course who was currently doing bar work and who would love to have a change. Matthew thanked her for this. "You've never let me down," he said. "Never."

With that disposed of, the rest of the morning had passed in amicable companionship, with only the occasional reference to their new situation.

"You'll find somebody else," said Matthew at one point. "There are plenty of boys. Plenty."

"Not all of them are nice," said Pat. "In fact, some of them are really awful."

Matthew nodded. "Wolf, for example."

Pat said nothing.

"And others," said Matthew quickly. "But there are some nice ones. And you'll meet them, I'm sure."

"I don't know if I want to," said Pat. "I think I might have a boy-free time for a while. It's nice to be single, you know. It's . . . it's uncluttered."

Matthew was not so certain about that. He had endured long periods of being uncluttered, and, on balance, he preferred to be cluttered. He thought of Elspeth Harmony. He would see her that night—he had asked her to have dinner with him and she had agreed. He would cook something special—he had a new risotto recipe that he had mastered and he would give her that. And champagne? Or would that be a little bit too much? Yes, it would. Perhaps they would have a New Zealand white instead. Or something from Western Australia. Margaret River, perhaps.

And what would he wear? That was more difficult, as he obviously could not wear his distressed-oatmeal sweater—not after those remarks that Pat had made. It was not beige! It was not! But there was no point in going over that—it was obvious that distressed oatmeal was not a colour of which every woman approved, and in that case he would wear . . .

"Pat," he said. "What should I wear? I mean, what should I wear for special occasions?"

She guessed at what he was talking about. "For

when you're seeing what's-her-name? Elspeth Harm . . ."

"Harmony."

"Yes, her. Well, let me see. Don't think that . . ."

"I won't wear my sweater. Don't worry."

"Good. Well, look, Matthew. You have to decide what your colour is. Then go for that. Build around it."

Matthew looked interested. "Build around my colour?"

Pat looked at him intensely. "Yes. And your colour, I would have thought is . . . ultramarine."

Matthew stared at her. "As in Vermeer?"

"Yes," said Pat. "Do you know how Vermeer got that lovely shade of blue? By crushing lapis lazuli."

"Of course I knew that," said Matthew.

"And that's why there's that terrific light in his pictures. The girl with the pearl earring, for instance. That blue in her headscarf."

"Do you think I should wear that exact blue?"

Pat nodded. "I think so. But you shouldn't wear everything in that blue, of course. Maybe a shirt in that blue and then get some trousers which are . . . well, maybe blackish, but not pure black. Charcoal. That's it. Charcoal trousers, Matthew, and an ultramarine shirt."

"And a tie?"

"No, definitely not. Just the shirt, with the top button undone. And don't, whatever you do, have a

406

button-down collar. Just have it normal. Try to be normal, Matthew."

Pat went off to the university at lunchtime, leaving Matthew to spend the afternoon in the gallery by himself. He closed early, and made his way up to Stewart Christie in Queen Street. The window was full of brown and green clothes—a hacking jacket, an olive-green overcoat with corduroy elbow patches, green kilt hose—but they were able to produce several blue shirts which struck Matthew as being close to ultramarine. He chose two of these, along with a pair of charcoal trousers and several pairs of Argyle socks, which he needed anyway. Then he made his way down Albany Place, crossed Heriot Row, and was in India Street, where his flat was.

India Street was, in Matthew's view, the most appealing street in the New Town. If he thought of the streets in the immediate vicinity, each of them had slight drawbacks, some of which it was difficult to put one's finger on, an elusive matter of feng shui, perhaps, those almost indefinable factors of light or orientation that can make the difference between the presence or absence of architectural blessedness. This, he thought as he walked down his side of the street, is where I want to live—and I am living there. I am a fortunate man.

And he discovered, as he thought of his good fortune, that what he wanted to do more than anything else was to share it. In recent days, he had given two valuable gifts, and the act of giving had filled him with pleasure. Now he would give more; he would sweep Elspeth Harmony up, celebrate her, take her from whatever place she now lived in, and offer her his flat in India Street, his fortune, himself, everything.

He looked at the parcel he was carrying, the parcel in which the ultramarine shirt and the charcoal trousers were wrapped. He saw himself in this new garb, opening the door to Elspeth Harmony, ushering her into the flat. In the background, the enticing smell of cooking and music. I have to get this right, he thought. If this doesn't work, then there's no hope for me.

He climbed the stairs to his front door and let himself in. On the hall table, a red light blinked insistently from the telephone: somebody had left a message.

He dropped the parcel and pressed the button to play the message. It will be from her, he thought.

It was.

83. The Matthew He Wanted Her to Know

Matthew listened to the message left for him by Elspeth Harmony. In the rather sparsely furnished hall of his flat in India Street, the recorded voice, with its clear diction—it was, after all, the voice of a teacher—echoed in the emptiness. And it seemed to Matthew that the chambers of the heart were themselves empty, desolate, now without hope.

"I'm really very sorry," Elspeth began. "It was very sweet of you to ask me to dinner, but I can't make it after all. I'm a bit upset about something and I don't feel that I would be very good company. I'm so sorry. Maybe some other time."

He played the message through and the machine automatically went on to the next message, which was from a company that had tried to deliver something and could not. The company spoke in injured tones, as if it expected that people should always be in to receive its parcels. Matthew ignored that message; his thoughts were on what Elspeth had said. Women had all sorts of excuses to get out of an unwanted date: family issues—my mother's in town—I'd much prefer to be seeing you, but you know how it is. And then: I've had a headache since lunchtime and I think I should just get an early night, so sorry. He listened again to what Elspeth had to say. There was no doubt that the tone was sincere, and from that Matthew took a few scraps of comfort. This was not a diplomatic excuse concealing a simple reluctance to have dinner with him; this was the voice of somebody who was clearly upset, and for good reason.

He switched off the machine and stood up from the crouching position in which he had been listening to the message. How he reacted to this would, he thought, determine whether he saw Elspeth again. If he did nothing, then she might think that he simply did not care; if, on the other hand, he tried to persuade her to come, in spite of everything—whatever everything was—then he might appear equally selfish. He decided to call her.

As the telephone rang at the other end, Matthew tried to imagine the scene. Her address was on the other side of town, in a street sandwiched between Sciennes and Newington, and he thought of her flat, with its modest brass plate on the door, HARMONY, and its window box with a small display of nasturtiums. Or was that mere romanticism? No, he thought, it is not. Her name is Harmony, and there's no reason why she should not have a window box with nasturtiums, none at all.

"Elspeth Harmony."

The voice was quiet, the tones those of one who had been thinking of something else when the telephone had rung.

"It's Matthew here. I got your message. Are you all right?"

There was a momentary pause. Then: "Yes, I'm all right. But I'm sorry about tonight. I just couldn't face it."

Matthew's heart sank. Perhaps it had just been a lame excuse after all. "Oh," he said. "But . . ."

Elspeth interrupted him. "It's nothing to do with you. Please don't think that."

He imagined her sitting in a chair in the kitchen, looking out at the nasturtiums.

"Has something happened?"

"Yes," she said. And then, after a momentary hesitation, "I've lost my job. Or rather, I'm about to lose my job."

Matthew gasped.

"Yes," Elspeth went on. "There was an incident at the school yesterday and . . . and, well, I'm afraid that I've been suspended, pending an inquiry. But they think that it might be best for me to go before then. I'm rather upset by this. Teaching, you see, has been my life . . ."

She broke off, and Matthew for a moment thought that she had begun to cry.

"I'd like to come and see you," he said firmly. "If I get a taxi now, I'll be at your place in ten, fifteen minutes."

She sounded tearful. "I don't know. I really don't . . ."

"No, I'll be there," said Matthew. "Ten minutes. Just wait for me."

He put down the receiver and went into his bedroom to change into a new ultramarine shirt. But then he stopped. He looked at the shirt that he had laid on the bed. No, that shirt was not him, that was Pat's idea of what she thought he should be. The real Matthew, the one that wanted to go and help Elspeth Harmony in whatever distress she was suffering, was not the Matthew of ultra-marine shirts and charcoal trousers; it was the Matthew of distressed-oatmeal sweaters

411

and crushed-strawberry trousers; that was who he was, and that was the person whom he wished Elspeth Harmony to know.

The taxi arrived promptly, and Matthew gave the driver instructions. They travelled in silence and, in the light traffic, they were there in little more than ten minutes.

"Number eighteen?" asked the driver, as they entered the small cul-de-sac. "I had an aunt who lived at number eight. Dead now, of course, but she used to make terrific scones. We used to go there for tea as children. There were always scones. And she made us kids eat up. Come on now, plenty more scones. Come on!"

Matthew smiled. There used to always be scones. The taxi driver was much older, but even Matthew's Scotland had changed since his own childhood, not all that many years ago. Things like that were less common—aunts who made scones. There were career aunts now, who had no time to bake scones.

They stopped outside number 18 and he looked up towards the third floor, where Elspeth Harmony lived. There were window boxes at two of the windows and a small splash of red. Nasturtiums. He smiled.

She let him in, and he could tell that she had been crying. He moved forward and put an arm around her shoulder.

"You mustn't cry," he said. "You mustn't."

"I feel so stupid," she said. "I feel that I've let everyone down."

"Tell me exactly what happened," said Matthew.

She told him, and he listened carefully. When she had finished, he shook his head in astonishment. "So all you did was give her a little pinch on the ear?"

Elspeth nodded. "There was really no excuse," she said. "But there are one or two of the children who are seriously provocative. There's a boy called Tofu, who really tries my patience. And then there's Olive, whose ear . . . whose ear I pinched."

"It's entirely understandable," said Matthew. "Teaching is so demanding, and you get so little support. That pinch will have done Olive no harm—probably a lot of good."

"Do you really think so?"

"Yes," said Matthew. But then he went on, rather sadly, "But I suppose that's not the world we live in, with all these regulations and busybodies about." He paused. "I think you've struck a blow for sanity. Or rather, pinched one."

She thought this very funny and laughed.

"I'm rather fed up with teaching anyway," Elspeth said.

Matthew thought: if you married me, then you'd never have to work again. Unless you wanted to, of course.

84. A Tattooed Man Stirs Up a Painful Past

Dr Hugo Fairbairn, author of that seminal work of child psychotherapy, *Shattered to Pieces: Ego Dissolution in a Three-Year-Old Tyrant*, was walking in from his flat in Sciennes, on the south side of Edinburgh, to his consulting rooms in Queen Street. It was as fine a day as Edinburgh had enjoyed for some weeks, with the temperature being sufficiently high to encourage shirt-sleeves, but not so high as to provoke some men to remove their shirts altogether. A few more degrees and that would, of course, happen, and many men who should, out of consideration for others, remain shirted, would strip to the waist, treating passers-by to expanses of flesh that was far from Mediterranean in its appearance, but was pallid and perhaps somewhat less than firm. After all, thought Dr Fairbairn, this was what Auden had described as a beer and potato culture—in contrast to the culture of the Mezzogiorno, which he had then been enjoying; and beer and potatoes led to heaviness, both of the spirit and of the flesh.

Of course, it was not every male who felt inclined to strip down in the better weather; lawyers did not, and for a moment Dr Fairbairn imagined the scene if lawyers, striding up the Mound on their way to court, were to take off their white shirts in the same way as did building workers; such a ridiculous notion, but it did show, he thought, just how firmly we are embedded in social and professional roles. He, naturally enough, did not dress in a manner which in any way showed an acceptance of imposed roles. His blue linen jacket, with matching tie, could have been worn by anybody; it was classless garb of the sort that said nothing about him other than that he liked blue and linen. And that was exactly as Dr Fairbairn wanted it.

He had been looking down at the pavement; now he looked up, to see a young man approaching him, without his shirt. The psychotherapist suppressed a smile: never believe that you will not see something, he thought—because you will. This does not mean that the thing that you think you will not see will crop up—what it does mean is that you may think that you have seen something which you actually have not.

But this young man, walking along the pavement in the slanting morning sun, was real enough, as was the large tattoo on his left shoulder. It was an aggressive-looking tattoo, depicting what appeared to be a mountain lion engaged in mortal combat with what appeared to be a buffalo. Or was it a wildebeest? Dr Fairbairn imagined himself stopping and asking the young man if he could clarify the situation. Is that a wildebeest? One might ask, but such questions could be misinterpreted. As

Dr Fairbairn knew, men could not look too closely at the tattoos of others, without risking misunderstandings. But it was a mistake, he knew, to assume that somebody who provided the canvas for such a scene of combat would have an aggressive personality. This was not the case; a real softie might have a tattoo of a mountain lion for that very reason—he was a real softie.

These reflections made him remember that Wee Fraser, the boy whose analysis he had written about in *Shattered to Pieces*, had a tattoo, even though he was only three years old. He had had inscribed in capital letters across the back of his neck *Made in Scotland*, just below the hairline. When he had first noticed it, Dr Fairbairn had been astonished, and had wondered if somebody had written this in ballpoint ink on the boy's skin, as some form of joke. But closer examination had revealed that it was a real tattoo.

"You have something written on the back of your neck, Fraser," he had said gently. "What is it?"

Fraser had replied in very crude terms, indicating that it was no business of Dr Fairbairn's, using language which nobody would expect so young a child to know; but then, Dr Fairbairn reflected, he would have heard these words on the BBC, and so perhaps it was inevitable. And some people had always wanted their children to speak BBC English and were now getting their wish fulfilled in this unusual way.

"You mustn't talk like that, Fraser," he said. "Those are bad words. Bad!"

At the end of the session, Fraser's father, a fireman, had appeared to collect his son and Dr Fairbairn had taken the opportunity to ask why Fraser had *Made in Scotland* tattooed on the back of his neck.

"Because he was," said the father simply, and had winked at the psychotherapist.

That encounter was never mentioned in *Shattered to Pieces*. Nor was that fateful occasion on which Dr Fairbairn had smacked Wee Fraser after the boy had bitten him, an episode which Dr Fairbairn had attempted to forget, but which kept coming back to haunt him, reminding him of his weakness. Indeed, the memory came back to him now, as he walked past the tattooed man, but he put it out of his mind, muttering, "We do not go back to the painful past."

Dr Fairbairn was looking forward to the day ahead. He had a few hours to himself at the beginning, which would provide an opportunity to deal with correspondence and to do some further work on a paper that he was preparing for a conference, in collaboration with a well-known child psychotherapist from Buenos Aires. The conference was to be held in Florence, and for a moment he reflected on how pleasant it would be to be in Florence again, enjoying the always very generous hospitality of the Italian Association for Child Psychotherapy, an association whose corpulent president placed great emphasis on the importance of elaborate conference dinners and a good cultural programme. At the last such conference, when Dr Fairbairn had given his paper on early manifestations of the Oedipus complex, the delegates had been taken to a restaurant on the banks of the Arno where, as the sun set, they had been treated to a chocolate pudding borne in on a trolley, the pudding being in the shape of Vesuvius (the chef was a Neapolitan). The pudding's very shape had been enough to draw gasps of admiration from those present, which turned to exclamations of surprise when fireworks within the chocolate crater had erupted into incandescent flows of sparks, like bright jets of lava, like tiny exhalations of fiery gold.

85. A Dangerous Turn in the Conversation

Dr Fairbairn was pleased with the amount of work he had got through by the time Irene arrived in his consulting rooms at eleven o'clock.

"I have had a very satisfactory morning, so far," he said, as he ushered her into the room. Then he thought that the words "so far" might suggest that the morning was about to change, which had not been the meaning he had intended to convey. So he quickly added: "Not that I'm suggesting the tenor of the day will change because of your arrival. *Au contraire.*"

Irene waved a hand airily. "I did not interpret it in

that way at all," she said. "Have you been seeing patients?"

Dr Fairbairn waited until Irene had sat herself down before he continued. "No, not at all. I'm working on a paper, long-distance, with Ettore Esteves Balado," he said. "He's an Argentine I met on the circuit, and we found ourselves interested in much the same area. We're writing on the Lacanian perspective on transference." He paused, smiling at Irene. "And it's going very well. We're practically finished."

Irene looked at his blue linen jacket. Linen was such a difficult material, with its propensity to crumple. She had a white linen blouse with a matching skirt which she loved to wear, but which crumpled so quickly that after five or ten minutes she looked like, well, Stuart had put it rather tactlessly, like a handkerchief that had been left out in the rain. It was an odd analogy, that, and she wondered what the Lacanian interpretation might be. We did not choose our words simply for their expressive power; our words were the manifestation of the conflicts of our unconscious, indeed, they themselves formed the unconscious itself. Lacan had made that quite clear, and Irene was inclined to agree. She did not think that we could find a stable unconscious; our unconscious was really a stream of interactions between words that we used to express our desires and conflicts.

So when Stuart had made those remarks about a

handkerchief in the rain, he did not mean that her linen outfit was a handkerchief left out in the rain, or indeed even looked like one. What his words revealed was that he feared disorder (or rain) and that he wanted her, Irene, to be perfect, to be ironed. And that, of course, suggested that he looked to her for stability to control his sense of impermanence and flux, his confusion. No surprises there, she thought: of course he did. Stuart might have many good points, but in Irene's view, strength—what people called backbone, or even bottom—was not Stuart's strong suit. Mind you, it was strange that people should use the word "bottom" for strength or courage. What was the Lacanian significance of that?

Her eyes returned to Dr Fairbairn's blue linen jacket. He had said something, she recalled, about the combination of fibres in the jacket, and that must be the reason it looked so uncrumpled. The question in her mind, though, was: at what point did the insertion of other fibres deprive the material of the qualities of real linen? If it was merely a treatment of the linen, then that was one thing; if, however, it involved polyester or something of that sort, could one still call it linen?

Dr Fairbairn, aware of her gaze, fingered the cuff of his sleeve self-consciously. "I'll give you a copy of the paper," he said. "When it's finished. I know of your interest in these things."

"Argentina?" said Irene.

"Yes, Buenos Aires. My friend Ettore is one of their best-known analysts there. He has a very extensive practice."

Irene nodded. She had heard that there were more psychoanalysts in Buenos Aires than anywhere else in the world, but was not sure why this should be. It seemed strange to her that a country associated with gauchos and pampas should also have all those analysts. She asked Dr Fairbairn why.

"Ah!" he said. "That is the question for Argentine analysts. They're immensely fortunate, you know. Everyone, or virtually everyone, in Buenos Aires is undergoing analysis. It's very common indeed."

"Surprising," said Irene. "Mind you, the Argentine psyche is perhaps a bit . . ."

"Fractured," said Dr Fairbairn. "They're a very charming people, but they have a somewhat confused history. They go in for dreams, the South Americans. Look at Peronism. What did it mean? Evita? Who was she?"

For a moment, they were both silent. Then he continued. "I think the reason Freud is so popular in Argentina is, like most of these things, explained by a series of coincidences. It just so happened that at the time that Freudian ideas were becoming popular in Europe, the Argentine public was in a receptive mood for scientific ideas. You must remember that Argentina in the twenties and thirties was a very fashionable place."

"Oh yes," said Irene. She was not going to let

him think that she knew nothing about all that. "The tango . . ."

"Hah!" said Dr Fairbairn. "The tango was actually invented by a Uruguayan. The Argentines claimed him, but he was born in Uruguay."

"Oh."

"But no matter," he went on. "The point is that *La Jornada*, one of the most popular newspapers in Buenos Aires, actually started a daily psychoanalytical column in the early thirties. It appeared under the byline 'Freudiano,' and readers were invited to send in their dreams for analysis by Freudiano. The paper then told them what the dreams revealed—all in Freudian terms."

"But what a brilliant idea!" said Irene. "Perhaps *The Scotsman* could do that."

"Are we not perhaps a little too inhibited in Scotland?" asked Dr Fairbairn.

"But that's exactly the problem," said Irene heatedly. "If we were to . . . to open up a bit, then we would all become so much more . . ."

Dr Fairbairn waited. "Like the Argentines?" he ventured.

Irene laughed. "I'm not sure," she said. "They've had a tendency to go in for dictators, haven't they?"

"Father figures," said Dr Fairbairn.

"And generals too," added Irene.

"Military figures," said Dr Fairbairn.

"But they do dance so marvellously," mused

Irene. "And there's something deeply appealing about a Latin American type. They're so tactile."

Dr Fairbairn watched her. This conversation was fascinating, but it was straying into dangerous territory. He should bring it back to the topic in hand, which was not the history of Freudian theory in Buenos Aires, nor Latin American sultriness, but Bertie. How was Bertie doing? And, in particular, how was he getting on with his new brother, Ulysses? But that triggered another thought in his mind: where exactly was Ulysses? He asked the question.

86. Bertie and the Baby: an Expert Explanation

"Ulysses is in the waiting room," said Irene. "In his baby buggy. Sound asleep."

"I see," said Dr Fairbairn. "And how is Bertie reacting to him?"

Irene was always ready to see psychological problems, but she had to admit that in his dealing with his brother, Bertie showed very little sign of resentment.

"He's very accepting," she said. "There appears to be no jealousy, although . . ." She hesitated. She had remembered Bertie's comments on the baby that had been mistakenly brought back from the council nursery. That had been slightly worrying.

Dr Fairbairn raised an eyebrow. "Although?"

"Although he did make a curious remark about exchanging Ulysses."

This was greeted with great interest by Dr Fairbairn, who leaned forward, eager to hear more. "Please elucidate," he urged Irene. "Exchange?"

Irene had not intended to discuss the incident in which Ulysses had been parked in his baby buggy outside Valvona & Crolla—she was not sure how well either she or Stuart emerged from that tale—but now she had to explain.

"It was a most unfortunate slip on my husband's part," she said, almost apologetically. "He left Ulysses outside Valvona & Crolla."

"A handbag?" said Dr Fairbairn and smiled; he thought this quite a clever reference and was disappointed when Irene looked at him in puzzlement.

"*The Importance . . .*" he began.

"Of being Ulysses!" capped Irene. She had understood all along of course, and had merely affected puzzlement.

Dr Fairbairn had to acknowledge her victory with a nod of the head. "But, please proceed. What happened?"

"Well, he was found," said Irene. "Somebody must have called the police and they took him off to the council emergency nursery. We went there very quickly, of course, and retrieved Ulysses, or the baby we thought was Ulysses. In fact, it was a girl." She paused. "And unfortunately, Bertie made the discovery. He saw that this baby didn't have . . .

well, he thought that the relevant part had fallen off."

Dr Fairbairn made a quick note on his pad of paper. "That's most unfortunate," he said. "But it clearly reveals castration anxieties. As you know, most boys are worried about that."

"Of course," said Irene. And she wondered for a moment about Stuart.

"And the interesting thing is this," went on Dr Fairbairn. "As you'll recall, one of the main concerns of Freud's famous patient Little Hans was that he would suffer this unfortunate fate through the agency of dray horses." He paused and looked at Irene with bright eyes. "Isn't it extraordinary how real life mimics the classic cases. Don't you agree, Dora?"

Irene frowned. "You called me Dora."

Dr Fairbairn shook his head. "No," he said. "You're mistaken."

"No, you made the mistake. And a classic one, if I may say so. Surely you don't regard me as Dora?"

Dr Fairbairn smiled urbanely. "Of course not. Perish the thought. But I didn't call you Dora, anyway, and so let's return to this issue of baby exchange."

"He suggested that we keep the girl," said Irene. "For some reason, he seemed quite happy that Ulysses had been mislaid."

"Well, there you are," said Dr Fairbairn. "He obviously feels that a girl would be no threat to him in his mother/son relationship with you. He's Oedipus, you see, and you are Jocasta, mother of Oedipus and wife of Laius. Bertie resents his father—obviously—because he, Bertie, wants your unrivalled attention. Ulysses is a rival too, and that's why Bertie secretly wishes that Ulysses did not possess that which marks him out as a boy.

"When he saw that the baby whom he took to be Ulysses did not have that, then it was the fulfilment of his wildest dream. Now there was no danger for him—and that, you see, is why he would have wanted to keep the other baby."

Irene had to agree with the perspicacity of this analysis. He was really very clever, she thought, this doctor in his crumple-free blue linen jacket; so unlike virtually all other men she had ever met. Men were such a disappointing group, on the whole; so out of touch with their feminine side, so rooted in the dull practicalities of life; and yet here was Dr Fairbairn, who just understood.

She sighed. Stuart would never understand. He knew nothing of psychodynamics; he knew nothing of the unconscious; he knew nothing, really.

"Of course," she said suddenly. "There's always Ulysses."

Dr Fairbairn said nothing. He picked up his pen and stroked it gently. "Oh yes?" he said noncommittedly.

"Ulysses will have identity conflicts, will he not? When he's old enough to question who he is?"

"We all wonder who we are," said Dr Fairbairn distantly. "Who doesn't?"

"So Ulysses will look at his family and think: who are these people? Who's my mother, who's my brother, who's . . ." She broke off. She had almost said "Who's my father?" but decided not to.

Dr Fairbairn was staring down at his desk. Then he looked at his watch. "Gracious! Is that the time?" He looked up. "I have somebody coming, I'm afraid. Is there anything else you need to tell me about Bertie before I see him tomorrow?"

There was. "He's had a bit of trauma at school," said Irene. "That will probably come out. His class teacher has been suspended, and he'll no doubt lose her. She pinched one of the girls. A nice child called Olive."

"Goodness me!" said Dr Fairbairn.

"Yes," Irene continued, "I heard about it from Bertie, and of course I had to raise it with the school."

"You reported it?"

"Yes," said Irene. "I couldn't stand by."

He thought for a moment. "But Bertie was very fond of that teacher, wasn't he? He always spoke so warmly of her. Don't you think that he might blame you for the fact that he's losing her?"

Irene was silent.

Dr Fairbairn, realising that Irene seemed unwilling to pursue the matter, gave a shrug. "No matter. These losses are an inevitable part of life.

We lose so much, and all we can hope is that our separation anxiety is kept within reasonable bounds. I have lost so much. You, no doubt, have done so too."

He looked out of the window. He was a lonely man, and he only wanted to help others. He wanted to help them to recover a bit of what they had lost, and it gave him great pleasure when he did that; it was like making something whole again, mending a broken object. Each of us, you see, has a secret Eden, which we feel has been lost. If we can find it again, we will be happy, but Edens are not easily regained, no matter how hard we look, no matter how desperately we want to find them.

87. A Fantasy Sail on
That Slow Boat to China

The break-up with Matthew was a great relief to Pat. She had been worried by Matthew's completely unexpected proposal at the Duke of Johannesburg's party; she was too young for that, she knew, and yet she was unwilling to hurt Matthew, who was, she also knew, in his turn unwilling to hurt her. She would never settle down with him; she would never settle down with anybody, or at least not just yet. She stopped herself. That was simply untrue. If somebody came who swept her off her feet, who intoxicated her with his appeal, well, it would be very pleasant to settle down with such a person. If one is really in love, really, then the idea of spending all one's time in the company of the person one loves, tucked away somewhere, was surely irresistible. That was the whole point, was it not, about slow boats to China—they provided a lot of time to spend with another. And would she have wanted to get on a slow boat to China with Matthew? The answer was no. Or with Wolf? The thought was in one sense appalling—Wolf was bad—but, but . . .

For a moment, she thought of the cabin on this slow boat, in which she and Wolf were sequestered, and she saw herself and Wolf in this cabin, and there was only a half-light and the engine of the boat was throbbing away in the distance somewhere and it was warm and . . . She stopped herself again. This was a full-blown fantasy, and she wondered if it was a good thing to be walking down one side of George Square, fantasising about a boy such as Wolf, while around her others, whose minds were no doubt on higher things, made their way to and from lectures. Or were they fantasising too?

She had reached the bottom of the west side of George Square, the point where the road dipped down sharply to a row of old stables on one side and Basil Spence's University Library on the other. She had not been paying much attention to her surroundings, and so she was surprised when she found herself drawing abreast of Dr Geoffrey

Fantouse, Reader in the History of Art at the University of Edinburgh, expert in the Quattrocento, and the man whose seminars on aesthetics she attended every Wednesday morning—together with fifteen other students, including Wolf, who sat, smouldering, on the other side of the room and who studiously averted his gaze from hers; as well he might, given his history of deception and attempted seduction.

"Miss Macgregor?"

Pat slowed down. "Dr Fantouse. Sorry, I was thinking. I wasn't looking." And she had been thinking, of course, though he would never guess about what.

Dr Fantouse smiled. "As an aesthetician," he said, "I would be inclined to suggest that one should first look, then think."

Pat thought for a moment. She did not immediately realise that this was a joke, but then she understood that it was, and she laughed politely. Dr Fantouse looked proud, in a modest sort of way.

It was clear that they were both walking in the same direction—across the Meadows, that broad, tree-lined expanse of park that separated the university area from the semi-Gothic nineteenth-century tenements of Marchmont—and so Pat fell into step with the aesthetician.

"You're enjoying the course?" he asked, glancing at her in his mildly apologetic way.

Pat suspected that nobody ever told Dr Fantouse

that his course was enjoyable, and yet she knew how much effort he put into his work. It must be hard, she thought, being Dr Fantouse and being appreciated by nobody.

"I'm really enjoying it," she said. "In fact, it's the best course I've ever done. It really is."

Dr Fantouse beamed with pleasure. "That's very good to hear," he said. "I enjoy it too, you know. There are some very interesting people in the class. Very interesting."

Pat wondered whom he meant. There was a rather outspoken, indeed, opinionated girl from London who was always coming up with views on everything; perhaps he meant her.

"Your views, for example," went on Dr Fantouse. "If I may say so, you always take a very balanced view. I find that admirable." He paused. "And that young man, Wolf. I think that he has a good mind."

Pat found herself blushing. Wolf did not have a good mind; he had a dirty mind, she thought, full of lascivious thoughts . . . like most boys.

Dr Fantouse now changed the subject. "Do you live over there?" he said, pointing towards Marchmont.

"I used to," she said. "Now I live at home. In the Grange." It sounded terribly dull, she thought, but then Dr Fantouse himself was very dull.

"How nice," he said. "Living at home must have its appeal."

They walked on. Dr Fantouse was carrying a

small leather briefcase, and he swung this beside him as he walked, like a metronome.

"My wife always makes tea for me at this hour," said Dr Fantouse. "Would you care to join us? There is usually cake."

Pat hesitated. Had the invitation been extended without any mention of a wife, then she would have said no, but this was very innocent.

"That would be very nice," she said.

Dr Fantouse's house was on Fingal Place, a stone-built terrace which looked out directly onto the footpath that ran along the Meadows. Pat had walked past these houses many times before and had thought how comfortable they looked. They were beautiful, comfortable in their proportions, without that towering Victorianism that set in just a few blocks to the south. That an authority on the Quattrocento should live in one seemed to her to be just right.

The flat was on the first floor, up a stone staircase on the landings of which were dried-flower arrangements. The door, painted red, bore the legend FANTOUSE, which for some reason amused Pat; that name belonged to the Quattrocento, to aesthetics, to the world of academe; it did not belong to the ordinary world of letterboxes and front doors.

They went inside, entering a hall decorated with framed prints of what looked like Italian cities of the Renaissance. A door opened.

"My wife," said Dr Fantouse. "Fiona."

Pat looked at the woman who had entered the hall. She was strikingly beautiful, like a model from a pre-Raphaelite painting. She stepped forward and took Pat's hand, glancing inquiringly at her husband as she did so.

"Miss Macgregor," he explained. "One of my students."

"Pat," said Pat.

Fiona Fantouse drew Pat away into the room behind her. Pat noticed that she was wearing delicately applied eye shadow in light purple, the shade of French lavender.

88. *Some Tea and Decency with the Fantouses*

The sitting room into which Fiona took Pat was an intimate one, but big enough to accommodate a baby grand piano, along with two large mahogany bookcases. The wall behind the piano was painted red and was hung with small paintings—tiny landscapes, miniatures, two silhouetted heads facing one another. A low coffee table dominated the centre of the room, and on this were books and magazines, casually stacked, but arranged in such a way that they did not tower or threaten to topple. A large vaseline glass bowl sat in the middle of the table, and this was filled with those painted wooden balls which Victorians and Edwardians liked to collect. The balls were speckled, like the eggs of some exotic fowl, and seemed to be, like other things in the room, seductively tactile.

Pat noticed that to the side of the room there was a small tea table, covered with a worked-linen tablecloth. On this was a tray, with a Minton teapot and cups and saucers. Then there was a cake—as Dr Fantouse had said there would be—a sponge of some sort, dusted with icing sugar, and a plate of sandwiches—white bread, neatly trimmed.

"We sometimes have people for tea," said Fiona. "And so we keep an extra cup to hand."

She sat herself beside the tea tray and asked Pat how she liked her tea. On the other side of the room, facing them, Dr Fantouse perched on a high-backed chair, smiling at Pat and his wife.

"Miss Macgregor belongs to the coffeehouse generation," he remarked. "Afternoon tea will not be her usual thing. Perhaps you would like coffee?"

"I like tea," said Pat.

"There are so many coffeehouses," said Fiona. "And they are all full of people talking to one another. One wonders what they talk about?"

Both Dr Fantouse and his wife now looked at Pat, as if expecting an answer to what might otherwise have seemed a rhetorical question.

"The usual things," said Pat. "What people normally talk about. Their friends, I suppose. Who's doing what. That sort of thing."

Dr Fantouse smiled at his wife. "More or less

434

what we talk to our friends about," he said. "Nothing has changed, you see."

The two Fantouses looked at one another with what seemed to Pat to be relief. There was silence. Fiona passed Pat a cup of tea and Dr Fantouse rose to his feet to cut slices of cake.

"There's something very calming about tea," remarked Fiona. "I sometimes think that if people drank more tea, they would be calmer."

Pat looked at her. The Fantouses were very calm as it was; was this the effect of tea, or was it something more profound?

Fiona seemed to warm to her theme. "Coffee cultures can be excitable, don't you think?" she said. "Look at the Latins. They never talk about things in a quiet way. It's all so passionate. Look at the difference between Edinburgh and Naples."

There was a further silence. Then Dr Fantouse said, "I don't know. Perhaps we might become a bit more . . ."

All eyes turned to him, but he did not expand on his comment, but lifted a piece of cake and popped it into his mouth. Fiona turned to Pat, as if expecting her to weigh in on her side and confirm the difference between Edinburgh and Naples, but she did not.

Dr Fantouse licked a bit of icing sugar off a finger. "*Un po di musica,* as Lucia would say. Would you care to play, my dear?"

Fiona put down her teacup and smiled at Pat.

"It's something of a ritual," she said. "I usually play for a few minutes after we've finished tea. Do you play yourself? I would be very happy for you to play rather than . . ."

Pat shook her head. "I learned a bit, but never got very far. I'm hopeless."

"Surely not!" said both Fantouses in unison. But they did not put the matter to the test, as Fiona had now crossed the room and seated herself at the keyboard.

"This is the Eriskay Love Lilt," she announced. "In a rather charming arrangement. It was Marjorie Kennedy Fraser, of course, who rescued it. And the words are so poignant, aren't they? *Vair me or ro van o / Vair me o ro ven ee / Vair me or ru o ho /* Sad I am without thee."

Pat found herself watching Dr Fantouse as his wife played. He was watching her hands, as if transfixed. When she reached the end of the piece, he turned to Pat and smiled.

"We could have more," he said, "but we ration ourselves. People have so much music—don't you think?—that they don't bother to listen to half of it. Music should be arresting, should be something which makes one stop and listen. But we're inundated with music. Everywhere we go. People are plugged into their iPods. Music is piped into shops, restaurants, everywhere. A constant barrage of music."

"But you will have more tea?" asked Fiona.

Pat shook her head. "I must get on," she said. "You've been very kind."

"You must come again," said Fiona. "It's been such fun."

"Yes, it has," said Dr Fantouse. "That's the nice thing about Edinburgh. There are so many pleasant surprises."

They saw Pat to the door, where Pat shook hands with both of them. She saw again the delicate eye makeup on Fiona's eyes. Who was it for? she wondered. For Dr Fantouse? Did he notice such things?

As she went downstairs, a boy of about eleven or twelve was coming up. He looked as if he had been playing football, his knees muddied, his hair dishevelled. She looked into his face, a face of freckles, and saw that he had grey eyes. For a moment, both stopped, as if they were about to say something to one another, but then the boy looked away and continued up the stairs. Pat felt uneasy. It was as if she had seen a fox.

She went out into the street and glanced up at the windows of the flat. Dr Fantouse was standing at the window, his wife beside him. They noticed Pat and waved. She waved back and thought: how many people in this city live like that? Or was this a caricature, an echo of what bourgeois Edinburgh once was like but was no more? Or, again, had what she seen that afternoon been simple, quiet decency, nothing more? As she walked up the narrow road that led past the Sick Kids Hospital, she remembered what she had once read somewhere, words of little comfort: for most of us, nothing very much happens; that is our life.

89. *A Peculiar and Yet Harmless Enthusiasm*

"So, Lou," said Robbie Cromach. "Tuesday's your birthday, and you and I are going somewhere special! You choose."

Big Lou smiled at Robbie, her boyfriend of two months, the man whom she felt she knew rather well, but in a curious way did not know at all. He was a thoughtful man, and paid much more attention to Lou's feelings than had any of her previous boyfriends. They had been a disaster—all of them—selfish, exploitative, weak; indeed, one or two of them all of these things at the same time. But Robbie was different; she was sure of that.

"Well, that's really good of you, Robbie," she said. "Only my birthday's on Monday, not Tuesday and . . ."

She did not finish. Robbie was frowning. "Monday . . ." he began.

"Yes. So we'll have no difficulty getting in anywhere."

Robbie was still frowning, and Big Lou realised that he must have something on that evening. She had told him several times that her birthday was on

438

Monday—he had asked her and she had told him. Now it appeared that he had made other arrangements for that night. She sighed, but she was used to this. Big Lou's birthday had never been anybody else's priority in the past, and it looked as if that would not change now; she had thought that it might be different with Robbie, but perhaps it was not.

"You've got something on?" The resignation showed in her voice. "You can't change it?"

Robbie, who had called in on Big Lou's coffee bar to accompany her to her flat on closing time, shifted his weight awkwardly from foot to foot.

"Sorry, Lou," he said. "Monday is a really important evening for me." (And for me? thought Lou.) "I'd love to be able to change it, but I'm afraid I can't." He paused. "But I don't want you to spend your birthday by yourself, Lou. So why don't you come with me? There's an important meeting. Really important."

Big Lou rubbed at the gleaming metal surface of the bar. It would be the Jacobites, she thought: Michael, Heather, and Jimmy, and others no doubt, all equally obsessed, all equally poised on the cusp of delusion. She looked at Robbie, who smiled back at her encouragingly. When you take on a man, thought Big Lou, you take him on with all his baggage. So women had to put up with football and golf and drinking in pubs, and all the things that men tended to do. In her case, she had to take on

Robbie's peculiar historical enthusiasm, which, when one came to think of it, was harmless enough. It was not as if they were some sort of guerrilla movement, dedicated to changing the constitution by force, and prepared to blow people up in the process—these were mild, rather ineffective people (or at least Michael, Heather, and Jimmy were), who hankered after something utterly impossible. And there were plenty of people who harboured unrealistic, unlikely beliefs, who wanted the unattainable in its various forms. There was a saint for them, was there not? Saint Jude, she thought, patron of lost causes and desperate situations.

"All right," she said. "I'll come along. And maybe we could have a late dinner—afterwards. The meeting won't go on forever, will it?"

Robbie's relief was evident. "Of course not. And thank you, Lou. Thank you for being . . . so understanding."

Big Lou smiled. "That's all right," she said. "As long as you're happy, Robbie. That's the important thing."

"I am, Lou. I am."

"But what's the meeting about?" she asked. "Why is it so important?"

Robbie thought for a moment. "Michael asked for it," he said. "He's going to give us the details of the arrival . . ." He broke off, evidently uncertain as to whether or not he should continue.

"Go on," encouraged Big Lou. "The arrival of . . ."

"Of the emissary," said Robbie. "As you know, he's coming very soon. He's coming, Lou!"

Big Lou raised an eyebrow. "This Pretender fellow they were talking about last time?"

"He's not a Pretender, Lou." Robbie's tone was aggrieved, and Big Lou immediately relented. He believed in this.

"Sorry," she said. "I didn't mean to be rude."

"This is serious, Lou," said Robbie. Now he lowered his voice. "This man is a direct descendant, a direct descendant of Prince Charlie himself. And he's coming here to make contact with his people again. He's entrusting us—us, Lou—to look after him. We're going to meet him at Waverley Station and then we're going to have a press conference to introduce him. It's going to be all over the newspapers, Lou. It's going to make people think." He paused. "And I've been asked to take him up to the west."

Robbie waited for a reaction to this, but Lou did not know what to say.

"He wants to follow in the steps of Prince Charlie," Robbie continued. "So I'm going to take him over to South Uist. Then we'll cross over to Skye, just as Prince Charlie did."

Big Lou stared at Robbie. "That means crossing the Minch," she said.

"Aye, it does," said Robbie.

"In a wee boat?"

"I haven't made arrangements yet," said Robbie. "I think that the prince was rowed, wasn't he? Him and Flora MacDonald."

"And you're going to row?"

Robbie shrugged. "Maybe. Maybe we'll have a small outboard motor, something like that."

Big Lou nodded. "The Minch can get pretty wild," she said. "You wouldn't want to sink. Not with a New Pretender on board. That wouldn't look too good, would it?"

Robbie looked at her reproachfully. "I'm serious, Lou. I know that this may not mean much to you, but it means a lot to us. It's a link with our country's past. It's part of our history."

Big Lou was placatory. "I know, Robbie. I know."

"Do you, Lou? Do you? You aren't laughing at me, are you?"

She moved from behind the counter and went to stand beside Robbie. She reached out and put her arms around his shoulders. "I wouldn't laugh at you, Robbie. I'd never laugh at you. You're a good man."

Big Lou was tall, but Robbie was slightly taller. He looked down at her. "I love you a lot, Lou," he said. "I really do. You're kind. You're clever. You're beautiful."

She caught her breath. Nobody had said that to her ever before. Nobody had called her beautiful, and now he had, this man, this man with all his funny notions, he had called her beautiful. So

442

perhaps I am, she thought. Perhaps I've been wrong to think of myself as plain. There is at least one man who thinks otherwise, and that, for many women and certainly for Big Lou, was enough.

90. *A Theme for the Definitive Masterpiece*

For Angus Lordie, the return of Cyril from durance vile had been a transforming event. The sense of emptiness, the listlessness, that had afflicted him during the period of Cyril's absence faded immediately, like a blanketing haar that suddenly lifts to reveal a morning of clarity and splendour. This, he thought, is what it must be like to be given a reprieve, to be told that one was well when one had imagined the worst. Now he had energy.

His first task was to pick up the brush that he had so dispiritedly laid aside. The group portrait over which he had been labouring was finished with alacrity, and the sitters, who had appeared sombre and depressed, were invigorated by a few bold strokes: a smile there, a jaunty dash of colour there—they were easy to rescue. Once that was done, though, there was the question of the next project, and Angus had been giving some thought to that.

The previous night, while taking a bath, it had occurred to him that there was no particular painting to which he could point and say: "That is

443

my masterpiece." Certainly, he had executed some fine paintings—although he was modest, Angus had enough self-knowledge to recognise that—but the best of these was no more than *primus inter pares*. Two of them were in the collection of the Scottish National Gallery of Modern Art, and one of them had gone abroad, to vanish into the private collection of a Singaporean banker—or was it a Singaporean baker? The dealer in Cork Street who had written to tell him of the sale had handwriting which was difficult to interpret, but Angus had hoped that it was a baker rather than a banker. He could imagine his Singaporean baker, a rotund man with that agreeable, genial air that seems to surround those who have made their money in food. He liked to think of him sitting there in his Singaporean fastness, appreciating his painting, nibbling, perhaps, on a plate of pastries.

Of course, Singapore was close to Malacca, where Domenica had conducted her recent researches into the domestic economy of contemporary pirates, and Angus had asked her on her return if she had ventured south.

"I went there for a few days after I left Malacca," she had said. "You'll recall the dénouement of my researches? I felt that after that I should treat myself to a bit of comfort, and so I went to Singapore and stayed in the Raffles Hotel. Such luxury, Angus! The Indian doorman at Raffles has the most wonderful mustache—apparently the most photographed thing in Singapore!"

"There can't be much to see if a mustache is the main attraction," observed Angus.

"Well, it's a small place," said Domenica. "And a big mustache in a small place . . . Mind you, it's getting bigger."

"The mustache?"

Domenica smiled, but only weakly. There was occasionally something of the schoolboy about Angus, at least in his humour. "No, Singapore itself is getting bigger. They have land reclamation projects and they're inching out all the time. Their neighbours don't like it."

Angus was puzzled. "I don't see what that's got to do with them. Presumably they're reclaiming from the sea."

"Yes, they are. But the Indonesians have stopped selling them sand to do the reclamation work. And Malaysia gets jumpy too. They don't like to see Singapore getting any bigger, even if it's just a matter of a few acres."

"Neighbours can be difficult," said Angus.

Domenica thought for a moment of Antonia and the blue Spode cup. There were parallels there, perhaps, with relations between Malaysia and Singapore. "Dear Singapore," she said. "They're frightfully rich, and as a result nobody in Southeast Asia likes them very much. But I do. They make very rude remarks about them; it's

445

very unfair. And Singapore gets a little bit worried and feels that she has to expand her air force. But that leads to problems . . ."

Angus looked at Domenica quizzically.

"They can't really fly very easily," she explained. "Singapore is terribly tiny in territory terms. When the air force takes off, it has to take a sharp right turn or it ends up flying over Malaysian airspace, which they're not allowed to do. So it somewhat hampers their style."

Angus smiled. "I see."

"So they keep the air force elsewhere," went on Domenica.

Angus raised an eyebrow. "One would hope that they don't forget where they put it," he said. "It would be a terrible shame if one put one's air force somewhere and then forgot where it was. I'm always doing that with my keys . . . Easily done."

Domenica laughed again. "I think they have a book in which they write it all down," she said. "Actually, they keep their air force in Australia."

"Well, at least Australia's got the room," said Angus.

Domenica agreed. "Yes, but it's a bit strange, isn't it? Rather like the Bolivians and their navy."

"No sea?"

"Not anymore. And the tragedy is that they really want a navy, the Bolivians, poor dears. They've got a lake, of course, and they keep a few patrol boats on that and on the rivers, but what they want is a pukka navy . . . like the one we used to have before . . . Anyway, Navy Day in Bolivia is the big day, and everybody gives money for the cause. And they have numerous admirals, just like we have now. No ships, alas, but bags of admirals. And then there was the Mongolian navy, of course. They only had one boat and seven sailors, only one of whom could swim!"

"Interesting," Angus began. "But . . ."

"But the point is this: the Uruguayans, to their credit, let the Bolivians keep a real ship in Montevideo. It's rather like the Australians allowing Singapore to keep its air force in Darwin or wherever it is. So kind."

"There's not enough kindness in the world," said Angus.

With that the subject changed, and now Angus remembered it as he went over in his mind possible themes for what he hoped would be his master-piece. Kindness, he thought—there's a subject with which a great painting might properly engage! But how might one portray kindness? There were those Peaceable Kingdom paintings, of course, in which all animal creation stood quietly together—the wolf with the lamb, the lion with the zebra, and so on. But that was not kindness, that was harmony, which was a different thing. Angus wanted to paint something which spoke to that distinct human quality of kindness that, when experienced, was so moving, so reassuring, like balm on a wound, like a gentle hand, helping, tender. That was what he wanted to paint, because he knew that that was what we all wanted to see.

91. Angus Opens His Front Door to . . . Trouble

Angus Lordie was still thinking of kindness, and of the great painting he would execute in order to portray that theme, when the doorbell sounded. Cyril, half-asleep on a rug on the other side of the room, lifted his head and looked at his master. He knew he should bark, but what was the point? Whoever it was on the other side of the door would not be deterred by his barking, and if he continued, and barked more loudly, God (as Cyril thought of Angus) would simply get annoyed with him. So he glanced towards the door, growled briefly, and then lowered his head again.

Angus looked at his watch. It was just before ten in the morning, and he was still seated at the kitchen table, the detritus of his breakfast on the plate before him: a few crumbs of toast, a small piece of bacon rind, a pot of marmalade. He was dressed, of course, but had not yet shaved, and he felt unprepared for company.

He rose to his feet, crossed the hall and opened the front door.

"Mr Lordie?"

There was something familiar about the face of the woman who stood on his doorstep, but he could not place her. There were new neighbours several doors down; was she one of them? No. The Cumberland Bar? No, she was the wrong type. Perhaps she was collecting for the Lifeboats; they had plenty of women like that who raised money for the Lifeboats—so much, in fact, that the Lifeboats were in danger of positively sinking under all their money.

He nodded. "Yes."

The woman's lips were pursed in disapproval. Surely I can go unshaven in my own house, thought Angus. Surely . . .

"You may not recall our meeting some time ago," she said. "It was in the gardens. At night."

Angus smiled. "Of course. Of course." He had no recollection of meeting her, but she was one of the neighbours, he assumed. There would be some issue with the shared gardens; keys or benches or children breaking branches of the rhododendrons.

"Good," said the woman. "So you'll remember that your dog . . . your dog paid attention to my own dog. You'll remember that, then."

It came back. Of course! This was the owner of the bitch whom Cyril had met in the gardens. It had been most embarrassing, but it was hardly his fault—nor Cyril's, for that matter. One could not expect dogs to observe the niceties in these matters when a female dog was in an intriguing condition. Surely this woman . . .

449

"And now," said the woman, staring at Angus, "and now my own dog is experiencing the consequences of your dog's . . . your dog's assault."

Angus stared back at her. Cyril had not assaulted the other dog. They had got on famously, in fact, and this woman must know that.

"But I don't think that my dog . . ." Angus began, to be cut short by the woman, who sighed impatiently.

"My dog is now pregnant," said the woman. "And your dog is responsible for it. There are six, the vet says."

"Six?"

"Six puppies, Mr Lordie. Yes, the vet has performed an ultrasound examination of Pearly, my dog, and has found six puppies."

Angus swallowed. "Well, well. That really is . . ."

"Most unfortunate," snapped the woman. "That's what it is. There are six puppies for whom I cannot be responsible. I live in a small flat and I cannot keep seven dogs. Which means that you are going to have to shoulder your responsibilities."

For a few moments, Angus said nothing. He did not doubt that the puppies were there, and that Cyril was the father, but was he really responsible for them? He knew all about the Dangerous Dogs Act (after Cyril's unfortunate brush with the law), but were the laws of paternity and aliment of puppies the same as those that applied to humans? Surely not.

The woman broke the silence. "And so what I'm proposing to do is to pass the puppies on to you the moment they are ready to leave their mother. That will be . . ." She consulted a small red diary which she had taken out of her handbag, and gave a date. "I take it that that will be convenient."

Angus stared at her in astonishment. "No," he said. "We can't have six puppies here. This is . . . this is my studio as well as my flat. I simply can't have six puppies."

"You should have thought of that before you allowed your dog to . . . to approach my dog," said the woman. "You should have thought of the consequences of your dog's actions."

Angus felt a wave of annoyance come over him. He had been polite to this woman, but she had been hectoring and imperious. Had she spoken to him courteously and sought his assistance, he might have made some proposals about sharing the care of the puppies until they were found a new home, but she had not done that, and now he felt like digging in.

"I'm sorry," he said. "From my point of view, you took the risk when you took a bitch in heat out into the gardens. You should have known better. You cannot blame my dog for behaving as he did. In fact, you should count yourself lucky that the puppies will have good blood. Cyril, I would have you know, is a pedigree dog, while yours, if I may say so, is undoubtedly a mongrel of some sort. Cyril lowered himself when he consorted with her . . ."

"How dare you!" hissed the woman. "You . . . you impossible man!" She paused, as if to summon up further insults, but there were none; instead: "The puppies will be brought on the appointed day. I shall leave them at the bottom of the stairs, in a box, if you are not in. And that is all there is to it."

She turned round and began to walk down the stairs. Angus watched her for a moment. He wanted to call out, to shout out some final, resounding comment that would stop her in her tracks, but he did not. He was incapable of being rude, just as his father before him, and his grand-father, had been incapable of rudeness, particularly towards a woman. So he closed the door behind him and went back into the flat.

Cyril watched him. He knew, in some extraordi-nary, nonconceptual way, that the events at the door concerned him. But what had he done wrong? He could think of nothing. All he had ever done was to be a dog, which deserved no blame—and perhaps no praise either. But the ways of the gods were arbitrary, as in Greece of old, and the manner in which Angus was looking at him now made Cyril realise that this was serious—extremely so.

92. A New Version of the Fateful Olive Incident

When it was announced to the class that Miss Harmony was to be replaced, there was a sudden, shocked silence. For a few minutes, the children were left alone, waiting for the arrival of the new teacher, and it was in this period that recriminations were fervently aired.

"Somebody told on her," said Tofu. "Somebody's mummy went and complained because she had heard about Miss Harmony's act of self-defence."

People reacted in different ways to this. For his part, Bertie froze. He had an inkling of the fact that it was his mother who was responsible for the downfall of Miss Harmony, but he had no intention of revealing this.

"Not my mother," he said, in a small voice.

Everybody looked at him, and he blushed. He was a truthful boy and he would not normally tell a lie, but, in this case, he felt he could say what he said because he had no actual proof that Irene had been the cause of Miss Harmony's departure. Moreover, on a strict construction, all he had said was "Not my mother," which was a sentence capable of many interpretations. "Not my mother" could mean: May misfortune strike others, but not my mother (the first phrase being understood). Or it could be a general denial of maternity; there were many senses in which the statement could be read. So it was not really a lie.

"Nobody said it was her," said Larch suspiciously. "Although . . ." He left the rest of the sentence unfinished, and Bertie quaked.

"Bertie only said that because he knows that everybody hates his mother," said Tofu kindly. "Isn't that so, Bertie?"

Bertie swallowed. "Well . . ." He trailed off. They knew what his mother was like—there was no point in trying to hide it, but did they actually hate her?

Tofu's pronouncement evoked a very different reaction in Olive. "Self-defence?" she said, glowering at Tofu. "What do you mean by self-defence, Tofu?"

"I meant what I said," retorted Tofu hotly. "Miss Harmony only pinched your ear because you were threatening her. I saw you. I saw you try to scratch her. And I'm going to tell everybody. I'm going to tell the other teachers."

Olive's eyes opened wide in outrage. "Scratch her? I never did. You're a liar, Tofu! Everybody knows what lies you tell. Nobody will believe a liar like you."

"I will," said Larch. "I'll tell them that Tofu's telling the truth. I'll tell them that you had your hands round Miss Harmony's neck and that she had to pinch you to bring you to your senses."

"Precisely," said Tofu. "And Bertie will say the

same thing. And Lakshmi. And everybody, in fact, because everybody knows how horrid you are, and they'll blame you when Miss Harmony commits suicide. In fact, she's probably done that already. That's what people do when they're falsely accused of things."

"Yes," said Larch. "She's probably climbing up the Scott Monument right now . . ." He leaned forward and pointed an accusing finger at Olive. "And it'll be your fault, Olive! Your fault!"

Olive opened her mouth to say something, but was prevented from doing so by Tofu. "So," he said, "we have to find out who told on Miss Harmony and we have to get that person to say that it was all made up and that it was self-defence, as I've said."

"And then we'll get Miss Harmony back," said Pansy. "Because she was the nicest teacher we could ever hope to get. She was kind, and she liked all of us."

"Except Olive," said Tofu. "She knew what Olive was like. That's why she pinched her."

"I thought you said it was self-defence," crowed Olive. "Now you're saying it was because she hated me."

"Both," snapped Tofu. "She hated you and she had to defend herself. Both are true."

The argument might have continued had it not been for the arrival of the new teacher, a man in his midtwenties, who walked into the classroom and

455

stood smiling at the top of the class. He introduced himself as Mr Bing.

"I'm your new teacher," he said, "now that Miss Harmony . . ."

"Is dead," supplied Tofu.

"Oh no," said Mr Bing. "Miss Harmony's not dead! Where on earth did you get that idea? She's just reassessing her career. People often do that, boys and girls—they have another look at what they're doing and decide whether they aren't better off doing something quite different. That's all."

"But did she want to reassess her career?" asked Tofu. "Or was she forced to go because she had to defend herself against Olive?"

Mr Bing frowned. "I'm not sure that I understand you . . . what's your name, by the way?"

"Tofu."

Mr Bing hesitated for a moment. "Well, Tofu," he said, "it's possible that Miss Harmony might have become a little bit stressed. And it's possible that she might have done something a little bit impulsive."

"It was self-defence," said Tofu, looking around the class for support. "Olive tried to strangle her, and it was the only way in which she could calm her down. She gave her a little pinch to get her to loosen her grasp round her neck. That's true, isn't it, everybody?"

A chorus of support was raised.

"Yes," said Larch, his face contorted into an

expression of sincerity. "She's quite dangerous, Mr Bing. We all know that. But Miss Harmony still wants to protect her, and so she probably didn't say anything about Olive trying to strangle her. Miss Harmony is so kind, you see. If somebody tries to strangle her she never says anything about it."

Mr Bing seemed flustered. "Well, we might talk about this later," he said. "For the time being, I should like to get to know you all. So what we're going to do is to write a little piece about ourselves—just a page or so. And then we'll put our names on top of that, and in that way I'll know all about each of you! Now isn't that a good idea?"

"Some people can't write yet," said Larch. "Olive can't."

"No," said Tofu. "She's illiterate, Mr Bing."

Olive glared at Tofu, but was steadfastly ignored.

"Well," said Mr Bing. "In that case, those who can write will write, and those who can't can draw pictures for me! How about that? They can draw pictures of themselves and of their favourite things to do."

"How do you draw fibs?" asked Tofu. "Because Olive will have to draw them."

"Now Tofu," scolded Mr Bing. "We mustn't say such things. What you've just said about Olive creates negative karma. But I'm sure that you didn't mean it, and so we'll move on and start our little project. I'll give you each a bit of paper and you can get down to work. What fun we shall all have!"

457

93. *The World of Bertie—in His Own Words*

Giving the tip of his pencil a lick for good luck, Bertie began to write:

The world according to Bertie.

My name is Bertie Pollock, and I'm a boy. I live in Scotland Street, which is a place in Edinburgh. Our house is at No. 44, which is easy to remember. It is hard to get lost in Scotland Street, because it just goes up and down and you can see each end if you stand in the middle. I have a brother called Ulysses, who is very small and can't talk or think yet. My Daddy's name is Stuart, and he works for the Scottish Executive, where he makes up numbers. I think that he is very good at that because he has been promoted and given more money.

My Mummy's name is Irene. She is quite tall and she talks more than Daddy, who sometimes tries to say something but is told not to say it by Mummy. Mummy has a friend called Dr Fairbairn, who is mad. He wears a blue jacket which Mummy says is made of stuff called linen. Dr Fairbairn lives in Queen Street. Most people have a living room, but he has a waiting room. He keeps copies of a magazine called *Scottish Field* in his waiting room so that people can read it before they go in to talk to him. I like reading *Scottish Field* because it has pictures of dogs and castles in it, and also pictures of people having fun. Often I see a picture of Mr Roddy Martine in it and also Mr Charlie Maclean. They go to parties and have lots of fun. I am not sure what they do apart from having fun, but I still think that they are quite busy.

Dr Fairbairn does not have much fun. I think that this is because he knows that they are going to send him to Carstairs one day. That is where they send all the really dangerous mad people. I think that they have booked a place for him there, but he is not ready to go just yet. Mummy will probably visit him there because she likes talking to him and she will miss him when he gets sent to Carstairs.

When she is not talking to Dr Fairbairn, Mummy likes going to the floatarium in Stockbridge. That is where she floats, in a special tank that makes you feel as if you are lying down on top of something. Mummy took Dr Fairbairn to the floatarium one day to show him how to float. I think that the tank is big enough for two people. Dr Fairbairn liked it because he seemed much more cheerful afterwards and did not just talk about inkblots and dreams. Mummy said I should not tell Daddy about how we took Dr Fairbairn to the floatarium, as that would make Daddy want to go too and he would not like floating as much as Dr Fairbairn liked it. Mummy said that Daddy is happier with sums and numbers and that is the best thing for him to do.

My brother Ulysses looks just like Dr Fairbairn, but I do not think that he is mad like him. My friend Tofu tells me that there are lots of mad babies in

Carstairs and that they have special padded playpens for them. I am not sure if this is true, because Tofu tells a lot of fibs and you never know when he is fibbing. One day his pants will go on fire and that will serve him right for all those fibs he has told.

We do not have any pets. I would like to have a dog, and a cat too. I would also like a rabbit and a hedgehog. Mummy says that all of these things are smelly and are best left in the wild. She says that dogs are really wolves and would be happier in the forest. She said that cats hate people and are spiteful too. She says that rabbits are an evolutionary mistake and that hedgehogs have lots of fleas. So I am not allowed to have any of these animals.

There is a dog who lives in Drummond Place. He belongs to a man called Mr Lordie, who paints pictures and who smells of turpentine. The dog is really nice. He is called Cyril and he has a gold tooth. When he opens his mouth to stick out his tongue you can see the gold tooth inside. He is a very smiley dog and everybody in Scotland Street, where I live, likes him, except for Mummy, because Cyril bit her when she called him bad and smelly. He was arrested for biting other people, but it was not him, and they got him out of the pound before they shot him. Now he is back and can go to the Cumberland Bar again. That is where people go to drink beer in the evenings. You cannot go there unless you are eighteen. There is a different rule for dogs. Dogs can go there even if they are only one.

When I am eighteen I am going to go to live in Glasgow or Australia, or maybe Paris, where I have already been. Once I went to Glasgow and I met a very fat man there called Mr O'Connor. Mr O'Connor eats deep-fried Mars bars and is very proud of Glasgow. Mummy did not like him when he came to see us, but my Daddy likes him, a bit.

That is everything about me. I am happy with my life except for some things. I do not want to have anymore psychotherapy and I do not want to go to yoga anymore. I would like to go out with my Dad more and I would like Olive not to come and play at my house. I would like to have some nice friends, nicer than Tofu, and I would like to make a fort in the gardens with these friends. I would also like to go fishing with my friends, on a boat, but I cannot do that now because I do not have a boat and I do not have those friends yet.

I think the world is nice. I think that it is very sad that there are people who are unkind to one another. I also think that it is sad that there are people who want to kill other people just because they do not like them. I think that we should share things, and not be selfish, like Tofu.

Miss Harmony was a very kind teacher. We all loved her and she was very kind to us. I hope that wherever she is she is happy. I want her to come back, though. I want things to be the same again and for everybody to be happy. That is what I want.

Bertie Pollock (6).

461

94. Some Battles Are Destined to Be Lost

Domenica had arranged to meet her old friend Dilly Emslie for coffee in the Patisserie Florentin in North West Circus Place. They had last met shortly after Domenica's return from the Malacca Straits, and Domenica had given Dilly an account of her anthropological research project among contemporary pirates—a project that had ultimately led to the discovery that the pirates stole intellectual property rather than anything else. Dilly had greeted this news with some relief; it was she who had encouraged Domenica to take on a new piece of research in the first place, although she had not envisaged that she would choose to work among pirates. Had Domenica come to an unfortunate end, she would have felt a certain responsibility, and so now, if Domenica again showed signs of itchy feet, she would certainly not give her any encouragement.

The two old friends had much to discuss.

"I take it that everybody behaved themselves while I was off in the Malacca Straits," said Domenica, as she contemplated a small Italian biscuit that had been placed on the side of her plate.

"I'm afraid so," said Dilly. "Or if they didn't, then word hasn't reached me yet."

Domenica sighed. "So disappointing. That's Edinburgh's one, tiny little fault: most people behave rather well."

"On the surface," said Dilly, smiling. "But there are some people who are still capable of surprising one."

"Next door, for example," said Domenica. "My erstwhile friend, Antonia—she of the work-in-progress on the lives of the Scottish saints, and, incidentally, the person who removed a blue Spode teacup from my flat, but that's another story—she has just finished an affair with a Polish builder, would you believe it? A man who had only one word of English, and that was 'brick.'"

"The strong and almost silent type," said Dilly.

Domenica laughed. "Yes, but it's over now, and she's decided to look for a better sort of man. Where she'll find somebody like that, I have no idea, but hope springs eternal. Meanwhile, she continues to write about her saints.

"A very popular field at the moment," she went on. "Do you know that Roger Collins is writing a great work on the lives of the popes? He's got quite far with it. I had tea with Judith McClure and she showed me the new study they've built. There are two desks in it—one for Judith and one for Roger, with a rather comfortable-looking chair that Roger can swing round in while he's writing about popes."

"This city, taking a broad view of its boundaries, is becoming very productive," said Dilly. "Roger Collins and his book on popes. And Allan Massie, with those marvellous historical novels of his.

Even if the Borders claim him he's almost Edinburgh. And . . ."

"Ian Rankin writing all about criminal goings-on," interjected Domenica. "Such an active imagination, and a very fine writer too. And then there's Irvine Welsh, with his vivid dialogue!"

"Quite an impressive range," said Dilly.

Domenica nodded. "And that's only mentioning the books that make it into print. Imagine all the others. On which subject, do take a look at Stuart Kelly's *Book of Lost Books*—it's all about books that people have talked about but which were never really written or have been lost. Great missing masterpieces. Books that never were, but which may still contribute to their authors' reputations!"

They moved on. Had Domenica seen the latest article by Lynne Truss?

"A real heroine," Domenica said.

"Yes," said Dilly. "But I can't help but feel that she's fighting a losing battle. The other day I saw an article about grammatical mistakes that had two grammatical mistakes in it. And these weren't the examples—they were in the text itself."

"Of course, language changes," said Domenica. "And how do we decide what's correct? What did Professor Pinker say about the songs of the whales?"

"Oh, I think I remember that," said Dilly. "Didn't he say that it would be nonsensical to point out that the whales made mistakes in their songs? That whale songs were what whales sang?"

"Something like that," said Domenica. "He implied that grammatical rules should merely reflect the language that people used, because that's where they came from in the first place."

Dilly smiled. "So they weren't handed down on tablets of stone? No Académie Française?"

"No. So if you were to ask me how I was, I suppose I could now reply either 'Fine,' which is what I'd actually say, as would you, or 'Good,' which is what lots of other people now say. They say: 'I'm good.'" Domenica paused before continuing. "And I always think: how immodest! Because good is a moral quality when used without a noun."

"There are some battles which are destined to be lost," said Dilly.

Domenica lifted up her biscuit, examined it, and popped it into her mouth. "You're right. And I suppose that if we don't have an Académie Française to authorise words we must rely on what happens in the street, so to speak. Mind you, not all new words come into existence like that. Some new words are really very clever. Somebody must have made them up."

Dilly thought for a moment. "Like *Robinsonade*. Do you know what that is? No? It's a word for a book which deals with people being taken out of their normal surroundings and dumped somewhere where they have to struggle to survive. It comes from Robinson Crusoe. So *Lord of the Flies* is a Robinsonade."

They sipped at their coffee. "Well, words aren't the only things that change," Domenica went on. "Look at Edinburgh. What used to be a prim, maiden aunt of a city is now something quite different. Should we embrace these changes?"

"If they're for the better," said Dilly. "And lots of them are, surely?"

Domenica looked wistful. "Yes, some are. But I'm not sure if all of them are. I'm not sure if I think that crudity of language and attitude are things that we should embrace with enthusiasm. You know, I went to a Burns Supper a couple of years ago and I had to sit through a tirade against men from one of the speakers—a very aggressive performance. The speaker thought it appropriate to speak like that at a celebration of Burns' birthday. But I found myself wondering: why is it considered smart to be crude and combative?"

"There are quite a lot of people like that," said Dilly.

They were both silent for a while. The sun came in through a high window, slanting. There was the smell of olive oil, of freshly baked bread; there was the murmur of conversation at a nearby table. For a brief moment, Domenica closed her eyes and imagined a parallel Scotland, one of kindness and courtesy, where the vulgarity of our age had no place, other than a shameful one. Was it wrong to dream of such a thing? Or was it just "uncool"?

95. *Faster and Yet Faster—with a Surge of Panic*

Matthew knew that he was moving too quickly, but he was like a man driving a car down a very steep hill; there were brakes, of course, but the car itself wanted to go faster and faster. He knew that what he should do with Elspeth Harmony was to get to know her better and then, if he was still sure that she was the right person, he could suggest whatever it was that he wanted to suggest. And what he wanted to suggest was marriage—just that. Matthew was now over twenty-eight. In fact, he was twenty-nine and would be thirty on his next birthday. Thirty!

People, or some people, would begin to look at him with something approaching pity. He would begin to get better insurance rates and he could start going on those overthirty holidays that he had seen advertised. The advertisements, of course, did not say anything about a top age limit—all they said was that the holidays were for those over thirty, and that meant, he realised, that he might find himself on holiday with people of forty or even fifty!

No, he would have to do something about finding somebody, and that is exactly what he had done. He had not looked for Elspeth—she had just turned up, on his doorstep, or the doorstep of his gallery, and they had immediately taken to one another.

And now all he wanted to do was to make sure that she would stay with him and that she would move in to India Street. They would become a couple—a couple!—and they would build up a bank of memories, of things they had done together, places they had been. They would travel. They would go to Barbados, to the Seychelles, to India. They would take photographs of one another riding camels and sitting on a houseboat in the backwaters of Kerala while the sun went down and birds flocked to the trees. They would lie on a beach in Thailand, on Ko Samui, and listen to the waves. All this lay ahead, and Matthew wanted it to start as soon as possible.

His visit to Elspeth Harmony's flat was going well enough. She was distraught over her suspension from the school, but he was succeeding in getting her to see the positive side of this.

"Look on it as a career change," he said. "Lots of people have them. And everybody says that it's a good thing."

She thought about this for a moment. "But I haven't got another career to go to," she said. "And do you think anyone will give a job to somebody who's been fired? Do you think that?"

"Not fired," said Matthew. "You can resign before they fire you. You can resign right now."

"But everybody will know that I've only resigned because I was about to get fired," she pointed out. "You know what this town's like. Everybody knows everybody else."

Matthew decided that it was time to be more direct. "So what if they know?" he said. "I know, and I'm still going to offer you a job."

She stared at him in surprise.

"Yes," he said. "You can have a job in my gallery. Straightaway. You can start tomorrow, if you like." He paused. "Not that you'd have to do any work. Not real work. All you'd have to do is look after the gallery sometimes—when I go to auctions or to meet a client. Things like that."

"But I don't know anything about art," she protested. "Nothing at all."

Matthew was about to say: "And nor do I," but did not. Instead, he said, "That doesn't matter. You can learn as you go along. You can read Duncan Macmillan's book on Scottish art. There's lots of information there. And you'll pick it up. But you really don't need to bother."

Elspeth laughed. "This sounds like a most peculiar job," she said. "I have no qualifications for it, and I won't have to do much work. Will it be paid? Or will it be one of these jobs where you have to pay yourself to do it?"

"It'll be paid," said Matthew eagerly. "And the pay is really, really good."

She hesitated. She did not want to ask what the salary was, but this was such a peculiar situation that she might as well. "How much?" she inquired.

Matthew shrugged; he had not thought about the

salary. "Oh, about . . ." He waved a hand in the air. "About sixty thousand a year."

Elspeth said nothing for a moment. Then, her voice quiet: "I really don't think we should talk about this anymore," she said. "It's very kind of you, but . . ."

Matthew felt a surge of panic. I'm going to lose her, he thought. I've mishandled this. She thinks that I'm trying to . . . to buy her!

He knew that he had to act, or he would have a lifetime to regret not acting. "Elspeth," he said earnestly. "I may as well tell you that the job . . . Well, you can have the job of course, if you want it, but what I'm really talking about is something quite different. I want to ask you something, and I want you to know that whatever I've said up until now doesn't count for anything. But what I'm about to say to you now, well, I really do mean it. I want to ask you if you will marry me. That's all. I know that we hardly know one another, I know that, but I feel that you and I are . . . well, I just think that it feels right. It feels so right that I want you to know everything that I'm thinking, and it would be dishonest to pretend that I'm not thinking this. I want you to marry me. Please. Please. I really mean it."

She said nothing for a few moments, but she was thinking, quickly. Nobody had ever asked Elspeth Harmony to marry him before. And she wanted to get married. She wanted to have a husband and

470

children of her own. She liked Matthew; she liked him a great deal. Liking can become love. In fact, it had just done precisely that. Right then. She loved him.

"I'll marry you," she said. "Yes, I'll marry you." But then she thought: I should check up on one thing first.

"Would you want a family?" she asked. "Children?"

"Hundreds," said Matthew. "Or at least four or five."

"But we probably wouldn't be able to afford that many," she said, smiling at his enthusiasm.

Matthew watched her as she spoke. Perhaps he should tell her. He did not want to tell her before she had said yes, but now he felt that he could.

96. Bruce Samples the Porsche Experience

On the day that Matthew proposed—success-fully—to Elspeth Harmony, Bruce went to see a motor dealer. The dealer knew Bruce's future father-in-law and had received a call from him several days earlier on the subject of Bruce's car; instructions were given, and the dealer in due course telephoned Bruce to arrange the appointment.

For Bruce, this was the first result of the agreement he had reached with Graeme Donald following their meeting over dinner in Julia's flat. Bruce had been surprised by the directness with which the older man had spoken. There had been no beating about the bush, no tactful references to vague possibilities: it had all been spelled out in the most unambiguous terms. Graeme Donald would see to it that his daughter's husband would be well looked after.

There would be an engagement, followed by a wedding, and once that was over, then the real benefits would begin to flow. Nothing could be simpler.

The car, which went with the soon-to-be-assumed directorship of the holding company (that would be put into effect after the wedding), would be an earnest of things to come, and, besides, with Bruce shortly assuming operational responsibility for the wine bar in George Street, transport would be necessary. So the call to the dealer was made.

The dealer, who operated from a small showroom in Morningside, was of course a freemason, and was a member of the same lodge as Graeme.

"Julia's young man is not in the craft yet," said Graeme. "But that will be arranged soon enough. I think he's sound enough."

As it happened, the dealer was not listening when Graeme said this, with the result that when Bruce arrived at his garage, he gave him a warm and prolonged handshake, in the course of which, using his thumb, he firmly pressed Bruce's middle knuckle. At the same time, the dealer kept his heels together and the toes of his shoes out, thus forming an angle of exactly ninety degrees with his feet. This is what is known as being on the square and is a sure sign of masonic status.

When Bruce felt his knuckles being pressed in this peculiar fashion, he misunderstood the signal. Of course these chaps go for me, he thought. Quite understandable, but he would have to give a signal that he played for the other team.

"My girlfriend couldn't come with me," said Bruce, repeating, for emphasis, "Girlfriend."

The dealer smiled. "We're better off without them," he said, meaning, of course, that in his view the choosing of cars was really a male matter, best done by men.

They moved on to the cars. "I have four Porsches in stock," said the dealer. "All of them low mileage. Would you like to take a look?"

Bruce nodded, and was shown over to the first of the Porsches, a silver model, a low-slung, sneaky-looking car.

"Great cars," said Bruce.

"They go from nought to sixty like that," said the dealer, snapping his fingers. "This one here is a 911 Turbo." He patted the top of the car. "You'll be wondering about the difference between it and the GT3? A few facts and figures?"

"Great," said Bruce, bending down to look in the window.

"Maximum Torque (Nm) at rpm in the Turbo is

620 Nm (with overboot to 680 Nm)," the dealer began. He paused, while Bruce absorbed this information. "Whereas, with the GT3—and that red car over there, that's a GT3—the max torque is 405 Nm. Also," and here he raised a finger, "also, there's a different compression ratio. 9.0:1 in the Turbo, and 12.0:1 in the GT3. Mind you, there's a bottom line."

"There always is," said Bruce.

"Yes," said the dealer. "The bottom line is this: the maximum speed in each case is 193 mph. Tops. That's the max."

Bruce looked thoughtful. "Not bad," he said.

The dealer nodded. "Dr Porsche is working on pushing that up a bit, but for the time being, 193 mph it is."

Bruce opened the door of the silver car and slid into the driver's seat. He held the leather-covered steering wheel and gazed at the array of instruments. This was very good. At 193 miles per hour, it would take him how long to reach Glasgow from Edinburgh? That was about three miles a minute, which meant that one would divide forty by three, to get just over thirteen. So he could reach Glasgow in fourteen minutes!

Bruce looked up at the dealer, who was standing by the door, looking down on him, smiling. "Could we take this for a test drive?" he asked.

The dealer nodded. "Of course. If you hold on a moment, I'll get the key."

Bruce moved his hands gently up and down the steering wheel and then felt the gear lever. The head of the lever was covered with leather and silver, with a little Porsche symbol on the top. The dealer came back, lowered himself into the passenger seat and passed the keys over to Bruce. "It's all yours," he said.

Bruce switched on the engine and listened appreciatively to the throaty roar which resulted. "You can get that sound as a ring-tone for your mobile phone," said the dealer. "That's what I have on my own phone."

"Great," said Bruce.

"All right," said the dealer. "Let's take her out."

The silver car slipped out onto the road outside the showroom. Bruce felt the power of the engine as he pressed down on the accelerator, a strong, throbbing feeling, as if there were something live within the machine, some great, stirring creature. He pressed the accelerator down farther, and the roar, and the power, grew.

They soon found themselves up in the Braids, where the comparatively empty roads allowed Bruce to increase his speed. This was heady, intoxicating.

"Feel the G-forces!" said Bruce, giving the engine its head for a few seconds.

"Serious," said the dealer. "Really serious G-forces."

They turned round, the car engine making a

satisfactory growl even at idling speed. Then they drove back to the showroom.

"Fantastic," said Bruce. "That's the one."

The salesman looked awkward, and Bruce frowned. Had he already sold that model—in which case, what was the point of letting him take the vehicle out for a test drive?

"Well, actually," the dealer began, "your father-in-law, if I may call him that, has already chosen something for you."

Bruce looked puzzled. "Chosen?"

"Yes," said the dealer. "You're to get a GT3, I'm afraid. The red one over there."

Bruce bit his lip. "Then why let me drive the Turbo?"

The dealer smiled. "I wanted you to have the best Porsche experience you could," he said. "And that's with the Turbo. But the GT3 is still a great car."

Bruce turned away. It had suddenly occurred to him that he was walking into something for which he might not have bargained. Trapped, he thought; I'm trapped. But was it better, he wondered, to be trapped with a Porsche or not trapped without a Porsche?

The former, he decided.

97. Do We Have to Love Our Neighbour?

Domenica Macdonald looked at her watch. Five o'clock in the afternoon. As Lorca observed, she thought, at that terrible five in the afternoon. *A las cinco de la tarde.* It was five in the afternoon by all the clocks, said Lorca. And five sounded so sinister, so final (in spite of the existence of six o'clock). Three-thirty had no such associations. Somehow, it did not seem quite so sombre, so tragic, to say: it was at three-thirty in the afternoon. Ah, that terrible three-thirty in the afternoon! Three o'clock seemed somehow more innocent, less brooding, than five, as Rupert Brooke sensed when he referred to the church clock standing at ten-to-three. Nothing ominous happened at ten-to-three, as opposed to five minutes to midnight (a dreadful, worrying time) or, of course, five in the afternoon.

She looked out of her window onto Scotland Street, where the evening shadows were beginning to lengthen. It was a fine evening, something for which she was grateful, as she had chosen it for the dinner party she had long been planning to mark her safe return from the Malacca Straits, back to Edinburgh, into the bosom of the New Town and those who made up her circle of friends. She remembered how, before she had left for Malaysia, she had been joined in this very room by those self-same friends. She remembered how

Angus had made a speech, as he always did on such occasions, and how his speech—which was quite touching—had modulated into a poem about small places, as she recalled. The poem had said something about being grateful for the small scale, for the local, for the minor things that gave meaning to life. And Angus was right: these things were being forgotten in the headlong rush into globalisation, which drained identity out of life, rendered it distant, impersonal. Thank heavens, thought Domenica, for the Royal Bank of Scotland, which still had people round the corner to whom one could speak on the telephone, unlike others, who put one through to India, or Sri Lanka, or even Wales. That was a good object lesson for the rest: the Royal Bank of Scotland was a global bank, but they still knew how important it was to remain rooted. That made Domenica proud. People made a big fuss about sporting heroes— some of whom were pretty ghastly, she thought— but nobody seemed to make a fuss of bankers. And yet they did great things and made piles of money. The big challenge, though, was to get them to share it . . . and also to make sure that they were nice to people with overdrafts.

Domenica herself had no overdraft, but she suspected that virtually everybody else had one. An overdraft was a rite of passage, in a sense; one went from pocket-money as a child straight into the world of overdraft as a student. And many people remained there, never graduating to the really adult phase when their bank account was in credit. Anthropology had paid little attention to this, she reflected. There were plenty of studies on debt bondage patterns elsewhere, but few, if any, on such bondage in urban Western societies. In some countries, one might be reduced to virtual slavery, saddled with debts incurred by one's grandfather, and labouring endlessly just to pay the interest. But here, for many, the sentence was not all that dissimilar, even if the debt was not inherited.

She thought about her friends and wondered how many of them lived on an overdraft. Angus Lordie, she thought, was one. His finances were a closed book to her; she knew that he received commissions for portraits, but these were sporadic, and she doubted if he made a great deal from them. Angus occasionally painted opulent people, and charged accordingly, but his strong democratic instincts, so deeply rooted in the Scottish psyche, also inclined him to paint those whose pockets were not so deep, indeed were shallow, or had large holes in them; these people he painted for nothing, or next to nothing. Which was wonderful, thought Domenica, and meant that the future record of what Scottish people looked like would be a far more balanced one than the record we had from the past, when artists painted only the wealthy. So we know what rich faces looked like in those days, but we had little idea of what the features of the indigent were like. No, that, she decided, was nonsense, but it had been an interesting thought.

Yet how did Angus survive? Of course he had relatively few outgoings, as he appeared to eat very little, probably rather less than that dog of his. And his studio was really rather cold most of the time, which suggested that he did not have large gas bills. So perhaps he was all right after all, and she need not worry. Of course it was tempting to speculate on the personal finances of others—what greater pleasure is there than to see somebody else's bank statement, a guilty pleasure of course, and a furtive one, but tremendously interesting? But it was not a healthy thing to do, and Domenica decided that if she saw Angus Lordie's bank statement lying around, she would fold it up and return it to him, without looking. Or perhaps without looking a great deal.

But for this evening, as she stared out at Scotland Street, at the sun on the tops of the roofs, so beautiful, so beguiling, she reflected that she had spared no expense, or trouble, in preparing the meal for her friends. With their pre-dinner drink they would have Spanish olives from Hasta Mañana in Bruntsfield, generous olives the size of small ping-pong balls.

Then they would sit down to table, to a salmon timbale made with smoked salmon from the smokehouse in Dunbar, followed by a venison cassoulet, and finally a sort of apple tart which she had constructed and covered with strips of pastry in Celtic designs (a touch of which she felt inordinately proud).

She looked at her watch again. Twenty minutes had passed in reverie, and it was time to get things ready. She hesitated. She had not invited Antonia, and now she felt the first twinges of guilt; perhaps she should go and ask her right now, at the last moment. But do we really have to love our neighbour? she wondered. Really?

Domenica looked out of the window again. The sky was clear, with just the slightest trace of cloud, high, attenuated, so delicate. And the answer came to her quite clearly: yes, we do. Thus do epiphanies come in Scotland Street, as elsewhere in Edinburgh, across the tops of roofs, from an empty sky, when the city's fragile beauty can touch the heart so profoundly, so unexpectedly.

98. The Domenica Connection Becomes Clear

"Olives!" said Angus Lordie, reaching out to the bowl which Domenica had placed on the table. "Yes," said Domenica. "For you—and others. So please don't eat them all. Exercise restraint if you can, Angus."

Angus gave her a reproachful look—as if he, of all people, with his ascetic attitudes—would exercise anything but restraint. But if he looked reproachful he did not feel it; quite the opposite in fact: Angus liked to be told off by Domenica, and the more she scolded him, the more he liked it. What a masterful woman, he thought, so calm, so assured; so much like . . . Mother. The realisation came to him quite suddenly. Domenica was his mother. That was why he liked her; that was why he did not mind being told what to do and what not to do, especially at the table. Now it was olives; all those years ago it had been soor plooms that the late Patricia Lordie, wife of Fitzroy Lordie, innovative agriculturist and pioneering figure in the Perthshire soft-fruit industry, told her son Angus not to eat in excess; but the tone, and the authority, was much the same. Women are here to tell us what to do, thought Angus; that is why they are here, and we are here to do their bidding.

Angus looked at Domenica with moist, admiring eyes. How comfortable it would be to be married to her, to have her running his life for him, looking after him. They would breakfast together in this very room, looking out over the tops of the roofs, with the glorious day before them. They could discuss what was in the news—or such bits as bore discussion—and then they would take a walk and Angus would go to Valvona & Crolla, with a list drawn up by Domenica, to purchase whatever it was that she needed in order to prepare the evening meal. Oh bliss! Oh sheer matrimonial bliss!

But then it occurred to him that none of this

would be possible, fond though its imagining might be, for the simple reason that Domenica did not like Cyril. She had made this perfectly clear to him—and to Cyril—on a number of occasions, and she would never agree to having the dog live with them. But this practical obstacle did not stand too much in the way of fantasy, and in his mind's eye he saw the pair of them standing before the altar at St John's in Princes Street, he in his kilt, Domenica in an elegant cream-coloured outfit, while beside him, neatly groomed, Cyril watched proceedings with interest. They could modify the vows, perhaps: do you, Domenica, take this man, and his dog . . . No, it was impossible. And Angus could hardly fire Cyril after all those years of devotion that the dog had shown him. No, it could never be.

Domenica looked at her watch. Angus always arrived half an hour early at her parties, something which she encouraged, as it gave them time to discuss the guests before they came. She often consulted Angus on the proposed guest list and was prepared to strike people off if he raised a sufficiently weighty objection.

"Oh, we can't have her," Angus once said, pointing to a name on Domenica's list for an earlier dinner party. "She talks about nothing but herself. All the time. Have you noticed it? Yak, yak, yak. *Moi, moi, moi.*"

"True," said Domenica, drawing a line through the name. "Mind you, that is the most perennially fascinating subject, don't you find? Ourselves."

Angus thought about this. He did not talk about himself, and so he could not agree, but when he thought of others he could see the truth of Domenica's observation. Most people were delighted to talk about themselves and their doings, asked or unasked.

"And we can't have him," he said, pointing at another name. "Because if we have him, then we can't have her. And if one had to choose, I would have thought that she was the one we really wanted."

Domenica scrutinised the list. "Yes," she said. "I'd forgotten about that. Was it true, do you think? Do you think that he really did that?"

"Apparently he did," said Angus, shaking his head over the foibles of humanity. Edinburgh was a city that took note of these things. Indeed, he had heard that there was a book somewhere in Heriot Row in which these things were all written down, so that they could be remembered. The book, he had been told, was in the hands of a carefully chosen committee (although anybody was entitled to nominate an incident for inclusion), and went back as far as 1956. It had once been proposed that the record should be expunged ten years after an event, but this suggestion had been turned down on the grounds that many of the older scandals still gave a great deal of enjoyment to people and it would be wrong to deprive them of that.

The guest list that evening had been fully approved by Angus, and he was looking forward to the good conversation that he knew would take place. As he sat there, watching Domenica carry out a few last-minute preparations, Angus thought about the painting he had begun a few days before and which now dominated his studio. It was an extremely large canvas, ten feet by six, and he was at present sketching in the outlines of his planned great work on kindness: a seated woman, beneficent, portrayed in the style of Celtic illuminations, comforts a crouching boy, a figure of modern Scotland.

"I'm working on an important picture," he said to Domenica, "on the theme of kindness."

Domenica, who had been peering into a pot on the top of the stove, looked over her shoulder at Angus. "A very good subject for a picture," she said. "I approve. Do you have a title for it yet?"

Angus shook his head. He thought of it simply as *Kindness*, but he knew that this sounded a bit weak, a bit too self-explanatory.

"In that case," said Domenica, "I suggest that you call it *Let the More Loving One*."

Angus frowned. *"Let the More Loving One?"*

Domenica turned away from the stove. "It's a line from Auden," she said. " 'If equal affection cannot be / Let the more loving one be me.' "

They were both silent for a moment. Behind Domenica, the pot on the stove simmered quietly;

485

there was a square of light on the ceiling, reflected off window glass, shimmering, late light. Angus thought: yes, that is precisely the sentiment. That's it exactly. That's all we need to remember in this life; two lines to guide us.

99. Mr Demarco Sees Danger for the Fringe

They sat at the table, Domenica's guests, all in perfect agreement, at least on the proposition that the first course was exceptional. At the head of the table sat Domenica herself, anthropologist, widow of the late proprietor of the Cochin Sunrise Electricity Factory, author of numerous scholarly papers including, most recently, "Intellectual Property and Piracy in a Malaccan Village." At the opposite end of the table, in a position which indicated his special status in this house as old friend and quasi-host, sat Angus Lordie, portraitist and occasional poet, pillar of the Scottish Arts Club, and member of the Royal Scottish Academy. On Domenica's right sat James Holloway, art historian and a friend of Domenica of many years' standing, whose advice she had sought on many occasions, and followed. On his right, Pat, the attractive but somewhat bland student who had got to know Domenica when she lived next door as tenant of Bruce Anderson, the surveyor—now the fiancé of Julia Donald—an unrepentant, a narcissist, a success. Then there were David Robinson and Joyce

Robinson, both old friends of Domenica; her neighbour, Antonia, invited at the last moment out of guilt; Ricky Demarco, that great man, the irrepressible enthusiast of the arts, artist, impresario; Allan Maclean of Dochgarroch, chieftain of the Macleans of the North, and Anne Maclean; and, of course, Humphrey and Jill Holmes. That was all, but it was a good sample of Edinburgh society, and there were many who were not there who, had they known, would have given much to have been present.

Angus looked about the table. He had been charged by Domenica with responsibility for ensuring that everybody's glass was well filled, and they were. Now, sitting back, he savoured both the timbale and the conversation.

"It's a disaster," said Ricky Demarco. "A complete disaster."

Silence fell about the table as all eyes turned to Demarco. Was he referring to the timbale?

"Yes," he said. "The Festival Fringe is in great danger."

Most were relieved that the subject was the arts and not salmon timbale; David Robinson, in particular, looked interested. People were always predicting the demise of the Edinburgh Festival, he reflected, but somehow it always got better. And the same was true of the Fringe, the Festival's unruly unofficial partner, which seemed to get bigger and bigger each year.

"Danger of what?" asked David.

"Drowning in stand-up comics," said Demarco. "Haven't you seen how many of them there are? They flock to Edinburgh, flock like geese over the horizon." He waved a hand airily. "Thousands of them."

Pat picked at a small fish bone that had become lodged in her teeth. She rather enjoyed going to hear stand-up comics, even if there were rather a lot of them.

"I quite like them," she said quietly.

Fortunately, nobody heard her, and she was only twenty anyway.

"I must admit, for the most part, they're very unfunny," said Angus. "Or am I out of touch?"

"You're out of touch," said Domenica. "But you may nonetheless be right about their unfunniness. I find most of them rather crude and predictable. No, I agree with Ricky. These people are getting a bit tedious."

"They are," said Demarco. "And the problem is this: they charge so much, some of them, that they mop up all the ticket money. The Fringe should be about the arts, about drama, music, painting. And all these people do is stand there and tell joke after joke. Just think of it: the world's biggest, most exciting arts gathering reduced to a motley collection of comedians telling jokes. Is that what we've come to?"

Angus looked down at his plate. "I wish I found

more things funny," he said. "But I don't. The only people who can make me laugh anymore are Stanley Baxter and Myles Na Gopaleen."

David Robinson agreed about Na Gopaleen. "Yes, Flann O'Brien was a very funny writer. Do you remember his book-distressing service for the nouveau riche?"

"Of course I do," said Angus. "They would come and make newly acquired books look suitably used. And for an extra fee they would write appropriate marginalia so that people thought that you had actually read the books."

"Irish writers can be very entertaining," said Domenica. "But what about public life? How long is it since we've had an amusing politician?"

There was a complete silence. Mrs Thatcher had been tremendously funny, but she had gone now.

"Harold Macmillan," said Humphrey, after a while. "He made the entire United Nations laugh once, although the laughter took a long time to travel round the Assembly as his remark had to be translated into numerous languages. The Germans laughed last, only because of their word order, I hasten to add."

"What did he say?" asked Domenica.

"Well," said Humphrey. "Mr Khrushchev started to get very heated when Macmillan was making his speech and he took off his shoe and started to bang it on the table. Whereupon Macmillan looked up and said, in a very cool drawl: 'Could we have a translation of that, please?' The whole place collapsed."

They all laughed. Then Humphrey raised a finger in the air. "Mind you, I know an even funnier story about Khrushchev."

They looked at him.

"This story concerns Chairman Mao," said Humphrey. "He was said to have had a very good sense of humour. He was asked once what he thought would have happened had it been Nikita Khrushchev rather than President Kennedy who had been assassinated. He thought for a moment and then said: 'Well, one thing is certain: Aristotle Onassis would not have married Mrs Khrushchev!' "

Angus let out a hoot of laughter, but he noticed that Pat looked puzzled. Leaning across the table he whispered to her: "Mrs Khrushchev, my dear, was a terrible sight. One of those round, squat Russian women whom one imagined picking potatoes or working in a tractor factory.

"Mind you," he went on, "Russian women weren't the only frumps. I had a friend who was once invited to meet a foreign leader (a delightful chap, now, alas, deceased) and was being shown around the leader's tent—he lived, you see, under canvas. Anyway, he saw this picture of a very ugly-looking chap hanging on the side of the tent and he was about to ask: 'Who's that man?' when an official leaned forward and whispered to him: 'That, sir, is our beloved leader's mother.' "

100. Not an Ending—More an Adjournment

The salmon was entirely consumed, and at least one pair of longing eyes was directed to the empty plate on which the large timbale had stood; but there was to be no more, and those who had hoped for a second helping were sent empty away. But more was to come; now they progressed to the venison cassoulet, accompanied by Sardinian Rocca Rubia, a wine which Philip Contini himself had pressed into Domenica's hands; and beyond that to the apple tart with the Celtic-inspired pastry strips.

The conversation around the table was noisy and enthusiastic, as wide-ranging as it always was in Domenica's flat—that was her effect upon others, a freeing of the tongue, an enlargement of confidence. Even Pat, who might have felt inhibited in such accomplished company, found herself expounding with ease on obtuse topics, emboldened by Domenica's smile and encouraging nods of agreement. And outside, slowly, the light faded into that state of semi-darkness of the Scottish midsummer; not dark, not light, but somewhere in between, a simmer dim perhaps, or something like it.

At one point, at an early stage of the dinner, Domenica heard, but only faintly, the sound of Bertie practising his saxophone downstairs, and grinned. She glanced at Angus and at Pat; they as well had both heard, and smiled too, for they could picture Domenica's young neighbour at his music stand, under the supervising gaze of his mother. Poor Bertie, thought Angus, what a burden for a boy to bear in this life, to have a mother like that, and how discerning Cyril had been when he bit her ankle in Dundas Street. And although on that famous occasion he had been obliged to look apologetic and to administer swift punishment to Cyril, his heart had not been in the retribution, and, as soon as possible, he had rewarded the dog with a reassuring pat on the head and the promise of a bone for his moral courage.

And as Angus remembered this incident, Domenica found herself thinking of how well Auden's words in his poem on the death of Freud fitted Bertie's situation. He had written there of the child "unlucky in his little State," of the hearth from which freedom was excluded; such powerful lines to express both the liberating power of Freudian insights, but also to describe the plight of a child. Of course, Auden had believed in Freud then, had imagined that the problem of human wickedness was a problem for psychology, a belief which he had later abandoned when he had come to recognise that evil could be something other than that. On balance, Domenica thought that she agreed here with the younger rather than the older Auden. What tyrant has had a happy childhood?

When they rose from the table to go through for coffee, Angus came up to Domenica and took her hand briefly. It was an unusual gesture for him, and Domenica looked down, almost in surprise, at his hand upon hers, and he, embarrassed, let go of her.

"I wanted to thank you for the apple tart," he said. "You know I like it."

"That is why I chose it," she said.

"Well, thank you," he said.

"You heard Bertie playing back then?" she asked. "I believe it was 'Mood Indigo.'"

Angus nodded. "It was." He paused for a moment. "He'll be all right, that wee boy. He'll be all right."

Domenica hesitated before she replied. But yes, she thought he would be, and this comforted her. As they entered the drawing room, she turned to Angus and whispered to him: "You will say something, won't you? They'll be expecting it, you know. You always have a poem for these occasions."

Angus glanced at his fellow guests. "Are you sure they want to hear from me?"

Domenica was sure, and a few minutes later, when everybody was settled with their coffee, she announced to her guests that Angus had a poem to read.

"Not exactly to read," he said.

"But it is there, isn't it?" pressed Domenica. And she thought, as she spoke, perhaps I would get used to canine company after all. Yes, why not?

493

Angus put down his cup and moved to the window. There was still a glow of light in the sky, which was high, and empty, the faintest of blues now, washed out. Then he turned round, and he saw then that every guest, every one present, was a friend, and that he cherished them. So the words came to him, and he said:

Dear friends, we are the inhabitants
Of a city which can be loved, as any place may
    be,
In so many different and particular ways;
But who amongst us can predict
For which reasons, and along which fault lines,
Will the heart of each of us
Be broken? I cannot, for I am moved
By so many different and unexpected things:
    by our sky,
Which at each moment may change its mood at
    whim
With clouds in such a hurry to be somewhere
    else;
By our lingering haars, by our eccentric skyline,
All crags and spires and angular promises,
By the way we feel in Scotland, yes, simply that;
These are the things that break my heart
In a way for which I am never quite prepared—
The surprises of a love affair that lasts a lifetime.
But what breaks the heart the most, I think,
Is the knowledge that what we have

We all must lose; I don't much care for denial,
But if pressed to say goodbye, that final word
On which even the strongest can stumble,
I am not above pretending
That the party continues elsewhere,
With a guest list that's mostly the same,
And every bit as satisfactory;
That what we think are ends are really adjourn-
    ments,
An *entr'acte*, an interval, not real goodbyes;
And perhaps they are, dear friends, perhaps
    they are.

Center Point Publishing

600 Brooks Road ● PO Box 1
Thorndike ME 04986-0001 USA

(207) 568-3717

**US & Canada:
1 800 929-9108**
www.centerpointlargeprint.com